An Iron Yoke

S.L. Russell

Published by New Generation Publishing in 2015

Copyright © S.L. Russell 2015

Cover design by © Naomi Russell

First Edition

The author asserts the moral right under the Copyright, Designs and Patents Act 1988 to be identified as the author of this work.

All Rights reserved. No part of this publication may be reproduced, stored in a retrieval system or transmitted, in any form or by any means without the prior consent of the author, nor be otherwise circulated in any form of binding or cover other than that which it is published and without a similar condition being imposed on the subsequent purchaser.

Scriptures and additional materials quoted are from the Good News Bible ©1994 published by the Bible Societies/Harper Collins Publishers Ltd UK, Good News Bible © American Bible Society 1966, 1971, 1976, 1992. Used with permission. www.biblesociety.org.uk

www.newgeneration-publishing.com

New Generation Publishing

A M D G

With particular thanks to Claire, David, Derek, Liz and Nikki

Scotland: 1972

I'm so cold in here. But the sweat's pouring off me.
   She huddled deeper into the old oak wardrobe, drawing her knees up to her chin, wrapping her arms round them, shivering.
   Perhaps I'm ill. If I was ill I could go to hospital. Then no one could get to me. But would anyone notice? Would they care? Maybe they'd just let me get worse and worse. Maybe I'd die.
   A tear leaked out of her eye and dribbled down to her chin. She sniffed quietly.
   Quin, I keep wishing and wishing you were here. You make me feel safe. Why couldn't they have sent me away to school too? I asked him, it was about two weeks ago, I don't know how I dared, but I asked him, I said, I want to go away to boarding school, like my brother. He was in one of his good moods. He put his arm round my shoulders – he was in the kitchen, warming his hands at the fire – and he said, Whatever for? Laughing, and showing his horrible brown teeth. That's why we've got Catriona, to teach you. Can't have you away at school too, can we? I'd be lonely. And he squeezed me, and I'm holding myself stiff as a broom, hoping he didn't notice me shudder. Of course they were there, they're always around, and he's grinning and she's grinning and I wanted to be sick.
   Sitting hunched and stiff in the wardrobe, making the smallest possible movements, she remembered another time, years before, when she was no more than six years old, crouching in the dark, crying with cold and fear, but with her brother's arm around her. Then the memories vanished as she tensed, every sense alert, hearing, she thought, a sound outside the room, a quiet footfall on the stone staircase. She sat utterly still, like a threatened animal, her breath held till her lungs gave way and she had to exhale, slowly, silently. There was no more sound, and her shoulders slumped.
   I thought there was someone on the stairs, but it's gone. I don't know how long it'll be, though, till someone notices. I was remembering that time

– snivelling and crying, when you were so brave. But I'm not crying now, Quin. Or not much. It's been a bad day: she, Catriona that is, told him I'd been slacking, and he started to shout, and I ran. They've been drinking again too, him and Neil. It's always worse then. That's why I'm hiding. And it's so cold! I haven't had a fire in my room for weeks, and you know how draughty this place is. There's a lot of snow. Nobody's been out for days. They just drink, and laugh, and give me those looks. Quin, you don't know how lucky you are. I can just hear them now, downstairs, laughing. Someone must have opened the kitchen door. It's a horrible, scary laugh, like a donkey braying, only worse. Everything I fear, everything that makes me want to be sick, is in that laugh.

She flinched, ears on alert. Footsteps, heavy and stumbling, audible even through the massive door, sounded on the stairs.

No! They're coming up! I can hear them – or is it only him? Neil has egged him on, I know that. In a minute he'll be outside my door, calling me, all soft and sweet – the stinking liar! I have to pretend to be asleep. If he believes me, maybe he'll give up and go away. But if he doesn't he'll start roaring like he does, and pounding on the walls. It's got worse as I've got older, worse since you went away. It makes me feel shivery right to my backbone. He's outside my door now. I've put my chest of drawers there so he can't get in. He's knocking! I've got my fingers in my ears, but I can still hear him. Please, God, make him go away. I'm so afraid. I just know that soon I'll be there when he's in one of his rages, and I won't be able to escape. I'm quick, but I'm still only small and skinny, and he's so big, like a great lumbering bear. Quin, he's changed – he hardly goes to town any more, and he takes his guns everywhere. His hair and his beard have grown so long, he looks like a wild man. I sometimes think he is truly mad. I am locked up with a mad man and his horrible sneaking servants.

She shrank back into the darkness, gasping as a hanging coat brushed her cheek. As she realised what it was that had touched her, a shudder rippled through her body and a quiet moan escaped her. She could feel her heart pounding wildly against her ribcage.

He's gone. I don't know why he changed his mind. But I do know he'll be back, maybe not today, but soon. I'm telling you, he's bad, but they are truly evil. And you know what? I don't believe they are married like they say. She's at least twice as old as him, Neil and his stupid moustache like a squashed spider, strutting about like a turkey-cock, with his horrible

jeering voice, and her all prim and proper, with her mouth like a letterbox and her hair all tight and crimped. Ugh. They make me sick.
I wish it was Easter. Then you'll be here for the holidays. Then I'll be able to breathe again. I know you won't let him hurt me. But it's still only February – Easter's weeks away. And how can I tell you what's going on?

She moved carefully, trying to ease her stiff muscles, and felt her bladder protest. She shuddered, imagining herself having to leave her sanctuary, opening the wardrobe door and crawling out, creeping across the room, trying not to make a sound as she moved the chest of drawers that she had pushed there, opening the door and dashing down the corridor to the bathroom. But who might be on the stairs, or on the landing?

And then came a sudden crash, making her stomach lurch wildly and her mouth gape.

He's back! I didn't hear him, he must have crept up the stairs. And Neil is with him, and they're shouting out, pretending they are worried about me, but it isn't true, they're laughing at the same time. They're hammering on the door, they've got something to break it down, they're shouting, I can hear the chest of drawers starting to move, they'll be in here, they'll find me! Oh, Quin, please, help!

3

2002: Compton

'Aunt Erica, how am I supposed to get in here?' The tall young woman stood in the alley at the end of the garden, the other side of a rampant stand of brambles heavy with dusty fruit, her arms wrapped round a cardboard box. The woman in the wheelchair looked up, squinting in the strong sunlight, from where she had been deadheading roses that had gone wild.

'Oh, hello, child. What are you doing at the back anyway?'

'I thought I'd save you the bother of opening the front door. But these brambles are too dense.'

'Come round to the front and I'll let you in.'

Five minutes later, after much puffing and sighing and squealing of ill-oiled bolts, the front door creaked open. The woman backed down the narrow hallway in her wheelchair, bumping the walls as she went. 'Sorry to have been so long, but this passage is only just wide enough for the chair, and not for my elbows.'

'That's why I came round the back. It's rather dark in here, isn't it?'

At the end of the hallway Erica swivelled the wheelchair round in one swift movement. 'Your father has all sorts of plans, one of them to knock down that wall and do away with the hallway altogether.' She made a face. 'Another is to put in a fence all round the garden, complete with a locked gate to which, no doubt, only he will have a key.'

'I shall have a key as well,' the young woman said. She bent to kiss her aunt's cheek. 'How are you, Aunt Erica?'

'I was all right till you biffed me with that box. And could we do without the "Aunt" part? It makes me feel a hundred.'

The young woman laughed. 'When you frown like that you look a hundred. And you are my aunt whether you like it or not. But what would you like me to call you?'

'Plain 'Erica' will do. What's in that box, anyway?'

'It's a cake, for you. I made it myself. Every time you cut a slice you can think of me.'

'Cake, indeed! I shall get fat, sitting in this contraption all day eating cake. Are you going somewhere, then? That I have to think of you while eating cake?'

'Don't be obtuse, dear Aunt, I mean, *Erica*. You know where I'm going in a couple of weeks – back to uni.' She put the box down on the kitchen surface. 'Shall we have some now? With a cup of tea? Since you haven't offered, I could make it myself.'

'Yes, yes, you were going to anyway. You know where everything is.' She watched her niece as she busied herself in the kitchen, humming quietly, her long, light red hair flying about as she moved. 'Helena.'

'Yes?'

'Thank you for the cake. You are full of kind thoughts.'

'You're welcome. It's probably horrible, but it was made with love.'

The older woman folded her arms and scowled. 'And you couldn't say that about many people.'

Helena laughed, her blue eyes lighting up. 'Who can wonder at it, you're such an old grump. Anyway, everyone knows Daddy is devoted to you. Hence the home improvements and all the security measures. He's most anxious for your safety.'

'Hm. Not that I have anything whatsoever to steal.' Her expression softened. 'But yes, my brother is a very good man. One of the few people who have always been there and never let me down.'

'And I shall be another,' Helena said cheerfully. 'Here's your tea. Try not to spill it, you poor old invalid.'

Erica glowered. 'Wash your mouth out!'

Helena leaned against the kitchen counter, grinning. 'So, how's it going in this little old backwater? Met anybody yet?'

'No, but it appears I'm about to. Your father has organised someone to look after me. As if I need anybody! I'm quite capable of looking after myself.'

'Who is it?'

5

Erica sighed. 'Oh, I don't know, some woman. Some well-meaning old busybody. She's coming round tomorrow. Perhaps I'll send her away with a flea in her ear.'

'That wouldn't be sensible,' Helena said gently. 'Would it? There may come a time when you need more help, and she may be perfectly nice. So don't upset her before she's even got a foot in the door.'

'Oh, Helena.' Erica shook her head. 'Everybody's "perfectly nice" in your eyes, I think. Even your ma and those two rather dreadful brothers of yours.'

'They have their points. And don't complain they never come to see you, because you'd hate it if they did.' Helena bent down and took a plate out of a cupboard. 'Where's your sharp knife? I'll cut this cake. It's gone a bit gooey, I'm afraid.'

Erica shrugged, and the movement made her wince. 'Sorry, it's in the garden. I was using it to deadhead the roses. I need to get some secateurs.'

'You are such a heathen, using your kitchen knife on roses. I'll go and fetch it.'

Erica followed her to the back door, rolling the wheelchair slowly with one hand. 'Speaking of heathens, I had a visit from the vicar the other day.'

Helena paused with her hand on the latch. 'Oh, really? What's he like?'

'Well, of course you'd think he was "perfectly nice", I dare say,' Erica said acidly. 'Not at all a bumbling old buffer with hairy nostrils who looked as if he should have retired years ago.'

Helena laughed aloud, shaking her head so that her fine wild hair whipped about her face. 'Poor man. I wouldn't want the likes of you in my congregation. I'll just go and get the knife.'

In a moment she was back, brandishing a soiled blade. 'So you won't be going to church, then?'

'I might, if this carer woman will take me. I'll have to see.'

Helena washed the knife under the kitchen tap and dried it on a tea towel. 'Well, maybe the old vicar *is* coming up for retirement and they'll send a nice young one instead for you to ogle from the pews.'

'Good gracious, child! "Ogle," indeed! What must you think of me?'

'I think you are a terrible sinner. Here's your cake. Please don't choke on it, or Daddy will never forgive me.'

2002: London

Helena put her key in the lock and turned it quietly, closing the door soundlessly behind her. But the door to the kitchen was ajar, and Fiona was sitting at the table with a magazine open in front of her.

'I suppose you've been down to Compton, seeing your aunt,' she said. She made the words 'your aunt' sound as if she had something unpleasant in her mouth.

'Yes, that's exactly where I've been,' Helena said calmly. 'I told you I was going some time this week. I took her a cake.'

Fiona closed her eyes briefly and sighed. 'Well, it's a pity. I had Barbara Buchan here, and you missed her. But perhaps you meant to.'

'Did I know she was coming?' Helena wondered. 'And surely she was coming to see you, not me. She's your old crony from school, isn't she?'

'She's a friend, not a crony,' Fiona said irritably. 'And you know perfectly well why I wanted you to be here when she visited.'

'For goodness' sake!' Helena said. 'You're not still trying to set me up with her son, are you? Andy Buchan is a buffoon.'

'He's also in the Dragoons, and they've been in Kosovo,' Fiona countered.

Helena folded her arms, standing in the doorway. 'All right, so he's a brave buffoon. But he's still a buffoon, I'm afraid. And a drunken one.'

Fiona narrowed her eyes, not looking at her daughter, pretending to scan the pages of her magazine. 'You can hardly blame soldiers for letting their hair down when they're on leave. After all the awful things they've seen and done.'

'I can,' Helena said darkly. 'Especially if they have the habit of groping you when they've had six too many.'

Fiona sniffed. 'I suppose you prefer those louts you've met at university.'

'Since you haven't met any of my uni friends you can't know if they are louts or not,' Helena retorted. 'Just because they're not Scottish blue-bloods with ancestral seats. Anyway, I went to uni to get a degree, not a husband. I'm much too young to be thinking about marriage.'

'You're almost twenty-one, Helena! I wasn't much older than you when I married your father.' Fiona bit her lip, realising what she had laid herself open to.

Helena gave her a long, unsmiling stare. 'I'll refrain from making the obvious comment.' She kicked off her shoes and flexed her bare toes. 'Anyway, how was dear old Barbara Buchan? Still spending a fortune doing up that old ruin of hers? I bet you were jealous, mother – a castle *and* a son in the Dragoons.'

'Sarcasm really doesn't suit you, Helena,' Fiona said coolly. 'It just shows you up as rather pathetic. You should know I am just looking out for your interests.'

Helena laughed. 'Sorry, Mother, I don't believe you. You're looking out for your own interests, and they don't coincide with mine.'

Fiona stood up abruptly, closing her magazine with a snap. 'You've been got at by your father, that's the trouble. You've been thoroughly spoilt.' She peered at Helena disdainfully, her mouth turned down. 'The way you talk no man would want you anyway, it seems to me.'

Helena shook her head and picked up her shoes. 'Honestly! What century are you living in? I do have ideas of my own, you know. And I hope there's more to my future than desperately searching for some well-bred fool to get hitched to. Anyway, you can hardly claim to have given me a very positive view of marriage, can you?'

Fiona's nostrils flared. 'Well, we all know whose fault that is.'

'Do we? As far as I know, it takes two. Anyway, I must have a shower. I'll be going out later – to find some louts for company. Don't wait up, will you?'

2008: Compton

Oh, no, surely that's not the time! Drat, I'm going to be late. She hates it if I'm late, and I'll get a tongue-lashing. It was Jamie's fault, not that poor Jamie can help it, and his mother would talk and talk, though I dare say the poor woman's got few enough people to talk to, stuck in that house with a disabled boy all day. Man, I should say. Jamie's thirty-five if he's a day. Bother, bother.

'Ben, for heaven's sake, don't get under my feet! I'll take you both out for a walk when I'm done with Mrs P. It's too hot for walking anyway. Yes, I promise. Now, I must go.' *Have I got everything? Goodness knows.*

'All right, boys, I'll have to shut you in now. I know, you didn't like going to the vet. But it's for your own good. Don't fuss, I'll be back in an hour, and maybe it'll be a mite cooler then. Be good, and don't chew anything, please.'

She banged her front door shut and crossed her tiny garden to the road where her battered Beetle sat parked slightly askew. *Phew, this car's hot. I should have put it in the garage. Open the windows, Nettie. Let a bit of air in. Now let's see if the old girl will start first time.* She turned the key. *Great! Who says miracles don't happen?*

I wonder what sort of mood she'll be in this evening. No telling these days, though I have to say she's getting more and more snappy. I suppose it's not surprising, poor soul, with all that pain. It's so hot today too; that frays your temper. I should be used to it, anyway, after all these years. And if I don't put up with it, I don't know who will. There's not many who can suffer her moods for too long. She's worn out a good many people's kindness. Not Joseph's, though. He's always kind, bless him. She lurched out of her cul-de-sac onto the main road, the car's engine coughing in protest. *Bother, the lights have gone red. Another few minutes late, another nail in my coffin! Oh well, if she rages, I'll just have to shut my ears. I wonder what she wants for her supper. Probably just a bit of salad, it's so hot, though she says she can't chew, her teeth*

11

hurt, and she won't see the dentist. Got no time for him. Anyway, it won't take too long to get her something to eat, that's if she eats it at all. I throw so much away, and she's thin as a rail, all bones. I just hope there's no mess to clear up. I know she can't help it, but it makes her even more bad-tempered. It's the humiliation of it all, I guess. She hurtled down the High Street, turned abruptly left and swerved, narrowly missing two ambling, oblivious teenagers. Then she climbed the long incline of Plough Lane and parked with a jerk as the tyres grazed the kerb. *Anyway, here we are. Just another hour and I can go home and put my feet up. They ache these days, my feet. Getting old, Nettie. Need to retire. But then who'd look after Mrs P? The others would find someone soon enough. But she's none too popular.* She climbed out of the hot car with a sigh, gathered up her voluminous bag and started up the front path. For a moment she paused mid-stride. *I wonder why I've never been able to call her by her first name. Funny, that. She's asked me to a few times. 'For Pete's sake, Nettie, call me Erica, can't you? We've known each other long enough, and you've had to do some pretty personal things for me. We should be bosom buddies.' How she sneers, as if she hates me, or herself. I don't know, though, I can't seem to call her Erica, she's my employer after all.*

Nettie made it to the front door and put her bag down, bending over, rummaging through its contents. *Why is it that keys always seem to get right to the bottom of your bag? My goodness, it's hot. Did I remember to open her windows at lunch time?*

Hundreds of years ago the town of Compton stood on low cliffs above the sea; now that sea lies twenty miles to the east, the river flowing into it is silted up, and instead of breakers there are salt marshes and tussocky fields where sheep graze. At the far end of the town the road peters out into a track leading up onto sandy bluffs, all that now remain of the cliffs. When the wind is strong gulls come to rest there, as if the sea were still in sight. Sometimes, in the heat haze, it almost seems that it can still be seen, shimmering in the distance, but it is an illusion, fostered by the indistinct boundary between sky and horizon.

Plough Lane leads to the track, and nowhere else. If you had business in Plough Lane you might go there, but not otherwise. A row of modest bungalows, set behind long gardens, lines one side; on the other side is a head-high railing and beyond that scrubby bushes and waste ground. It is a quiet street, quiet to the point of moribund, or, as now, somnolent under a July sun. At six o'clock in the evening the pavement is still baking, but the sun is climbing slowly down, as if with a weary sigh.

An old man sits on a weathered garden bench set at the side of the road. He has a shopping bag beside him, and his ragged collie is taking shelter under the seat. The man is leaning with both hands on his stick, his head bowed. Further down the road a young woman is pushing a pram. Every few steps she stops to rearrange something around her baby, or to wipe her hand across her sweating face.

Then, in the sun-drugged silence, comes an unexpected crash, as a door is flung open with violent force, banging on the wall, and the sound of hurrying sandalled feet slapping against the concrete path. There at the gate of one of the bungalows is a dumpy woman in a floral apron. Her eyes are bulging and her breathing is laboured. The collie looks up, its ears pricked. The old man's head turns in the direction of the sound, and the mother with the pram stops dead, her eyes wide. The woman at the gate is standing quite still, staring at her hands. They are covered in blood.

Patrick Carver looked gloomily out of the train window. He rubbed his hands across his cheeks, and his stubble rasped. 'Not what you'd call pretty, is it?' He waved a hand in the direction of the landscape. 'Not like what you're used to, eh, Bertie boy? You and your sunny English acres.'

His companion looked up from his book, frowning. 'The acres are still, strictly speaking, my father's. And please don't call me Bertie. It's just as aristocratic as Francis Bertram Greville. Just Bert will be fine, there's a good chap.'

Patrick smirked. 'Well, no doubt the rolling estates will be yours one day. And you do realise, don't you, that this strange inverted snobbery of yours, this attempt to appear one of the lads, is a complete waste of time. Calling yourself Bert doesn't cut it. Your clothes are much too nice in their understated way. And the illusion fails as soon as you open your mouth. Old chap.'

'Whatever. Stick to Bert, please. And keep your anthropological observations to yourself.'

'I like it. "Anthropological observations." I suppose I do rather see you as a fascinating alien species.'

'Now who's an inverted snob? You're the worst of the bunch. *And* with a chip on your shoulder that gives you a permanent sideways lurch.'

Patrick laughed. 'You're on form today, Bert, I see. What's brought that on? Surely not just this little bit of freedom from the divine Amanda?'

'If freedom from your wife is such a fine thing you should be singing, Patrick.'

'Ha! Perhaps I will! Shall I?' Patrick looked around the compartment, empty but for themselves. 'Perhaps not. Anyway, in case you'd forgotten, conjugal freedom is not something I've actually chosen.'

'Perhaps you should have behaved better,' Bert said.

'Who says I don't always behave impeccably?' Patrick said, his voice rising in self-mocking indignation.

'You've changed, then, have you, out of all recognition? No more Carver the Casanova, the man whose trousers don't recognise him? You can't swing that one, old man. Remember that College reunion a couple of years back? You were leering at a lot of the assembled ladies, I seem to recall, including Amanda.'

'You can hardly blame me. That girl of yours is absolutely delicious. Not to mention the dress she was wearing!' His eyes rolled upwards. 'What there was of it. Phew!'

'I shall not rise to your pathetic attempts to make me jealous, Carver. Amanda loves only her horse and Professor Whitewell. Oh, and probably me and the boys as well, when she remembers. She probably never noticed you at all.'

'Story of my life. Who's Professor Whitewell?'

'The chap that's in charge of this dig she's gone on.'

'What's he like?'

'I haven't met him. But to hear Amanda speak you'd think he was the wisest, most knowledgeable, most attractive, wittiest man in Christendom.'

Patrick whistled. 'Tough competition, then. Even for someone as wise, knowledgeable, attractive and witty as you.'

'Tough indeed. Let's hope he's more interested in ancient artefacts than starry-eyed female dirt-shovellers. Anyway, Carver, enough of this infantile bitching. What about Joseph? At least you and I still have a wife.'

'True. Possibly, in my case, not for much longer.'

Bert looked at him sideways. 'Are you serious? Has divorce actually been mentioned?'

'Not in so many words. But she took the children to her parents', and it was obvious I would not be welcome. Hence my presence with you.'

'Well, if you really want to, perhaps you could make a supreme effort and patch things up. Rachel is a nice woman and might forgive you.'

Patrick's eyebrows arched. 'Forgive me for what? I haven't done anything.'

'Hm. Forgive you for being you? What I'm saying, Carver, is that maybe there's still hope. Which is more than you can say for Joseph.'

Patrick leaned back, folding his arms. 'I suppose so. Tell me again, how did you find out about – what's her name again?'

Bert closed his book, making sure the marker was in place. 'Caroline. It's a very strange thing, but she and I are, were, distantly related. The Kings are cousins on my mother's side. Never had anything to do with them as a child, didn't know any of them. But it was my mother who told me, via her mysterious network. Any happenings like that, especially the tragic ones, or the scandals, seem to reach her by way of the jungle drums.'

'When was this?'

Bert waved his long fingers in an expansive gesture. 'Oh, not long ago, weeks, a couple of months at most. But Mother's informants aren't always completely up to date. And she doesn't always tell me things straight away. She dropped in for coffee one morning on her way to town, and she said quite casually, "Oh, by the way, darling, have you heard?"' Bert's voice rose by half an octave as he mimicked his mother's patrician vowels. '"Caroline King, you know, my second cousin Veronica's daughter, terribly sad, dead in a car accident. Didn't she marry that old university chum of yours?" Of course I was shocked, but when I asked her when it had happened she said all airily, "Oh, ages ago, a year at least, but I've only just heard about it through the grapevine." So I'm afraid I didn't find out until long after the event.'

'Did you contact Joseph straight away?'

'I tried to. I rang him on several occasions, but never got hold of him. In the end I sent him a card, you know the sort, white lilies and Victorian verse. And he sent me an e mail. Turned out I had an out-of-date number for him. Anyway that started things off. I said would he like me to visit some time, and he said, why not, and bring Patrick. So here we are. A perhaps not-so-jolly weekend in sleepy commuter-land.'

Patrick whistled softly. 'So the poor chap's been a widower for maybe eighteen months? He must think we've been dilatory to the point of heartless.'

'No, he understands. I explained the circumstances.'

'How did he seem?'

'Oh, you know, all right. Joseph was never much of a talker, was he?'

'No, he just did a lot of thinking. My God, Bert, I'll never forget my astonishment, not to say horror, when I found out he'd given everything up to get ordained. He was ten times cleverer than you and me put together. Got a brilliant degree. What a waste.'

'It would only seem a waste to an atheist like you, Carver. Obviously not to him. Nor, as it happens, to me.'

Patrick scowled. 'Oh, and you're a stalwart Christian, I suppose.'

'In my own traditional way, yes.'

'Traditional as in keeping up the family reputation? Going through the motions at Christmas and Easter? Lord of the manor stuff?'

'Do desist, old man. Your prejudices are unappealing.'

'Well, I hope Joseph doesn't expect me to go to his church.'

'I'm sure he won't.'

'What about your second cousin any-number-of-times-removed – Caroline? Was she religious?'

'I have no idea. The only time I ever met her was at their wedding. I thought it was a happy wedding, as they go. You were there too, I remember. You had Rachel and the children with you.'

'So I did.' Patrick scratched his head, remembering. 'Betsy was two, so it must have been about five years ago. She slept all the way through the service. Very convenient. But Oliver kept complaining about his itchy suit. Loudly. I told Rachel the suit was a mistake.'

'Was he a vicar then?'

'Who, Oliver?'

'Don't be ridiculous. Joseph, of course.'

'Yes, I'm sure he was. Surely all that happened ages before. But anyway, I seem to remember a dog-collar. And didn't the Bishop do the honours?'

'Could be.' Bert yawned and stretched. 'What's the time, Carver? I dropped my watch in the shower last week.'

'Five forty. When does this trundling beast get in to, what is it, Compton?'

'Compton Magna, to give it its full title. It doesn't, Carver. I'm sure I told you. Compton isn't on a railway line. We get off at Stockley and catch a bus.'

Patrick closed his eyes and groaned. 'I knew it. As soon as you leave London behind things get positively medieval.'

'Even for you that's a stupid remark. If this was the middle ages you'd be travelling, at best, by cart. And if you hadn't been late we might have caught a faster train.'

'Hm. Part of me is regretting this trip already.' He held up his hands, as if to ward off Bert's protest. 'I'm sorry for poor old Joseph, of course, and if our company helps then I don't

17

begrudge it. But I have a horrible feeling we're going to be bored to the point of catatonic.'

The two men stood outside the bus station. Patrick looked around, his arms spread wide. 'Where are all the commuters?'

Bert hefted his bag onto his shoulder. 'It's Friday. They all scurried away from their offices as soon as they could and caught that *earlier train*.' He looked at Patrick meaningfully, but was ignored. 'It's a hot summer weekend. They're probably relaxing in brightly-coloured shirts and firing up their barbecues.'

'But it's uncannily quiet. Apart from us nobody got off the bus except that short woman in the extraordinary hat.'

'There's nothing uncanny about it. Your view of things has been warped by years of metropolitan living. This is a sleepy country town, old man. Probably a lot livelier than where I live, though. Anyway, shall we move on, or are you planning an extended stay in the street?'

Patrick picked up his bag. 'Do you know the way, by any chance?'

'Not really. But I imagine Joseph inhabits the vicarage, which I assume is near the church, and if I'm not mistaken that looks distinctly like a church spire.' He pointed to where the roofs of the town rose at the end of the street.

'On the other hand,' Patrick said, grimacing, 'there could be more than one church. And Joseph's vicarage might have been condemned because of termites, so that now he lives in the middle of an impenetrable housing estate.'

'Well, do *you* know the way?'

'Of course not.'

'We'll just have to ask for directions if there's any problem.'

'But there isn't anybody. It's a ghost town.'

'Do give over, Carver. You're becoming irritating.'

Patrick sighed. 'That's what Rachel says. If I'm normal, I'm cynical. If I'm in a good mood, I'm irritating.'

'Poor Rachel. Let's walk, shall we, rather than stand here jabbering?'

'But I was thinking, Bert, should we perhaps take something? An offering, for Joseph? Will there be any shops open?'

'Probably. What did you have in mind?'

'A bottle? It might ease the weekend along.'

Bert frowned. 'I'm not sure. Joseph had some kind of breakdown, didn't he, after we all graduated? I lost touch with him for quite a while. Was it anything to do with alcohol?'

'I thought there was some issue with drugs, homelessness, mental stuff, wasn't there? Don't know if drink was involved.'

Bert stopped abruptly and turned on his friend. 'What do you mean by "mental stuff", for goodness' sake?'

Patrick shrugged. 'Didn't he go to the dogs for a few years? I don't know, it was only on the grapevine, like your ma's jungle drums. He dropped off the radar. Didn't his father die, or something? Causing him to lose his way a bit? Which is odd, since I seem to recall he didn't get on with his old man.'

'Not odd necessarily. If his father died, and they'd fallen out, it could've been guilt that set him off.'

'Still doesn't answer the question about whether or not we should invest in something strong and fiery.'

'Perhaps we should see which way the land lies first. Look, here we are, Carver you doubter, in the High Street. Plenty of people about, and there's the church.'

'Plenty? I count six at most. And they all look half dead.'

'For heaven's sake, come on, or I swear *you* will be fully dead.'

On the other side of town Nettie sat in the back seat of a sweltering police car. She twisted a large white handkerchief round and round in her hands, stopping only to wipe her sweating face. The handkerchief, once crisply laundered, was stained with blood.

'Feeling any better, Mrs Carew?' Louise Gordon leaned against the seat-back and rolled up her sleeves, watching Nettie under her blond lashes.

'Yes, I'm all right, Sergeant,' Nettie whispered. 'It was just the shock. Such an awful shock.'

Louise nodded. 'Of course. Anybody would be upset. What about your hand? Let me see.'

'Oh, it's nothing, really,' Nettie said. She held out her right hand for inspection. Two shallow cuts crossed her palm. 'It stopped bleeding very quickly.'

'You'll need to keep an eye on it. Just in case there are any tiny slivers of glass in there.'

'I'll wash it thoroughly when I get home and wrap it up.'

'All right, Mrs Carew,' Louise said. 'Just run it past me once more, will you, please? From the time you arrived here at the bungalow. In case we've missed something.'

Nettie looked up, past Louise, out of the open car window, and her brows contracted. 'There are policemen knocking on the doors down the street. The neighbours are all looking out.'

Louise nodded. 'That's right. We have to check if they noticed anything. Go on, Mrs Carew. Just as you remember it.'

Nettie took a deep breath. 'I was coming back to Mrs Pole's, to get her supper, and see if she was all right for the night. I'd have asked her what she wanted to eat, and got it on a tray next to her wheelchair. Then I'd have got her washing things ready in the bathroom, and taken her to the toilet if she needed to go, and I'd have got her night things out. She can just about get herself to the bedroom, though it costs her dreadful pain. I never wanted to come out at night, you see. She could have had someone else, but she chose to battle on by herself. Anyway, I let myself in, and went to the back of the bungalow. It was so hot today I'd left her in the conservatory, with the door ajar and the windows open, just to catch the breeze.'

'You'd been to see her at lunchtime, yes? What time did you leave?'

'Oh, about half past one.'

'And you got back at six?'

'Perhaps a bit after. I was running late. But you see, normally I would have gone back.'

'Oh?' Louise looked at Nettie, her head on one side.

'Yes, usually I go back about three, and take her out for a bit of air, just for an hour or so, up onto the bluffs or round the quieter streets. She gets so claustrophobic, shut away all day.'

'You do that every day?'

'Not on Sundays. I take her to church on Sunday morning, if she's up to it. But you see, today was different. I couldn't go back. I had to take my Ben to the vet's, because he's having trouble with his teeth. Mrs P said she didn't mind, it was too hot to be tramping round anyway.' She rubbed the handkerchief over her face. 'Oh, Sergeant, I wish I had gone back!'

Louise patted Nettie's arm. 'It can't be helped, Mrs Carew,' she said gently. 'All right. So you went back at six. Did you call out to her when you went in?'

'Oh yes, of course. I always do.'

Louise shifted in her seat and smoothed down her skirt. 'Did anyone see you arrive?'

Nettie shook her head, frowning. 'I don't know. I didn't see anyone. Well, there was an old man with a dog on the seat up the road. But he looked half asleep. Oh, and a young woman with a pram. I didn't recognise either of them.'

'Were you surprised or worried when Mrs Pole didn't answer?'

'No, not really. Sometimes she can't be bothered to answer. She can be quite abrupt, you know. Rude, almost. But I'm used to her.'

'Go on.'

'The first thing I noticed was there was, well, *stuff* all over the place. Things were in a mess – a lamp on the floor, drawers hanging open. I didn't leave it like that, and I was puzzled. I wondered if Mrs P had been looking for something. Then I went into the conservatory. She was sitting in her wheelchair, looking out into the garden.' Nettie glanced up anxiously at Louise.

'Did you have a clear view of her face?'

'Only sideways.'

'What did you do then?'

21

'Well, I noticed her water glass had fallen onto the tiles and broken. Really she was dangerous with glass, but she refused to have a plastic beaker. She was most haughty when I suggested it. There was glass and water everywhere. I bent down to pick it up, and I spoke to her, I can't remember what I said, something like, "Oh dear, what's happened here? Did you knock it?" And then while I was squatting down, picking up pieces of glass, I looked up at her, and I knew something was wrong.'

'Hold on a moment, Mrs Carew.' A uniformed constable was leaning in at the car window. 'Is everything secure, Des?'

The constable nodded. 'Yes, Sarge. All done.'

'All right. Make sure no one steps inside that tape. Is someone at the back?'

'Constable Simmons, Sarge.'

'Thank you.' Louise turned back to Nettie. 'All right, Mrs Carew. You say you knew something was wrong. What made you think so?'

Nettie swallowed. 'She, Mrs Pole, had her scarf round her neck. I know when I left it was just loosely wrapped round, you know? She doesn't like draughts. But now it was tied tightly, really tightly, and there's no way she could have done it. Her hands, her poor painful hands – they were kind of held up, as if she was trying to pull the scarf away. And her face! Oh, Sergeant, her face was terrible. All twisted and red, and her eyes were –' She faltered. Louise waited. 'That's when I cut myself. I was holding pieces of glass, and I must have gripped them, not thinking. But I could see she was dead. Poor lady. Who would do such a thing? She was helpless.'

'All right, Mrs Carew. Just remind me, how long have you been looking after Mrs Pole?'

'About five or six years. Ever since she moved to the town. At first she didn't need me so much. But she's got worse.'

'And it's a private arrangement, you say?'

Nettie nodded. 'People know me here. I've lived in Compton all my life. After my John died I needed something to do. I've got other clients, you see.'

'Yes, so you said. Did Mrs Pole set up the arrangement herself?'

'No, it was a man. A very charming man, by the sound of him. He said he was her brother. I've never met him, you see. We did it all over the phone. He said his sister had not long moved in, that she needed help, so he'd made enquiries and people had recommended me. He posted me a key, and he pays money direct into my bank account.'

'All right, Mrs Carew. Thank you for being so helpful.'

'Can I go home now?' Nettie looked at Louise, her hands gripped together.

'Not just yet. I'll need you at the police station to make a statement. Just what you've told me. It won't take long.'

'Oh, dear! But I need to get home soon. My dogs are shut in, and it's terribly hot.'

Louise thought for a moment. 'Would you be happy for a constable to go down to your place and let your dogs out? You could go with him in your car, then leave your car at home while you come down to the station.'

'Well, I suppose so. If that's how it has to be. I need to take them out before it gets dark, though.'

'It won't take as long as that. And someone will drive you home.'

Patrick looked around the small front garden. The grass was mown, and red geraniums flourished in a tub beside the door.

'I suppose Joseph must have a gardener,' he said. 'And what do you think, a housekeeper? Now he's on his own?'

'Good grief, man, what century are you living in? Clergy don't have that sort of people any more. Your view of the church is positively Trollopian. Joseph probably does all his laundry, trims his hedges, runs the mop over the kitchen floor, bakes his own bread and cleans out the gutters all by himself, in between consoling the sick and composing uplifting sermons.'

'Joseph doesn't quite do *all* those things, as it happens.'

Unheard the front door had swung open, and Joseph Stiles stood in the doorway, smiling his lopsided smile.

'Joseph, old chap!' Bert shook his friend's hand vigorously. 'How are you?'

'I am all right, thank you,' Joseph said. 'Tired out, of course, after all that baking. Hello, Patrick. Good to see you. Come in.'

The three men stood in the shady hallway and looked one another up and down.

'You're looking a bit careworn, Joseph,' Patrick said without preamble. 'But then we're all looking older, I suppose. Except Bert, of course. He manages to retain his youthful good looks. Must be his upper-crust genes. But you still have hair as well. It's most unfair.'

Joseph laughed and clapped Patrick on the shoulder. 'Yes, but it's a bit grizzled round the edges, and in need of a trip to the barber. You've gone for the hard man look and shaved it all off, I see.'

'It was a case of pre-empting nature,' Patrick said sourly. 'Male-pattern baldness, back to front. But at least,' he brightened, 'none of us have run to fat. Not yet. And if Bert is right and you do all your own work, you probably won't.'

'Bert is almost right,' Joseph said. 'But I do have a little help with the admin stuff. A nice lady volunteers once a week and keeps the paperwork in order. Otherwise I'd be wading in it.' He caught Patrick's eye. 'And no, in case you were wondering, she isn't young and nubile. Irene is a retired headmistress, terrifyingly efficient, and at least seventy. But come through to the kitchen. Would you like some tea, or is it time for something stronger?'

Patrick and Bert followed Joseph down a passage and through a door to the back of the house, where a large light kitchen overlooked a long, wide back garden bordered with hedges and trees. 'We were thinking of bringing a bottle,' Patrick said, 'but we weren't sure if it would be quite appropriate.'

Joseph raised an eyebrow. 'What, do I drink or not, do you mean?'

'You had a bit of an issue, didn't you, at one time? We weren't quite sure –'

Joseph shook his head. 'A long time ago, old fellow. And alcohol wasn't really a problem. I couldn't afford it, which was probably fortunate. I've cooked us a meal, ready in twenty minutes or so. Bottle of red suit you? Sit down, take the weight off. I'll get the glasses.'

An hour later, plates and bottle empty and another half-consumed, Bert leaned back in his chair and loosened his belt with a groan. 'Joseph, you have become something of a cook. I have to say that was delicious.'

'Just a bit of beef and a few vegetables,' Joseph said. 'Nothing fancy. Top up?'

'I won't, thanks.'

'But I will,' Patrick said, pushing his glass across the table. 'Wicked to waste it. Thanks. Well, Joseph old chap, we've brought you up to date on our fascinating lives – Bert and his ancestral estates and his horses and his heirs at public school and what-not, and me attempting to teach environmental science to a body of students most of whom don't speak the Queen's English, and living in a house I can't afford to get my offspring to the right schools. When are you going to fill us in about your doings? We've heard the odd snippet over the years, but the last time we saw you was at your wedding.'

Joseph lowered his eyes and picked at the tablecloth. 'Yes,' he said quietly. 'Five years ago, almost to the day.' He looked up, and his smile was melancholy. 'What do you want to know?'

'Everything, of course.'

'Birth onwards?'

'If you like.'

'No, we'd be here all night. Perhaps the unexpurgated biography can wait. Preferably for ever.' He sighed. 'Look, you know I really appreciate your coming down to see me, giving up your weekend, and I'm sure it's out of kindly fellow-feeling for the bereaved widower. But I should come clean. When poor Caroline was killed in that motorway pile-up she was in the act of leaving me. So you can understand I can't really be sorry on my own account. Of course I'm appalled for Caroline herself, and for her family. It was obviously a disaster for them – Caroline was only thirty-two at the time, far too young to die.

But I could hardly grieve for a life I wouldn't have had anyway. I hope that doesn't sound callous.'

'You poor old thing,' Bert murmured. 'I had no idea.'

'You knew she was leaving you?' Patrick asked sharply.

'Yes, she made that clear. Couldn't stand the life, she said. Couldn't stand me, when I was so often depressed.'

'But she knew about the life, surely? You were ordained before you married.'

Joseph nodded. 'Caroline was at home in the smoke,' he said. 'And at first I was working in an inner-city parish. That's where we met. But my old troubles came back, which is one of the reasons I got moved here. And Compton was far too sleepy for someone like Caroline. Too sleepy, too provincial, not enough going on. She was scathing on the subjects of flower-arranging and cleaning rotas and all those other small services that keep a parish ticking over.' There was silence for a moment as the friends absorbed Joseph's story. Then Joseph cleared his throat and looked up. 'What I didn't know, and what came out at the post-mortem, was that Caroline was pregnant.'

'Good heavens!' Bert said. 'How dreadfully sad.'

'You're sure it was yours?' Patrick said abruptly.

'Carver, really!' Bert protested.

Joseph waved his hand. 'Don't worry, Bert. I suppose it's a fair question. I have assumed so, Patrick. I have no reason to believe otherwise. But I'll never know for sure. I just know if things had been different I might have been living here with a wife and child.'

'Sorry, old chap. Rather tactless.'

'No problem.' The phone rang in the hall. 'Excuse me for a moment.' Joseph pushed his chair back, wiped his hands on his napkin and left the room, closing the door quietly behind him. A moment later they heard him pick up the phone and speak.

'That was a bit brutal, Carver,' Bert said. 'The poor chap's obviously been through the mill, however much he plays it down.'

'I suppose so. I never did have much grasp of diplomacy. Good job you're around, Bert – keep me in check.'

They heard the phone go down and Joseph came back in. 'I'm sorry, I'm going to have to go out for a while.'

'A parishioner in distress?' Patrick said with insincere sympathy. 'A death-bed confession, perhaps?'

'Not exactly,' Joseph said, and his voice was unusually stern. 'One of my congregation is at the police station. That was her on the phone, asking me to come and be with her. She's just found another member of my flock dead.'

'But why the police station, Joseph?' Bert asked.

'Because she was murdered, it seems.'

'Good grief!'

'Look, fellows, I'm sorry, you'll have to fend for yourselves for a while. Your rooms are at the top of the staircase, bathroom opposite. If you want anything help yourselves. I'll be back as soon as I can.' Joseph pulled a jacket from a hook behind the door and stuffed his arms into the sleeves.

'You can't drive, old man, not after all the wine you've drunk,' Bert said.

'I don't have a car,' Joseph said. 'Caroline took our car and smashed it up, and I haven't bothered to replace it. I'll take my bike. Please, make yourselves at home.'

A moment later the front door slammed shut.

'Well,' Patrick said softly. 'Maybe it's not going to be quite so dull after all.'

Bert got to his feet. 'Really, Carver, sometimes you are quite insufferable.'

'I just say what other people are thinking. I may be insufferable, but most people are hypocrites.'

'Have it your own way.' Bert pulled a tea towel down from a drying-rack. 'But we can at least make ourselves useful and do the washing up.'

Nettie dabbed at her pink, puffy eyes. 'I hope you don't mind, Joseph. Calling you out like this.'

'Of course I don't mind.'

She sniffed. 'Isn't this the weekend you were having visitors?'

'Yes, two old friends from university days.' Joseph shifted uncomfortably on the hard wooden bench. 'Couldn't they have found somewhere pleasanter for you?'

'I had to make a witness statement. I don't know what's keeping them. They were supposed to be taking me home.' She began to cry again, her lips trembling as fat tears rolled down her cheeks. 'Oh dear, I'm so sorry. I was quite calm at first, but now I can't seem to cope at all.'

'That's very normal, Mrs Carew,' Louise Gordon said as she came into the room. 'Delayed shock. Here, I've brought you a cup of tea. We'll drive you home when you've drunk it. Would you like one, sir?'

'No, thank you. Will you need Mrs Carew again, Sergeant?'

'Yes, I'm afraid so. She's a very important part of the investigation. So no leaving the country, Mrs Carew.'

Nettie took a sip of tea. 'Where do you think I'd be going, for goodness' sake!' She turned to Joseph. 'Oh, but isn't it awful, Joseph! Poor Mrs Pole! Who could do such a thing? What wickedness there is in this world.'

'Sadly, Nettie, you're right.'

Louise Gordon, holding the door open, looked out into the corridor. 'Ah, here's the Inspector. He'll want a word, Mrs Carew. Then you really can go home, till we need you again.'

She left the room, pulling the door closed behind her. Joseph and Nettie heard her speak, and the low tones of a man's voice in reply. The conversation went on for several minutes, but nothing could be clearly heard. Nettie sniffed and wiped her face with her handkerchief, and Joseph patted her arm reassuringly.

Then the door opened again, and a moment later a very tall man came in, stooping as he entered. His dark eyes were baggy with fatigue, his hair and moustache peppered with grey.

'Mrs Carew, sir,' Louise Gordon said as she followed him in. 'The lady who found Mrs Pole's body. Inspector Hazell, from Stockley CID.'

Nettie Carew clapped her hands together. 'Well! If it isn't little Freddie Hazell! Haven't seen you for years, my dear! How are you?' Joseph, looking on, enjoyed the look of horror, replaced in a moment by amusement, on Louise Gordon's face.

'You know each other?' she said.

Hazell bent over and took Nettie's hand, smiling. 'Good to see you, Mrs C,' he said. 'You're looking well.'

'This young man was born and bred in Compton,' Nettie said. 'He was in the same class as my John in primary school. Often round our house, weren't you, my dear? How well you have done, Fred.'

'Thank you. I hear you've had an unpleasant experience this evening.'

Nettie sighed. 'Yes. Poor, poor Mrs P. She's not had an easy life.'

Hazell turned to Louise Gordon. 'If you're all done for now with Mrs Carew, Sergeant, I'll drive her home myself. Take the opportunity to catch up.'

'Right you are, sir.'

The Inspector turned to Joseph. 'And you are, sir -?'

'Joseph Stiles. I'm the vicar of Christchurch. Mrs Carew, and Mrs Pole for that matter, are, were, members of my congregation. Mrs Carew was upset and asked me to come.'

'Would you mind waiting till I come back, Reverend? I won't be long. It would save time if I could ask you a few questions this evening.'

'All right. You OK, Nettie? I'll phone you in the morning, see how you are.'

'Thank you, Joseph. I'm sure I'll be fine.' She put her tea cup down. 'Ready, Fred.'

Despite the discomfort of the narrow, slippery bench, Joseph dozed while he waited for Inspector Hazell to return, overcome by the weariness that seemed to follow his every step. Someone came into the room and left a cup of tea, but he did not hear them, and when voices in the corridor outside wakened him the tea was cold, an unappetising brown ring staining the edge of the white cup.

'Reverend Stiles.'

Joseph blinked. 'Yes.'

Hazell came into the room and sat at the table. He put a cardboard file down in front of him. 'Sorry to keep you waiting, sir. I went for a walk with Mrs Carew and her dogs. Just wanted to see that she was all right.'

'You know her well, then, Inspector.'

Hazell shook his head. 'I knew her when I was a lad at school. When I went to secondary school I saw her less often, though she was friendly with my mother. I went off to school in Stockley, and John went to a special school by bus.' He looked up. 'Would you come and sit at the table, sir?'

'Of course.' Joseph sat down opposite Hazell. 'Why a special school?'

'What? Oh, yes, John. John had Down's Syndrome, Mr Stiles. It was very sad – Mrs Carew was widowed early, and John died following a routine operation when he was thirty.'

'So Nettie has nobody, apart from her dogs.'

'And her friends, I hope.'

'Indeed.' Joseph frowned. 'I knew she was a widow, of course, and she'd mentioned her son occasionally, but she didn't elaborate and I have always hesitated to probe.'

'I see.'

Joseph shifted in his seat. 'What was it you wanted to ask me about, Inspector?'

Hazell leaned back in his chair and stretched out his long, thin legs. Beneath dark eyebrows his eyes surveyed Joseph, tired eyes full of intelligence. 'How long have you lived in Compton, Mr Stiles?'

Joseph pursed his lips. 'Three years, give or take.'

'Is it a large congregation at Christchurch?'

'Not normally, no.'

Hazell was silent for a moment. 'So would you say you knew your flock fairly well as individuals?'

'Some better than others. I thought I knew Nettie quite well, but I didn't know what happened to her son.'

'What about Erica Pole?'

Joseph nodded. 'I went to her place fairly regularly, at her request, to give her Communion.'

'Did she ever get to church?'

'When I first came here Nettie used to bring her quite regularly, but her health has deteriorated recently. It became a struggle for her to leave the house, and she was embarrassed for people to see her as she was. Also,' he cleared his throat, 'there's no toilet in the church, and I had the impression that might be an issue for Erica in recent months. But she still comes once in a while, when she feels well enough.'

Hazell folded his arms, still fixing Joseph with his intent gaze. 'I gather from Mrs Carew that Mrs Pole was not especially popular.'

Joseph smiled slightly. 'She could be very abrupt. I believe she'd fallen out with most of her neighbours as a result. She hated being helpless and rejected every offer of help, sometimes quite rudely. But at the same time she needed help, and she needed friends, so I didn't take her rants too seriously. She had a difficult life, and of course she was in considerable pain.'

'Do you know how she became disabled?' Hazell scribbled a note on the pad in front of him.

'It was a long time ago – at least fifteen years, I think. She was on a friend's yacht, on holiday. This is what she told me. She damaged her spine in a diving accident.'

'She must have had treatment, surgery, physiotherapy perhaps?'

'I really don't know all the details, Inspector. Just that in recent years she had become worse – more pain, less mobility. And latterly arthritis became a problem as well. She was less and less able to take care of herself or take charge of her life, more and more dependent. And she hated it.'

Hazell made another note: from what Joseph could see, an indecipherable hieroglyph. 'When was the last time you were in Mrs Pole's house?'

'Mm, last week some time. Wednesday.'

'Would you say you were an observant man?'

Joseph shrugged. 'About average, probably.'

'Would you, for example, notice if anything was missing?'

'From Erica's? I don't know. She didn't have many things, certainly. The house was quite sparsely furnished. She had an ancient television, a radio, a shelf of books. Presumably she had clothes in her wardrobe, but I don't think I ever went into her bedroom – or perhaps I did, once, to fetch something at her request. But I didn't take much notice of what was there. She always said she had nothing to entice a burglar, if that's what you mean. No jewellery, very little money, nothing of value. Sometimes I expressed concern that she seemed rather gung-ho about security, but she always maintained it was a bit pointless in the circumstances. She had a locked gate in her back garden, I think. I guess that wouldn't have deterred a determined burglar. It didn't seem to bother her, though.'

'What do you know about her background? Did she confide?'

Joseph shook his head. 'Not much. She'd been living here a few years before I arrived. We talked a fair bit, when she wanted to, but not much detail about her life. I wouldn't ever pry, Inspector. If someone wants to tell me something, I'll listen. But if they don't, I don't press them. Erica was a bit of a mystery, but it's not my job to probe into people's secrets. Perhaps I should have.'

Hazell shot Joseph a look. 'Why do you say that?'

'I'm asking myself, of course, why anyone would want to kill her.'

'Hm. So what did you talk about with Mrs Pole?'

'Matters of faith, principally. She had many questions.'

'I see.' Hazell tapped his pen quietly on his notebook, then laid it down. 'And were you able to answer her?'

A stain of colour appeared on Joseph's cheekbones. 'No, not always to her satisfaction, I'm afraid.'

Hazell got to his feet suddenly, his chair scraping against the floor. 'Thank you, Reverend Stiles. I appreciate your frankness. Mrs Carew told me you have guests, so I'll let you get back to them. We may very well need to speak to you again, so please don't go anywhere, will you?'

Joseph stood up too quickly, and his chair clattered to the floor. 'I'm not likely to abscond,' he said with a touch of sourness. 'The day after tomorrow is Sunday. I have services here and at Compton Parva.' He set the chair to rights.

'Of course.' Hazell offered his hand, and Joseph shook it. 'Thanks again. I'll see you out.' He opened the door and let Joseph through. 'Oh, and Reverend Stiles, I wonder, could you please let us have a list of your regular congregation? Names, addresses?'

For a moment Joseph seemed confused. 'Well – yes, I suppose I could do that. I'll drop it round in the morning.'

By the time Joseph wheeled his bicycle wearily into his garden shed it was past ten o'clock. The lights were still on and he found Bert and Patrick still sitting at the kitchen table with a bottle of whisky between them.

'There you are, Joseph!'

'Yes. I'm sorry to have abandoned you for so long. The Detective Inspector turned up and wanted to ask me some questions, but he kept me hanging around for quite a while, I'm afraid. I see you have found some entertainment.'

'We discovered a shop with a licence,' Bert said. 'Wouldn't dream of raiding your supply, of course.'

Joseph smiled. 'Just as well, as my supply is probably exhausted.'

'Has there been any progress with the investigation?' Patrick asked.

'I doubt it, not yet,' Joseph said, resting his hands on the table. 'And even if there were, I don't think they'd be telling me. All I know is that Erica Pole is dead, we assume murdered, we don't know by whom and we don't know why.'

'But shouldn't someone be informed?' Bert said. 'Does she have any family?'

'All that, it seems to me, is for the police to organise. Look, fellows, I hope you won't think me rude, but it's been a long day with a nasty shock at the end of it. I'm sorry it's happened when you're here, but if you don't mind I'm going to turn in, perhaps have a quiet read and collect my thoughts. I hope this business doesn't eat up your whole weekend, that's all.'

'Of course, my dear fellow, you go and rest. We're all right, aren't we, Patrick?'

'Yep – me, Bert and Old Man Scotch will get along just fine,' Patrick said, his voice a little thick. 'We'll see you in the morning, Joseph.'

Lying on his bed in the dark, fully clothed, Joseph tried and failed to clear his mind. His friends' laughter from the kitchen below battered him, and he could barely think. Chaotic images crowded his sleepless brain, images of Erica in the time that he had known her, driven out by the chilling thought that soon perhaps he would have to conduct her funeral. At last he heard footsteps on the stairs and hissed goodnights as Bert and Patrick finally went to bed. He endured the sounds of running water, a flushing toilet, a loud crash and cursing, until at last the house was quiet.

Slowly the sense of strain began to unwind and drain away. Still he found himself unable to think, let alone pray; and yet he knew his absolute need to spend time in touch with his God. The presence of Bert and Patrick in the house seemed to disrupt the very air he breathed.

He got up slowly, yawning, running his hand through his already-disordered hair, picked up his shoes and crept down the darkened stairs. The sound of gentle snoring came from one of the guest bedrooms. In the hall he took a key down from a hook and let himself out into the still-warm summer night. There was silence in the street, and the light of a half-moon gilded the clipped hedges of his neighbours.

He walked the few yards to the church and let himself in, switching on only one dim light. He closed the door softly behind him and sat in one of the back pews, like a visiting stranger. The shadows and the silence enfolded him, and he undid the top button of his shirt and slumped back, his eyes closed.

Oh, Lord, what a mess. What a mess I am in. What a mess I am. Now what am I to do? I know too much, and yet I know nothing. Whatever I say I will get someone into trouble, and yet if I say nothing it will probably be worse. I want to be clear and honest and above reproach, but somehow along the way I have lost the art. Sans peur et sans reproche – whose motto was that? It doesn't matter. Because I don't think it's possible, not in these times, not for me. And yet there are people who should be defended. One of them at least is innocent of any wrongdoing, and yet would be so hurt if the truth were known. Erica was convinced of that. But what is the truth? She didn't tell me all of it, I'm sure. It always seems to be the way – having to do too big a job with inadequate tools and insufficient information. Lord, what would you have done? Did anyone entrust you with a secret? If they did, it wasn't recorded. You were so open and transparent, even when you were being enigmatic. No wonder they killed you. But who killed Erica?

Hazell and Louise Gordon sat looking at each other silently across the table, each nursing a mug of tea.

'So, sir,' Louise ventured after a moment, 'what are you thinking?'

Hazell sighed. 'Sorry, Louise. And when we're on our own, call me Fred, will you? We worked together pretty well in the old days, didn't we?'

Louise smiled. 'Way back when! I was a lowly DC, and you were a demanding boss. By the way, congratulations – I hear you've just got the next rank.'

'Thanks. So was I that bad?' Hazell looked pained.

'No, you were a good boss. But you expected results.'

'I hope I still do. Anyway, I should have kept you updated sooner. It's been a long week and a long day, and this happened right at the end of it. I'll bring you up to speed.' He took a sip of his tea and cleared his throat. 'As soon as I got your call I drove straight to the scene.'

Louise nodded. 'I thought you would. Was everything OK?'

'It was all wrapped up tight, thanks to you. I met the Divisional Surgeon on the front path. He gave me the curtest of nods and confirmed that Mrs Pole was in fact dead. Then he got in his car and roared away. Probably not too amused at being called out on a Friday evening, but you did the right thing. Some smart-arse lawyer might have tried to make out she wasn't dead when we moved her – you can't be too careful. I got into protective gear and went into the house. Like you, I saw no sign of forced entry. Our photographer was there, so I told him what shots I wanted and he finished up quickly and left. I had the chance to look around for maybe five minutes before the SOCOs arrived. The only area where there was any obvious disturbance was in the living-room – drawers open, shelves ransacked, contents strewn over the floor. But nowhere else: bathroom, bedroom, kitchen all seemed normal. And there was a handbag on the kitchen worktop. Zipped up and tidy. I took a look inside, not much there, just a hairbrush, a pack of tissues, that sort of thing, but there was a purse with money – not a huge amount, about sixty quid. To my eyes it looked undisturbed. OK, it's just possible a burglar might have taken some and left some, but would he, really? And then closed the purse and zipped up the bag?'

Louise shook her head. 'Not likely. We'll have to see whether there are any fingerprints there that we can't account for. You're right, though: it's odd.' She thought for a moment. 'When did they take the body?'

'While I was still there.' Hazell frowned and cleared his throat. 'I'm thinking we need to move sharpish, Louise. A solitary disabled woman, violently murdered in her own home, right here in the quiet heart of safe middle England. The press are going to be out in force. I'm going to ring the pathologist at home, stick my neck out, see if he can get the say-so to do the PM tomorrow. Who is the pathologist these days?'

'Ben Crocker.'

Hazell noted Louise Gordon's sudden flush, but said nothing. 'So what happened to the old chap? Mortimer? Mortlake?'

'Morton. Retired about a year ago.'

'Right.' Hazell finished his tea. 'Look, it's getting late. We'll have a full-on day tomorrow. Just summarise for me, can you, what enquiries are in action at the moment.'

Louise took out her notebook. 'I had three constables available and they knocked on all the doors in Plough Lane. Obviously not every resident was at home. Nobody noticed anything unusual either today or in the last couple of days, except the next-door neighbour clocked an unfamiliar car parked outside the garages at the end of the alley that leads to the back gardens of the bungalows – a black BMW four-by-four. The neighbour didn't take the registration – he didn't think much of it at the time. People do park there, he said. He only noticed it because it seemed a bit smart for the area.'

'Anything else?'

'Well, as you said, there was no sign of forced entry, front door or back gate. We have no idea who possessed a key, apart from Mrs Carew herself, but we do know the conservatory door was ajar. Someone could have scaled the back fence with a ladder. I doubt we'll find any footprints with the ground so dry and hard, but we'll have to wait and see what the scenes of crime people find. I confess to being puzzled, though.'

'Go on.'

'Like you, I saw what looked like a burglary. But there was nothing obviously missing. Mrs Pole's TV was still there. Perhaps it wasn't something a burglar would want. Maybe he or she broke in and didn't find anything of value. I looked in the drawers that were hanging open, but they were just full of...stuff. The sort of stuff people keep in drawers, junk really. One thing I expected to see, though, and didn't.'

'What?'

'A phone, sir. Mrs Pole was disabled. A lot of the time she was alone. What if something went wrong, say she fell out of her chair? There was no landline anywhere, and anyway wouldn't she have had something portable within reach? So she could call for help? It doesn't add up – someone's set up care for her, but she can't communicate.'

'Which leads you to what conclusion, Louise?'

'I think she probably did have a phone. A mobile in her pocket, in her lap, on the table beside her. I reckon she had a phone, and the killer took it.'

Hazell nodded, frowning. 'That's something to check with Mrs Carew, first thing in the morning. But there was something else missing, I thought. I looked in the drawers because I wanted to find some clue about her next of kin – some paperwork with names, addresses, you know the sort of thing, certificates, insurances, deeds, bills, bank statements. But there was nothing.'

'I suppose,' Louise reflected, 'some of that stuff could be with a solicitor.'

'Or she had copies, and the killer took them. Along with her phone, maybe.'

'Why would he do that?'

'I don't know. It seems an odd thing to do if it was an opportunist burglary that backfired.'

'But maybe,' Louise said, frowning in concentration, 'maybe the killer had some idea of delaying us, stopping us finding out who she was, who knew her, who her relations were, who visited. Stupid, really. Nobody's anonymous. Chances are we're going to find out who she was straight away, from the neighbours. Not a very bright burglar, if it was a burglar.'

Hazell flexed his shoulders and stretched. 'Well, all that's speculation. I admit there are oddities here. But we have to think about tomorrow.' He stood up. 'You need to talk to Mrs Carew. I need to organize a lot more bodies than you have here in Compton to do a complete house-to-house, starting with the residents of Plough Lane who weren't in earlier today. Oh, and Louise, get one of your lads to go down to the bus station, have a word with the regular drivers, see if they noticed anyone they didn't know coming into Compton yesterday afternoon. Once we've covered all the streets, and who knows how long that'll take, I can stand the Stockley people down. I can't keep them away from their normal duties too long. I'll need a street map, addresses of every resident. What's the population these days?'

Louise shrugged. 'Not sure, Fred. Compton's not a big place. I can find out.'

'Right. I'm going home now, and I suggest you do the same.' He paused at the door. 'I've cleared for you to be part of the team, heading external enquiries. One man I'm going to bring in from Stockley for the whole investigation. DS Rivers. He'll be our Office Manager. Not known for charm and conversation, but I trust him. He has a lot of experience, and he's very thorough.' He thought for a moment. 'I'll be in early.

You'll need to organise getting elimination fingerprints from anyone who had a legitimate reason for visiting Mrs Pole's bungalow. And I want to have another little chat with that vicar, before he gets the chance to talk to Mrs Carew. He knows something he's not telling us, or I've lost my nose for trouble.'

1972: Scotland

'Marjie, why are you ringing me at school? It's only for emergencies! I could be in big trouble.'

'It *is* an emergency, Quin. I don't know what to do, and there's nobody else that cares.'

'Are you crying, M? What's the matter? I'll be home in a week anyway.'

'I know. But I had to tell you what's going on, so you can make a plan. Once you're here it won't be so easy.'

'All right, but stop sniffing and snuffling, I can hardly hear you. Tell me, Marjie, but be quick. The Old Man's just outside the door.'

'He's gone mad, Quin. Father. I'm sure of it. He drinks all the time, and yesterday he caught me with the back of his hand and I went flying. All because I'd got something wrong in my homework. I'm black and blue, Quin. I'm sure he'll kill me one of these days.'

'The evil bastard. I'll kill him first.'

'No, you need a proper plan. *Please*, think. I can't stay here much longer with him.'

'All right. Don't worry, I'll do *something*. I don't know what yet. How have you managed to get hold of the phone, anyway? He threatened he was going to lock it away.'

'He does normally. But he's gone fishing with Neil, and he forgot to lock his study. They got the old pickup going – they've been tinkering with it all week. He won't be back till tonight. They left me doing my lessons with *her*. But I think she's been drinking too. She suddenly went a funny colour and rushed off to the lav, and I heard her puking. Came back looking really green, mumbled something about me finishing my work, and scarpered off to their flat for a lie down.'

'Marjie, just keep your head down for a while. When I get home I'll deal with it, I promise. Don't be surprised at what I say to him. Just trust me, all right? Try to keep out of his way. If you find him half-way reasonable, apologise.'

'What?'

'Do it, Marjie. Say you're sorry you made him angry. Just survive till I come. I've got to go. I'll have to make up some story for the Old Man.'

'All right, Quin. I'm waiting for you. You won't leave me, will you?'

'You know I won't. Not ever. You and me, kid.'

'You and me, Quin.'

2008: Compton

Nettie was drying her hands on a kitchen towel when she heard the bell jangle. She looked at the clock: eight forty-five. She padded down the hallway and opened the door. The morning sunlight streamed in, blinding her, making her visitor a silhouette.

'Oh, Sergeant Gordon. Good morning.'

'Morning, Mrs Carew. May I come in?'

'Come in, of course. But I was just going to see Jamie, Sergeant.'

'Jamie?'

'Jamie Knowles. One of my other clients. He's disabled, and his mother can't do all the things he needs, because she's got problems with her hands. Mind you, I'm getting a bit old and creaky myself these days, and Jamie's no lightweight.'

'Is there someone else you could ask to see to Jamie today, Mrs Carew?'

Nettie frowned. 'Someone else?'

Louise Gordon nodded. 'What happens if you are unwell?' she said patiently. 'Surely you have back-up.'

'Oh, I see.' Nettie seemed confused for a moment. 'Well, I suppose I could ring Mrs Knowles and say I'll be late. Will this take long, Sergeant?'

'I don't really know, Mrs Carew. Depends where our chat leads to.'

'Oh. Well, I'll ring her then. I can't really call on anyone else at this short notice.' She gestured down the hallway. 'Go and sit down in the living room while I make the call. Do you mind dogs?'

'Not if they don't bite.'

A few minutes later Nettie joined Louise, who was sitting on an ancient brown sofa with one terrier on her feet and another on her lap.

'Bill! Get down, you rascal! I'm so sorry, Sergeant, your smart black trousers are all covered in hairs. I'll turf these two out.' She shooed the two dogs into the kitchen and shut the door. 'Oh dear,' Nettie fretted as she turned back to Louise. 'Mrs Knowles wasn't at all happy, and I didn't know if I was allowed to say anything about poor Mrs Pole, so I just said I was unavoidably detained. I do so hate letting people down.'

'Thank you for being discreet, Mrs Carew. You can explain to Mrs Knowles later. You understand that if someone has been murdered other things have to come second.'

'Yes, of course.' Nettie sighed. 'Would you like a cup of tea, Sergeant?'

'No, thank you. I'd just like to ask you a few questions and the sooner we're done the sooner you can get on with your day.'

'All right.' Nettie perched on the edge of an armchair opposite Louise, her face flushed, her hands gripped together in her lap.

Louise took a notebook out of her bag, and looked up at Nettie. 'There's no need to be anxious, Mrs Carew,' she said gently. 'I understand this has been a nasty shock for you. But there are things we need to know about Mrs Pole, and as far as we know you were the last person to see her alive. Apart from the murderer, of course.'

Nettie shuddered. 'I understand, Sergeant. Fire away.'

Louise nodded. 'One thing, Mrs Carew: does anyone visit you regularly? A friend, or family member?'

Nettie frowned. 'Well, once in a while, I suppose. A neighbour might drop by. I don't have any family, not round here. My sister lives in Cornwall, and I hardly ever see her. Why?'

'I'm wondering if anyone, someone you know, would have access to your keys.'

'I can't see how. Why would they want to?'

'Where do you keep your key to Mrs Pole's bungalow?'

Nettie's eyes widened. 'Oh! I see. Well, I am quite security-conscious, Sergeant. Mrs P being as she is, so vulnerable, and me responsible for her. You understand. I keep her key separate, in my kitchen drawer. It's not labelled, and nobody knows it's there but me.'

'So nobody could have taken it without your knowing?'

Nettie bristled. 'Certainly not.'

'All right, Mrs Carew. Thank you.' Louise cleared her throat. 'Another thing I'm puzzled about – Mrs Pole seemed to have no means of communication with the outside world. Strange for a person in her condition.'

Nettie blinked. 'No communication? But she had her phone. It sat on the table next to her chair, or it was in her lap. The one with the big numbers.'

Louise made a note. 'What was on this phone, Mrs Carew? You said Mrs Pole had trouble with her hands. Was she able to dial?'

Nettie shook her head. 'No. She had about ten numbers. I was number one, of course. She could just press the number, and my phone would ring.'

'Who else was on it?' Louise scribbled in her notebook.

'I don't know them all. That was her business.'

'So who set her up with this phone?'

Nettie shrugged. 'Her brother, I suppose.'

Louise thought for a moment. 'What were the arrangements if you needed help?'

'Me?'

'Well, what if something happened you couldn't cope with? Some decision regarding Mrs Pole? Say she was ill, or needed something, and she couldn't use the phone herself for some reason?'

'Oh, I see. Well, I used her phone to call her brother on his direct line. He was number two.'

'Did you ever have cause to contact him?'

Nettie thought. 'Once. In the early days. Mrs Pole had bad flu. She had a terribly high temperature. I didn't know her so well then, I had trouble getting through to the doctor's surgery, and I panicked, I suppose. I would be able to cope better these days.' She sighed. 'Not that I will ever have to now, of course. Poor lady.' A tear trickled down her cheek and she brushed it away. 'Sorry, Sergeant.'

'What happened on that occasion?'

'He said he would come down at once, and not to worry. He seemed a very kind man. Beautifully spoken.'

'And you don't know his name?'

'Of course I know his name. Mr Fraser. That was Mrs Pole's maiden name, Erica Fraser. But he didn't call her that.'

Louise looked up from her notebook. 'Oh?'

'He called her Marjie. I asked her why once, when she was in one of her better moods. She said it was because of a story their mother told them when they were very young, a story they liked and asked for over and over – you know what small children are like. Do you have children, Sergeant?'

'I'm afraid not. You were telling me about their special names, Mrs Carew.'

'Yes, in this story the two children, brother and sister of course, were called Marjorie and Quintin. So Mrs Pole and Mr Fraser were Marjie and Quin.'

Louise made a note. 'Is there any other way, do you suppose, Mrs Carew,' she said quietly, 'that we can contact Mr Fraser?'

'Well, there's his daughter, Helena. She was fond of Mrs P and came to visit regularly.'

'And you met her?'

'Oh, yes, quite frequently. A lovely young lady, and very fond of her aunt. Mrs P said to me once she was the only member of her family she had any time for, apart from her brother.'

'I see. Was she another number stored in Mrs Pole's phone?'

'Yes, but I have Helena's number in my address book too. Shall I get it for you?'

'Please. The family need to be informed.'

'Of course they do. What am I thinking of? I'm all of a dither today.'

She left the room, and after a few minutes of scrabbling and muttering came back in with a scrap of paper which she handed to Louise. 'Here you are, Sergeant. Poor dear girl, she'll be terribly upset.'

Louise got to her feet. 'One more thing, Mrs Carew, before I go and leave you in peace. Did Mrs Pole have any paperwork? You know, the kind of thing we all have, perhaps stored away safely somewhere, marriage certificate, title deeds, driving licence, birth certificate, insurances, that kind of thing?'

Nettie frowned. 'Well, of course that was none of my business, but I believe she had a brown cardboard folder in one of the drawers in the living room. I never looked inside it, but I guessed that's what it contained.'

A thought struck Louise. 'Did she have a safe anywhere in the house?'

'Not that I know of. She always said she had nothing worth stealing. I don't think she was very well off, Sergeant. It seemed to me her brother provided for her, for everything. But I had the impression that she might have been quite wealthy at some time in her life. Not that she said anything much. That's all it was – an impression.'

Louise paused by the door. 'You said something there about her mother, Mrs Carew. Did Mrs Pole ever speak about her early life?'

Nettie shook her head. 'Only once, a long time ago. I asked her what her childhood had been like, just in the way of making conversation, you understand, and she said one word: "Horrible." Then she clammed up. I kept quiet after that. It was none of my business, really.'

Louise made her way down the hall, with Nettie bustling behind. 'Sadly, Mrs Carew, it's become your business now. But I'd appreciate your continuing discretion. Please, don't say anything to anyone beyond the basic facts. Yes, Mrs Pole is dead. Yes, the police are involved. It's a small town, and there'll be gossip.' She opened the front door, and the sunlight bathed them in warmth. 'Especially as we are in the process of calling on every resident. And, I'm afraid, the press will be out in swarms.'

'Don't you worry, Sergeant,' Nettie said. 'I don't talk about my clients, dead or alive.'

'Thank you, and for your help this morning, Mrs Carew. We'll be in touch.'

In the kitchen of the vicarage on the other side of Compton, Joseph pushed his chair back and got up. 'If you'll excuse me, I need to go and dream up a sermon for tomorrow. With all this going on I've got a bit behind. Have some more coffee if you want it. I shouldn't be long – then I'll give you a guided tour of the sights, such as they are.' He smiled, and the creases round his eyes made him look even more tired. 'Maybe we'll finish up at the Nag's Head for lunch.'

'Now you're talking, Joseph,' Patrick said. 'Don't mind us – you go and sermonise.'

They heard him cross the hall and shut the door of his study behind him.

'Poor old Joseph,' Bert said, sipping his coffee. 'He does look worn out.'

Patrick stretched, his hands gripped above his head. 'Well, we must help him with a spot of relaxation. Lunch in the pub sounds a good start. Maybe we can relive a few of our youthful follies and bring a smile to that sombre visage.'

The doorbell rang, and Patrick sat up, staring in the direction of the sound like an attentive dog. The two men heard Joseph leave his study and open the front door. Patrick got up quietly, went to the door of the kitchen, and opened it a crack.

'Carver, what the heck are you doing?' Bert hissed. Patrick waved him to silence. Voices came from the hallway, footsteps, a closing door.

Patrick turned back to Bert, his eyes alight. 'It's the Old Bill,' he whispered. 'A very tall bloke with a moustache.'

'How do you know it's the law?'

'I heard Joseph call him Inspector. I'm going to creep out and listen.'

'Carver, you can't do that!'

'Says who?' Patrick came back to the table and finished his coffee in one gulp. 'You can be as scrupulous as you like, but I

47

want to know what's going on, and I'll wager your sunny acres Joseph won't tell us much.'

'I shall go out for a walk.' Bert's face was thunderous. 'Once I've finished the washing up. With the door closed. Eavesdropping, Carver – really isn't done.'

'I'm immune to guilt trips, Bert, especially of the socially-unacceptable variety. You should know that. Anyway, I bet you'll want to know what I find out when you come back from your stroll, you old hypocrite.' He grinned.

Bert said nothing. He got up from the table and carried his dishes to the sink, turning his back. Patrick took off his shoes and crept out of the kitchen.

'Do take a seat, Inspector.' Joseph indicated a chair and sat down behind his desk, sweeping away some of the open books and scribbled notes that littered it. 'What can I do for you?'

'Perhaps I could ask you a technical question, Reverend Stiles.'

Joseph nodded, his brows contracting slightly. 'You can ask whatever you like, of course.'

Hazell smiled, but there was little humour in it. 'The implication being that I can ask, and you can choose whether or not to answer.'

'I hope I am always willing to help the police with their enquiries.'

'In that case – you are an Anglican, I think.'

'Yes.'

'Of any particular persuasion?'

Joseph shrugged. 'I am more or less middle-of-the-road, I suppose. It seems to be suitable for Compton.'

'So, what's the Anglican position on the secrets of the confessional?'

Joseph's eyebrows shot upwards. He paused for a moment, and Hazell sat motionless, waiting. 'In the strict sense, I don't think it exists, Inspector. What are you driving at? Are you asking if I am obliged, as a minister, to keep secrets? or perhaps to divulge them?'

Hazell nodded. 'Yes, I suppose that is what I am asking, more or less.'

Joseph sighed and stretched out his legs under the desk. 'In the normal way of things, I don't do confession as such. If a parishioner wants to confide in me, of course I will keep that confidence, provided it isn't too inflammatory. But I would go that route as a private person too, not just in my priestly role. I might, if the situation seemed to require it, warn the person that I could not in all conscience keep a confidence that involved something illegal, immoral or harmful. And if I was in doubt there are those I could consult.'

'The Bishop?'

Joseph shrugged. 'Among others.'

'What about Erica Pole?' Hazell said abruptly, seeing, as he expected, Joseph's expression become guarded.

'What about her?'

'Did she ever ask for confession? Or should I say, unburden herself on the understanding that the confidence be kept?'

'Erica had many problems, Inspector. Physical, emotional, spiritual. I thought of myself as a friend as well as her vicar, but that doesn't mean I was privy to her deepest secrets.'

'All right, sir, just tell me what you do know.'

'For instance?'

Hazell frowned. 'Her early life. Her family. Her marital history. Anything that might help us discern a motive for murder.' He waited, seeing Joseph's silent struggle. 'You hesitate.'

'She told me things about herself, Inspector. Not much, it's true. I've probably based my own conjectures on insufficient evidence. But there are issues of confidentiality here. She was most insistent. There were other people she was very concerned to protect. Some of them innocent.'

Hazell's eyes narrowed. 'I imagine you are almost as dubious on the subject of innocence as I am myself,' he said. 'It's a very relative concept. I might consider a small baby innocent, but not much beyond infancy. Maybe you would consider even the baby corrupt.'

'Would I?'

'The doctrine of original sin.'

'Oh. Yes, well in practical terms I would probably consider a baby innocent too.'

'So what relatively innocent person are you defending, Mr Stiles? Or should I say who was Mrs Pole seeking to defend?'

Joseph's expression hardened. 'If I tell you that, such protection as I could offer by being silent would be blown to bits.'

'I shouldn't have to remind you that there is a murderer somewhere out there. Your anonymous "innocent person" may be in danger.' He noted the look of dawning dismay on Joseph's face. 'I think you'd better tell me what you know, sir. Let's start with Mrs Pole. Is there, was there, a Mr Pole?'

Joseph nodded, biting his lip. 'Erica was married in her twenties. It was not a happy marriage, and ended in divorce after about six or seven years, I believe. There was a child, a son. Custody was awarded to the father, and he took the boy away, to America. As far as I know she didn't see her son after that. I told you she hadn't had an easy life.'

Hazell thought for a moment. 'It's unusual for a court to give custody of a young child to its father,' he said. 'She must have been seen as a particularly unsuitable parent.'

'She drank,' Joseph said. 'In her own words, like the proverbial fish. She was an alcoholic, Inspector – or as near to being one as makes little difference. With, again in her own words, an unsavoury lifestyle. She dried out and tried to set things right after the boy was taken away, but it was too late.'

'Was this before or after the accident that led to her disablement?'

'Oh, before.'

'I see.' Again Hazell fell silent. 'Are the Poles, father and son, still in America?'

'As far as I know.'

'Well, we'll have to follow them up, of course. Mrs Pole had a brother, I believe.'

Joseph shifted in his chair. 'Who told you that?'

'It's our business to find out these things, Mr Stiles. So you don't need to pretend ignorance, and I would very much prefer it if you were frank with me. We know Mrs Pole had a brother, and a niece, and that their name is Fraser. Can you shed any more light?'

Joseph swallowed. 'He is Ewan Fraser, the construction millionaire who founded the Haven.'

Hazell drew a deep breath. 'I see.' He paused for a moment. 'The thing is, Reverend Stiles, the only contact we have is a telephone number for Helena Fraser, furnished by Mrs Carew. I thought it would be kinder, as well as more appropriate, to inform the brother rather than the niece. We could find out all these things, as I'm sure you realise, but it would be laborious. So much easier to ask someone – in this case, yourself. We must inform Mrs Pole's family of her death, of course.'

Joseph's pale face flushed. 'And is this why you've been asking me all these probing questions? Just to find out how to contact her relatives?'

'Among other things, sir, yes. I must say you've been most helpful. Saved that most precious commodity, police time.' He pushed his chair back and stood up, resting his hands momentarily on the edge of the desk, towering over Joseph. 'I may have to ask you more probing questions, I'm afraid. But I hope, now that we know who the next of kin is, I won't have to trouble your conscience any further. At least, not today. I'll see myself out.'

Hearing the front door click quietly shut, Joseph leaned back in his chair, closed his eyes, and let out a long, sighing breath.

Lord, I am not sure whether I have done well or ill. I want to be open, transparent, innocent – like the Inspector's baby. He grimaced. *But it doesn't seem possible, not in this world we have tainted and sullied. Erica asked me to keep her secret, the secret that had her locked up, heart and soul, for so many years. And I said I would. No doubt I shouldn't have. But what was I to do? Oh, Lord, why is everything so difficult? She's recruited me into her world, and I want to get out, out into the light that I haven't seen for so long. Holding on to this thing for her has made the load heavier, Lord – the load that came down with a crash when I read that note from Caroline. Perhaps I am particularly dim. Perhaps it's as*

Caroline said on more than one occasion, so bitter and taunting, that I suffer from the dimness peculiar to men, that single-minded obliviousness that leaves those we should care for out in the cold. I am guilty, I know. As to confession, I find the idea unbelievably appealing right now. To tell all, to shed this burden of dark knowledge. I said Erica was a friend, and she was, but it was a lopsided friendship, and she has left me with a load I can't carry. If only I could just tell Inspector Hazell everything. But I can't. Because there's the destruction of lives. In the case of Ewan Fraser, a life founded on something at least dubious, and yet producing great good. And there's Helena. If only for her, I have to think of the consequences. Lord, I need to know what to do, what to say, what not to say. I'm all at sea. Please, help me.

Patrick was hovering in the doorway of his bedroom. 'Bert? You're back, good. Come in here a moment.' Patrick took Bert by the elbow and drew him into the room, shutting the door behind him.

Bert stood with his arms folded. 'I'm still disgusted with you, and I don't want to know.'

'Of course you want to know,' Patrick said. He was sitting on the edge of his bed, where his laptop lay open. 'Anyway, aren't you overreacting a bit, old chap? I haven't done anything all that heinous, when it comes down to it. I know one isn't supposed to listen at keyholes, but I haven't actually committed a felony, just a little social blunder.'

'Hm.'

'Do sit down, Bert, you make me feel uncomfortable.'

Bert scowled. 'Just how you should feel, you utter peasant.' He slumped in a chair by the window.

'Don't insult the peasantry, old fellow,' Patrick said serenely. 'Especially as your forebears relied on them to do all the work and accumulate your hereditary fortune by the callouses on their hands.'

'Do give over, you verbose little Marxist,' Bert said. 'I can see by your wolfish grin that you've found something, so I suppose you'd better get it off your chest.'

'The most interesting thing I overheard,' Patrick said, 'was the identity of the dead woman's brother. Ewan Fraser.'

Bert sat upright. 'What? Not the chap who heads up that charity – what's it called?'

'The Haven. It's for the homeless.'

'That's it. Isn't he some kind of saint?'

'How would I know? I do know he's quite disgustingly rich, though. *And*, Bert old thing, I have met him.'

'Really? How come? I wouldn't have thought saints were regular members of your social circle.'

'It was a couple of years ago. I had the job of organizing guest speakers at my college. Broadening the little dears' knowledge beyond their narrow specialisms, that sort of idea. Fraser was one of the people I invited. Given his background in innovative architecture, affordable housing, and a charitable foundation for the homeless, I thought he might be of interest to my students.'

Bert leaned forward. 'Was he any good?'

'Yes, very, as it happens. He was also charming and surprisingly approachable. But that's not it, Bert. Before he came I did a bit of digging on the internet. I like to know the background of people I invite into the college. You can't be too careful. Some people are respectable on the surface and absolute stinkers when you look deeper. I can't afford to make that sort of howler in my job, especially as my college has Christian connections.'

'Yes,' Bert murmured. 'I have often wondered how you managed to swing that. Didn't they ask you about your religious affiliations, or lack of them, at your interview?'

'Of course,' Patrick said. 'But I don't have your scruples, and I needed the work. But that's not the point, Bert. I found out some interesting things about our friend Mr Fraser. Who, I have heard it said, might even be in the running for a knighthood one day.'

'Go on.'

'He grew up in a castle in Scotland. What they call a castle – more of a fortified manor. Quite remote and rather primitive, I understand. He inherited, and later sold, his ancestral seat in wildest Perthshire after his father died. The boy was only sixteen at the time. It was with the proceeds of that sale that he set up Fraser Homes and later the Haven.'

'Quite a fellow.'

'Yes. But I wonder if there was more to it than meets the eye.'

'You and your suspicious mind! I thought you said he was rather saintly.'

'I just can't believe in all that, Bert. People are people, full of cunning and self-seeking. That saintly exterior is probably a cover for something mucky.'

Bert shook his head. 'It must be wearisome, living with such cynicism.'

'On the contrary,' Patrick said briskly. 'It's refreshingly unsentimental.'

'So what are you saying? That there's some scandal surrounding Fraser? How did the father die, anyway?'

'He drowned while fishing. Drunk as a lord, apparently. Well, I suppose there's nothing much else to do but drink, is there, stuck out in some hideous old ruin in the middle of a peat bog. No, no scandal that I could unearth. But that's where you come in, Bert.'

'What are you talking about?'

'You upper-crust types are a close-knit little society, I think,' Patrick said. 'If you don't all exactly know each other, you know someone who knows someone, and they know someone else, and on it goes. So I have heard.' He raised his eyebrows enquiringly.

Bert pursed his lips. 'There's some truth in that, I suppose,' he said grudgingly. 'Especially when you consider my mother and her ilk. They seem to know about everybody and everything, north and south of the border.'

Patrick nodded. 'So I thought you could do a bit of research.'

'What?'

'A timely word in mama's ear? I'll bet the contents of Betsy's piggy bank she knows a thing or two.'

'But what for, for heaven's sake?'

'Background, Bert. My way of helping the police with their enquiries.'

'More like sticking your long nose in! Do show some sense for once, Carver! You'll get us all in hot water.'

'Ssh, Bert! Don't yell. We don't want Joseph getting wind of our schemes. He wouldn't approve at all.'

'Your schemes, Carver, not mine.'

'Don't deny you're interested. Just a bit of background, Bert. Is that so much to ask?'

Bert frowned. 'I still don't understand why you're so interested.'

'Well, here we are, spending our weekend in somnolent Compton Magna, home of the barbecuing commuter. Deadly dull. And something interesting happens – a murder, on our doorstep. A solitary woman whose brother is a national figure. Whose drunken father died in a mysterious accident. It livens things up a bit, don't you think?'

Bert shook his head. 'You've missed your vocation, Carver. You should be writing for the tabloids – it would suit your sleazy turn of mind right down to the ground.'

'Probably. But maybe you could find a moment at some point this weekend to turn on that flashy little phone of yours and have a word with your dear mater. See what you can dig up on clan Fraser. Just as a favour for your old chum Carver, who is ever so slightly bored.'

Hazell walked briskly into the police station, letting the door swing to after him. The constable on duty looked up.

'Davies, isn't it?' Hazell said.

'That's right, sir.'

'Look up a number, will you, please. Ewan Fraser. Somewhere in London. I'd like his home number ideally, but his office may have to be your first call.'

'Fraser, sir.' The constable frowned, perplexed.

'Fraser, yes, of Fraser Homes and the Haven.'

'That Fraser, sir! Right away.'

'I'll need a printout on anything we can find on him and his company. Soon as you can. Meanwhile I'll be upstairs in DS Gordon's office. Is she here?'

'Yes, sir.'

'Bring the number to me as soon as you get it.' Hazell bounded up the stairs. The door to Louise Gordon's office was ajar. He knocked lightly and entered. Louise was on the phone, and she waved him to a chair.

After a moment Louise said, 'All right, thanks,' and wrote a note on a pad as she hung up.

'This case?' Hazell asked.

Louise nodded. 'You asked for a preliminary opinion from the pathologist, Fred. I just rang to see if there'd been any progress. We won't get anything detailed until the PM's done, but he's a friend of mine –' Hazell raised one eyebrow, and Louise looked away '– and he owes me a few favours. He's not sticking his neck out, but there are no obvious marks on the body, apart from the neck. And he can't account for the blood, not yet.'

Hazell grunted. 'That fits with what we know of Mrs Carew's movements. And we were pretty sure the blood was Mrs Carew's too. That'll have to be confirmed.' He frowned and paused. 'What time do we have for that black BMW?'

'The neighbour wasn't sure. He saw it when he watered his garden, but it had gone by the time he went in for a cup of tea.'

Hazell sighed. 'Less than helpful.'

Louise leaned forward, her elbows on the desk. 'Did you find out anything from the vicar, Fred? Oh, incidentally, he dropped in the church electoral roll earlier, with names highlighted, people who were regular attenders. I've passed it on to the uniforms doing house-to-house. But we may need to follow some of them up.'

Hazell shook his head. 'He knew Erica Pole well, I'm sure. And she told him something he doesn't want to tell us. He's protecting someone. I didn't press him, not yet. If we need the information he's keeping to himself, we'll nail him down. If we can get it without alienating him, so much the better. But I did find out the identity of Mrs Pole's brother – none other than

Ewan Fraser, head man of Fraser Homes, founder of the Haven charity for the homeless, adviser to governments, often on panels or interviewed on television.'

Louise's eyebrows shot up. 'Wow. And here was the sister, secluded in Compton.'

'I rather think that was the point, don't you, Louise?' Hazell said. 'It's almost as if he was hiding her away.'

'But – '

A tap came on the door.

'Hold on. Come in, Constable.'

Davies edged into the room and cleared his throat. 'I found the number for the charity offices, sir,' he said. 'Got a very snooty lady who said, "No, you can't have Mr Fraser's home number. It's the *weekend*." So I told her it was the police on a matter of life and death and perhaps she'd like to speak to the Inspector. She humphed a bit, but anyway, here's the number, sir. And the information you wanted is being printed out now.'

'Thank you, Davies. Good work.'

Davies grinned and backed out of the door.

Hazell turned back to Louise. 'I'll use your phone, if I may, Louise.'

'Of course. Shall I go?'

'No need.' He picked up the handset, glanced at the scrap of paper Constable Davies had given him, and dialled. He waited. Then, 'May I speak to Mr Fraser, please?' A pause. 'This is Detective Inspector Hazell, of Stockley CID. It's extremely urgent. You are Mrs Fraser, madam?' Hazell listened again. 'I see. Have you any way of contacting Mr Fraser on the tennis court? By mobile, perhaps?' He waited for a few seconds, then interrupted brusquely. 'Please tell Mr Fraser that I will be calling on him at two o'clock this afternoon. You say he should be home for lunch. No, I would rather not discuss it on the phone, but I can assure you this matter is more important than any other claim on Mr Fraser's time. Goodbye.' He replaced the receiver with precision.

'That's telling her,' Louise said with a gleam of humour.

'Frosty upper-crust hag.' He cleared his throat and sat up. 'Don't quote me on that. I can't stand these self-important harpies that treat us like clod-hopping peasants.'

'Mrs Fraser?'

'The same.' He got to his feet. 'I shall be all civility and restraint when we meet the lady, Louise, I assure you.'

'I have faith in you, Fred,' Louise said wryly. 'Where now?'

'You can drive me up to London,' Hazell said. 'There's a nice pub I know on the way, the other side of Stockley, where we can get lunch. We've just got enough time, I think. Fortify ourselves for the interview with the Frasers. I only hope he has a better manner than his wife.'

'That's what they say.'

Hazell sighed. 'Well, whatever he's like, we have to tell him his sister is dead. It may be news to him, it may not. Come along, Louise. Get your keys and we'll be off. Incidentally, what do you make of the missing phone and papers?'

Louise followed him out of the room. 'It looks like an opportunist burglary, on the face of it. But there's still something that doesn't ring true. Taking the papers and the phone, and leaving the cash, doesn't make sense.'

Hazell paused at the top of the stairs and looked down at her from his considerable height. 'What makes you say that?'

'Say it was a hired killer, for instance. Or even a casual burglar. They'd never bother with trying to put us off the scent. Taking her stuff is the work of an insider, someone who doesn't want us to look too closely at her nearest and dearest. Amateurish, really. Almost as if he or she was disturbed, and panicked.'

Hazell nodded. 'I agree. Something tells me we might meet the killer in the next day or two – or even perhaps today.'

Gordon raised her eyebrows. 'It might be a good idea, then, to get those elimination prints done. Reverend Stiles, Mrs Carew, all the family members, anyone else we can think of who might conceivably have a reason to visit Mrs Pole.'

'Yes. I'll get someone to organise it on our way out. And I must ring my DCS. He'll give me a long rein, but I need to keep him informed.'

At a quarter to two Louise drove down a tree-lined road in a quiet suburb. The houses were large, set back behind railings and high walls, many with gates and visible security systems. 'Just drive past, Louise,' Hazell murmured. 'We have a few minutes to spare. Go up to that side street and turn round, then come back and park just past the entrance.' He looked keenly out of the window, turning his head, his eyes narrowed against the sun's glare.

'Are you looking for anything in particular?' Louise asked.

'A car. A black BMW, to be precise. It may be a red herring, but I would be very happy to see one all the same.' As Louise turned the car and crawled back down the road he sighed. 'Nothing. And the Fraser cars are probably all safely tucked away in the garage.'

'We can ask him what he drives.'

'And we will. All right, Louise. Just here'll do.' Louise parked, and they got out of the car.

Hazell straightened his tie. 'This heat's a bit overpowering. I hope the Frasers have got air con.'

'I imagine so, Fred.' She grinned. 'I'd better call you sir from here in.'

'Right. On we go, Sergeant.'

As they approached the front door across the gravelled drive the sound of large dogs barking came from inside. Hazell lifted the heavy knocker and let it fall, hearing it echo hollowly in the hallway beyond. Then came a shout, instantly stifled, and the barking ceased. They both looked up sharply, then at each other. Hazell made a face.

They heard light footsteps, and the door opened. A man stood there, a man of medium height, slim but compactly-muscled. His hair, swept back from a broad forehead, was white, but his ruddy tan and freckled arms betrayed him as a redhead born. When he spoke, his voice was soft, retaining vestiges of his Scottish accent.

'Detective Inspector Hazell? I'm Ewan Fraser.' He held out his hand, and Hazell shook it.

Hazell showed Fraser his warrant card and nodded towards Louise. 'This is Detective Sergeant Gordon.'

'Good to meet you, Sergeant. Do come in.' He led them into a cool hallway. 'Please excuse my informality.' He indicated his polo shirt and loose cotton trousers. 'I've been bashing a ball about on the local tennis court with my son.'

'Is your son here, Mr Fraser?' Hazell said.

'He's in the shower, I believe.'

'And your daughter?'

Fraser frowned, but answered courteously. 'No, Helena is not at home. This way, please.'

'Your daughter lives here, sir?' Hazell pursued.

'Yes, but my sons do not. Alexander is only here because we've been playing tennis.'

'You have another son?'

'Robert, yes.' Fraser opened a door onto a large, light room. There were rugs on the polished wood floor, and a long oval table in the centre. A woman was sitting in one of the high-backed chairs round the table.

'Inspector Hazell and Sergeant Gordon,' Fraser said. 'My wife, Fiona.'

'Good afternoon, Mrs Fraser.'

The woman sat with her hands tightly clasped together. She gave the officers a curt nod, the least possible acknowledgement. She was slim, dressed entirely in white, with a silver chain round her neck. Her hair was dark blonde, expertly cut to achieve a look of expensive simplicity. Under perfectly-arched brows her pale blue eyes were icy.

Fraser stood beside her, his hands resting on the back of a chair. 'How may I help you, Inspector?'

'Unfortunately, sir, I have bad news. The worst. Can I confirm that Mrs Erica Pole of 42, Plough Lane, Compton Magna, is your sister?'

Fraser stiffened. 'Yes. Has something happened to her?'

'I am very sorry to have to tell you sir, that your sister died yesterday afternoon. She was, I'm afraid, murdered.'

Fraser's mouth dropped open, and he seemed to sag, held up only by his hands gripping the chair-back. 'What? What are you saying? Erica – murdered?'

Fiona Fraser pushed her chair back slightly and put a hand on her husband's arm. Louise, watching, saw that her expression, one of bored suspicion, had barely changed.

'Perhaps you'd like to sit down, sir,' Hazell said gently.

Fraser collapsed into the chair, gripping his hands together in front of him. 'What happened, Inspector?' he said, his voice hoarse.

'We aren't sure yet,' Hazell said. 'She was discovered by her carer, Mrs Carew, just after six o'clock. Mrs Carew had been to see her that lunchtime and was going back to get her evening meal, just as she did every day.'

'How –' Fraser gulped, unable to finish his question.

'We believe she was strangled, sir.'

Fraser bowed his head, shaking uncontrollably. Then he looked at Fiona, his eyes wide, as if searching for some explanation, some comfort. She shook her head and looked away. Fraser turned to Hazell. 'Who could have done this? Who would want to? Was anything taken? She had hardly anything of value. I tried to make her house secure, but it wasn't easy.'

'It's possible burglary might have been a motive,' Hazell said. 'The living room was in some disarray, and some things seem to be missing – her phone, and all her documents. Can you throw any light on that, Mr Fraser?' Ewan shook his head. 'It's almost as if whoever killed her wanted to delay tracing her relatives for as long as possible, which is quite odd. That's why we weren't able to be in touch with you sooner.'

'Erica, my poor sister,' whispered Fraser. Now tears were running down his face unchecked. Louise kept a fascinated watch on Fiona, and saw her expression change from guarded suspicion to cold contempt. 'She was helpless, Inspector. She didn't have a chance. I tried to protect her, and I failed.'

'Do you have any ideas, sir, why anyone would want to harm your sister?'

'It is inconceivable to me, Inspector.'

'All right. Please don't misunderstand me, Mr Fraser, but for the sake of elimination, I need to ask you, and Mrs Fraser, and your children, where you all were yesterday afternoon.'

Fiona Fraser broke her silence, and her voice was full of self-justifying disdain. 'Surely you can't imagine my husband would kill his own sister!'

'It's just routine, madam. We must cover every possibility, and eliminate anyone we can.'

'Routine!' Fiona scoffed.

Hazell looked at her from his great height. 'Perhaps you'd like to tell me where *you* were yesterday afternoon.'

'I was at the hairdresser's at two. Then I went shopping with my friend Dee Willson.'

'The address of the hairdresser and your friend's phone number, please.'

Fiona gave them, barely controlling her indignation, and Louise wrote them down.

Hazell turned to Fraser. 'You, sir?'

'I was in my office at the charity, doing some long-overdue paperwork. My secretary saw me when I got back from lunch, but she left for home at five. She put her head round the door to say goodbye. I was still working.'

'What time did you get home that evening?'

'About seven, I think.' Fraser took a handkerchief from his trouser pocket and wiped his face.

'Can you confirm that, Mrs Fraser?'

'I heard him come in, yes.'

'Would you be kind enough to call your son, please? You said he is in the house.'

Fiona Fraser stood up abruptly. 'I'll go.'

When the door closed behind her Hazell said, 'If I may ask, Mr Fraser, did the rest of your family share your care and concern for your sister?'

Ewan looked up, and smiled wearily. 'You aren't stupid, Inspector, nor are you blind. My wife has never got on with my sister. Perhaps she, Fiona that is, sees my fondness for Erica as excessive. I don't think Fiona would commit murder, though.' He sighed. 'My wife doesn't really approve of me, either. We live more or less separate lives under the same roof, united only in our children these days. Won't you both sit down? I'm sorry, I'm forgetting my manners.'

'Thank you, sir, but we would rather stand. There are questions I will need to ask you, but I won't keep you any longer today than is absolutely necessary. I realise this is a very difficult time for your family.'

'The family won't be very bothered, I'm afraid, Inspector. Horrible as no doubt it seems to you. Apart from myself the only other person who will mourn the loss of Erica is my daughter, Helena.'

'One question, sir – how often did you visit your sister?'

Ewan sighed deeply. 'It's varied over the years. There were times when we were both too busy. But we were always connected. And if you're talking about the years she lived in Compton, when she was close geographically and couldn't go anywhere, I tried to go and see her once a week, sometimes more.' He looked up, and his stare was a challenge, all tears gone. 'Don't be deceived, Inspector – I am no saintly brother oozing kindness. My visits to my sister were as much for me as for her. She is probably the one person on earth I feel at home with.'

'And when did you see her last, Mr Fraser?'

'It was Thursday. Thursday afternoon.' He gripped his hands together. 'Just to think – I had no idea that I'd never see her again, that just the next day –' His voice failed.

The door opened, and Fiona came back in, followed by a young man of medium height, slim but broad-shouldered. His thick dark hair was damp from the shower, and his chin was unshaven.

'Ah. My older son, Alexander,' Fraser said.

Alexander shook hands with Hazell and Gordon, then went over to his father and draped an arm round his shoulders. 'This is a nasty turn, Dad,' he said. 'I'm so sorry. Poor old aunt.'

Fraser smiled faintly. 'The officers want to know where you were yesterday afternoon, Alex.'

'Between one-thirty and six o'clock,' Hazell added.

'I was on the golf course, as a matter of fact,' Alexander said. 'It was a beautiful day, much too good to be indoors. Rob was with me. We both skived off.' He looked at his father with an apologetic grin. Louise was still watching Fiona, and saw her expression change from annoyance and contempt to self-satisfied complacency.

'Did you go to your regular club, Mr Fraser? Assuming you have one?' Hazell asked.

'Yep, Golden Lawns,' Alexander said. 'We signed in around midday, had a spot of lunch in the club-house, and roamed the fairways all afternoon.'

'What about your daughter, Mr Fraser?' Hazell asked, turning to Ewan.

'I'm afraid I don't know. I assume she was at work. All three of my children work for me, Inspector. Alex is an accountant, Rob a project manager. They work for Fraser Homes HQ here in London, though Rob's work does take him round the country a fair bit. Helena works for the Haven. I don't know where she is at the moment – does anyone?' He looked at his wife and son.

'She went out this morning to take her car in for a service,' Fiona said. 'After that, I have no idea. She lives here, but she's a grown woman with her own life. She doesn't consult me. You might imagine that as her mother I would have a more intimate knowledge of my daughter's life. But it appears our interests don't coincide.'

'Does she have anywhere else she stays?' Hazell asked.

Fiona shrugged. 'She stays with friends once in a while, but she has no other home.'

'Perhaps someone can ask her to contact us when she returns,' Hazell said. 'I'll leave my card. One more thing: speaking of cars, perhaps you can tell me what each one of you drives.'

'I have a Mercedes E class,' Fraser said. 'Silver. But it doesn't come out of the garage all that much. I quite often take the tube to work and save myself the stress of negotiating the traffic. My wife has a one-year-old red Lexus IS 250. You can see them if you like.'

'Mine's parked round the back,' Alexander said. 'You can't be too careful in London these days. It's a Merc A45, awful colour, a sort of murky bronze, but it goes like a bomb.'

'I imagine it would, sir,' murmured Hazell.

'Rob drives a blue Audi Sportback. It's only a few months old and still gleaming. I keep telling him he needs something like mine to impress women, but he won't listen.'

'And your sister?'

Alexander rolled his eyes. 'Helena has a Golf. It's at least four years old, but she says she likes it. It's – what, Mum? Navy blue? Really boring, but that's Helena all over.'

'Thank you. We will leave you in peace now. Again, I'm sorry to have been the bearer of such tragic news. Obviously we'll have to be in touch over the next few days – I'll need more information about Mrs Pole's background – and you, sir, will need to come down to Compton for the formal identification.' He saw Ewan flinch. 'I wonder, Mr Fraser, if I could have a direct number for you? We had to go via your office to contact you, and we were not well received.'

Ewan smiled sadly. 'Yes, that would be Mrs Bryant. She's very protective. Of course, Inspector. I'll write it down for you before you leave.'

Once they were back on the motorway Hazell broke the silence.

'Did we get anywhere, do you think?'

Louise shook her head. 'I don't know, Fred. Mr Fraser didn't seem to know much about his sister's everyday life, did he? Not that he was telling us. Is it possible the only people she knew well were Mrs Carew and her vicar? Surely there must have been friends, neighbours, other people from her church.'

Hazell sighed. 'We need to ask all of them a lot more questions. We need more details for Criminal Records. What did you make of them, anyway?'

'The Frasers? He's all right, genuine I thought, but as for her, and the son…'

'Could any of them have done it?'

Louise thought. 'Any of them could, theoretically. We can't really say, not till we've checked the alibis, and dug a bit deeper into motives. The brothers were just a bit too pat, though.'

'I'll ring the nick, get Davies or someone to check with the Golf Club. And with the Haven, for the daughter's movements yesterday, and Mrs Fraser's hairdresser and friend. Remind me to ring the local station nearest to the Frasers to let them know we've been operating on their patch. Then we must have a meeting, get the team together, see what we know. Something might set off a spark in someone's mind.'

Louise glanced at him. 'I sense you have an idea, Fred.'

'Maybe. But let's get the facts straight before we indulge in too many theories. We haven't spoken to either Helena Fraser or her brother Robert. There are many things we still don't know.'

'And many we'll never know.'

Hazell smiled. 'Now you're talking like a philosopher, not a copper. We need to know only just enough to send a murderer to prison.'

'True. One thing did strike me, though, and I wonder if you noticed it too. When Mr Fraser talked about his sister, he didn't say they were always in touch, or at the end of the phone, or whatever. He said "connected." To my ears that has a very far-reaching ring to it.'

Hazell nodded. 'Yes, I did pick that up. But it doesn't mean he didn't kill her.'

Louise indicated and swung off the motorway onto the Stockley exit. 'No, that's true. We have to keep an open mind. And we need to know about the locals, and any itinerants that might have been hanging around. Plus whatever any of the known criminals might be up to.'

'Even Compton has its share of those.'

Louise smiled. 'Oh, yes. But I have a feeling that brother-sister thing could well be at the centre of this.'

At eleven thirty on Sunday morning Bert rang the vicarage doorbell to be admitted by a puzzled Patrick.

'Hello. You on your own?'

'Let me in and I'll tell all. Coffee would be good too,' Bert said, following Patrick into the kitchen.

'Got some on already,' Patrick said. 'I thought you and Joseph might be in need after an hour of spiritual communing.' He looked at his friend and frowned. 'You look rather agitated, Bert. Something is ruffling that calm patrician exterior. What's up? I can't believe Joseph's sermon was that exciting.'

Bert sat down at the table. 'Well, it was rather more intriguing than a normal Sunday morning. Joseph was announcing the notices at the beginning of the service. Everyone was sitting there, taking it all in, or not – all the announcements, sick people to pray for and so on – when the door opened and this woman came in.'

Patrick put a mug of coffee in front of Bert and sat down opposite him. 'A woman, eh? Young and beautiful?'

'Well, yes, as a matter of fact. Late twenties, I'd say. Tall, slim but strong-looking, nice legs. Pale skin, long titian hair.'

'Titian? Whatever colour is that? The only connection I make with Titian is a rather rude limerick.'

'It's a light red, ignoramus. Anyway, someone gave her a hymn book and she sat in one of the back pews, but when Joseph looked up and saw her, the effect was electric. I swear he nearly fell over.'

'How fascinating. What a dark horse Joseph is. He hasn't mentioned any redheads.'

'It may not be as you surmise, Carver. He looked worried all through the service, only just held it all together, and *she* was weeping. Quietly, but obviously distraught.'

Patrick sipped his coffee. 'He's worried, she's crying,' he muttered. 'Must be he's knocked her up and he's embarrassed she's there among his congregation, blowing his respectable reputation apart.'

'Careful, Carver, your cynicism is showing again,' Bert said.

'So where is the young lady now?'

'Joseph ushered her into the vestry after the service while he went to say goodbye to people at the door. Presumably that's where they are now.'

'Good heavens,' Patrick said thoughtfully. 'Well, at least he's got his cassock on.'

'Do be serious for once, you irritating man,' Bert said. 'She's obviously in some distress, and I'd say poor old Joseph has had quite enough trouble, wouldn't you? Still, I suppose that's par for the course in his line of business. If it's not your own worry, it's someone else's.'

Both men looked up as they heard Joseph's key in the door and the sound of quiet voices.

'Get some more coffee on, Carver,' Bert said. 'Looks like we may be about to find out.' He turned in his chair. 'In here, Joseph.'

The door opened and a young woman came through it, tentatively, her eyes searching round the kitchen before they lit on Bert and Patrick and darted away again. Joseph was behind her, his hand on her back.

'Come in and sit down,' he said. 'Just for a while.' He turned to his friends. 'Helena Fraser, meet Bert Greville and Patrick Carver, my old friends from university.'

Bert leapt to his feet, stretching out his hand, which Helena shook briefly. Patrick, eyebrows raised, dark eyes gleaming, saluted her from across the table.

'Good to meet you, Miss Fraser,' Bert said.

'Helena, please,' she murmured.

'Helena is the niece of Erica Pole,' Joseph said, a faint colour rising in his cheeks.

'Oh! Your aunt, of course,' Bert said. 'What a terrible thing. I'm so sorry, Miss – um, Helena. What a shock for you.'

'Yes. Thank you,' Helena said faintly.

'Make the poor girl some coffee, Carver,' Bert said. 'Don't just sit there grinning like an ape.'

Patrick shot him a look but said nothing, got up and busied himself with the coffee-pot. With exaggerated care he put a mug of black coffee and a jug of milk in front of Helena. She added milk to her coffee with a shaking hand.

'I think it might be good to take a stroll before lunch, don't you?' Bert said to Patrick. 'It's a beautiful day, and I'm sure

Joseph and Helena need time to talk without us in the way. Come on, Carver, stir yourself.'

Patrick stood up with a baleful look at his friend. He turned to Helena. 'Good to have met you,' he said politely. 'I'm sorry about your aunt.'

She looked at him silently, her eyes welling with tears.

In the hallway, closing the door behind him, Patrick hissed, 'Bloody marvellous, Bert, isn't it! Anyone would think I was your valet! Carver, do this, do that, snap to it, man!'

'Sorry, old chap,' Bert said contritely. 'Old habits. I just thought we should leave them alone.'

'Now what?'

'Look, do unfold your arms and stop looking like a disgruntled schoolboy. I've said I'm sorry. Let's go out. It occurs to me this might be a good moment to phone my mother. Discreetly.'

Patrick brightened. 'Right. I'll get some shoes on.'

On the corner of the street Constable Winston Davies, off duty, in sandals, cotton trousers and a baggy T shirt, was speaking into his mobile phone, at the same time trying to control an excited spaniel puppy on the end of a lead. 'Sarge? You're in, good. It's Win Davies here. Yes, I know I'm off duty. Look, I'm in Church Street, corner of Melville Road. Just been to get my paper and give Dennis an airing. Yes, daft name for a dog, my wife's idea. Sarge, wasn't there something about a black BMW round the back of Mrs Pole's place? It may be nothing, but there's one parked in the drive of the Vicarage right now.'

1972: Scotland

'Father.'

The man looked up. He was slumped in his usual ancient leather chair in front of the dying fire, still wearing his dusty brown greatcoat against the cold. There was a small table next to him, on it an unstoppered decanter and an empty glass.

'What?' He looked at his son as if he was seeing him for the first time, and frowned, screwing up his eyes. 'What do you want, boy?'

'I'd like to come fishing with you tomorrow. If you are going.' The boy was standing by the door of the kitchen, his hand on the handle as if prepared to flee. But his expression was calm, his stance determined.

'Hmm.' The man's voice was a subterranean rumble from a chest full of phlegm. 'I will be fishing tomorrow, if it doesn't snow.' His accent was strong, his voice deep. He paused, and cocked his great head in the direction of the kitchen table, where another man, slim and dark, sat nursing a tumbler of amber liquid. 'Gilmour goes with me.'

The boy darted a glance in the direction of Gilmour, who raised the glass in mocking salute. 'Must he, Father? Could we not go alone? You can go with him any time.'

The big man's eyes narrowed. 'Gilmour goes. Why the sudden interest in fishing? I thought you only cared for books.'

'No, this last term at school I've been doing a lot more sport. Rugby.'

The father laughed, a hollow cavernous growl that shook his belly. 'About time you got some muscles, I agree. Look at him, Gilmour. Skinny like you. Who'd think he's a whelp of mine, eh?' Gilmour gave a thin, sycophantic giggle.

The contrast between father and son was stark: the man huge, six foot four and seventeen stone, massively muscled, though the muscle was slowly turning to flab. His hair and beard, a rusty brown, uncut for months, lay tumbled and greasy round his broad shoulders, and when he laughed he bared long stained teeth. His son was a little above middle height, but slender, still with the unformed look of a boy growing too fast. He was pale, blue-eyed, with aquiline features and a mop of wavy red hair.

'I'd like to come, Father. May I?'

'Hark at him, Gilmour! "May I?" He talks like a girl!' The father laughed, and the man Gilmour echoed him. Suddenly the laughter stopped, and the father stared at his son, breathing noisily through his nose. 'Aye, you can come. Maybe these next weeks we can make more of a man of you. Be ready by six.'

'Thank you, sir.' The boy turned to leave.

'Ewan!'

'Yes, Father?'

The big man waved the decanter at him. 'Want some whisky?'

The boy was startled, hesitated, swallowing. 'I'm not old enough. Thank you.'

The father bellowed with laughter, spilling some of the precious stuff. 'Hark at him, Gilmour! He's such a girl! We'll have our work cut out with him!'

Gilmour grinned, his sly eyes roving round the room. Ewan pulled the door open and vanished through it.

'But, Quin, what are you actually going to *do*?'

'I'm not absolutely sure yet. Don't worry, though. I've said I'll sort it out, and I will.'

They were sitting together on the window seat in her bedroom, wrapped in an old grey blanket from her bed, looking out of the mullioned window, though there was nothing to see in the darkness.

'I'm afraid, Quin.'

'I know. But you won't have to be afraid any more.'

'I'm not just afraid of him. I'm afraid of what you might do. Please, Quin, don't make him even angrier. If they thought for a moment that you were here now, we'd both get a hiding.' She clutched at his sleeve and looked at him pleadingly.

'Don't worry, Marjie. I'll be careful. And they won't know I'm here.' He looked at his watch. 'It's two in the morning. They're all in their beds, sleeping off the whisky.' He groaned. 'I *hate* the smell of that stuff.'

The girl shuffled closer and leaned against him. He slid his arm round her shoulders. 'I don't feel so bad now you're here,' she said, her voice muffled. 'But you have to be careful. Sometimes he can seem all right. But he can turn into a monster faster than you can blink.' She pulled away and looked at him, her eyes reflecting the light of the sailing moon. 'This fishing trip. If you make him angry he could quite easily pick you up and throw you in the river.'

'Maybe I'm stronger than I look. You wait and see.'

'Oh, Quin! You've forgotten what he's like! He doesn't care about *anything*.' She rolled up her sleeves. 'Look here.' Both arms were a mass of purple bruises. 'The day before yesterday he punched me in the stomach. I've got belly-ache all the time now.'

'He's a bullying bastard, and I'm going to fix him. You'll see, Marjie. You're going to be safe.'

'But will *you* be safe, Quin?'

Lachlan Fraser lumbered from his chair by the dead fire at six o'clock, and shambled to the downstairs toilet. The laces trailed from his massive brown boots. Ewan, waiting by the open back door, shivering in the chill early air, saw Gilmour in the yard, loading the pickup. Gilmour looked up and gave him a tiny smile that was somehow complicit. Ewan turned his back. Through the open kitchen door that led into the passage, he heard his father's grunt and the loud stream as he urinated with the toilet door ajar. A few minutes later Lachlan emerged, zipping his fly. He looked at Ewan but said nothing, shoving past him into the yard, rubbing his calloused hands together with a dry, rasping sound. He said something to Gilmour, and for a moment the two men's heads were together. Ewan slipped back into the passage, looking over his shoulder, and into a small room beside the toilet. He found a key in its habitual hiding place, opened a glass-fronted cabinet and for a moment his eyes flew over the bracketed guns. Fleetingly the words "hung for a sheep as a lamb" flashed through his mind as his hand lit on his father's sweetest prize: a 12-gauge side ejector Purdey shotgun, won in a drunken wager by his own father in 1935, when Lachlan was a boy of eight. Lachlan coveted it all through the years till his father's death, and it was the only thing he treated with loving care. Even in his moment of heart-jangling terror it seemed to Ewan that it was his only choice. He took it down, closed and locked the cabinet, and returned the key, then slid the gun under his knee-length coat, ramming the barrel beneath his belt. He hastily buttoned the coat, and in a moment of clear thinking slipped into the toilet and flushed it.

'Boy!' his father's voice roared from the yard.

'Coming!'

He hurried across the kitchen and into the yard. His father was behind the wheel of the pickup and the engine was running. Ewan's eyes darted round the yard. Where was Gilmour? He climbed into the back, aware of his awkward gait with the gun against his chest. Lachlan noticed nothing. One gnarled hand was resting on the steering wheel, the other was already lifting a silver flask to his lips. Ewan suppressed a shudder.

'Cold, are you?' his father asked.

Ewan shook his head. 'Where's Gilmour?'

His father grunted. 'Forgot something.'

Then there was Gilmour, coming through the kitchen from the passage. He climbed into the pickup beside Lachlan, and shot a sly glance back at Ewan. Ewan's stomach clenched and he fought down an urge to vomit. Clearly Gilmour had entered the castle by another door, but had followed Ewan out: had he seen that the Purdey was missing?

The five-mile ride to the river, a small but strong-flowing tributary of the Ericht that ran along the border of Lachlan's land, its deep pools providing a home for brown trout and grayling, made Ewan glad he had had no time for breakfast. Lachlan drove like a man infested by a score of demons, one-handed, bouncing over ruts and rocks, plunging into potholes, from time to time yelling with fierce glee as he swigged from his flask. Once in a while he offered it to Gilmour, who refused with a shake of his head. Ewan saw that he too was pale to the point of green, and seeing his passengers suffering Lachlan roared with delight.

The track narrowed and deteriorated, and Lachlan slowed at last, hearing the ancient pickup protest. He turned off the headlights, and Ewan saw the dawn light spreading over peat and heather and stunted trees. They climbed a long rise, and from the top the landscape rolled away under the pale spring sky. At the bottom of the slope the track petered out, and there the river ran, narrow and bubbling over flat rocks, pausing in its headlong flight to form deep pools before rushing on again. Trees misshapen by the wind crowded its edges and dropped dead branches into the water. Lachlan brought the pickup to a juddering, gut-wringing halt.

'Well, my fine boys.' He looked at his passengers with open contempt. 'Here we are. Get the tackle out, Gilmour.'

'Hang on a minute,' Gilmour muttered. He stumbled out of the pickup and disappeared behind an outcropping of rocks, and they heard the sound of puking. Lachlan roared with laughter, climbed down and strode towards the river, with Ewan behind, hard-pressed to keep up. For the moment Gilmour was out of sight.

Lachlan stood on the river bank, legs planted apart, greatcoat flaps flying in the morning breeze, swigging greedily from the silver flask. He turned suddenly.

'What! Where's the – ' he began angrily, and then the words failed, and he was staring at his only son, a boy he barely knew, in whose two hands was his own precious Purdey, aimed steadily at his heart.

'What's this?' he growled, and moved to lunge forward, but Ewan lowered the gun until it was pointing at Lachlan's groin.

'I'll take you just where it hurts most,' Ewan said. His voice sounded thin in the cold air.

'That's my gun, you snivelling little thief,' Lachlan snarled, his eyes flitting from the dull barrel to Ewan's pale face and back again. He licked his lips.

Ewan took a step forward. The gun was pointing at Lachlan's belly now.

'You going to kill me, boy?' The words were taunting, but there was uncertainty in the big man's voice.

'I'd like nothing better, you filthy bastard,' Ewan said. 'But I won't swing for you. I might just put a bullet in your gut, though. So I can see you bleed and squirm. This is for the hand you lay on my sister, you coward. Look at you! You great bully! Preying on a skinny helpless kid.' He moved forward slowly, pointing the gun at Lachlan's eyes now. Lachlan took a step back, doubt crossing his coarse face like a shadow. At the sight of it a fierce joy surged in Ewan's stomach, and he pushed forward.

Lachlan took another step back, holding out his hands. 'You take a shot at me, they'll put you away,' he growled.

'Not before I put you in hell where you belong, you devil,' Ewan said, his voice still low.

Then Lachlan stumbled, and the bank crumbled under his boots, and for a moment he seemed to hang immobile, arms flailing, before he toppled backwards into the water with a shout of sheer panic.

Ewan rushed forward, his boots snagging in the coarse grass of the river bank, and almost fell. Righting himself he looked into the deep pool where the water was disturbed in widening ripples, and then he saw something that would stay with him for the rest of his life, asleep or awake, as if the image was printed indelibly on the back of his eyelids. Lachlan rose slowly to the surface, his arms and legs, his coat and hair and beard spread out, just as he had fallen. Worst of all were his bulging eyes, his long brown broken teeth bared in a hideous grin as the water washed over his face. For a moment he seemed to stretch out a hand, but then the current took him, and the heavy boots and waterlogged coat dragged him down, and he was whirled away and turned over in the stream, only to lodge in tree roots on the other side of the river. Ewan stared, his breath coming in gulps, his chest heaving, as he almost absent-mindedly put the gun away under his coat.

How long he stood there he never remembered, seconds most likely, though it seemed like an eternity. Then Gilmour came panting up behind him.

'What the hell happened here?' Gilmour yelled. He was wiping his mouth with a grubby handkerchief.

'He fell in.'

Gilmour stared at Ewan. 'Well, we'd better get him out!' he shouted. 'Come on, help me! What's the matter with you?'

Ewan stared back at Gilmour as if seeing him for the first time. 'It's no use,' he said quietly. 'That river comes straight off the mountains, full of snow melt. It's so cold it'll probably have stopped his heart the minute he hit the water. It's too late.' He backed away, feeling himself begin to tremble uncontrollably, the panic and revulsion rising like an icy tide, and he turned and ran. All that mattered at that moment was to put as much distance as he could between himself and the horror that was his father. He raced back to the pickup and leapt in, turning the key till the engine sputtered into life, yanking the wheel round, bumping along the track back in the direction of the castle. He heard Gilmour shout in protest as he tried to catch up, and for a moment he ran alongside, but was inexorably left further and further behind. The boy pressed his foot down on the accelerator and the pickup lurched forward. His bright red hair streamed in the wind, and his mouth was open in a great shout of liberty and terror.

2008: Compton

'Joseph, I should go.' Helena looked at him from the sofa. She sat with a damp handkerchief gripped between her hands. Her eyes were red-rimmed, and every few moments a sob broke unbidden from her throat and fresh tears welled.

'Don't go yet,' he said. 'I don't like the idea of you driving when you are so upset.'

She sighed, sat up straight, and shook out her cloud of hair. 'Daddy is worse than upset,' she said sombrely. 'He's in pieces. You know how he and Erica were. Now I'm the only one he can talk to. Poor Daddy. This is very cruel. Who could want to hurt her? I just don't understand.'

Joseph shook his head. 'How would you understand?'

'What, you mean I've had a sheltered life? It's true, I suppose.'

'No,' Joseph protested softly. He had been leaning against the door-frame; now he pushed himself upright and came over to where she was. He sat down beside her and took one of her hands in his. 'I didn't mean that, just that *you* wouldn't hurt a fly. Anyway, sheltered or not, you've seen a bit of the less attractive side of life since you've been working for the Haven, surely?'

Helena smiled faintly. 'My life has still been one of ridiculous privilege,' she said. 'Unlike yours. Not that you ever say much about it.'

'It's not a pretty story. If I don't tell you it's because I don't want you to know what an utter fool and failure I have been. Maybe still am.'

Helena laughed sadly. 'You really must let me make my own mind up, you know. I'm quite old enough.'

He let go of her hand. 'You're right. But it's such a risk.' He heaved a deep sigh. 'If you must go, you must. Of course your father needs you. Just don't stay away too long.'

'I won't.' She smiled faintly. 'Joseph, I think I owe you an apology.'

'Whatever for?'

'When I was here just a few days ago, I wasn't at all kind or fair to you. I behaved like a spoiled brat. I'm sorry.'

'It's forgotten, Helena.'

The door bell jangled, and they both looked up.

Joseph frowned and got to his feet. 'They could have stayed away a bit longer.'

Helena smiled. 'They've been gone at least an hour, Joseph. I thought they were most sensitive – well, Bert was. They are your guests after all.' She pushed her hair back from her face. 'Do I look a complete wreck? I can't seem to stop crying.'

'You look as lovely as always,' Joseph said. 'Perhaps slightly less composed, that's all.'

The bell clanged again. Joseph grunted disapprovingly and went to the front door. But when he pulled it open it was not Bert and Patrick on the doorstep, but Louise Gordon.

'Reverend Stiles, I'm sorry to bother you, but do you have a visitor who owns the black BMW in your drive?'

Joseph frowned. 'I think you'd better come in, Sergeant.' He led the way into the sitting room. 'Sergeant Gordon, Helena Fraser.'

The two women shook hands. 'Miss Fraser, you're Mrs Pole's niece, I believe. We have been trying to track you down. May I ask a few questions?'

'Yes, I suppose you must.' Helena looked up at Joseph, and her face radiated anxiety. 'Can Joseph stay?'

'Of course. May I sit down?'

'Please do,' Joseph said. 'Would you like tea?'

'No, thank you. Miss Fraser, I need to ask you where you were on Friday afternoon.'

Helena swallowed. 'I was in my office at the Haven. Lots of people saw me. I had a meeting that overran. I left at six.'

Louise scribbled a note. 'All right. Is the BMW yours? I thought you drove a blue Golf.'

Helena nodded. 'Yes, I do. I took my car in for a routine service yesterday and then went to do a bit of shopping. The garage rang me on my mobile to say the car needed some work done and they wanted to keep it for a few days. The BMW belongs to the business.'

Louise looked at Helena, her expression a studied blank. 'I see. Are there other cars that belong to the business?'

'Yes, all BMWs, all black. Two of them are estates, like this one, and two are four-by-fours. Those are mostly used by Fraser Homes.'

'Can anyone borrow them?'

'Well, not *anyone*, exactly. But they are there for employees with a good reason.' She paused. 'Or family members without one, sometimes.'

'Is there a strict procedure for taking the cars out?' Louise asked.

'Yes, officially. But my brothers and I have been known to bend the rules on occasion.'

Louise tapped her pen against her chin. 'Would it be possible to take one of these cars without telling anyone, in practice?'

'Yes, at a pinch. What are you getting at, Sergeant? I booked this one out quite legitimately.'

'No, I don't doubt that, Miss Fraser. Just a bit of background, that's all.' She paused. 'May I ask why you are here this afternoon? Forgive me if I seem nosy, but what is your relationship to Reverend Stiles?'

Helena sat bolt upright, and Joseph moved behind the sofa where she sat, resting a hand on her shoulder. 'Joseph is a friend,' Helena said stiffly. 'He is, was, a good friend to my aunt as well. When I heard of Erica's death, I wanted to come and see him, just to talk, if you must know.'

'Thank you.' Louise bent her head and wrote in her notebook. 'Miss Fraser, I believe you were close to your aunt and visited her regularly. Is that so?'

'Who told you?' Helena said, her brows knitted together.

'Mrs Carew. She spoke highly of you.'

'Oh, Nettie. That's all right. She's a good soul.'

'Has there been some problem with visiting your aunt?' Louise said.

Helena sighed, staring down at her hands as they rested in her lap. 'No, not really, but my mother doesn't approve, and it's easier not to get Mummy going.' She looked up and saw Louise's gaze intently upon her. 'Mummy and Erica have never got on, you see.'

'Why was that, do you think?'

Helena shrugged. 'Mummy was jealous, I guess. Because Daddy and Erica were such a tight twosome. Nobody else came close. Even I was second.'

'No, Helena, that's not true,' Joseph protested. 'Not to your father. I can't believe that.'

Helena looked at him and smiled sadly. 'It is true, Joseph. Of course Daddy has always been lovely, very supportive, very kind and generous. These last few years he has talked to me more as well. But everyone knows the most important person in his life was his sister. It's something to do with their early life, when all they had was each other. Daddy won't talk about it if he can avoid it, so I don't know the details, only hints. You've only got to count up how often he went to see her. No wonder Mummy was bitter about it.'

'Miss Fraser,' Louise interjected, 'who actually owned your aunt's bungalow?'

Helena looked startled. 'I'm not sure. She did, I think. Of course Daddy bought it, but as far as I know it was in her name. He would have wanted her to have that security, in case anything happened to him.'

'Have you spoken to your father since yesterday?'

'Of course.'

'Did he tell you about the missing items?'

Helena nodded slowly. 'Yes. That does seem strange.'

'Did you know where your aunt kept her documents?'

'Yes, in the drawer in the living room. But I never saw any of them. Why would I?'

Louise made a note and there was silence for a moment as she thought. 'Have you any idea,' she said finally, 'what might have been in that drawer?'

'Well, I suppose the usual things. The house deeds, perhaps, although they might have been with the solicitor. Bills and receipts. Her certificates of birth, marriage and divorce. Maybe some stuff from the Inland Revenue. I'm struggling a bit here, Sergeant. If I thought about it at all, I assumed it was the usual stuff people keep.'

'Did your aunt make a will, do you know?' Louise asked.

'I have no idea,' Helena said. 'She had very little to leave, I imagine. She had money once, long ago, but she blew it all. So my mother says, anyway. Daddy paid for everything. I don't know why Mummy resented it, because we have plenty for ourselves. Daddy's a very successful man, you know that. If Erica did have a will I guess that would be with the solicitor too.'

'Do you happen to know who the solicitor is, Miss Fraser?'

'Of course. It's Bob Hamilton. Well, he's Daddy's solicitor, anyway, and he's an old family friend.'

'Could you let me have his address and telephone number?'

'He's in the phone book. Robert Hamilton and partners, Western Avenue.'

'Thank you.' Louise stood up. 'That's all I need to ask you for now, Miss Fraser, though it's likely there'll be more questions at some point. And we need your fingerprints, please – for elimination. Could you call at the station and get that done on your way home? And you, sir –' she turned to Joseph. 'We'll need yours as well.'

'Well, yes, all right,' Helena said uncertainly. 'Joseph can come down to the police station with me. But I should go now, if you are done. I really need to see my father. He's in a terrible state.'

'Yes, of course. Many thanks for your help, and please accept my condolences.' She paused at the door, and Joseph and Helena waited. 'What was she really like, your aunt? I get the impression she wasn't one to suffer fools gladly.'

Helena smiled, sadness clouding her eyes. 'She was often misunderstood,' she said softly. 'In fact, she was a very fine person – honest, intelligent, brave. She wasn't always polite, that's true. But she was in so much pain a lot of the time, so she could be irritable and impatient. She had a lot of suffering in her life, but she still kept a generous spirit and a sense of humour.' She looked at Joseph. 'You'd agree with that, wouldn't you, Joseph?'

Joseph nodded, and to Louise Gordon's sharp eyes the look he gave Helena told more than any words. 'I would,' he said. 'She was a good friend to me on many occasions. I'll miss her – even her acid wit. She liked to deflate me when I pontificated.'

'Thank you both,' Louise said. 'Goodbye for now. We'll be in touch.'

1972: Scotland

'Marjie! *Marjie!*'

The pickup lurched into the yard and stalled. Ewan leapt out, stumbled to the kitchen door, and into the passage. The sight of the gun cupboard through the open door restored him to his senses, and for a moment he stood still, shaking, sweat dripping from his hairline.

He drew the Purdey out from under his coat, unlocked the cupboard, put the gun back carefully and relocked the glass door. Then he stood back and looked at it for a few moments, wondering that such a lovely, deadly thing could have done what it did in his hands.

He hurried down the passage and up the stairs, hanging onto the battered handrail. 'Marjie!' The castle was quiet: it was only just after seven o'clock. He banged on his sister's door.

'Quin, is that you?' he heard her whisper.

'Let me in, please!'

He heard heavy furniture being shoved aside. The door opened a crack.

'Let me in, Marjie. It's all right, I promise.' He slid round the door, shoved it shut and leaned against it.

Erica stood there in her nightie, her feet bare on the wood floor, a blanket thrown round her thin shoulders. 'What's happened?' she whispered. Her eyes were round as saucers. 'Why are you back?'

Ewan swallowed. 'He's dead, Marjie.'

'What? Father? No, Quin! Did you kill him?'

'Kind of.' Ewan stumbled across the room and sat on the edge of the bed, hunched, his hands deep in the pockets of his coat. 'I took a gun. The Purdey. I threatened him. He'd been drinking again, of course. Maybe he was drinking all night, I don't know. He fell into the river, Marjie. He drowned.'

Erica sat beside him and put her arms round him. 'You didn't actually kill him, Quin. You won't go to jail.'

'I meant to hurt him, though. I hated him.'

'I hated him too. I'm glad he's dead. Now he can't hurt us any more. Thank you, Quin.'

Ewan turned to her, his young face anxious. 'What are we going to do?'

'What do you mean?'

'We have to tell someone, don't we?'

'Mrs Gilmour?' Erica said tentatively.

Ewan laughed, the bark of a fox. 'I don't think so. I didn't bring him back, Neil Gilmour, I mean. I left him at the river with all the fishing tackle.'

'Did he see anything?'

Ewan shook his head. 'He was too busy spewing up his guts. But he might have seen me take the gun. I didn't realise he was somewhere behind me in the passage before we went. He gave me such a look. Like he could see straight into my head.'

Erica shivered. 'I hate those two almost as much as *him.*' She pulled away from her brother and studied him closely. 'Quin, you look awful. You're like a ghost. And you're shivering! Here, wrap this blanket round you.'

'No, I'm all right.' A thought came to him. 'I know, Marjie. I'll ring that old solicitor in Crieff – what's his name?'

'Mont- something. Montgomery?'

'That's it.' He got up in one swift movement and strode to the door.

'Wait, Quin. I'm coming with you.' Erica stuffed her feet into a pair of shoes and followed him.

Before they reached the door there was a rapping from the outside and the heavy accent of Catriona Gilmour. 'Young man! What have you done with my husband? *Where is he?*'

Ewan opened the door. He looked at Catriona with utter disdain. She had obviously dressed in a hurry, and her face, devoid of makeup, showed the ravages of the night before with cruel clarity.

'Your husband, madam, if that's what he is, is on his way back on foot. There has been an accident and my father is dead. Now I have no more to say to you. Please get out of my way.' He shoved past, taking Erica's hand and pulling her after him, leaving Catriona gaping like a fish. Then together, gasping with barely-suppressed snorts of laughter, they ran down the stairs.

Two hours later Neil Gilmour arrived back at the castle. Ewan and Erica, watching from the upstairs window, saw him trudge across the yard, carrying the fishing tackle, or some of it. His clothes and hair were soaked.

'He must have gone into the river,' Ewan said. 'I told him it was no use. That water is freezing.' He shuddered. 'I saw Father rise to the surface. Marjie, he looked – he looked *horrible*. Like something from the underworld.'

'Quin,' Erica said hesitantly, 'if he hadn't fallen in, would you have, you know, actually shot him?'

Ewan shook his head. 'The Purdey wasn't even loaded. I didn't have time to get any ammunition.'

'What would you have done if he hadn't fallen? If he'd come at you?'

'I don't know, Marjie.'

'Never mind, Quin. Don't think about it. Have some more toast.' She put the plate on his lap. 'What do you think's happening? They're taking a long time.'

'Mr Montgomery said he would have to alert the police. They'll have to get a truck out to the river. But he said they'd send a car for us. Some busybody will take us somewhere. We might have to go to our aunt Joan in Edinburgh.'

'I don't care, as long as we get away from here.' Erica leaned against her brother's side and closed her eyes, and for a time they sat in silence. Ewan chewed his toast, his eyes staring without seeing, and Erica rested against him, feeling the roughness of his coat against her cheek.

'I hear a car.' Ewan jumped up and ran to the window. He gasped. 'Quick, Marjie, come and see!' He turned to her, his eyes wide. 'It's the pickup! The Gilmours are in it – they're driving away!'

Erica came to the window and peered out. 'They've got suitcases with them, Quin. They're leaving!'

'And stealing our car,' Ewan said grimly.

Erica turned to him, her face alight. 'Who cares? Let them have the old junk-heap. We're free, Quin!'

2008: Compton

'Sir, sorry to call you at home, but you did say to keep you up to date.'

'Go ahead, Louise. Hang on, I'll just shut the door. It's my daughter's birthday, and she's got some noisy friends here. Good. Fire away.'

'I've been talking to my friend at the lab. Off the record.'

'And?'

'Very little to work with, it seems. Nothing under the vic's fingernails. The SOCOs lifted some prints, but we won't have those results yet. I'm speculating here, I know, but just supposing all the prints from the house are eliminated – all the ones for the people who had a legitimate reason to visit?'

Hazell thought. 'In that case, either our killer is one of those people, or else he or she was wearing gloves. Which makes me wonder…' There was a long pause, and Louise Gordon waited. Hazell cleared his throat. 'I'm ruminating here, Louise. Did whoever it was come intending to murder? Or was there some other reason?'

'I don't know,' Louise said soberly. 'But maybe whoever it was didn't expect Mrs Pole to be there. Which, in the normal way of things, she wouldn't have been.'

'And that means he or she knew Mrs Pole's normal routine. Much food for thought, Louise.'

'Yes, there is.'

'Who has the flimsiest alibi of the people we've spoken to so far?'

'On the face of it, Ewan Fraser. Mrs Carew was at the vet's with her dog. Miss Fraser was in her office with a lot of other people. Reverend Stiles was visiting a housebound parishioner, then went to the butcher's in the high street to buy meat for a meal he was cooking for his visitors. All of that checks out.'

'Hm. There are still a lot of gaps. That car, for a start.'
'Another thing to follow up.'
'How's the house-to-house going?'
'Going along all right, but nothing much to report. Should be all done tomorrow.'
'Speaking of tomorrow, I'm hoping to have a breather. I've only just finished up on another case. I could do with time to think. Maybe even fit in Sunday lunch with my family.'
'Sounds good. But you want me to keep you informed?'
'Of course. Even though my wife would much rather I didn't work on Sundays.'
'I'll get off the line, then, sir. Goodnight.'

At two o'clock the following afternoon Hazell was stretched out in his favourite armchair in the sunny conservatory of his house on the outskirts of Stockley, attempting to digest his Sunday lunch and wishing he were asleep. Even had it not been for the enigma of Erica Pole winding around in his brain, sleep would have been prevented by the loud squabbling of his adolescent son and daughter who were supposed to be washing up. He sighed, raised himself into a sitting position and rested his head in his hands.

The phone rang, he heard it answered and a moment later his wife called out. 'Fred! Phone for you. It's the station in Compton. Goodbye, Sunday afternoon.'

Hazell heaved himself to his feet, padded through to the hallway and picked up the handset. He listened intently for a moment or two.

'All right, Louise, seems to me we need to move now. Who have you got there at the moment? Can you call anyone else in? Good. Send two men to Golden Lawns, check on the brothers' alibi. There'll be plenty of regulars there today, I imagine. See if any golfers saw Alex and Rob Fraser during the afternoon. Be as specific as you can about times. Then get them to check out the perimeter, see if there's anywhere a car could be parked discreetly. Potentially, if they were on the golf course all afternoon, there might have been time for one of them to hop over the fence and get to Compton and back. Talk to residents around the edges of the golf course. Someone might have been mowing his lawn on Friday afternoon and noticed a car he didn't recognise. Send men you know can use their initiative. It's a big place and it'll take them the rest of the day, realistically. So we'll need to get everyone together first thing in the morning, everyone who's been involved in the door-knocking, any forensics that might be available, all of it, have a bit of a brain-storming session and see what we've got and what we can come up with. But meanwhile perhaps you can drive over to Stockley and pick me up at home. You and I need to have an urgent chat with Robert Fraser.'

Patrick and Bert lounged on the rumbling train later that afternoon on their way back to London.
'Carver? Are you asleep?'
Patrick opened one eye. 'If I was, I'm not any more. Why aren't you asleep, anyway? That vast lunch at the pub was enough to knock out an elephant.'
'I'm concerned about Joseph. There's something awry there.'
Patrick yawned and rubbed a hand over his shaven skull. 'Anything in particular?'
Bert thought. 'When we got back from our little walk, the delightful Helena Fraser was gone, unfortunately for us. Joseph said little, but he did say the police had been and talked to her. How do you think he seemed?'
Patrick shrugged. 'Joseph is never that forthcoming. He was quiet, I suppose. But then, his girlfriend has just been quizzed by the Old Bill. He has plenty to think about.'
'No, Carver, that's not it. As to whether Helena is Joseph's girlfriend is another thing, but what did he do when we got back from the pub?'
'Right,' Patrick said slowly. 'I see where you're going. He went into the back room and played the piano.'
'Yes. He made sure we were comfortable and he disappeared for an hour. Isn't that exactly what he did when we

were students, when things were difficult? For example, when he got thrown over by some girl, or when his old man was kicking off? I don't think it's this murder that's the problem, Carver, though I guess that makes things worse. I just get the feeling he never really came back up after that bout of depression in his twenties. If that's what it was.'

'But that was *years* ago.'

'I know. And in the meantime, he's got ordained, and as far as we know he does a good job. Maybe at one time he was doing ok. But his wife's death has hit him hard, harder because she was on her way out of his life anyway. If Joseph has a sense of failure that will have confirmed it.'

Patrick frowned. 'Joseph isn't a failure. He got an excellent degree. He survived a difficult parent. He pulled himself up out of his early troubles. He holds down a stressful job.'

'No,' Bert said patiently. 'He isn't a failure in our eyes, but it's not our eyes that count. I think that dark cloud is always there, and right now it's looming rather menacingly.'

Patrick grimaced. 'I can't see we helped in any way.'

'No, maybe not. But I am determined about one thing – I'm not going to let him slip away from us. I'm going to keep in touch.'

'Fair enough. So, what role does the delectable Helena play in all this, do you suppose?'

'Well, to me that's another mystery. I wish I could say she's a love interest that will heal his woes. But it's rarely as simple as that.'

'Don't I know it,' Patrick said gloomily, folding his arms across his chest. 'Women tend to make things much more complicated, in my experience.'

Bert laughed. 'Oh, Carver, you of all people can't say that! You would have died of boredom if your life hadn't been enlivened by your amorous escapades.' He shook his head. 'And that reminds me, you told me you were going to straighten things out with Rachel when you got home.'

Patrick opened his mouth to reply, but then Bert's phone rang shrilly from his jacket pocket. 'Hold on.' He took it out, opened it and put it to his ear. 'Oh, hello, Mother. Is all well?'

He waved Patrick to silence and turned to face the window. He listened, his face intent. 'I see. Hm. Lots of gossip, not very conclusive, then. It was indeed all a long time ago. You should be a detective yourself, I think. Yes, Mother, of course I'm joking.' He turned to Patrick and grinned conspiratorially. 'Yes, we're on the train now. It gets in at five forty-five. I should be home in time for a drink before dinner. No, I haven't heard from Amanda. Have you?' He shook his head. 'Well, if she wants to stay longer I dare say we'll manage. Joseph? Bearing up, I'd say. But I'll give you all the news when I get in. Father all right? Excellent. Thanks so much for your help, Ma. See you later. Bye.' He closed the phone and put it back in his pocket. 'Interesting.'

Patrick leaned forward. 'Did Mater manage to dig anything up on clan Fraser?'

'Yes and no. Yes, she found out lots, but no, most of it is probably irrelevant.'

Patrick looked at his watch. 'We've got twenty minutes. What did she say?'

'I'll condense.' Bert cleared his throat. 'The family into which Ewan Fraser and his sister were born was a quite minor branch of the clan, and, if Mother is correct, rather looked down upon. She found a friend who knew some old lady who died this year and who knew a fair bit about the family, so you see my information is third hand at best.'

'Caveats noted.'

'Well, Ewan and his sister lost both their parents in childhood. No one really seems to know exactly what happened. As you found out, they lived in a castle –Mickle Castle, it was called. It was one of the border defences originally, built in the seventeenth century to repel raiders. I gather it was pretty remote. The children's mother died of some illness when they were very young. The father's death was a bit odd, as you discovered.'

'Odd how, according to Mater?'

'Unusual, certainly. It was as you said – he fell in a river and drowned while on a fishing trip. In the presence of his sixteen-year-old son.'

Patrick whistled. 'Major trauma, then.'

'According to Mother's sources, the father was permanently drunk and considered to be at least a bit mad. Ewan attended a public school for boys near Edinburgh, so he knew various boys from other families, but Erica was hardly seen or heard of until after her father's death.'

Patrick rested his chin on his hand. 'There must have been an inquest on the father, surely? Or the Scottish equivalent.'

Bert frowned. 'I dare say. Is your suspicious mind working overtime?'

'Not as such, but it might be an intriguing avenue to pursue on the internet over the long summer holidays. So, Ewan inherited and became Laird of Mickle. Quite a responsibility for a sixteen-year-old. Or did he have to wait till he got to eighteen?'

'Under Scottish law one can inherit at sixteen, so says my informative parent.'

'Plenty to think about here, Bert.'

'Yes, but I don't see how any of this has the slightest relevance to our old friend Joseph.'

'Maybe not,' Patrick said softly. 'Well, if I find out anything, I'll keep you posted.'

Bert's brows knitted together. 'I'm not as susceptible to rumour and scandal as you seem to be, Carver. I have an estate to run. And perhaps, during these long school holidays, you might like to take your children to the zoo or something.'

'Ha! You sound like Rachel. I tell her I work in a zoo all term.'

'Ugh, Carver, you are impossible.'

Patrick beamed. 'I do my best.'

'Where to, sir?'

Hazell and Gordon sat in the car outside Hazell's house.

'I don't know. We need to contact the Fraser parents. Can you do that? Find out where Robert lives and also where he's likely to be on a Sunday afternoon.'

Louise took her phone out of her bag. 'Pity to alert him, really, sir.'

Hazell grunted. 'He'll have been expecting a call from us all weekend. I can't see that he's going to be fool enough to run. But if he's not at home, if he's gone to the gym or the beach or just to the pub, we could be looking at wasted time.'

'True.' Louise dialled the private number that Ewan Fraser had given them. There was a long silence. In Hazell's quiet street they could hear laughing children in a garden somewhere and the muted sound of traffic on the motorway. 'Mrs Fraser? Good afternoon. It's Sergeant Gordon from Compton police here. I beg your pardon, madam? Well, unfortunately a murder investigation goes on whatever the day of the week it happens to be. Could you please confirm the address of your younger son? Yes, Robert.' She scribbled a note. 'Thank you. Perhaps you could also hazard a guess as to his whereabouts this afternoon. No, of course you aren't his keeper. Possibilities will do. Right, thank you.' She held the phone away from her ear and grimaced. 'I'm not making any assumptions at the moment, Mrs Fraser. Just a process of elimination. That's right, routine.' Louise shook her head. 'Thank you. My apologies for disturbing your weekend.' She ended the call and turned to Hazell. 'For heaven's sake. Her sister-in-law is murdered and she is complaining about me ringing her when she has guests. And of course her darling boys couldn't *possibly* be involved in anything so sordid.'

'Everyone, even the most violent offender, is someone's darling boy or girl, it seems,' Hazell said wryly. 'Shall we go?'

Louise started the engine. 'How are we going to recognise Robert Fraser if he's in some public place?'

They found Rob Fraser sitting in the garden of his local pub, talking to a group of friends, one arm loosely draped round the shoulders of a sparsely-clothed young woman wearing huge sunglasses, the other hand gripping a pint of beer. Recognising him had been no problem: he was a shorter and more heavily-muscled version of his brother. As Hazell and Gordon

93

approached the table, heads turned and conversations faltered. Among the sun-dresses and sandals, the colourful shirts and cut-offs, the police officers in dark suits looked like crows or mourners at a funeral.

'Mr Robert Fraser?' Hazell said quietly.

The young man looked up, a broad unconvincing smile on his handsome features. 'That's me, and who are you?'

'DI Hazell of Stockley CID,' Hazell said, showing his warrant card. 'This is DS Gordon. We need to ask you a few questions, sir. Is there anywhere more private we can go?'

Robert gestured expansively round the pub garden. Several people were staring, but he made a show of unconcern. 'Nowhere here, Inspector, as you can see. Can't it wait?'

'I'm afraid not. Rather than disturb your friends, perhaps you could come and sit in our car. Unless, of course, you'd prefer the local police station.'

Robert stood up. Louise, her sharp eyes missing little, saw that he had paled beneath his tan. 'Well, I suppose so,' he said huffily. 'See you in a minute, guys.'

His friends were silent, but as Hazell and Louise walked away with Robert between them, they heard gusts of laughter. They made their way to the car, which was parked down a side street away from the pub. Robert slid into the back seat and Louise sat beside him. Hazell got into the front passenger seat and turned to look at Robert.

'We are investigating the murder of your aunt, Mrs Erica Pole,' Hazell said. 'Your brother has told us that the two of you were playing golf that afternoon, but we'd like to hear your movements from you, please, sir.'

Rob folded his arms and shrugged. 'It was a nice day. We thought it would be good to get out of a stuffy office.'

'Whose idea was it?'

'Er, mine, I think.'

'Whose car did you travel in?'

'Alex's. He says my car is boring. I'm going to get it done up.'

'And what time did you arrive at the Golf Club?'

Rob made a face. 'About midday, I think. We signed in, then we had a bit of lunch in the clubhouse restaurant. There were plenty of people there who saw us.'

'Would you say you were well known at the Golf Club, Mr Fraser?'

Rob shifted in the seat. 'Well enough. Don the barman knows us, anyway.'

'And then?'

'Then we went and played golf. Till around six. I remember the time because I told Alex I had to get back. I was meeting someone.' He smirked, then saw the sombre expression on Hazell's face.

'May I ask, sir,' Hazell pursued, his voice still quiet and calm, 'if you ever use any of the fleet of cars belonging to your father's business?'

'All the time, for work.'

'Have you ever borrowed one of the vehicles for purposes other than work?'

'Like what?' Rob said. He unfolded his arms and rested his large, red hands on his bare knees.

'Leisure activities, for example,' Hazell said blandly.

'Sometimes, maybe,' Rob mumbled. 'If my car was off the road.'

'But on Friday you travelled to and from Golden Lawns in your brother's Mercedes. Did he drop you off after the golf?'

Rob nodded, licking his lips.

'Mr Fraser, how did you get on with your late aunt?'

'All right. Hardly ever saw her. She was a cripple, wasn't she? Couldn't get around easily.'

'Yes, but she wasn't always disabled. Did you see much of her when you were younger?'

Rob shrugged. 'Sometimes. Not for a while.'

'So when did you last see her?'

'No idea. Years, must be.'

'Where was that?'

'Can't remember. Some family gathering.'

'Did you like her?'

'Like I said, Inspector,' Rob said, lifting his chin and looking at Hazell, 'I can't say I really knew her that well.'

'What about the rest of your family?'

'What about them?' Rob said with a tinge of defiance.

'Did they get on well with Mrs Pole?'

Rob clenched his hands into fists. 'Well, Dad adored her, but you probably knew that. Helena too. Thought she was something special. Alex and me, not so much.'

'And your mother?'

'Why don't you ask her?' Rob said with sudden heat, glaring at Hazell.

'We will. But I'd like your take on it too, sir.'

'I don't think they ever got on. But I don't know why. I didn't want to be bothered with all that. Got my own life to live.'

'Yes, I see.' Hazell was silent for a moment, looking at Rob thoughtfully.

'Can I go?' Rob said. 'I've told you where I was. My friends are waiting.'

'A moment, sir, if you don't mind. Did you ever go to Mrs Pole's bungalow in Compton?'

'Once. When she first moved in. I helped take some furniture.'

'Thank you. I think that wraps it up for now. But don't go anywhere, will you, Mr Fraser? We'll need to speak to you again, I expect.'

Rob opened the car door and climbed out.

'Oh, just one more thing.'

Rob turned, scowling, every muscle tensed.

'Would you consider yourself a fit man, Mr Fraser?'

'Fitter than most,' Rob growled. 'I run. I go to the gym and do weights. I work on building sites. I have to be fit. Fitter than my brother, anyway. He's stuck in his poky office all day, staring at a computer screen. No wonder he has to wear glasses.' He jammed his thumbs into his belt. 'What's my fitness got to do with anything?'

'Probably nothing,' Hazell said with imperturbable smoothness. 'Thank you for your help, Mr Fraser. Have a good afternoon.'

The Major Incident Suite at Compton Police Station consisted of two hastily-cleared rooms, neither of them large. One housed the computers, overseen by pock-marked middle-aged Sergeant Rivers, brought in from Stockley. Into the other room, where tables had been cleared out and chairs were at a minimum, some of the inquiry team – Hazell, Gordon, Sergeant Rivers, and Constables Davies, Simmons and Walsh – were gathered, squashed up against the walls and perched on window sills. Despite the sensitivity of the proceedings the door had to be open to avoid asphyxiation, but the rooms were on the first floor and the team was unlikely to be disturbed. They stood, some lounging, others upright, arms folded, hands in pockets, but all with their eyes on Hazell.

'Right, we've heard from Tom Rivers with the overview so far, and what we've got is pretty thin in terms of concrete evidence. We've got plenty of intelligence and I've a few ideas of my own, but let's hear what happened yesterday at the Golf Course. Davies, over to you.'

Constable Winston Davies extracted his notebook and cleared his throat. 'Simmons and I went up to Golden Lawns. The barman, a chap called –' he glanced at his notes – 'Donald Pickering, confirmed that Alexander and Robert Fraser were in the clubhouse restaurant soon after midday but he said they didn't stay long and they didn't drink. He noticed this because it was unusual – orange juice, he said. We had a look at the register and the brothers did sign in at twelve and out at just after six. We had a word with some of the golfers who were in the bar but there were only a few there, because most of them were out playing, and the ones that were there when we were asking around either hadn't been playing on Friday afternoon or didn't see the brothers. Mr Pickering said he would put the word out over the next few days and let us know if he found anything helpful.

'Then we drove slowly round the perimeter. There were places we had to get out and walk because the Golf Course gave onto a residential street or a belt of woodland, for example. We split up to save time and kept in touch by radio. I'm sure we covered the lot but it took a long time and it was getting towards dusk. The Golf Course is generally well secured with high fences but we did identify a few places where someone could climb or scramble over with a bit of help. We didn't see any evidence of anyone having made a hole in the fence. So then we knocked on doors in the vicinity. Not a lot of luck until right at the end of our search, and it still may be nothing.' He looked up and caught Hazell's eye. 'Well, anyway, one elderly gentleman, a Mr Palmer, said there had been a vehicle parked in a cul de sac parallel with his place, about a hundred yards from the Golf Course fence. He didn't think much about it at the time – if he thought anything it was that one of his neighbours had a visitor and because it was a big vehicle the visitor had parked it where it wouldn't be in the way. He didn't clock the make but he did say it was a four-by-four and it was black. He wouldn't have noticed even that, he said, if he hadn't had to stop while his dog had a good sniff around and peed on one of its tyres.'

There was a general muted chuckle. Then Hazell said, 'Not the first time we might be thankful for the activities of dogs. That's something to alert the forensic team about. Right. Thank you, Win and Barry, good work.' He looked around at the rest of the group. 'As you can see, it's theoretically possible that one or both of the brothers constructed an alibi but left themselves time to drive to Compton and back undetected. From Golden Lawns to here takes about an hour, a bit longer if the traffic is heavy. If this is the case it was totally premeditated – they had to find a place where the fence was weak, somewhere to park the BMW out of the way, and so on. Sergeant Gordon and I have spoken to both the brothers. It seemed to us that Alexander, the older one, is quite a bit brighter than Robert and if there was a conspiracy it might have been him who cooked up the plan and his brother that executed it. But,' he said warningly, 'that's all conjecture at this stage. Apart from the neighbour who thinks he saw a black BMW parked by the garages at the back of Plough Lane, we have no concrete evidence that the brothers were anywhere except on the Golf Course. As to the other family members, Mrs Dee Willson backed up Mrs Fraser's alibi that they were shopping together. Of course it's not unknown for friends to cover for each other, but we'll assume she was truthful – for the moment. Miss Helena Fraser was seen by at least four or five colleagues during the course of the afternoon and I think we can rule her out. Mr Ewan Fraser himself was in his office, but he could have left without being seen and driven to Compton in that time period. Given his lifelong devotion to his sister he seems an unlikely suspect, but we have to keep him in the frame for now.' He took a breath and his gaze swept over them all. 'You may be wondering why we are concentrating on the family. One reason is that we have no other suspects, although obviously we are looking into the possibility of itinerants or known criminals in the area, as well as establishing the whereabouts of the neighbours. Mrs Carew, the carer, the only local person with a key, was at the vet's with her dog that afternoon, and when she wasn't, she was seen by, and spoke to, her neighbour. Another reason is the theft of Mrs Pole's phone and paperwork. A casual burglar might have taken the phone, but what would he do with a bunch of personal documents? And why wouldn't he have lifted the contents of her purse?' He paused. 'What we don't have at the moment is a clear-cut motive. We've heard hints that there was bad blood between Mrs Pole and her sister-in-law. Whether it amounts to a motive for murder we have yet to learn.' He smiled faintly. 'So as soon as this meeting is over Sergeant Gordon and I will be off up London again to see what we can prise out of Mrs Fiona Fraser.'

Once again Louise parked the car on the corner of the street where the Frasers lived. She stifled a yawn.

'Are you weary, Louise?' Hazell asked, his dark eyebrows raised.

'A bit, yes, sir. Fred.'

'Right, then, you ask the questions and I'll watch and listen. And I'll drive back.'

'Fine by me.'

They crunched across the gravel drive, and Hazell ran a hand over his hair.

Louise rang the doorbell. 'That's odd,' she said. 'No barking dogs.'

'I don't think there are any. If I'm not mistaken what we heard the first time was a recording. They must have switched it off.'

'Right.'

There was a long pause before they heard a set of clacking heels on the other side of the door. Fiona Fraser opened it and looked them up and down. 'You're early.'

'The traffic was light,' Louise said, with a hint of acidity. 'May we come in?'

'I suppose you must.' Fiona turned her back and led them through to a sunny sitting room, leaving Hazell to close the front door. He noted the high heels, the upswept hair, the immaculate makeup, the crisp dress and understated jewellery. Was she dressed to go out? Or was this for their benefit, an attempt to seem taller, cleverer, more imposing and in control?

She indicated a cream leather sofa. 'Please sit down.' She sat opposite them on the edge of a matching armchair, her back straight, her knees tightly together, her expression one of suppressed fury. She said nothing. Hazell, his eyes discreetly roaming the room, noted on the otherwise immaculately-empty and highly-polished coffee-table a stack of magazines. On the glossy cover of the topmost was a photograph of an imposing castle-like building against a backdrop of heather-covered hills. Fiona Fraser saw where his gaze had fallen and her lips tightened.

'Mrs Fraser,' Louise began, 'could you please describe to me your relationship with your sister-in-law Mrs Pole?'

Fiona looked up. 'Relationship? It barely existed.' Hazell, listening for every nuance, thought he could detect a whisper of her Scottish accent under the Home Counties vowels.

'What did you think of her?'

Fiona's eyes narrowed. 'Surely my thoughts are my business.'

'Normally, yes, of course they are,' Louise answered calmly. 'But in a murder investigation it's a question we might be interested in.'

Fiona turned to Hazell. 'Why is *she* asking the questions?' she said. 'You're the senior man, I think.'

Hazell turned on her the full force of his intimidating stare, and Louise smiled inwardly to see Fiona almost imperceptibly cringe. 'Sergeant Gordon is quite senior enough to conduct this interview,' he said. 'Proceed, Sergeant.'

Louise took a notebook and pencil from her bag. 'I'll ask you again, Mrs Fraser. Did you get along with Mrs Pole?'

'No, I did not,' Fiona Fraser answered, her eyes a blue blaze and her accent more pronounced. 'I considered her a waster, a sponger, a leech. She barely did a day's work in her life. She lost her husband and her son through alcohol abuse. Of course it is a pity she was disabled, but perhaps you don't realise the accident that caused it happened on the yacht of one of her many lovers. He was cheating on his wife, and both of them were drunk. All these years she has been dependent on her brother, my husband, who refused to see what a liability she was. In my view she was almost as mentally unstable as her father.'

'Do you have evidence for that, Mrs Fraser?'

Fiona lifted her chin. 'Not what you would consider evidence, perhaps, but you asked me what I thought.'

'You spoke of her father. Did you ever meet him?'

'Happily, no. But one hears stories. Our circle in Scotland in those days was quite small. We all knew each other, at least by repute. Lachlan Fraser was widely regarded as a lunatic.'

Louise made a note. 'May I ask how long you have been married to Mr Fraser?'

'I suppose you may. It is common enough knowledge. We had our thirtieth wedding anniversary last year.'

'Mr Fraser presumably knows of your antipathy towards his sister. Has that been a source of conflict?'

Fiona stood up suddenly. 'Conflict?' she said, her voice suddenly shrill. 'What can you know of the conflict in our family?'

'Not much, unless you tell me. Please, Mrs Fraser, do sit down.'

Fiona subsided into the chair. For a moment she was silent, and Hazell saw her struggle for control. She looked up at him, breathing hard, and he felt a sneaking admiration for her.

'My husband,' Fiona said bitterly, 'is regarded as an excellent man by everyone we know and everyone who meets him. A Christian gentleman of high integrity. A generous and modest man. But of course no one is a hero to his valet – or his family. He has never loved me, that much I know. Perhaps he has never loved anyone except his precious sister – oh, and Helena too, I'd almost forgotten *her*. Maybe his mother also. He has, on the surface, treated me well. But love? Never. His preference for Helena over his sons is another thing. You speak of conflict? *That's* been a frequent source of conflict over the years.'

'Did you hate Mrs Pole enough to kill her?' Louise asked the question in such a quiet, unthreatening voice that Fiona took a moment or two to process it.

'What? For heaven's sake! That's quite ridiculous! Of course I didn't murder her. I am not, I hope, so stupid.'

'Your husband knew how you felt about his sister, but what about your children? What was their attitude to Mrs Pole?'

'We always tried not to quarrel in front of them,' Fiona said. 'But children are not deaf, nor are they insensitive to atmospheres. So I dare say they knew how I felt. Alexander and Robert usually took my side. If my life has not been totally unbearable it is due in large part to the loyalty of my sons. I can be proud of *them*.'

'Why do you say 'unbearable', Mrs Fraser? You lead a privileged life, surely?'

'You might say so,' Fiona said stiffly. 'But a loveless marriage is a cruel trap. Not to mention all the other issues I've had to face because of my husband's family background.'

'Oh? Such as?'

'Oh, many things, some of them quite small, I suppose. And perhaps other successful men have these problems. What would I know? My husband has been the victim of blackmail, among other things.'

Louise frowned. 'When was this?'

'Quite some years ago. Some horrible little man from his past. I don't know the details.'

'Do you have a name for this man?'

'Oh, really, I don't recall – Gilbert, Gilchrist, some such name. I believe,' Fiona added with palpable disdain, 'he was an ex-convict.'

'I see.' Louise sat silently for a moment, then she turned to Hazell. 'I have no more questions for Mrs Fraser at the moment, sir. Do you want to ask her anything?'

Hazell shook his head and stood up. 'No, I think we've covered it for today.' He looked down at Fiona from his great height, unsmiling. 'Thank you for your time, Mrs Fraser. We can see ourselves out.'

'Did you sniff out any lies, Fred?' Louise asked as they drove back to Compton.

'One major one, at least one evasion, and a great deal she wasn't telling,' Hazell said. 'What do you think the lie was?'

Louise shook her head. 'I have no idea.'

'I think,' Hazell said, as he overtook a large and evil-smelling lorry full of rubbish, 'that Mrs Fraser knew exactly who was blackmailing her husband, and probably also why. I would say she's a party to many of his secrets, even the ones he thinks are safe. Whatever else she is, Fiona Fraser isn't stupid.'

'She's very angry,' Louise said thoughtfully. 'I wonder why. Apart from the obvious reasons, the ones she gave us.'

'It seems to me she's a disappointed woman, despite her life of privilege. I think she expected something quite different when she married Mr Fraser. Did you see the magazines on the table? If I'm not much mistaken they're aimed at super-rich people who fancy refurbishing a mouldy old ruin and turning it into a baronial pile, something to establish your aristocratic credentials. Well. Enough of my amateur psychology. I'm asking myself why Erica Pole was murdered now. Why not a year ago? Why not in six months' time? If she was killed by a family member, there has to be a reason that caused it to happen now. We need to find that reason.'

'Any clue as to what it might be?'

'Maybe. Remind me to ring Ewan Fraser as soon as we get back to the station. He needs to come down to identify his sister's body. There's a question I want to ask him, and I want to see his face when I do.'

1972: Scotland

St Serf's School for Boys
15 October 1972

Dear Miss Cordier,
    Since I understand that you are now the legal guardian of Ewan Fraser following the untimely death of his father, I am writing to express my concern, and that of some members of my staff, regarding this boy.
    Naturally I understand that he has undergone a significant trauma in recent months, and we at the school have tried to deal with Ewan accordingly. However, his academic studies have declined to such an extent that I am somewhat alarmed. From being a most promising and able student his level of achievement has dropped across the board. In addition, his performance on the playing fields, which had improved over the last year, has also suffered.
    I had hoped that the summer holidays might have restored some of this young man's equilibrium. He is now in the sixth form and undertaking A level courses, good results in which will, of course, be vital to his future career whether or not he chooses to apply to university.
    There is another matter that has come to my attention which has perturbed me. You are no doubt aware that at St Serf's we actively encourage our students to follow Christian principles. All pupils attend chapel on a regular basis, and Religious Studies form an essential part of the curriculum. You may also know that I myself am an Honorary Canon of St Agnes' Cathedral. Of course, an interest in religion is something I welcome in any of our boys. But Ewan has developed what may, without undue exaggeration, be described as an obsession. This has been, I believe, a significant factor in the deterioration

of his work. When I questioned him about it he told me that he was now what he called a "real" Christian. I tried not to take offence at the implications of his statement and took it, in the interests of charity, to mean that his level of commitment had seen an important change. However, as he left my office, he confounded me by announcing his intention of entering a monastery when he leaves school. It need not be said that I have anything but the deepest respect for such a calling; however, Ewan is only seventeen and I am not convinced that he has thought it through.

I felt that you should be apprised of these developments. I would be most grateful if you, as his guardian, could use your influence to persuade Ewan of the necessity of careful thought as to his future career.

Yours sincerely,
J.P.Crundall DD, Headmaster.

4, Arran Gardens,
Edinburgh
23 October 1972

Dear Dr Crundall,
Thank you for your letter. I am grateful too for your concern for my nephew.

Unfortunately I am rather at a loss to know what to do. I hardly know my sister's children, although now that Erica is living under my roof I have the opportunity to get to know her a little better. Ewan is another matter, because he is away at school so much of the time.

If I might explain the circumstances, you will understand my difficulty. My sister, the children's mother, was much younger than me – thirteen years. Tragically she died at the age of thirty-four, when Ewan was seven and Erica four. I saw them occasionally when she was alive, but after her death I was banned from Mickle, for no reason that I can fathom. I did send gifts and small amounts of money to the children on their birthdays and at Christmas, but I have no idea whether they received them. My brother-in-law, the late Lachlan Fraser, was a very strange man, and I have no idea why my sister married him. It is my belief that she and the children lived a secluded life until Lachlan decided, who knows why, to send Ewan to your school at the age of thirteen. Before that both children attended the village school, but after that, when Ewan went to St Serf's, Erica was taken out of the school and educated at home – again, by whom I don't know. I have only found this out from the girl herself. It must have been a patchy kind of education, because she has had a lot of catching up to do since she has been at St Catherine's.

Both children are polite and well-behaved – in my view, unnaturally so. When they are together, they speak almost exclusively to one another. I really have no influence over Ewan at all. If anyone knows him, it is his sister. But if I ask her about him she is evasive.

I have no children of my own, having never married, and I am now medically retired from my work as a civil servant. I am in poor health and it is as much as I can do to ensure that Ewan and Erica have adequate food and clothing and a decent education.

I will of course try to speak to Ewan about the problems you mention, but I cannot hold out much hope of success, for which I am truly sorry.

Yours sincerely,
Joan Cordier

2006: Compton

'Shut that window, can you, Joseph? There's a draught.' Erica spun her wheelchair into the centre of the room, away from the door, and clutched her cardigan more tightly around her.

Joseph closed the window and came to stand in front of her. 'You look frozen,' he said. 'Do you want something else to put on? Can I fetch something?'

'Yes, please – there's a sort of woolly jacket on the end of my bed.'

Joseph found the jacket, came back and draped it round Erica's shoulders. 'It's warm in here,' he said, looking at her closely. 'Perhaps you're getting a cold.'

'I might as well have something else while we're about it,' Erica said wryly. 'Mangled spine, arthritis, bad temper, Martian flu.'

'Never heard of Martian flu,' Joseph reflected. 'Venusian, now, that's spreading like a bush fire.'

'Ha, ha. Do you fancy putting the kettle on? Or are you in a hurry?'

'Not in the least.' Joseph crossed over to the kitchen, filled the kettle at the sink and plugged it in. 'Tea?'

'Please. Does it go with communion wine?'

'I reckon.'

'It's good of you to come and do the magic for me,' Erica said. 'Especially when you have a young bride to go home to.'

Joseph propped himself on the kitchen counter. 'Caroline is hardly a bride after almost three years,' he said. 'Anyway, she's out.'

He spoke with a finality that invited no further comment, but Erica was not to be deflected. 'How *is* Caroline?' she asked.

'Well enough,' Joseph said.

'Does she like being the vicar's wife in laugh-a-minute Compton?'

'Almost certainly not,' Joseph said. 'Where do you keep the teapot?'

'Oh, just fling a bag in a mug, for heaven's sake,' Erica said. 'Never mind the niceties. There's some milk in the fridge, courtesy of the wonderful Nettie. No biscuits, though. Pity.'

'I could go down to the shop on the corner and get you some, if you are feeling deprived.'

'No, no, I'd much rather you sat and chatted for a while. Just remember, I am a poor lonely old lady that nobody visits.'

'Except her brother, her niece, her carer, her vicar, and the bravest of her neighbours. And she's hardly old. All right, I'll bring you some biscuits next time I come. What sort do you like?'

'Chocolate.'

'Done.'

'Now, Joseph, come and sit down. You look weary. I hope it's because you've been up half the night making babies.'

'No, it isn't. Not that it's any of your business, Mrs Nosy. I am more likely to be burning the midnight oil wrestling with troublesome texts for Sunday's sermon. Here's your tea. Don't spill it.'

'Thanks. Well, that's a terrible waste! I am almost beginning to feel sorry for Caroline.'

'I feel sorry for her myself.' He stretched out on Erica's sofa and tried not to smile.

'It's a pity you're married, Joseph.'

'My dear Erica, you know I'm too young for you. And much too poor.'

'Ha! Funny man.' Erica took a sip of her tea, gripping the mug in claw-like hands. 'Ouch, that's hot. I'm not talking about me, as you well know. I have a lovely niece, though. Talented, beautiful and good-hearted.'

'I know you have,' Joseph reminded her. 'I have met her. In fact, it was because of Helena that you and I got acquainted.'

'So it was,' Erica said. 'The cheeky brat decided I needed spiritual sustenance and brazenly knocked on your door.'

'You should be grateful to Helena. Not necessarily for having met me, but for her kindness and concern.'

'I am indeed grateful,' Erica said softly. 'For both those things. So you see that I am telling you nothing but the truth when I say she is lovely.'

Joseph shook his head. 'She is. But it's a bit pointless your match-making, Erica. I am still married.'

'Yes. It's most inconvenient of you.' Erica fell silent for a moment, then she said abruptly, 'Take this cup for me, can you? It's burning my hands.'

Joseph swung his feet to the floor, took the cup and put it on a side-table. 'Let me know when you want some more.'

'I was married myself years ago,' Erica said. 'Did I tell you about that?'

'You said something once. No details, though.'

'Shall I tell you the details?' Erica said in a small voice.

Joseph frowned. 'Of course, if you want to.'

Erica sighed. 'My marriage was a disaster. Not from the beginning, but as good as. You say you feel sorry for Caroline, but I definitely feel sorry for Michael. He had no idea what I was really like. I married him after several years of dissolute living. Do you believe me? I mean that I was dissolute?'

'Absolutely,' Joseph said gravely.

'My brother Ewan was married very young,' Erica said. 'And just as disastrously, in my opinion. I suppose it wasn't very likely that either of us would be good at stable relationships, not after our rocky childhood. I was lonely in my twenties. I drifted from silly job to silly job. Ewan was busy with his work and his growing family. When I met Michael I thought I might as well follow suit, do the respectable thing, be a nice conformist housewife.' She sighed deeply. 'But frankly, I hated it.'

'Why was that?' Joseph said.

'Oh, I don't know. Well, no, of course I know. I'd had a freewheeling sort of life, knocked around with a few unsavoury characters, seemed to be having a ball, but I was always lonely inside, if you understand me.' She looked at him with narrowed eyes. 'Yes, I think you definitely understand. Anyway, Michael was a banker. Frightfully sensible. Utterly dull. A nice man, but with no imagination. I'd been a thoroughly bad girl, lots of men in my life, and I'm afraid Michael didn't match up where it counted, so I was lonely and purposeless and unfulfilled. All that changed when I had Stephen, at least for a while. He was my little beam of light. But you know what, it's another sort of loneliness, being at home with a tiny baby. I was exhausted, frustrated and bored. Looking back, I reckon I probably had post-natal depression for a while. But back then I didn't really know much about it. I thought you just had to battle through. And that's when I started drinking.'

'Bad idea,' Joseph said with feeling.

Erica looked up sharply. 'You too?'

'It was mostly my friends that drank. I could never afford to drink or do drugs, even if I'd wanted to. That wasn't really my problem. But that's another story. You were telling me about you.'

'Yes. It all unravelled.' Erica was silent for a moment, her eyes clouded. 'I kept it together for a little while, for Stephen's sake. I lurched along for a few years. But in the end I couldn't stand it any longer. I lost it completely, went on a bender, finished up in the cells. Nice story, huh?'

'There's got to be a lot more to it, I think,' Joseph said gently.

'Of course there is,' Erica snapped. 'But it's a nasty sordid little tale. Michael divorced me. There was a horrible court case for custody. I lost.'

'Did you see Stephen after that?'

'Yes, once a month, supervised. Then Michael got transferred to Chicago. It was a big step up. He took Stephen with him.'

'The court allowed it?'

'Yes. I was battling with the drinking, and thought I was winning, but they disagreed. I wasn't a suitable parent. It wasn't many years after they went to America that I had the accident. So I couldn't have looked after a child anyway.'

'What about later? Did you see Stephen as he was growing up?'

Erica was silent for so long, her head bent, that Joseph thought she had nodded off to sleep. 'Erica?'

When she lifted her head and looked at him, her eyes were red, her mouth twisted in a caricature of a grin. 'I'll have that tea now. It might be cooler.' Joseph took the mug and placed it carefully in her hands. She took a sip. 'Ewan offered to pay for another court case.' Her voice grated. 'Because Michael made excuse after excuse. But then I thought about it long and hard. Stephen had a good life. He would hardly have remembered me, or anything about living in England. Michael remarried when Stephen was eleven, and had another son. Stephen had a mother and a brother and friends. I thought, why does he need me? I wrote him a letter, explaining my decision, to be opened on his eighteenth birthday. I don't know if Michael ever gave it to him, but he has never replied. So no, I haven't seen my son since he was six years old. And yes, it broke me into pieces. Short of his death, I don't know what could be more cruel.'

Joseph leaned over and took her hand. 'I'm so sorry.'

She snatched her hand away. 'Don't be sorry for me,' she spat. 'I brought it on myself.' She glared at him, but he held her gaze, shaking his head.

'We often are to blame for our own misfortunes,' he said. 'That doesn't make them easier to bear.'

'I hate sympathy,' Erica said. 'I'm weak enough already. So I shall tell you about my brother instead – the story of his foray into matrimony. Ha! Almost as grubby and pathetic as mine, though most people wouldn't think so.'

'Should I be hearing this?' Joseph said mildly.

'You're very scrupulous, but don't worry,' Erica said. 'I'll just tell you about the party that changed his life.'

'That sounds dramatic.'

'It wasn't. Well. My brother inherited the title and the castle when he was sixteen. The will was archaic but legal, and everything was left to him. As if I didn't really exist.' She shrugged, and winced. 'Ewan was still at school, of course. Before he left school he was converted.'

'From what to what?'

'From not much to a full-blooded believer.'

Joseph raised his eyebrows. 'I thought you said it wasn't dramatic.'

'That bit might have been, but that's not the bit I'm telling you about. I can't tell you about his conversion – that was between him and God. Anyway, to everyone's consternation, especially mine, as soon as he left school he entered a monastery. Somewhere in Hampshire. At that point he was just a sort of enquirer. Testing his vocation, I suppose. For two years he lived with the brothers and worked in the kitchen and dug the vegetable patch. I was horrified.'

'Why?'

'Because, because –' To Joseph's dismay Erica's eyes filled with sudden tears. She dashed them away with a jerky impatient hand, almost knocking her cup over. 'Because I thought I'd lost him. I wrote to him, pleading with him: Don't stay there forever, I can't bear it. I don't know if it was me being so feeble, or whether he just changed his mind. Whatever, he never took his vows and left the monastery when he was twenty. At that point he still owned the castle. He hadn't decided what to do with it. He didn't even want to think about it at that point. Anyway, as soon as he left the monastery he went straight to the other extreme – crazy parties, rivers of booze, and some pretty unpleasant hangers-on. He was so innocent and helpless, really. You bored yet?'

Joseph, sitting on the edge of the sofa, shook his head. 'Hardly.'

'I'll cut to the chase. I was in my last year at school. Ewan invited me to a party at his flat. There were lots of foolish young people there – not his friends, quite honestly I don't believe he had any, they were just people who liked free drink – if he had lost it they would all have melted away, I'm convinced of that. I've experienced the same thing myself. We learned one lesson over and over again – that when it came right down to it Ewan and I only had one friend, and that was each other.' She took a deep breath. 'Hey, I'm getting away from my story. We hadn't seen one another for a while, and he made a big fuss of me. One particular girl had her eye on him, and she had it in for me from the off. I don't think she really wanted him, she just wanted to compete, to spite me. And she probably thought he was loaded, what with owning a castle and all that. She was a well-endowed blonde called Fiona Beaton. Ring a bell? That night Ewan was very happy and drunk as a lord. Fiona whisked him off to his bedroom at two in the morning and didn't come out till lunchtime the next day. I stayed over in his spare room, and when she emerged, eye makeup all down her face and hair like a bird's nest, I was eating a bowl of cornflakes among all the empties. She gave me a look that was pure spiteful female triumph, as if to say, "He's not all yours, skinny little sister." She resented me from the moment we met.'

'You said it changed his life,' Joseph prompted.

'Yep. That was the night Alexander was conceived. I wouldn't be at all surprised if Fiona had it all planned. She was a year or two older and much more worldly-wise. She also had a very alarming father. But Ewan, even then, was an honourable chap. He married her. They are still married. And she still hates me. Because in the end she never got what she wanted. She never got her castle, and in every way that matters, she couldn't take my brother away from me.'

'He's very important to you, I think,' Joseph murmured.

'There isn't anyone else,' Erica said simply. 'There never has been. For him too. There's nothing dodgy about it, nothing remotely incestuous. It's just the way it is.' She looked up at him, and her face was sad. 'But there's more, you see. Ewan went to work for Fiona's father, but they never got on. Ewan wanted to work for himself, and for that he needed money. There was some after my father died, but most of it had gone on paying off debts, and Ewan had blown a lot of it after he left the monastery. But he had a wife, and a baby on the way, and he had to sober up. I know for sure that Ewan decided for himself to sell Mickle, but Fiona was convinced I persuaded him against his better judgment. She was all for keeping it and living there – she had some fantasy of being the mistress of a baronial hall, which was laughable. She'd never been there, or she might have changed her mind. It was very remote, and only barely habitable. Anyway, Ewan sold it to a distant Fraser cousin who eventually turned it into some kind of hotel for sporting types. Ewan used the capital to set himself up in business. But Fiona was furious, and blamed me. It's true, Ewan knew how much I hated the place. But what was worse in her eyes, he gave me money from the proceeds so that I could have somewhere to live and be independent. Fiona thought I should go out to work and struggle like anyone else. There's a lot of bad blood.'

1976: Scotland

Dearest Quin,

When I read your letter I danced around the room, singing and shouting for joy. Aunt Joan must have thought I'd gone mad. I am *so happy* that you have decided not to take your vows and stay at the monastery for ever. How could I have borne it, to see you only once in a blue moon, or maybe never? Thank you, dear Quin, even if you didn't do it for me. I dare say I am terribly selfish wanting you to walk away from such a noble calling. When you come home you can tell me all about why I should be a Christian, and that will be my penance and your reward for your kindness.

I expect you will find me quite worldly and corrupt these days. I even have a boyfriend! His name is John, but everybody calls him Jock (of course.) You will probably find it hard to turn me into a good person, but if anyone can do it, you can. It's just that without you I have got very lonely. Jock is a nice boy and it is good to get hugs sometimes (plus all the rest!) but he doesn't really know me. Nobody does, except you.

I will meet you at the station. In case you don't recognise me I will be the one with the biggest, sunniest smile.

All love,
Marjie x

My darling Marjie,

You are such a fool! As ever! When I got your letter I realised just how much I have missed you these last two years. And, not to make you too conceited, I did decide to leave the monastery because of you, although that wasn't the whole reason. It's been a good experience here, and the brothers are wonderful, but I have come to understand it's not the life for me. (I am still a Christian though, and so should you be, heathen sister!)

As for a boyfriend called Jock, how could you even contemplate such a thing? Isn't he some kind of cartoon character? No, I mustn't be nasty. But I am a bit worried by your hints of an immoral life. I can see you need your brother's steadying influence.

I can't wait to see you. We have so much to catch up on! Do you really think I won't recognise you? I guess you're terribly grown-up these days.

See you soon,
Love from Quin x

2008: Compton

Ewan Fraser arrived at the mortuary of Stockley Hospital precisely at two o'clock. He drove himself in his sleek silver Mercedes. Despite the muggy heat of a cloudy afternoon he emerged from his car immaculate in a suit and crisp white shirt. He locked the car and walked slowly across the baking tarmac of the car park to where Hazell waited in the shadow of the doorway.

The two men shook hands. 'Inspector.' Fraser took off his sunglasses, revealing tired eyes. He squinted up at Hazell, who was almost a head taller. 'Shall we get this over with?' he said quietly.

'Are you ready, sir?'

'As ready as one can be for such a horrific task.'

'Understood. This way, then.'

Hazell led the way into the cool interior, down a passage, through a door, and signed discreetly to a white-coated technician, who followed them. 'Through here.' He took Fraser into a bare room, its walls a murky beige, a stark central light shining down on the table in the centre. The mortuary assistant drew the sheet carefully away from the body that lay there, taking care to keep the bruised neck covered.

Ewan stared at the drained white face of his sister, his own face a rigid mask. 'Yes, this is Erica,' he whispered. His eyes were wide, his hands clenched at his sides. 'Oh, my poor dear girl.'

The assistant replaced the sheet and glanced at Hazell, who nodded. There was silence as the man left the room. 'Thank you, Mr Fraser,' Hazell said softly. 'Shall we go out?'

Fraser bit his lip, turned too quickly and stumbled. Hazell caught him by the elbow and steadied him. Fraser nodded silent thanks, and walked briskly out of the room. Hazell followed, closing the door behind them. Fraser was ahead of him along the passage, and by the time Hazell caught up he was outside again, leaning against the wall, his eyes closed.

'Are you all right, sir?'

Fraser opened his eyes and looked at the Inspector. 'I know I am expected to say, yes, thank you. But the truth is, I don't think I will ever be all right again in this life.' He smiled faintly. 'It's always been a close-run thing.' He pulled a handkerchief out of his trouser pocket and wiped it over his face. 'Are you a praying man, Inspector?'

Hazell was startled. 'Sometimes.'

'Perhaps you would remember me, then. I shall need all the prayers I can get. I am thankful that you were here in person today. Now if you'll excuse me, I must return to London.'

'Are you fit to drive back right away, Mr Fraser? Wouldn't you like a cup of coffee first, perhaps? We can take a formal statement later.'

'You are kind, but no, thank you.'

'Then I'll walk you to your car. Mine is parked alongside.'

Fraser unlocked his car and took off his jacket, stowing it carefully on the back seat. He opened the car door and seemed about to say something but Hazell got in first. 'Mr Fraser, forgive me for questioning you on such a day, but it will save making another appointment. May I ask if you have changed your will recently?'

Fraser looked up at him and gaped. The sun was shining into his eyes and he raised his hand to shield them. 'How very extraordinary,' he said. 'Why would you ask me that? No, that is stupid, of course I know why. But why would such a thing occur to you?'

Hazell smiled slightly. 'I think it's called twenty-five years' experience, sir.'

Fraser sighed and shook his head. 'Yes, I changed my will a month ago, or thereabouts.' He narrowed his eyes. 'You'll want to know what changes I made. Well, as you no doubt suspect, I left a large sum to my sister.' He grimaced. 'She will not need it now.'

'Was she a beneficiary in your earlier will, Mr Fraser?'

'Yes, but not substantially. I was going to change it at some point in the future, but I thought I had plenty of time.'

'And now?' Hazell prompted.

Fraser smoothed his hair back from his forehead. His hands were freckled, sinewy and ringless. 'I have had some medical problems in the last few months. There have been tests. Not all the results are in yet, but I thought it best to alter my will now, just in case things turned out to be as serious as I feared. I wanted Erica provided for if I was ill, demented or dead. It gave me peace of mind. She had her house, of course, and I paid money into her bank account for all her current needs, but the fact is her condition was getting worse, she would have needed more and more help, and I knew that if I were to be incapacitated others might not care for her so well.' He frowned, squinting in the strong sun. 'Why are you interested in my will, Inspector?' He hesitated, and Hazell could see strong emotion in his face, quickly suppressed. 'Dear Heaven,' Fraser said. 'I'm afraid I have an idea of your answer, and it chills me to the bone.'

'At the moment,' Hazell said, 'we're trying to find out why Mrs Pole's private documents, as well as her phone, were stolen. Was a copy of the will in that brown folder in her drawer?'

Fraser nodded. 'The original is with my solicitor.'

'Apart from the solicitor, did you consult anyone about changing your will?'

Fraser's chin came up. 'No.'

'Did you tell anyone afterwards what you had done?'

'Yes. I told my wife. I felt I was honour bound to do that. Of course my family are still handsomely provided for.' Fraser spoke stiffly, his hand still resting on the open door of the Mercedes.

'How did Mrs Fraser react?'

'As I expected. With tirades of fury. You would have thought I'd left her destitute in the gutter.' He compressed his lips, as if he felt he had said too much.

'And your children?'

Fraser heaved a deep sigh. 'Who knows what she has said, and to whom,' he said sombrely. 'I have no control over that.'

'Thank you, sir. I'm sorry I have had to ask you these things, today of all days.'

Fraser looked at him, his face bleak. 'You have merely said out loud what I was trying not to think. Now my thoughts are tending in the same direction as yours seem to be. The difference is that I wish I was not thinking them.'

'Nevertheless, Mr Fraser,' Hazell said gently, 'your sister has been murdered, and it is my responsibility to discover the perpetrator, whoever he or she might be.'

'Yes. And I am sure you will. Thank you, Inspector. You know where to find me if you need me.' Fraser climbed into his car, turned on the ignition and wound down the window. Hazell leaned in. 'Let me say how deeply sorry I am for your loss. I mean that most sincerely.'

Fraser gave a ghostly sketch of a smile. 'I believe you do. Thank you, Inspector. Goodbye.'

carver@pcmedia.net to fbgreville@chelhall.org

Hello Bert old thing, how's it going down on Pater's farm? Hope you are back in the swing of things. I took your advice and did the good father bit at the zoo with my offspring. I plied them with ice cream and I have to say it went better than I expected. Rachel was pleased – an added bonus. So for the time being all is sweet in the Carver ménage.

Thought I'd report on my researches into the murky past of the Frasers. I hope you will be suitably impressed by my diligent ferreting. First off, things are different in Scotland – they don't have Coroners' Courts. If someone dies in what is deemed unusual circumstances, or unnaturally, they have a Fatal Accident Enquiry. I won't bore you with all the history, but I knew that Ewan Fraser inherited in 1972, and that's where I started my digging, into the grimy depths of the national archive. I used my native charm, plus a bit of blagging, quoting my academic status (true) and saying I was doing some research on behalf of one of my students (not so true.) A nice lady on the archive staff did the leg-work for me.

Your ma was right – Fraser pere (Lachlan) drowned in a river while fishing, drunk as usual. The son (Ewan) was quizzed at the hearing, but sympathetically. The interesting thing was a footnote about a possible witness who was called but failed to show up, a man called Neil Gilmour. This chap was a sort of informal factor to Lachlan Fraser. He and his wife lived at the castle, his wife having been employed to educate Erica. Here's the good bit: Ewan testified that Gilmour couldn't have seen his father go into the river because he was behind a rock vomiting. (Apparently all three of them, Fraser senior and both the Gilmours, drank like fish. Fish! Ha, ha.) However, when Gilmour arrived back at the castle (the boy had driven off without him, distraught) he was soaking wet. Shortly afterwards the Gilmours vanished, taking the Frasers' ancient truck, along with the contents of the gun cupboard – including a valuable gun – plus all the cash in the castle. An empty cash-box was found on the kitchen table. How did Gilmour open it? The key was kept *around Lachlan Fraser's neck*. So was Gilmour wet

123

because he had waded into a freezing river to rescue his boss? Or was he after the dead man's belongings? I know you'll say I'm cynical, but did he actually finish him off? The truck was found abandoned, but there was no sign of the Gilmours and their loot – or the key.

That was the sum of the enquiry, and they came to the conclusion that Lachlan Fraser's death was the result of an unforeseeable and tragic accident. But I was intrigued by the Gilmours, so I did a bit of internet research for myself. To cut a long story short, I found out that Neil Gilmour did time some years later for conning two elderly sisters out of their life savings. Not content with that he went back later to steal from them again – what a creep! After he was released I lost track of him, and his wife was never heard of again. But the valuable gun, a 1930s Purdey 12-gauge, (no idea what that means but no doubt you'll know) turned up in an auction in Glasgow about 5 years ago! Queer how these things pan out.

I've blathered on long enough. Hope this finds you in good fettle. All the best from your old pal.

fbgreville@chelhall.org to *carver@pcmedia.net*

Dear old pal, as you style yourself, I really don't think you have enough to keep you occupied. Are the long summer holidays beginning to pall? Why the obsessive interest in the distant past of minor Scottish lairds?

I must go – it's a busy time here. All the best, Carver. Do try and stay out of mischief.

I'm determined to keep in touch with Joseph, even if it's only on the phone.

2007: Compton

'Nettie? Is that you?'

'Yes, dear, just coming.'

Nettie arrived in Erica's sitting room in a flurry of coat, scarf and assorted bags. 'Oh, my dear, it's blowing a gale out there.'

'Nettie, you look flustered. Take your coat off and sit for a minute. I won't starve.'

Nettie took off her coat, folded it carefully and put it on a chair. Then she turned to Erica and burst into a gush of tears.

'Whatever is the matter, Nettie?' Erica said, propelling her wheelchair closer.

Nettie pulled a large handkerchief from the pocket of her cardigan and blew her nose. 'I'm so sorry, Mrs P, letting myself go like that. I do apologise. It's just that I've heard some dreadful news.'

Erica frowned. 'Well, what is it?'

Nettie swallowed. 'Caroline Stiles, you know, Joseph's wife, was involved in a pile-up on the motorway this morning. She's dead.'

'Good Lord! What a terrible thing! How did you find out so quickly, Nettie?'

Nettie sat down opposite Erica and sighed deeply. 'Mrs Rowe rang me, from Compton Parva. I'm on the prayer chain.'

'Ah. Ecclesiastical jungle drums. I see.'

'What?' Nettie looked up, bewildered.

'Never mind. Look, Nettie, you're obviously in a state of shock. Forget my lunch for now. Go and put the kettle on, and we'll have something hot and strong while you calm down a bit.'

'All right.' Nettie busied herself at the sink, sniffing loudly every few minutes.

'Nettie, have you seen Joseph?'

Nettie turned to face her, the tea caddy in her hands. 'Not yet. But there's going to be a…well, I don't know quite what, but a few people are going to gather in the church this afternoon to pray for him. And the rest of Caroline's family too, of course. I suppose he might be there. The police were at the Vicarage earlier, but they've gone now.'

'If you see him, Nettie, please will you say to him not to bother to come and give me Communion this afternoon? He may have forgotten anyway, but I don't want him thinking of unimportant things like me when he has this to deal with.'

'I'll make sure he knows. If he isn't in church, I'll ring him for you.' She put a steaming mug on the small table beside the wheelchair. 'Here's your tea.'

'Thank you.' Erica put a jerky hand over Nettie's in an unaccustomed gesture. 'What a shock, Nettie,' she said with none of her normal asperity. 'It's very sad when someone dies so young.'

Nettie's eyes welled with tears again, and she gulped them down. 'She was only thirty-two. Such a pretty girl. Poor Joseph.'

'Yes. Poor Joseph indeed,' Erica echoed.

At half past two Erica heard her front door grate open and bang shut. Her straight black brows knitted together. 'Hello?'

Joseph appeared, carrying a small brown leather case. 'Hello, Erica.'

'Oh, Joseph! I asked Nettie to tell you not to come.'

Joseph nodded. 'She did tell me. And lent me your key, so you didn't have to struggle to the front door. I made an appearance in church, just for a minute. Don't think I'm not thankful for their prayers – heaven knows I need all I can get, and not just now – but I couldn't face all the sad murmurings. I feel such a hypocrite. I'm thankful you gave me an excuse to escape.' He smiled faintly. 'No doubt they'll be thinking what a noble chap, soldiering on with his pastoral duties in the face of tragedy. I don't deserve their good opinion.'

'What about my good opinion?' Erica said, her eyes narrowed.

'I'm not at all sure you have one,' Joseph said. 'Let's do what I came for, at least. I don't want to add dishonesty to my list of failings. Then perhaps I can hide here for a while.'
'Hide for as long as you like. I should tell you my niece is coming down later, about four, she said.'
'Helena? I'll be gone by then. You ready?'

Joseph finished with a prayer, standing over Erica as she sat in her wheelchair, hands gripped together, head bent. Neither said a word for a few minutes, drinking in the silence. Then Erica lifted her head, looked up at him, and smiled.
'You know what,' Joseph said, 'you should smile more often. You look quite different.'
Erica clapped her hand to her heart, making even more of a parody of the gesture by her stiff awkwardness. 'At last he noticed her ravishing beauty.'
'Something like that,' Joseph said. 'Kettle on?'
'Good man.' She wheeled the chair slowly across the room, following him. 'Thank you for coming, Joseph. Though perhaps you shouldn't have.'
'No,' he said, turning to her from the kitchen counter. 'I made, for once, the right decision.'
'So, tell me, if I am not being too damn nosy, why does the natural sympathy of your parishioners make you feel like a hypocrite?'
Joseph looked at her sombrely as he put teabags into mugs. 'Because,' he said slowly, as if feeling his way, 'after Caroline left the house this morning, when I came back after doing assembly at the school, I found a note from her. Telling me she had had enough of life in the Vicarage, of life in Compton, and above all of life with me, and was leaving, permanently. I don't blame her, and I wasn't surprised. She's not really been happy since we came here. Poor girl, she had no freedom after all. She was on her way back to her parents' place, with her belongings all in the car with her, when the accident happened.' He poured boiling water into the mugs and stirred. 'So you see, I can't really cast myself in the role of heartbroken widower. But you

are the only person I could tell this to. Even if you think I am an unfeeling monster, you probably won't have a heart attack.'

'No, I won't, and I don't think you are a monster, just honest. I am usually unpopular because of honesty, but I value it above many things. To me, it's a sign of respect, and trust.' She sighed. 'I am very sorry a young person has lost her life in such circumstances. It's tragic, of course. Caroline may not have been my best pal, not by a long chalk – and I don't think she was right for you.'

'Nor I for her,' muttered Joseph, taking a gulp of his tea.

'Even so, as she drove off this morning no doubt she was hoping for a chance to be happy, and I wouldn't have denied her that. So, what now, Joseph?'

He shrugged. 'Oh, the usual rigmarole. I think her family will want to organise the funeral, and I won't object. I wouldn't normally be expected to conduct the funeral of my own wife, and if it's out of the parish there'll be less of a circus. I'll just put on my best kit and go and be a mourner in the family chapel. But there'll be an inquest. Caroline was involved with a speeding lorry, and unfortunately she wasn't the only fatality.'

'Grim. Two spoons of sugar, please.' Joseph raised his eyebrows. 'Well, I'm unlikely to get fat, and if I did, my doctor would probably be pleased. Also I don't worry about my health, since it's already shot to bits. Sugar, chocolate biscuits, no problem. I shouldn't drink alcohol, though sometimes I do. But if I were a bit more mobile I might go in for younger men.' She eyed Joseph with a look that was intended to be lascivious but was merely comical.

Joseph smiled, his eyes crinkling. 'Remind me to keep my distance. Here's your tea.'

'Thanks. Though what I meant was, what next in the longer term?'

'No idea. Soldier on, praying for guidance.'

'Fair enough.' She looked at him keenly as he came into the lounge area and flopped into a chair, momentarily closing his eyes. 'You look exhausted.'

'It's the thought of all that's to come over the next few weeks. The questions, the condolences, the pretence. Then the funeral, and Caroline's family, who will be devastated. They never thought me good enough for her. Just thinking about it makes me want to crawl under the carpet.'

'Do you mind if I ask you a personal question?'

'Go ahead. But I reserve the right to remain silent.'

'Not to beat about the bush,' Erica said, 'you and Caroline always seemed unsuited. Why did you marry her in the first place?'

Joseph groaned. 'How long have you got?'

'Longer than you, most likely. Well, this afternoon, anyway. Why don't you start at the beginning?'

'No, no. My infancy and boyhood were serene and dull. It was at university that things started to go bad. You sure you want to hear about my fall from grace?'

'Definitely.'

Joseph cleared his throat and thought. 'I had my heart broken a couple of times as a student, being a sensitive sort of chap, but otherwise not much happened out of the ordinary. I got my degree. My parents came up for the graduation ceremony, and I noticed that my mother wasn't looking well.' He bit his lip. 'They hadn't told me she had cancer. I'd seen her at Easter, and just thought she was more tired than usual. They didn't want to mess up my finals. That was my mother's last public appearance – the cancer spread with frightening speed, and she died in August.'

'Oh, Joseph.'

'I was completely shattered. Mother and I were very close. I have a much older sister, and they didn't think they could have any more children, so when I came along there was much rejoicing. Etcetera, etcetera. Then I fell out with my father. He thought I was moping and being generally unmanly. I thought his rough-and-robust attitude utterly insensitive. Instead of searching diligently for a job as he expected, I decamped to London and worked in a café washing dishes and living in a squat with six interesting young people. It's a good job my dad never saw them: he would have been horrified. All his prejudices would have been confirmed. Purple hair, tattoos, piercings, illegal substances, even a bit of petty crime. They are probably pillars of society now, if they lived through all that. I wasn't into drink and drugs that much – I was too poor, for a start. But I fell prey to the Black Dog, and wound up in hospital. My dad came to see me. He told me to pull myself together, stop malingering and get proper work.'

'Oh, dear.'

'Mm. Well, you'll be glad to know that after many years of not talking I went to see him when he was old and feeble, in a nursing home by then, and we forgave one another. But that was much later. At the time I felt cut adrift, alone, broke, sick and sad. But something good did come out of it.'

'You saw the light,' Erica said with heavy irony.

Joseph smiled. 'Mm, yes, not exactly the Damascus road, nothing so sudden nor so irresistible, more a long, slow process and the faithful friendship of a young man called Ivor who put up with my feebleness and backsliding and persevered. He's a medical missionary now, somewhere in Africa, I think. We still correspond from time to time. I have reason to bless Ivor. He was and is a very unselfish person, a true Christian.'

'What about you?'

'Ha. Well, I hope I am also a true Christian, or I shouldn't be in this job. I'm certainly nowhere near as selfless as Ivor. But if you want me to nail my colours to the mast, I will. I love the Lord. It's simple enough. He has the first call on my life. I fail all the time, but I get up again with his help. I'll pick myself up from this latest disaster, with his help. And carry on, God willing. I don't hope for spectacular successes, just the chance to serve his saints.'

'You have saints at Christchurch?'

'Every one. Even you, my dear Erica.'

Erica snorted her derision. 'Now I know you're crackers.'

'No, I'm perfectly serious. When I look round my congregation, I don't see a scattering of fragile humans, I see powerhouses of holiness, lights in the darkness of this world. They are extraordinary in their ordinariness.'

'All right, I believe you. But you still haven't told me how you met Caroline.'

'Do you want any more tea?'

'No, thanks. I had two cups with Nettie, and if I have any more now you will have the unenviable job of taking me to the toilet. You have a refill if you like.'

'No, thanks, I'll pass. I got a job in a bank, which was dreary but unthreatening. I recovered from depression, but it left me vulnerable. I hadn't got the energy for anything too demanding. Then I had a letter from Ivor, which set me thinking. By then I'd been attending my local church for a few years and making myself useful. Something Ivor said set in motion a train of thought which led, eventually, and via many tests and tortuous paths, to ordination. I'll whisk through that part.'

'Didn't they balk a bit when you told them about your dodgy past? Living in the gutter with druggies? Do they take headbangers these days?'

'Thanks for the ringing endorsement, Erica. No, it was an issue, of course. That was part of the tortuous path I mentioned. Anyway, it happened. But I had to get theological training first, and that took three years. So by the time I got through all the academic work and panels and what-have-you, I was twenty-nine. A different man altogether from the boy who got his degree and lost his mother.'

'Yes,' Erica murmured. 'I imagine so. And then?'

'I was still in London, and my first post was as a curate in a busy inner-city parish. We had a very charismatic chap in charge – charismatic in the non-technical sense – and there was another curate with me. We had a big congregation, a lot of young people, quite exciting and very different from here. Caroline was sharing a flat in that part of London then and she started coming along with some of her friends.'

'And you were smitten?'

'I'm afraid so. She was very pretty, very bright and full of life. What she saw in me is more mysterious.'

'Oh, I don't know,' Erica mused. 'For some women, at some times in their lives, there's a certain glamour, a certain mystique...one could imagine a priest might have greater certainties, and one would expect him to be more spiritual than most.'

'Misplaced, in my case,' Joseph said, amused. 'Who knows? My theory, for what it's worth, is that Caroline was in revolt against her family and their expectations. They were all rather upper-class. She thought perhaps to thumb her nose at them by marrying a proletarian Evangelical. She soon realised her mistake.'

'Joseph, you do yourself down,' Erica demurred. 'You are a very personable, educated, wise, lovable chap.'

'Praise indeed. Thank you. Caroline would probably not have agreed.'

'It takes two. So you married her after, what? A year or two?'

'Two months.'

'Crikey.'

'Yes, I know.'

'And then?'

'Well, perhaps inevitably, things started to get rocky. And I began to be depressed again, no surprise. It was hard for Caroline. She must have realised she'd made a mistake, I suppose, but to give her credit she didn't give up on me, not then. It became obvious that I couldn't hack the London parish any more. It was suggested a quieter place might help me. So we came here, but for Caroline it really didn't work.'

'What about you?'

'Apart from Caroline, I've liked it. The people I know are good souls in their quiet way.'

Erica sighed. 'It's a very sad day, Joseph. But I'm glad you might stay here, for the people of Compton, even if I'm not here to see it.'

'Don't you go and die on me, please.'

'Chances are I'll be getting my wings before you, my dear whippersnapper.' Her head jerked up abruptly. 'What's that?'

'Hello!' came a voice from the garden. 'Where are you hiding?'

'It's your niece,' Joseph said. 'I've stayed too long.'

'In here, Helena,' Erica called.

Helena arrived through the conservatory door, her hair ruffled, her cheeks flushed. 'Boy, it's windy!' She saw Joseph, stopped, and smiled. 'Hello.'

'You two have met, I believe,' Erica said, catching Joseph's eye and grinning wickedly.

'Good to see you again, Miss Fraser,' Joseph said, inclining his head.

'Oh, Helena, please.'

'And I'm Joseph. I was just leaving.' He turned to Erica. 'I'll see you soon.'

To his surprise she grasped his hand. 'There's something I need to talk to you about,' she whispered. 'Not today, of course, but soon. It's important. Can you come back tomorrow?'

'All right. About eleven?'

Erica nodded.

Joseph turned back to Helena. 'Goodbye.'

A few minutes later Helena came flying out of the front door and down the path after him, her eyes wide. 'Joseph!'

He stopped by the gate, eyebrows raised enquiringly, and waited for her to get her breath back.

'Erica has just told me your news,' Helena said. 'I am so, so sorry. How awful.'

'You didn't have to run after me,' Joseph said gently. 'But thank you.' He saw the sparkle of tears in her bright blue eyes, and was touched.

'And you still came to see Erica,' Helena said. 'Even today.'

'My staying at home locked away wouldn't have made anything different,' Joseph said. 'And my motives are quite selfish – your aunt is a tonic.'

Helena laid a hand lightly on his arm. 'I'm sure your motives are of the best. But I'm glad you aren't among those who think she is a rude, bad-tempered shrew. Not all the time, anyway.' She laughed through her tears. 'I won't hold you up. I'm sure there is nothing either Erica or I can do,' she added, 'but we will if we can.'

'Just pray, that's all. Not for me necessarily, but for Caroline's parents, and her brother.'

'Of course. We can do that. Goodbye, Joseph.'

'Well, young lady, as you see, Joseph is free now,' Erica said as Helena came back into the room.

'What? Oh, honestly, even you could leave the matchmaking for a few days!' Helena said.

'On the contrary, when you are a sick old wreck like me you have to be practical and make the most of every moment and opportunity. Of course I am sorry that Caroline Stiles is dead – but I won't deny I didn't care for her very much and I thought they were bad for one another. Life's too short for marital misery, Helena. As I should know.'

'You are disgraceful.'

'Yes, but I get away with it.'

'Why should he be interested in me, or I in him, for heaven's sake?' Helena exclaimed.

'I can't answer for you, but Joseph was mismatched and unhappy. He's an attractive man, in a slightly gone-to-seed way. He is also musical, sensitive, clever, honest and immensely kind. As indeed are you. I want to know you are taken care of when I am gone.'

'Oh, for goodness' sake, Erica! You'll live for ever, you are so wicked.'

'Perhaps. Now, my dear child, please make yourself useful. I have drunk so much tea today my bladder is bursting. Get me to the toilet before I have an accident. I really didn't want to have to ask Joseph. A girl's got to keep *some* dignity.'

2008: Compton

'We need something concrete,' Hazell said to Gordon before the team convened. 'It's all circumstantial.' He was staring glumly at a computer screen.

'Sir, we need to follow up the vehicles. Those BMWs. If what I think you're thinking is right, there might be some CCTV footage.'

Hazell sighed. 'I haven't really been all that frank with you, have I, Louise? The trouble is, I'm not sure. Once you say something out loud, even to yourself, it tends to solidify, and bit by bit your mind closes to other options, and things, vital things, get missed. That's what I'm trying to avoid.'

'I understand that, sir. All we have so far is suspicion – strong suspicion, maybe, but based on people's apparent motives. Which can be the foggiest thing of all to fathom.'

Hazell nodded slowly. 'But I think you're right. There are avenues we should be exploring now. Let's get people working on those cars.'

They went next door into the tiny, bare meeting room where Sergeant Rivers and Constables Davies, Simmons and Walsh were already arriving, muttering greetings, jostling for space to stand or perch.

Hazell flexed his shoulders. 'Right, everybody. We're going to follow up the black BMW. We know there are four connected to Fraser's business. A black BMW was seen behind the victim's house on the afternoon of the murder. An unfamiliar large black four-by-four was seen parked near the perimeter of Golden Lawns Golf Club at some point later that afternoon. The witness was vague about exactly when, but it fits the general time-frame.

'Miss Helena Fraser used one of the company's estate cars to drive down here on Sunday, and we have the registration plate for that. Rivers, you get hold of the plates for the other three, and you two, Walsh and Davies, no, take Simmons as well, examine the CCTV footage for the motorway on Friday afternoon, say between midday and six o'clock. Work out the route between Golden Lawns and Compton and go from there. If we get any hits we'll have something to work on, maybe something we can use to get a search warrant for premises associated with potential suspects. We can examine the cars, see if there are any discrepancies with the logged mileage, and check the satnav memory.'

'Sir,' Davies said, 'you're talking about suspects, but who are they? How certain are we that we're looking at a family member here?'

'We're not,' Hazell said. 'That's what it looks like to me, in the absence of anything else. There was no robbery, unless you count the victim's phone, which wasn't of much value. If it was some opportunist, why commit murder for a phone? The victim wasn't in a position to fight back, was she? That's what I'm thinking, that there's something deeper here. But I could be wrong. We have to keep an open mind.' He paused for a moment, thinking. 'What I don't want to do is alert any of the family that we might be questioning their alibis. I don't want to move until we've got it sewn up tight, as tight as we can. We need to cover every angle we can think of. OK, off you go. You know what to do. I'm going to stay here with Sergeant Rivers and try to get some kind of overview from what we've got so far.'

The phone rang on the desk, and Louise Gordon picked up the receiver. Hazell waved the others to wait. Louise listened, said 'OK, thank you,' and replaced the handset. She looked up at Hazell. 'Sir, that was the desk. They've just had a phone call from a resident of Plough Lane, one of the victim's neighbours, a Mr Jeffries. He lives at number forty-six, two up from Mrs Pole. He rang to report on a stranger snooping around the vicinity of Plough Lane in the last couple of weeks, making a nuisance of himself, he said. Mr and Mrs Jeffries only got back from a visit to relatives in Devon yesterday, which was the first they heard of the murder.'

Hazell thrust his hands deep into his jacket pockets and scowled. 'All right, Sergeant, you'd better go up there and see what Mr Jeffries has to say. It could be something, it could be nothing. While you're up there, see if the people at number forty are in. The neighbour that saw the BMW that afternoon. Ask him if there's anything else he noticed out of the ordinary that might have occurred to him over the weekend. Sometimes things come back to people after the event, but they think they're too insignificant to report.'

An hour and a half later, Louise Gordon returned to the station. She found Rivers and Hazell surrounded by computer screens, heads together, their voices low. 'Sir.'

'Hello, Louise. What have you got?'

Louise propped herself on the edge of one of the computer tables, ignoring a frown from Rivers. She flipped open her notebook. 'Mr and Mrs Jeffries said they saw this character because they live up the top end of the lane. Apparently this tramp, if that's what he was, was sleeping rough on the banks, on the benches the Council put up there. He was hanging around a few weeks ago, and Mr Jeffries was going to report him to us, because the man was dirty and drunk and abusive, and kids play up there. But then he disappeared. Mr and Mrs Jeffries went away to Devon and when they came back they found out about the murder. They were talking to neighbours about this tramp fellow and another neighbour, an elderly widow, Mrs Harvey, said she'd seen him at least twice, during the day when other residents were out at work, hammering on Mrs Pole's door and shouting.'

Hazell frowned. 'Shouting what?'

'Rubbish, apparently. Mrs Harvey was too scared to do anything except hide, and when I went to see her she was very vague about when she'd seen him. She was getting flustered and upset so I backed off. I thought I wasn't going to get anywhere by being heavy-handed. Obviously the neighbours are all in a state, with a murder on their doorstep. I went to see the man at number forty, and he hadn't got anything else to tell us, but he said Mrs Harvey had told him about the hammering and he thinks it was at the beginning of last week, when the Jeffries were away. But by then the man had gone, so they didn't report it. They didn't mention it when they were interviewed during the house-to-house, either, crazy as that seems. They didn't see the possible connection. Perhaps they were more interested in keeping themselves out of trouble. Their stories were a bit garbled, but I got a picture of someone scruffy and dirty, with long hair and a straggly beard, wearing an old grey overcoat even in this heat, and a felt hat. None of them could understand what he was saying, but they all agreed on one thing: he had a distinct Scottish accent.'

2007: Compton

'Joseph, you're soaked.'

'Yes, it started to pour down when I was half way here.'

'You walked?'

'I didn't have much choice, Erica. Our car is somewhere, maybe in some police back yard, or at a breaker's, crunched beyond salvation.'

Erica grimaced. 'Oh, Joseph, I'm sorry. I didn't think.'

Joseph ran his hands through his wet hair. 'I have a bicycle, but it's behind a load of junk in the garden shed. I haven't had time to get it out.'

'Take your coat off, hang it in the bathroom for a while. There's a towel in there you can dry your hair with if you like.'

'Thanks.'

A few minutes later he returned, towel in hand. 'I can't stay long, Erica. I have to go to Stockley to identify Caroline's body.'

'Of course. You poor man, what a hideous task. Where is she?'

'In the hospital mortuary.' He bit his lip. 'Yes, I am dreading it. It's the thought of seeing her mangled. Poor Caroline. Perhaps if I hadn't been the world's worst husband she might still be alive.'

'That's daft, and you know it,' Erica said gently. 'Put the kettle on and sit for a while. I'll have coffee, but you have what you like.'

'I'm sorry we didn't have time to talk about your issues yesterday,' Joseph said as he moved around the kitchen. 'I rambled on so long with my dismal story, and then your niece arrived.' He poured boiling water into two mugs. 'What a lovely young lady she is, Erica. After I left she came running out to offer sympathy, even though she barely knows me.'

'That's Helena all over,' Erica said. 'Big heart, just a bit naïve at times. She's been defended from life's dark side- rather, by her father. But you are short of time, and I don't want to hold you up.'

Joseph came through to the lounge area and put Erica's cup on the table beside her. 'Can you reach that OK?'

'Yes, thanks.' She looked up at him, frowning slightly. 'Joseph, I feel bad burdening you at this terrible time, but I'm worried about my brother.'

Joseph looked puzzled. 'I've never met him, Erica. How can I help?'

Erica sighed deeply. 'I don't know who else to talk to, quite honestly. And it's a spiritual problem, if anything. My brother seems so successful, doesn't he – so many achievements, and he's done such a lot of good. But Joseph, under all of that he is plagued, you could say tormented. I don't know how to help him, but I know for certain he never speaks of it to anyone else.'

'Not to his wife?'

The corners of Erica's mouth twitched in a bitter little smile. 'Oh, my dear! I don't think he and Fiona have had a proper conversation all their married life. I may be wrong – I hope I am. The fact is, they married because Alex was on the way. It should never have happened. And I am responsible too – if it hadn't been for me maybe Ewan and Fiona would have had to work something out. But he has always had me, you see. I tried not to interfere, especially when the children were growing up, and Ewan was building his business, and then later, founding the Haven. But if I kept away, he always sought me out, sooner or later. Perhaps Fiona can be forgiven for being aggrieved. But I assume being married to my brother has had its compensations – she loves life's material delights, and she has those in spades, kindly supplied by her hard-working husband. She has three children, and her two boys are her pride and joy. Helena counts for less in her eyes, which is another example of Fiona's warped values, it seems to me. Helena is very like her father, which might account for it. Whatever – I digress. But I can assure you that Fiona would not be the person you would want to talk to about spiritual things.'

'So what is it that's tormenting him, Erica?'

Erica stretched over painfully, and grasped Joseph's wrist. 'You must understand, Joseph – in a way I shouldn't be telling you this. It's his business. But I must, for Ewan's sake. As far as I am aware, no one else knows, and I don't want them to.'

'If you tell me something inflammatory, illegal, harmful, I can't promise to keep it to myself, Erica.'

'I understand.' She thought for a moment, then released his hand and took a deep breath. 'It's his conscience. It's always been more tender and sensitive than the average person's. Certainly more than mine. More than is good for his peace. Joseph, it's most unfair!' Her eyes sparked with indignation. 'My brother is the most humane of men, but his conscience rubs him raw. He is convinced that his life is built on a lie.'

'What lie?'

'Look, I know you don't have a lot of time. I'm going to have to tell you about our father. But I'll try to summarise.'

'No, don't worry. Caroline isn't going anywhere, is she? Poor girl. The living have to come first – there's still hope for them.'

'I'll just drink this coffee before it gets cold.' She picked up the mug and looked at him over its rim. 'Thank you, Joseph.'

'I haven't done anything yet.'

'Oh, but you have.' She took several gulps of her coffee and set the mug down with an unsteady hand. 'Well – my father, Ewan's father too – Lachlan Fraser. I have come to the conclusion over the years that he was suffering from some kind of mental illness, Joseph – his behaviour was often bizarre, and it was aggravated by his excessive drinking. Maybe that was a family weakness, because I was pretty much an alcoholic at one time. Not Ewan, though. He's always been quite abstemious – maybe he blamed that drunken party for his caving in to the scheming Fiona! Anyway, I promised not to wander off the point. Our mother died when I was four and Ewan seven. I barely remember her. For a while we went to the village school, sometimes we didn't go to school at all, but at thirteen Ewan was sent away to board at St Serf's in Edinburgh. My father took me away from the village school soon after, and employed people to home-school me. None of them lasted long. His rages were terrifying, especially when he was drunk. There were great gaps in my schooling, and it was only when he got letters from the authorities that he would employ someone else. There were long weeks, when Ewan was away at school, and I had no teacher, that my father and I were alone in the castle. I spent my days in fear, Joseph. He hounded me. He crept around, spying, breathing loudly, hiding...' She shuddered. 'And he became increasingly violent. In his fury he swung at me, threw things – if he caught me, he beat me. I was a mass of bruises and welts. I barricaded myself in my bedroom for days on end, creeping out only to use the bathroom or take food from the pantry – if there was any – or to get books from the library.

'Then things changed. New people came to the castle. They were called Gilmour.' She looked up at Joseph, her face dark with remembered pain. 'In some ways things were better – at first. The Gilmours were a distraction. Neil Gilmour became a sort of unofficial factor to my father, and Catriona taught me and sorted out the housekeeping. Things seemed to improve. But bit by bit everything started to go downhill. The Gilmours, I believe, saw where their best interests lay, and it wasn't in defending me. They encouraged my father to drink, gaining more power over him, so they thought. They didn't care how he behaved towards me. Why should they? The main chance was all they cared about, as their later behaviour showed quite clearly.' For a moment she fell silent, brooding, and Joseph said nothing, watching her face as expressions flitted over it in rapid succession. She lifted her head. 'There came an unguarded moment when I was alone. The men were out on the estate, Catriona Gilmour was sleeping off a hangover, and my father had forgotten to lock his study where the one and only phone was kept. In my despair I phoned my brother at school, and told him what was going on. He promised me that he would do something – I didn't know what and at that point neither did he, I'm sure – when he came home for the Easter holidays. So, somehow I survived the long weeks before Easter, and at last he came home. He managed to get included on a fishing trip, he stole a gun from the gun cupboard, he threatened my father with it, and my father fell backwards into a freezing river and drowned. He was a big, heavy man, wearing boots and a thick greatcoat. He was also still drunk. He didn't stand a chance.

'Ewan has always blamed himself, but in recent years that has intensified. Yes, my father was a dangerous madman, yes, Ewan did it to protect me, but he says if he hadn't waved the gun at our father he would still be alive. The gun wasn't even loaded, but Father didn't know that.'

'Where were you while all this was going on?'

'At the castle. Ewan came racing back in the truck. Neil Gilmour followed hours later, and then he and Catriona took the truck, some of the guns and the contents of Father's cash box and disappeared. But Joseph, just lately Ewan has been talking about it so much more. He comes to see me frequently, he always has, especially since I have been here in Compton, but it's almost all he wants to talk about, and he seems so *harried*. Why now, I don't know. I try to tell him he was just a boy, trying to defend his sister against a bullying maniac, that he couldn't have shot Father with an unloaded gun, that the Inquiry returned a verdict of accidental death, that he has more than atoned by how he has lived since then, all the good he has done, and for a while he seems pacified, but then it all comes back. I think he has nightmares about that day. He says he can still see our father's face under the water, his hair spread out, his eyes bulging, his teeth bared in a horrible grin.' She clenched her twisted hands together. 'Poor Ewan. What can we do for him, Joseph?'

Joseph shook his head. 'There's only one thing we can do, Erica. Pray for him. For peace.'

'Yes, I do that, every day. Will you pray for him too?'

'Of course.'

'Thank you.' She frowned. 'The thing is, Joseph, just lately he's been saying he needs to *do* something. Sometimes he talks of confessing – I'm not sure who to. But then he says if his reputation is stained it isn't fair on his family, his employees, and so on. He is so conflicted. And to my eyes it's making him ill. He even talks of going back to the monastery for a while, for some kind of retreat.'

'Maybe that wouldn't be such a bad idea,' Joseph said. 'Your brother needs to feel forgiven. It seems to us that he was more sinned against than sinning, but he has to accept that for himself.' He leaned forward and took Erica's crabbed hands gently in his own. 'Let's pray for him now.'

'All right,' Erica whispered.

Joseph bent his head and thought. Peace settled on the quiet room. 'Dear Lord. You promised that when two or three are gathered together in your name you would be there with them. Hear our prayer for Ewan Fraser today. By human standards he is a good man, your devoted servant for many years. Grant him peace in his heart, freedom from these nightmares, release from his past. Show him that there is forgiveness for the repentant sinner. Let him lay his burden down at the foot of your cross and walk away free. In Jesus' name, Amen.'

'Amen,' Erica echoed.

Joseph let go of her hands and looked up. Tears were running down Erica's face. He pulled a handkerchief out of his trouser pocket and put it into her hand.

'Has he heard us, do you suppose?' Erica said. 'God, I mean.'

'Yes, I'm sure he has. His hand defends your brother, just as it does you and me.'

'Well, we certainly need defending.'

Joseph got to his feet. 'I'd better go, Erica.' He smiled faintly. 'Got a necessary penance to perform.'

'Oh, yes, Joseph – of course. Thank you for everything. I'll pray for you too, that it won't be as hard as you fear. And that you'll be able to feel forgiven as well.'

He turned at the door and saluted her. 'Good point. I really must practise what I preach.' He laughed quietly. 'I'll see you soon.'

2008: Compton

Louise Gordon tapped on the door and went straight in to where Hazell and Rivers were studying a bank of computer screens. Both looked glum, brows furrowed, eyes dull.

Hazell looked up. 'Anything, Sergeant?'

'You'll like this, sir,' Louise said with an air of triumph. 'The lads have spent a good few hours running the CCTV footage for the motorway, both directions, for Friday afternoon. Nothing. A few big BMWs, even some black ones, but nothing matching the plates we have for the Fraser fleet. But Win Davies suggested we widen the search. I got him to check the CCTV in petrol stations on the minor roads between Compton and the outskirts of London. Not all of them have it, of course. But he got lucky. The camera only caught part of the registration, but it seemed enough for a closer look. He's gone down there with Des Walsh to have a word with the owner and see if he can remember anything. He should be ringing in within the next half hour, I'd say.'

'He's a good man, young Davies,' Hazell said. 'Maybe one to watch, to encourage.'

'I will, sir.'

'Did you let the rest of the team know about your findings up at Plough Lane?' Hazell said. 'The tramp, prowler, whatever he was?'

'Yes, sir, I briefed them all.'

'Good.' Hands in pockets, Hazell paced the room. 'We need a break. Something to justify getting a warrant to search all the Fraser houses, and all the cars. Something stinks, but so far we haven't found the source. There's a connection missing somewhere. And where does this tramp fit in – if he does? Is Scotland something to do with it? Is there some link with Mrs Pole's past? Or is that just a coincidence, irrelevant?' He heaved a sigh. 'Shall we have some tea while we're waiting? I'm parched.'

'I'll get that organised, sir. Do you want some, Sergeant Rivers?'

'No need to ask Tom. That man's an Olympic tea-drinker.'

Louise grinned and disappeared down the stairs. Ten minutes later she was back with a laden tray. 'Here we are, gents. Refreshment.' She handed out steaming mugs and took one for herself.

The phone on the desk in the adjacent room jangled shrilly. 'That might be Davies now,' Louise said. 'Shall I get it, sir?'

'Yes, do.'

Louise hurried out, and Hazell followed more slowly. When he entered the room she was perched on a corner of the table with the phone to her ear. She had kicked off her shoes and was rubbing one foot with her free hand. 'OK, Win, yes, got that. Good. You've done well.' She picked up her tea and sipped. 'What? Go and see, then. I'll hang on.' She looked up at Hazell, her eyes alight. 'Davies has found the garage, sir, and had a word with the owner. He remembers the black BMW. CCTV recorded it at two-fifty. He gave Davies a description – hang on a minute, sir. Yes, I'm here, Win. What's that? Speak a bit slower, can you? Where is this?' She listened, frowning in concentration. 'All right, yes, I'll tell him straight away. Good work, Win. Gold star, mate.' She replaced the receiver. 'Sir, the garage owner remembered the car, and he said the driver was a young bloke with dark hair. He doesn't think there was anyone else with him. He didn't say much, apparently, just paid for his fuel and left. And a sandwich, apparently. But the CCTV has the car there at the right time. If it is our car, of course. You can only see part of the plate – the middle bit, Davies said. But there's more. While he was on the phone to me telling me all this Walsh was waiting for him and chatting with the garage owner. There was a TV on the wall, no sound, but Walsh is one of those blokes who can't ignore a TV screen and he saw something that caught his attention and got the chap to put the sound on. It was the regional news, sir. They've found a body washed up on the beach at Bickham, where the river flows out to the sea. Can't be more than twenty miles from here, maybe less as the crow flies. The reporter was on the prom talking to the cameras, and there's people standing at the rail gawking down at the beach, and the reporter's describing a man in his sixties, bearded and unkempt, wearing a thick coat. No ID as yet, but it sounds a bit like our tramp, don't you think?'

'It's worth a look, anyway, Sergeant,' Hazell said. 'There's something about this tramp that's bothering me. Was it just a coincidence that there's a vagrant hammering on Erica Pole's door the week before her murder?'

'I don't believe in coincidence, sir,' Louise said. 'But I don't see that he's our murderer.'

'On the face of it, he's a better bet than anything else we've got, isn't he? So tell me why you're not convinced.'

'Well, for one thing the time frame's wrong. By the time Mrs Pole was murdered, he'd gone – as far as we know. OK, yes, he could have come back. But no one saw anything. Also, if he's grubby and scruffy, there'd have been something at the scene – dried mud, fibres, I don't know, but *something*. If he was going to murder Mrs Pole, why would he have advertised his presence to the street, shouting and hammering? And then worn gloves to kill her? I don't think so, sir. It doesn't hang together. And nothing was stolen. If he was after money, why didn't he take her purse?'

'I agree.' Hazell pondered for a moment. 'I'm going to stick my neck out and see if we can get warrants on the suspicions we've got. As soon as I've set that in motion you and I, Sergeant, are going to take a trip to the seaside. But don't bother to bring your sun-lotion and your beach ball. This is business. We have to follow this man up, whatever doubts we may have.'

'Fine by me, sir. You think they'll let us take a squint at the deceased?'

'I'm confident they will,' Hazell said. 'That's Eddie Squire's patch, and Ed and I go back a long way. You drive, and I'll phone him on while we're on the road.'

2007: Compton

Helena stood by the plate-glass window of the chemist's and looked out at the street. At half past four the Christmas lights had been on for half an hour, but in the steady rain and occasional wild gust of wind they were having a struggle to look remotely festive. A stream of dirty water was gurgling down the gutters and into the drains, and such shoppers as there were hurried past with coat-collars turned up.

'Haven't you got an umbrella, my dear?' asked the white-coated pharmacy assistant, a middle-aged man with owlish glasses. 'It's a horrible day.'

'I seem to have forgotten it,' Helena said, and smiled. Then, to the man's surprise, she muttered an exclamation and left the shop with a jangle of its old-fashioned bell, and he saw her hurry away, waving to someone across the street.

'Joseph!'

Joseph stopped under the striped awning of the butcher's, his back to the clean empty meat-racks in the shop window, cleared for the day. 'Oh! Hello, Helena.'

'You sound surprised to see me,' Helena said, joining him under the awning.

'I am. I wouldn't have thought Compton High Street would be your choice for Christmas shopping. I'd have thought you'd be at home somewhere more, I don't know, sophisticated.'

Helena laughed. 'Then you don't know me,' she said. 'Anyway, I wasn't here to do any Christmas shopping. I was collecting a prescription for Erica.'

'Is she not well?' Joseph said, frowning. 'She seemed all right on Sunday.'

'It's nothing major,' Helena said. 'She's developed a rash on the back of her hands. She was scratching it raw, so I ignored her protests and got the doctor to call. I thought I might as well come down straight away before the shops close and get the ointment. What are you in search of?' She looked behind him at the empty window. 'If you were after something for your dinner you seem to be out of luck.'

Joseph sighed. 'As it happens I'm trying, and failing, to find a Christmas present for my sister.'

'I see.' Helena's eyes sparkled with suppressed merriment. 'Would you like some help?'

'I would,' Joseph said, inclining his head in a sketchy bow. 'If you can spare the time.'

'No problem. I saw some pretty scarves in the shop at the bottom of the street. Would that be appropriate, do you think?'

Joseph looked relieved. 'It sounds perfect.'

'Right. Let's make a run for it.' Without waiting for him she hared down the pavement, almost knocking over a woman who was backing out of a shop, hauling a push chair after her. 'Sorry!' Joseph followed at what he hoped was a more sedate pace.

'Let's go in before they close,' Helena said. 'I see that Compton is that old-fashioned sort of place that starts to shut down when it gets dark.'

Joseph followed her inside. With her height and her vivid hair Helena seemed to fill the shop with flurry and light, and Joseph was immediately aware of the shop assistant, a skinny woman of indeterminate age, eyeing them with an inscrutable expression from the shadows at the back of the shop.

'Here we are,' Helena said, blithely oblivious. 'What do you think?' She showed him a rack of floating scarves, soft-textured, in many colours from muted green to eye-challenging purple.

'They're new in this week,' said the assistant, not moving from behind the counter.

Helena nodded. 'Lovely.' She turned back to Joseph, who was looking bemused. 'What's your sister's taste?'

'I have no idea.'

'Hm. Well, all right, what does she look like?'

Joseph thought. 'Rather like me, I suppose. On the tall side. Rather concave. But dark-haired, not mouse.'

Helena chuckled. 'What a description! "Concave!" I'm sure she wouldn't be flattered. And you're not mouse, you're still quite fair.' She looked at him critically. 'I bet you were very blond as a child.'

'I was,' Joseph said. 'Up to the age of about eleven. My mother said I looked like a little Swede. Not the vegetable, of course.'

'Ha! I should hope not,' Helena said, shaking her head. 'Well, what about this? This is nice. No one could possibly object to this one. Is she terribly conservative? Perhaps she might go for something a bit wilder.'

'I think not,' Joseph said solemnly. 'The blue one will be fine. I will go and pay for it.'

Outside the shop, the scarf wrapped and bagged, Helena said, 'Should we go for a cup of tea somewhere?'

Joseph pursed his lips. 'Apart from the fact that the only café around is almost certainly locking its doors and wiping its tables, I think that would be much too shocking.'

Helena looked at him, her eyebrows raised. 'You can't be serious.'

Joseph grinned. 'Not entirely. But you must have noticed the shop assistant eyeing you up and down with unhealthy interest. Wondering who the vicar is with, and so on.'

'You aren't wearing your dog-collar, though.'

'No. But believe me, they know. And if the café should happen to be open, and we went in and asked for tea, there would be mutterings. "Not even widowed a year yet, and he's out in public drinking tea with a strange young woman." Not that you are strange in any bad sense, of course. Perhaps exotic would be a better word.'

Helena shook her head. 'You're talking nonsense. Nobody at all is taking any notice of us. Except that we are stupid enough to be standing here getting wet. As for "exotic", you make me feel like an Amazonian parrot. Well, if not the café, what about the Vicarage? You could make me a cup of tea yourself. Or is that even more shocking?'

'It's eye-wateringly shocking,' Joseph said. 'But less visible. Where's your car?'

'At Erica's. I walked down – it wasn't raining then.'

'In that case, we'd better hurry.'

Joseph led the way at a brisk pace, down the length of the High Street, its lights now all on, past the church and into the Vicarage drive. Helena kept up easily, her long stride matching his, her low-heeled shoes squelching with each step.

'Ugh, these shoes are hopeless,' she said. 'My feet are soaked.'

Joseph unlocked the front door and ushered her into the darkened hallway. 'Take them off and put them under the radiator for a moment.' He was very aware of her nearness as she bent to remove her shoes in the narrow space, her hair falling over her face, her faint perfume in his nostrils, and he turned quickly and went into the kitchen, leaving her to follow.

'You're very tidy,' she said as she came in. 'Do you have a nice lady to clean up?'

'I wish I did,' Joseph said quietly.

She clapped her hand to her mouth and the colour flared in her cheeks. 'Oh dear, that was stupid. I'm so sorry.'

'It's OK.' He filled the kettle at the kitchen tap and set it to boil. 'So are you of the school of thought that believes all men are useless around the house?'

'No, of course not. It was just a thoughtless, tactless thing to say. Me and my big mouth.' She was silent for a moment, watching him take cups down from a cupboard and tea from a shelf. Then she said, 'Is it really a problem, protecting your reputation in a small town like Compton? It seems such an alien thought. Living where we do, and working in London, you get used to the feeling that nobody knows who you are or cares what you do.'

Joseph nodded. 'I lived and worked in London myself, a long time ago. My first parish was there, so I know all about anonymity. But it's very different here. Of course I was exaggerating, and folk on the whole are quite charitable. But you know, given most people's attitudes to the church, I prefer to avoid giving anyone cause to call me a hypocrite.' The kettle boiled, and he switched it off and poured water into a large brown teapot.

'I can't believe you are a hypocrite, Joseph,' Helena said, following his movements with her eyes.

'Well, I am,' Joseph said. 'So are you, I dare say – just because we are human. Those who accuse Christians of hypocrisy are right. Of course the accusers are hypocrites too, but that doesn't seem to occur to them.' He smiled, and his eyes crinkled at the corners. 'Unless, of course, they don't even aspire to good conduct, in which case they are wicked, but honest. I'll pour this tea. Are you drying off a bit?'

'Mm.' Helena slid into a chair at the kitchen table.

'We can drink this in more comfort, if you like,' Joseph said.

'I'm quite at home in the kitchen,' Helena said. 'So, now you have your sister's present, is that your Christmas shopping all done?'

'Yes, thankfully,' Joseph said. He put the teapot on the table. 'My brother-in-law will be content with a book, which I have already bought. They don't have children, just a dog. So Christmas is simple.'

'Is your sister your only family, then?'

'Yes, she is. Our parents are dead, and we have no other siblings or aunts and uncles now.' He poured the tea and passed Helena the milk jug. 'Things were different when my wife was alive – we visited her family too. But now things have gone back to the way they were.'

'I suppose Christmas is pretty busy if you're a vicar.'

'Well, Christmas Day is a busy working day for us, certainly.'

'Will you see her at all? Your sister?'

'Oh yes, I'll make my annual visit on Boxing Day and stay for a few days, go for long walks with my brother-in-law and the dog. They live in Carlisle, so I don't see them often. They are quiet people, so I get to do plenty of sleeping and reading. Things I don't have much time for the rest of the year.' He saw her gazing at him with a serious expression on her face, and he smiled. 'What about you? Lots of festivities?'

To his surprise she made a disgusted face. 'Don't tell anyone, but I detest Christmas at home,' she said. 'I wish I didn't, but there it is. If I ever have my own family I shall make sure Christmas is noisy, mad, fun and free.'

'So what happens in your house?'

'Ugh. My mother must have everything just so. She is a perfectionist and a snob, an unbearable combination, and we are all such cowards – at Christmas she is allowed full rein! The table, the decorations, the food, the wine, the tree, blah, blah. We all have to look like something out of a fashion magazine, perfectly groomed. If I wore the wrong earrings I'd know about it. In the run-up to Christmas she invites all sorts of people to parties and soirees and fashionable gatherings, not people she likes, not even distant relations, but people who might be useful, wielders of influence. They aren't friends, they're *connections*. I think I'd even prefer my tweedy, loud-voiced Beaton cousins. At least they can be fun. Mother doesn't believe in fun.'

'What about your brothers?'

Helena scowled, and Joseph saw the years fall away and a much younger Helena appear: gauche, stubborn, militant. 'They come along looking very smart, say all the right things, ooze rather unconvincing charm and disappear as soon as they decently can to their own celebrations. I am expected to stay at home, look decorative, and help. I am no help at all, even if any were really needed.' Her expression softened. 'But I do it to keep the peace, for Daddy's sake. I know he hates it too, although he's never actually said so.'

'What would he rather be doing, then?'

'I don't really know. He goes along with it all out of guilt, I suppose. Maybe he thinks he has given Mummy a raw deal marriage-wise. He goes to church early on Christmas morning, then he comes home, gets dressed up, and plays the gracious host to perfection.'

'And you? How would you celebrate Christmas if you had your way?'

'What, in an ideal world, or with things as they are?'

Joseph shrugged. 'You choose.'

Helena took a sip of her tea and thought. Joseph watched her while pretending not to. A slight frown made a wrinkle between her pale eyebrows, and as she pondered she unconsciously chewed her bottom lip. 'I can't say what I'd like in an ideal world,' she said slowly, 'because it's embarrassingly childish, and we don't know each other well enough yet for that sort of thing. As things are, I would rather spend Christmas with my tetchy, lonely, honest, lovely aunt, who is so desperate not to be a burden and a nuisance she is prepared to spend it by herself.'

'What? But she can't possibly manage,' Joseph said, horrified.

'Of course she can't, and she won't have to, because dear Nettie will see to her as she always does, even though Erica will probably complain and snap and generally be foul. Nettie is a saint.'

'I didn't know any of this,' Joseph muttered. 'But Erica can't easily go anywhere, of course. Why didn't I think?'

'I'm sure you have many parishioners who have all sorts of needs,' Helena said.

'No, no, your aunt isn't just anyone. Not to me.'

There was silence for a moment, and then Helena rapped the table lightly. 'Joseph, I have an idea.' Her face was alight with enthusiasm, and again Joseph saw the child behind the cautious veneer. 'When do you depart for Carlisle?'

'On Boxing Day morning, normally. If public transport allows.'

'So are you free after the morning service on Christmas Day?'

'I suppose I am.'

'Why don't we take Christmas to Erica? Nettie will make her a meal, she always does, even though Erica hardly eats any of it. She could easily make enough for three, in fact I think she'd love to cook for you, and it'd be much nicer for both of them if you were there. And I could come down later, when we've had our parody of a Christmas dinner, with Daddy trying to be festive and Mummy fussing and the boys getting tight. I could develop a convenient headache after the cheese.'

Joseph looked at her, shaking his head. 'Don't you think we should consult your aunt, since we'd be invading her home?'

Helena stood up abruptly. 'I'll talk her round. She likes to pretend she's all terribly "Bah! Humbug!" about Christmas, but

I think she will secretly like it. If you are there it will save poor Nettie from Erica's abuse. Think of it as an act of mercy, Joseph. Please say you'll come.'

Joseph pushed his chair back and got up slowly. 'I shall wait to be invited. Preferably by the lady of the house.'

Helena laughed. 'As opposed to her crazy niece.'

'Who, I am beginning to realise, is a formidable force,' Joseph said.

'I must go, Joseph. Erica will think I've been abducted. Thanks for the tea.'

Joseph followed her to the door, and watched while she hopped from one foot to the other, battling to put her damp shoes back on. He opened the front door for her, and stood back to let her out. The rain had stopped, leaving the air laden with misty moisture, the street-lights a fuzzy glow. She turned to him in the doorway. Her face was flushed. 'You know what, it might actually be fun. You'll be hearing from me!' Then she was gone with a careless wave, her feet crunching on the gravel of the drive, her fine hair flying. Joseph closed the door and walked slowly back into the kitchen, feeling slightly dazed, as if the earth itself had tilted precariously on its axis.

2008

carver@pcmedia.net to fbgreville@chelhall.org

Bert, old thing – a development! Flushed with the success of the trip to the zoo with my offspring, I succumbed to their pleading for a day at the beach. All of us went, Rachel too, down to Bickham, which is the nearest decent seaside to us. And while we were there, what a kerfuffle! Blue lights flashing, uniformed police and white vans and what-not, and we were herded off the beach! Apparently they'd found a body on the bank of the river that flows into the sea just to the north, less than half a mile from where we were. Seems a bit extreme to me; they could have whisked the corpse away quietly and not disturbed us jolly holiday-makers. Perhaps they were trying to secure the scene for evidence.

Anyway, when we got home I tried to console the children for their disrupted day by suggesting we did a bit of research on the story. There wasn't anything then, but young Ollie got the bit between his teeth and a couple of days later he came up with a news story which mentioned the name of the dead man: Neil Gilmour. Do you remember, Bert? He's the guy I told you about, the one who decamped with the Fraser belongings after failing to turn up to the Inquiry. Some coincidence, eh? Or perhaps it isn't one! What do you think?

fbgreville@chelhall.org to carver@pcmedia.net

I think you are probably losing your grip on reality, Carver.
It may not be the same man, and even if it is it may all be irrelevant. But if you're going to lose sleep over it, perhaps

you'd better have a chat with that tall Inspector – can't remember his name.

If I wasn't so busy I might be quite worried about you.

2008: Bickham

Hazell, Gordon and Sergeant Eddie Squire stood in a row, looking down at the draped, but otherwise naked, body on the metal slab. No one spoke for several minutes.

Hazell turned to Squire. 'You reckon you know who he is, then, Eddie.'

'Yep, fingerprints on file, did a stretch in Cordrum prison, six years and a bit, released in 2001. Nasty little con man, not above a bit of heavy stuff. Cheated two old biddies out of their savings, cased the joint while he was at it, then went back, took the family silver and the contents of the old brown teapot, and left them tied up for twenty-four hours. Trashed the house on his way out. One of the old girls didn't survive the shock – died a year later. Gilmour, his name is. Neil Gilmour.' He waved a hand at the grey-white corpse. 'See anything there that makes any sense, Fred?'

Hazell let out a deep breath. 'Not a lot. It doesn't look as if he's been in the water long, though. Any injuries?'

Squire shrugged. 'None I noticed. He looked quite a big bloke in his overcoat, but as you can see he's not too well-nourished by the look of him. Long hair and beard, a few teeth missing, but the water's not done much for the dirt. Too ingrained, I suppose.'

'Living rough for a while, maybe. What about his clothes?'

'In a bag. Feel free to have a look if you like. They're pretty smelly.'

'Anything in the pockets?'

'Piece of string, a few copper coins, one fingerless glove. But he had something round his neck – a small key on a chain.'

'Where is it?'

'Labelled and bagged in a drawer. You seen enough? Sergeant Gordon?'

Louise grimaced. 'More than enough. Never did like drowned bodies.'

They left the cold, tiled room and closed the door. Squire shook his head. 'Thing is, until they have a good look at him we won't know if he drowned or went into the water already dead. You got any reason to suspect foul play, Fred?'

'Not really. I'll have a look at this key, though, please, Eddie.'

'Be my guest.'

Back in his office Squire unlocked a drawer and brought out a small clear plastic bag. The key on its chain, though dulled by time, was an unusual design.

'Can you take a photo, Sergeant?' Hazell said to Louise. 'Then we must get back to Compton.'

Louise fished a small camera out of her bag and took several shots of the key and its chain. She heard Hazell and Squire asking after each other's families and remembering old colleagues. She inspected her handiwork, nodded, and put the camera back. 'Ready, sir.'

Hazell shook Squire's hand and clapped him on the shoulder. 'Good to see you again, Ed. Remember me to Moira. And thanks for your help.'

'Any time, Fred. Nice to meet you, Sergeant. Hope you get your murder cleared up OK.'

'I'll drive back, Louise,' Hazell said. He lowered himself into the driver's seat and adjusted it for leg-room. 'What do you make of our friend Mr Gilmour? Did he fall in the river and get washed down? Or did someone give him a helping hand?'

Louise slid into the passenger side and put the seat-belt on. 'There's no real reason to suspect he was murdered, is there? And we wouldn't be interested in him at all if he hadn't been sneaking around Mrs Pole's bungalow and banging on the door. Is there any chance it could be random? He could have been drunk, or mentally disturbed. Are we certain he even knew our vic?'

Hazell started the car and reversed slowly into the road. 'We don't know much at all. That missing connection is still missing, unless we're being very dim. Which way?'

'Left, sir. Back onto the B108.'

'Did you get that photo OK?'

'Yes. I took about five, from different angles. You think the key might be significant?'

Hazell shrugged. 'Who knows? If this man is connected to our enquiry in some way, it might jog someone's memory.'

For a few miles they travelled in silence. Then Louise said suddenly, 'Hang on, sir, Fred I mean, I just remembered something.'

'Oh?'

'When we interviewed Mrs Fraser. She talked about someone trying to blackmail her husband, way back. Said she couldn't recall his name. What did she say? "Gilbert, Gilchrist, some such name." Perhaps it was Gilmour she was trying to remember.'

Hazell looked at her with sudden interest. 'Yes…and perhaps it was Gilmour she remembered perfectly well all along. I think you're right. Mrs Fraser, it seems to me, might well know a lot more than she let on to us. Canny lady, Mrs Fraser.'

'You sound almost as if you admire her, sir. I thought she was quite unpleasant. Cold and sour.'

'Agreed. All that. But clever and determined. Maybe we need to have another chat. And with Mr Fraser.'

'Hm.'

A phone shrilled somewhere in the car.

'That's my mobile,' Hazell said. 'In my jacket pocket on the back seat. Lean over and get it, can you, please.'

Louise struggled out of her seat belt, twisted round and retrieved Hazell's jacket. The phone stopped ringing. 'Damn.'

'See who it was.'

Louise found the phone and flipped it open. 'It was the station, sir. Shall I call them back?'

'Yes, please do.'

Louise dialled and waited. 'Hello, yes, this is Sergeant Gordon. You rang us. No, Inspector Hazell's driving – you can tell me.' She listened for a few minutes, nodding and muttering 'OK' from time to time. 'All right, yes, thanks. I'll tell him.' She closed the phone. 'Fred, I don't know if you're going to like this. We've got a warrant all right, but only for the cars. We'll need something more concrete if we want to search the Fraser family premises.'

Hazell swore under his breath. 'What's the time? We could go over now and look at the cars.'

'Hold on a bit, sir. You might want to get back to the station right away. There's someone waiting, wants to talk to you about Neil Gilmour.'

Hazell frowned. 'Who is it?'

'Bloke called Carver. Dr Patrick Carver. Claims he's done some research on Gilmour.'

Hazell's eyebrows raised. 'Why? What's his interest?'

'Apparently, he's an old friend of Reverend Stiles, the vicar at Compton. You interviewed him.'

'I've never met any Carver.'

'No, sir, you interviewed Stiles. This Carver was visiting Mr Stiles last weekend. Got interested in the murder and did a bit of snooping. Only on the internet, as far as I know.'

'He's a medical man, you say?'

'No, I think he's some kind of university lecturer.'

'Right. This is what we'll do. Use my phone. Ring in to the nick. Get a team set up to go over those cars with a fine-tooth comb. If they can't get the right people today, first thing tomorrow. We can't afford to waste any more time. While the forensic lot are examining the vehicles, we interview whoever's in charge of recording who's using the cars and when, and we take a look at the mileages, see if there are any discrepancies. And check the satnav records.' He paused as a thought struck him. 'Plus we'd better make sure they look at the tyres, see if there's any trace of what that dog did. Meanwhile we get back to Compton now as fast as we can and see what this Carver has to tell us. Maybe he's some kind of crackpot. Who knows?'

Christmas 2007: Compton

Nettie arrived well-wrapped in a long black coat with dog hairs all around the hem. 'Here I am, Mrs P! It's raining again.' She battled up the passage, puffing and grunting, bags banging against the walls, and lumbered through to the kitchen, where she piled her baggage on the counter with a sigh of relief. 'I'll be with you in a minute!' She shed her coat, stuffed gloves into the pocket, and went back into the hall to hang the coat on a hook. 'Just washing my hands, then I'll be there.' She went into the bathroom, ran the water and gave her hands a thorough soaping. As she dried them she hummed a popular old hymn. 'There we are,' she muttered to herself. 'All ready.'

She opened the door to Erica's bedroom gently, almost tentatively. 'Morning, Mrs P. Are you awake?' She crossed the room and opened the curtains, letting in a dull grey light.

Erica, a slight twisted shape under the bedclothes, groaned and twitched. 'I'm always awake. Sleep's no friend to me, you know that.'

'Well now,' Nettie said, approaching the bed. 'It's Christmas Day, and a very happy Christmas to you, my dear.'

Erica opened one baleful eye and muttered some inaudible greeting in reply.

'As we have a guest today, would you like a bath?' Nettie said.

Erica's eyes flew open. 'Oh, my goodness, Nettie! I'd forgotten. Yes, a bath. You'll have to help me. What's the time?'

'It's only just after nine,' Nettie soothed. 'We've got plenty of time. I came early so we could get everything done without rushing. Come on, then, I'll help you up and into your chair, then I'll go and run that bath.'

An hour later Erica was back in her wheelchair, scrubbed and dressed, a bowl of cereal untouched on the table beside her. She clutched a mug of coffee in her crooked hands. 'Nettie, I want to look half decent today. This old T shirt won't do. And a bit of makeup, perhaps, and those earrings Helena gave me for my birthday. And, Nettie, my hair! It feels like a crow's nest.'

'One thing at a time, dear,' Nettie said. She emerged from a cupboard, her face red. 'I really must get the lunch on. Once everything is cooking I'll see to you. That T shirt will do for now – it doesn't matter if you spill something on that. We'll find something nice.' She bent down to the cupboard again, talking to herself.

A thought struck Erica. 'What time is Joseph coming?'

'After the morning service some time, I suppose,' Nettie said. She had a packet of stuffing mix in her hand. 'Found it at last. I knew it was here somewhere.'

'Oh, Nettie – I didn't think. Have I done you out of going to church on Christmas Day? I *am* rather a selfish old bat, aren't I?'

'Not at all, dear,' Nettie said with a smile. 'I went to the Midnight last night, and very lovely it was too with the flower arrangements, and the candles lit. Joseph did it all beautifully, and I have to say he looked splendid in the Christmas colours. It was quite uplifting. The morning service today is mostly for children, and I don't mind a bit missing it.'

'You're a saint in the making, Nettie.'

Nettie laughed. 'Hark at you spouting nonsense! Now I must get on. Give me half an hour to get this all on the go, then I'll see to you – make you beautiful.'

'Ha! Don't get too ambitious. It would take more than a dab of blusher and some sparkly earrings to achieve that impossibility,' Erica said. 'I'll settle for tidy and mildly festive. It's all we can hope for.'

Nettie, still clutching the packet of stuffing, looked at Erica thoughtfully, her head on one side. 'I'll bet you were quite a looker in your youth,' she said quietly. 'Before that horrible accident.'

Erica winced. 'Not specially,' she said. 'I was skinny and wiry with a mop of unruly black hair. What about you, Nettie? Were you the toast of Compton in your heyday?'

Nettie chuckled. 'Well, there were one or two lads after me, before I said yes to my Jack. I did have nice hair – wavy and coppery it was. But I've always been on the short side. In those days you might have said I was curvaceous. Now it's more like dumpy.' She turned and surveyed the cooker and the piled-up packages on the kitchen counter. 'To work, Saint Nettie.' She gave a little giggle.

At midday the doorbell rang, and Nettie bustled down the hallway and opened the door. 'Joseph, come in, come in. What a day! Let me have that wet coat.' She took it from him, gave it a little shake, and hung it up beside her own. She turned back to him. 'Happy Christmas once again, my dear.' She stood on tiptoe and kissed his cheek. 'Mm, you smell nice.'

Joseph smiled. 'I found some ancient after-shave in the bathroom cabinet. No idea who gave it to me. I wondered if it might have gone off, it's so old. But it didn't smell too bad, and you'll let me know if I turn green and my skin starts to peel.' He put his arm lightly round Nettie's shoulders. 'Happy Christmas to you too. I wore a tie as well, to mark the occasion.'

'My word, we are honoured!' Nettie said. 'Come through. It's time we opened up the sherry, I do believe.'

Joseph followed Nettie into the lounge and inhaled deeply. 'Mm, something marvellous is cooking here. Nettie is working her magic. Happy Christmas, Erica.' He took her hand briefly and surveyed her with a quizzical smile. 'I see we are all making an effort today. You look better than I've seen you for a long time.'

'A bit of war-paint, a clean top, a comb – hey presto!' Erica's tone was ironic, but her eyes twinkled.

'And I,' Nettie said from the kitchen, 'will try to measure up once I get this apron off. But for now you two sit and chat and take it easy. There's a bottle and glasses on the tray, Joseph. Perhaps you could pour.'

'Gladly,' Joseph said. He pulled the cork with the satisfying sound of suction defeated. 'But perhaps I can help you, Nettie. I'm not completely helpless in the kitchen.'

'I know that, dear. No, thank you – I can manage. Just look after Mrs P for me.'

'Not sure which of us has the tougher job,' Joseph said. He poured sherry into three sparkling glasses.

'Cheeky!' Erica growled. She took a glass from Joseph's hand. 'I've promised myself to be on good behaviour. Just for today, you understand. But don't provoke me. This tiger still has teeth. Just.' She took a swift sip of her sherry and set the glass down clumsily. 'Joseph, come with me into the conservatory, will you? I'm roasting alive in here. Nettie's been cooking for at least six hours.'

'How you do exaggerate!' Nettie exclaimed from the kitchen. 'Yes, go on, Joseph. I can get on much better without a certain person's interference. Shut the door, or it'll get all steamy.'

Joseph stood aside to let Erica roll past him. The conservatory was cool. 'Are you sure you're warm enough?'

'There's a cardigan on the chair if I need it,' Erica said in a low voice. 'The thing is, there may be things I need to say to you that I don't necessarily want Nettie to hear.'

Joseph closed the door. They could still see Nettie beavering away in the kitchen, but the sound of her singing was muted.

Joseph sat down opposite Erica. 'I've been meaning to ask you,' he said. 'How is your brother?'

Erica leaned forward, her hands clasped in her lap. 'That's just what I don't want to talk about in front of Nettie. She might quite innocently say something to Helena. You know there's not much I wouldn't do to defend Ewan. Well, Helena needs defending too.'

'She seems to me most resourceful and resilient,' Joseph demurred. 'Besides being grown up and able to take care of herself.'

'Of course she is, in the general way of things,' Erica said. 'I'm talking about defending her from knowledge that will hurt her. There's enough hurt in our family – if I can keep Helena clear of it I will.' She sighed. 'You ask me how Ewan is. He's very strange these days. Even I don't fully understand what he is thinking. He has a sort of focused, almost obsessed aura. He's not as open with me as he used to be, but I think that's because he's protecting me. He's done this before – he goes and does something without any consultation, and then presents it as a fait accompli. That way I can't argue with him.' She smiled sadly. 'Well, Ewan thinks he is clever, but I know him so well, he can't hide much from my eyes. The thing is, Joseph, Ewan has always had a terrible fear that he will end up like our father, out of his wits. He worries that he has inherited some fearsome mental illness. Oddly enough, he never thinks *I* might have inherited anything. He seems to be thinking more and more that he can actually detect early symptoms. I know he has been consulting doctors, very discreetly, but he hasn't told me any of the results yet, that's assuming that there's anything to tell. As far as I can see he is perfectly sane and as unlike our father as anyone can be. If he has any symptoms they might just as easily be put down to stress or tiredness – Ewan works really long days and he's always travelling. His home life isn't exactly stress-free either. And Joseph, when he's here, he never rests – he's for ever pacing and fidgeting. Like someone possessed by an idea. Oh, I don't know.'

'You're saying this behaviour is different from before?'

Erica nodded. 'He always used to come here to unwind. He'd sit where you are now, a cup of coffee or a glass of something in his hand, and we'd chat, and sometimes he'd fall asleep. But not now, not for about a year.' She bit her lip. 'I've been listening to him very carefully, saying nothing. Trying to find out just what is going on, what he isn't saying, what he lets slip. I'm pretty sure he is thinking of changing his will – maybe he already has. If I'm right it will be for my benefit, and I can tell you Fiona will be *livid*. He'd never leave her unprovided for, and I'm sure he'll have done right for the children, even though they all have good jobs. But Fiona would much rather I had nothing at all. She's one of those people for whom nothing can be enough, however much it might be. I've seen examples of it many times over the years, and her sons seem to be cut from the same mould, I'm afraid. Unless it's just taking on their mother's colouration. Perhaps I'm doing them an injustice. But really I barely know them now they're adults.'

Joseph shifted in his chair. 'So Ewan is restless, secretive and worried. Which means you're worried too.'

'Yes. But not only that, Joseph. If I had any doubt that Ewan was planning something, it would have been dispelled when he came down a week ago. Of course I doubted myself – after all, Ewan has always been level-headed. He wouldn't be as successful a businessman as he is if he'd been inclined to flights of neurotic paranoid fancy. Perhaps he had heard something, some medical test result, that confirmed his fears. I don't know. But he referred again to our father's undiagnosed condition. He'd been looking things up on the internet, conditions leading to dementia. He specified some of them, though I can't remember the names now. I was horrified. And then he said he wanted to leave London, leave Fiona, leave the business – in capable hands, he said – and come to live here, with me. Joseph, he's convinced himself he's facing his last months, if not of life, then of the ability to take care of himself.'

Joseph frowned. 'Which may be a sign that he really is ill, and his judgment is impaired. Because if he can't take care of himself, what would he be doing here with you, when you also need help? Nettie can't cope with two of you.'

Erica nodded. 'Exactly. But you know what, Joseph? I don't believe it. I know, you'll say I don't want to believe it. And of course I don't. But I asked him straight out, had he actually had any confirmation of his worries about his health? Had he had any tests? Who had he consulted? And he mumbled and muttered and looked sheepish, just as he did when he was a boy. There's no doubt something's preying on his mind, but I'm not convinced there's any foundation to it.'

Joseph shook his head. 'I hope you're right. Well, of course I'll continue to pray for him, Erica. And for you.'

'Thank you.' Erica sighed deeply. 'It's hard for me, not being able to help him. He has always, always helped me, even when I have brought it all on myself. He never complained or reproached me, he was just there when I needed him. Like when I had my accident.' She stirred restlessly in the chair, wincing with discomfort.

'Can I get you anything?' Joseph said.

'No, thanks, I'd better not drink any more, but you have a refill if you want it, and top Nettie up too.'

Joseph got to his feet. 'I'll see if she's all right. She might need a potato-peeling slave.'

'Ha! If I know Nettie, potatoes will have been peeled *months* ago.'

A few minutes later Joseph returned with a brimming glass in his hand. 'You were right, of course. Everything is under control. Nettie is flushed and singing hymns.' He put his glass on a low table. 'In fact, she says lunch will be ready in about twenty minutes, and I have to wield the carving-knife.'

'Nettie is nothing if not traditional.'

Joseph took a sip. 'You were telling me about your brother. He certainly seems many times more caring than the average brother. I have a sister, and I'm very fond of her, but I'm sure she wouldn't consider me devoted. It's unusual.'

Erica nodded. 'I know. For a long time when we were young we only had each other, and that's never really changed. It makes it hard for others, I see that. Fiona really didn't handle it well, though. I remember when I had my accident, how furious she was with Ewan. She'd been having things more her own way for a good few years, thought she'd got the upper hand at last, then I am disabled, Ewan comes to my rescue, and Fiona's loathing goes up another notch.'

'How did the accident happen, Erica?' Joseph asked softly.

'It's a long story, Joseph. Are you sure you want to hear it?'

'Yes, I do.'

'Well, all right, I suppose.' She twisted her empty glass between her fingers, and thought for a moment. 'When Ewan got married, I tried to keep in the background. I didn't want to make things difficult for him, and I knew Fiona didn't like me, though at the time I didn't really know why. Then Alexander was born, and Robert a year later. I suspect that Robert was no more planned than his brother. Anyway there they were with two small children, and Ewan was trying to set himself up in business and working incredibly hard, so inevitably we didn't see quite so much of each other. Then I met Michael, and we got married, and Stephen came along. It would have been nice for the two families to be closer, and it could have happened – if Fiona had been more accepting I wouldn't have wanted to meddle – but that wasn't to be. Well, the rest you know. Michael and I split up, he took Stephen to America, and my life nose-dived dramatically. I was in a pretty bad way, but you'd never have known it if you'd just seen the surface stuff. I partied and drank, and kept some really bad company. But underneath the superficial hilarity I was lonely and miserable. I'd lost everything, including my self-respect, but the worst loss was Stephen.

'I'll skim over the depressing details – you can imagine, I'm sure. I was invited on a yachting party in the Med, a whole bunch of wealthy sailing types, all with their own boats. I was with a man called Rory, and I knew even then how low I'd sunk, because I didn't really like him much, but I let things drift because I simply didn't care any more what happened to me. Quantities of alcohol blinded my eyes to the realities, and we sailed from port to port and got drunk every night.

'We all went diving off the boat at midnight one night, in the middle of an uproarious party. It's amazing there weren't more accidents. Almost everyone was completely sozzled. No one knew where anyone else was. It was ridiculously dangerous. People were throwing themselves in the water and generally behaving like idiots. I mistimed a dive and crashed into the side of one of the boats. Knocked myself out. I don't remember much after that. I could easily have drowned, but luckily one or two people had kept sober enough to stay on board and protect their opulent floating palaces, and someone must have seen me in the water, face down and pretty smashed up. The next thing I knew I was flat out in an Italian hospital, wires and tubes everywhere, and Ewan was sitting at my bedside.'

Joseph took a deep breath and let it out slowly. 'How long ago did it happen, Erica?'

'1993. Fifteen years. The Italian surgeons did a fantastic job, but there was only so much repair work they could do. Ewan flew back and forward to Italy every week for four months, till I was fit enough to be moved. Then he brought me home. I couldn't walk, of course, so it involved vast expense, with me on a sort of adapted hospital bed, and a hired nurse in attendance. After that I spent about a year undergoing more surgery, physiotherapy, whatever you can think of. Ewan bore the cost himself without complaint. Without him I would have been a lot more crippled. As it was I had some mobility, and for quite a while I was more or less independent. But then arthritis started to bite, and that got worse year on year. Till now. So you see, Joseph, I have everything to thank my dear brother for. It might have been better if he'd left me to die in Italy. But if I ever said such a thing, he said without me he would slowly die as well. Perhaps not physically, but in every way that matters. He has his faith, of course, and that has remained strong, but in human terms, according to him, I am the only person he feels that sort of connection with. Perhaps Helena might be an exception now – I hope so, for his sake. I don't know why it should be that way – heaven knows I can't be much of a friend or supporter for him, much as I wish I could. But there you are. Love is a funny thing, as I am sure you know very well from your own experience.'

Joseph nodded. 'I've seen some strange situations, it's true, in the pastoral side of my work. Under that crust of normality that most people like to maintain, that proud reserve, lie all sorts of mysteries. Sometimes you only find them out when someone calls on you to take a funeral. To be part of that is one of the privileges I have in this job.'

Erica was silent for a moment, evidently thinking and remembering. Then she looked up at Joseph. 'That's when I first found God,' she said. 'Or maybe he found me. Lying in bed in Italy, waiting for my brother to come. Ewan talked to me about his faith, he prayed for me *relentlessly.*' She grinned. 'My brother can be very persuasive. But in the end I guess God did his own work.'

The conservatory door flew open, and both Joseph and Erica looked up, startled. Nettie stood in the doorway, her hand on her hip. She had taken off her apron and looked festive in a floral dress and earrings in the shape of Christmas trees that flashed with red and gold lights. 'Lunch is served,' she announced with a triumphant grin. 'Bathroom first, Mrs P? And Joseph, perhaps you could sharpen the carving-knife. Everything's on the table.'

An hour later Nettie stood up with a clatter. 'Phew, it's terribly hot, don't you think? Now, my dears, I am more than happy to do the dishes, but I do need to pop home and let the dogs out. Is that all right, Mrs P? I would like to come back, if I may, just to see Helena for a while.'

'My dear Nettie, you must do whatever you need to. That was a truly magnificent meal, wasn't it, Joseph? You've excelled yourself.'

Nettie beamed. 'It's good to see you eating something for a change,' she said. 'Now, Joseph, please don't think you have to clear up. You sit and chat, you two. It's not often you have the opportunity without someone somewhere wanting something. I won't be very long.'

'I hope you're all right to drive,' Joseph said. 'You don't want to get done for drink-driving.'

'I'll go very slowly,' Nettie said solemnly. 'They won't suspect an old lady in an ancient Beetle. See you later.'

In a moment of bustle she had her coat, hat and gloves on and then the front door banged shut. They heard her car engine start up with a loud revving.

Erica shuddered. 'She doesn't steer straight when she's sober. I do hope nobody sees her. She would be absolutely mortified to be stopped by the police.'

Joseph stood up. 'I'm going to break Nettie's rules. She's worked very hard for us today, and it would be criminal to leave her with a pile of dishes. I'll clear the table.'

'I'm afraid I'm not much help,' Erica said.

'That's OK. Why don't you come into the kitchen and continue with your story while I get this lot washed and put away?'

'There's not much more to tell you. The rest is a dreary story of decline, I'm afraid. But if you like I'll wheel myself into the kitchen and park myself out of the way.'

Joseph followed her into the kitchen, watching the gnarled hands operate the toggle that changed the wheelchair's direction. 'Why don't you settle here by the fridge?' He looked around. 'You must have a tray somewhere.'

'Yes, on the top of the cupboard.'

Joseph began to pile dirty plates on the tray and bring them back to the sink. 'So where did you live when you came back home?' he asked. 'You've only been in Compton, what? Six years?'

Erica nodded. 'It took a long time to recover even quite basic functions,' she said sombrely. 'I was in a sort of rehabilitation unit for ages. But then I went back to my own flat. Ewan had got it adapted for me, and for a while it worked well enough. He was always there, even though he was so busy, and from time to time he'd bring Helena with him. She was just a teenager then, of course. I said to him not to make her come, why would she want anything to do with her crippled aunt, but he said she wanted to come and see me, and she always has. When she was born Ewan was keen for me to be her godmother, but Fiona wouldn't have it. She wanted someone more influential, one of her own circle. But as you might imagine, it didn't work. I don't suppose, whoever Helena's godparents are, that they have much to do with her at all, but Helena and I have always got along.'

Joseph filled the sink with hot water, pushed up his sleeves and started to wash the dishes. 'Helena seems to be the one most like her father,' he observed.

'She is, but she's more cheerful than Ewan. I suppose she hasn't had such trauma in her life, and she's only twenty-seven, but things haven't gone altogether smoothly for her.'

'Oh? How's that?'

'Nothing too major, I suppose, and she is quite reticent, but I've gathered her love life might have been a bit of a disappointment. The sort of men she meets, the sort her mama would no doubt like her to marry, aren't much use, in my opinion, despite their money and lineage.'

Joseph looked at her with raised eyebrows. 'What's wrong with them, according to you?'

'More ambition than brains. More testosterone than heart. Infantile sense of humour, loud braying laugh. Mercenary. Boring. Predictable. No conversation to speak of. How could such a creature appreciate my Helena?' She smiled wickedly. 'Are my prejudices showing?'

'Your prejudices are not just showing, they are ten feet high with flashing lights,' Joseph said. 'So what paragon of masculine virtue *would* suit Aunt Picky?' He held up a glass to the light and inspected his handiwork.

'Oh, well, as to that,' Erica said quietly, 'I have you cast for the role.'

'What? Me?' Joseph laughed. 'You're not serious, I hope.'

Erica fixed him with her implacable gaze. 'Whyever not? You are the reverse of those foolish young men, it seems to me. Before I go to my Maker I want to know my dear niece will be appreciated and cared for.'

'I'm running out of space here,' Joseph muttered to himself. 'I'll have to dry some of these plates and pans to make room.'

'Joseph, are you ignoring me?' Erica demanded.

'I'm afraid I am.'

'Why?'

'Because you are teasing.' He frowned. 'Aren't you?'

'No, not really. Helena is a fine young woman with many excellent qualities. I think if Fiona was my mother I'd have either run away or caved in and become just like her. But Helena is strong. You could do worse.'

Joseph gaped. For a moment he seemed struck dumb, and dried the dishes like an automaton, piling them up on the kitchen counter as he finished with each one. Erica watched him without speaking, a knowing expression on her face. At last he seemed to gather his wits. 'Erica,' he stuttered, 'you misunderstand me totally. I am not too good for Helena – she is far too good for me. Even supposing I was in the market, which I'm not. I'm too old, too poor and too battle-scarred. I'm a country vicar, only just on the right side of forty, with a history of depression and fourpence ha'penny in the bank. Why on God's good earth would a glorious creature like Helena want anything to do with me?'

Erica wagged a crooked finger at him. 'Ah, I don't say that she would. But who knows? It might be worth trying.'

Joseph shook his head. 'I can't believe we are having this conversation. It's quite ridiculous.'

'Not at all,' Erica said. 'She should have a good man and a clutch of children. As well as whatever work she wants to do. And you should have a bit more warmth and light in your life. QED.'

'You realise, I hope,' Joseph complained, 'that when Helena arrives I shall be thinking of what you have said and be far too embarrassed to utter a sensible word.'

'I'm sure you'll manage.'

Joseph uttered a barely-audible exclamation and went back to the dining table to clear the last of the debris. He threw paper napkins into the waste bin, together with bits of tinsel and crumpled Christmas crackers. Then he gathered the table cloth up carefully, took it to the back door and shook the crumbs out onto the wet lawn.

'I'll put this straight into the washing machine,' he said. 'Someone spilt their gravy.' He looked at Erica and shook his head. 'You know what, you get away with murder. You're quite outrageous.'

'I know,' Erica said serenely. 'But I am just fulfilling an ancient and venerable role – matchmaking elderly relative.'

A thought struck Joseph, and his eyebrows met in a scowl. 'Please tell me you haven't said any of this to Helena herself. I shall be too cringingly embarrassed even to look at her.'

'What nonsense. You will do very well. Have you finished the washing up? Because I would appreciate a cup of coffee with a slug of brandy in it.'

Joseph pursed his lips. 'I thought you'd abjured alcohol.'

'It's Christmas,' Erica said airily. 'I'll go back to abstemious sobriety tomorrow. I will, I promise.'

Joseph dried his hands. 'I don't know where most of this stuff goes.'

'That's OK. Nettie will put it away.' She looked up. 'Joseph, did I hear someone come in?'

'Helloo, here I am again,' Nettie's voice trilled from the hallway. She appeared, her hat and coat dewed with raindrops. 'Oh, this weather!' She took off her coat and hung it up. The she marched into the kitchen, saw the counter piled high with clean dishes, and frowned. 'Joseph, you are very bad. I would have done that.'

'Not a chance,' Joseph said, 'not after all your hard work this morning.' He patted her arm.

Nettie looked up and peered over Joseph's shoulder. 'And here's Helena, coming up the garden! What splendid timing.'

Helena came through the conservatory door, carrying a large carrier bag. 'I'll take these off in here,' she called. She put the bag down on a chair, spilling brightly-wrapped packages on the floor, and removed wellington boots covered in a pattern of dumpy cartoon penguins. She looked up at them as she tugged the boots off. All three were looking down at her, smiling. 'Happy Christmas, one and all,' she said. She grinned. 'I sound like Tiny Tim.'

Erica laughed. 'Not quite, my dear. I think he said "God bless us, every one." Close.'

'Well, that's a good thought too,' Helena said gaily. She padded into the lounge in her socked feet. 'Oh, it's lovely to be here with normal people.'

'If we're normal, I shudder to think who you are comparing us with,' Erica said.

'You know exactly who I'm talking about, you old fraud.' Helena bent to kiss her aunt. 'Happy Christmas.'

Erica held on to Helena's arms for a moment, then released her. Helena hugged Nettie, who enfolded her in plump arms. 'You look a treat, dear,' Nettie said. 'Lovely to see you.'

Helena came to Joseph and put her hands on his shoulders. 'I'm not leaving you out,' she said, and kissed his cheek. 'Happy Christmas, Joseph.'

'And to you,' Joseph murmured, for a moment inhaling her airy scent.

'Well, are you all full of turkey and Christmas pudding and brandy butter?' Helena asked. 'Is there any washing up to do?'

'No,' Nettie said, trying to look annoyed but succeeding only in crossing her eyes. 'Joseph sneakily did it while I was at home giving my boys a quick stroll. I told him not to, I really did.'

'Quite right,' Helena said. 'I like a bit of disobedience. I hope you three aren't thinking of taking any little siestas, because it's time for fun.'

Erica groaned. 'Please, Helena, no foolish games involving silly hats. I can't bear it.'

'All right, Mrs Scrooge, how about a nice sedate game of cards?'

'I suppose,' Erica said.

'But first – presents!' Helena turned and bounced back into the conservatory, where she gathered up the fallen parcels into her bag. 'Here we are – nothing much, so don't be embarrassed, anybody.' She spread the contents of the bag on the table. 'Nettie, for you. Here's yours, Erica. I'll help you open it if the tape's too tight and awkward. And Joseph – I had to ask my aunt's advice, and she said you play the piano. I hope you haven't already got it.'

'Thank you, that's really thoughtful.' Joseph opened the flat gold-and-blue striped parcel and found a volume of baroque suites and early classical sonatas. 'No, I haven't got it, and I shall enjoy exploring these.' He flicked through the pages. 'It's high time I did some proper practice. Thank you.'

'You ladies have got your favourite perfume, as usual,' Helena said. 'No one can say I'm not consistent.'

'I'm afraid I'm not very imaginative when it comes to presents,' Joseph said. 'Especially ones for women, as Helena knows.' He retrieved a bag from the hall. 'Here we are.' He looked at Helena with an apologetic smile. 'I went back to that shop in the High Street and asked the assistant's advice.'

The three women unwrapped soft scarves. 'You've chosen very good colours, Joseph,' Nettie said. 'Thank you, dear.'

Nettie and Erica exchanged small gifts, and gave Joseph books. 'Something for you to relax with while you're at your sister's,' Nettie said. 'I enjoy a good thriller myself. Nothing too heavy.'

'Excellent choice,' Joseph said solemnly. 'A relief from all that stodgy theology and collections of improving nineteenth-century sermons.'

'Hm. I did wonder where you got your inspiration from every Sunday,' Erica muttered.

'Now, Mrs P! How can you say that?' Nettie protested. 'Joseph's sermons aren't in the least stodgy. Don't listen to her, Joseph.'

'I shall try not to.'

Helena looked down at her aunt. 'Ready for cards, Mrs Curmudgeon?'

'No, I need the loo. And Helena, there are some more presents for you.'

'I'll open them in a minute,' Helena said.

'And I'll take you to the toilet, Mrs P,' Nettie said. 'You get the table clear of paper, Helena. And put the kettle on, if you will. I don't know about you good people, but I could murder a cup of tea.'

Ten minutes later Helena had all of them sitting obediently round the table, though Erica was pretending to scowl. Mugs of tea steamed gently.

'I'll teach you to play Black Lady,' Helena said. 'That's if you don't know how already. Daddy taught me when I was ten, so it can't be too hard. Oh – we need a pencil and paper. I'll get some in a minute. I'll tell you the rules, and then we'll have a dummy run.'

'I'm no use at cards,' Nettie wailed.

'And I can't hold that many in my hands,' Erica said. 'Shall we sit it out, Nettie?'

'No,' Helena said firmly. 'We can't play with just two. How about if you two play as a team? Nettie, you can hold the cards and put them down, and Erica can tell you what to do. Joseph and I will try not to listen to your discussions.' She looked at Joseph and shrugged. He shook his head and suppressed a smile.

'Well, guess who won?' Erica groused an hour and a half later. 'Little Miss Cardsharp herself.'

'Sitting this side of Joseph was definitely a bad idea,' Nettie said to Erica in a stage whisper. 'He kept giving us the most awful cards.'

'I never realised he was such a stinker, did you, Nettie?' Erica spoke as if only she and Nettie were in the room. 'You wouldn't expect such conduct from a man of the cloth. I will write to the Bishop and sign my letter "Disgusted of Compton Magna." See if I don't.'

Helena laughed and pushed her chair back. 'You two are such bad losers,' she said. 'Anyone fancy a sandwich?'

'I couldn't eat another thing,' Erica said. 'Nettie made us a huge lunch and I'm sure I haven't even begun to digest it. You make something for everyone, though, Helena. And I'll have another cup of tea to take my tablets with.'

'Oh, my goodness!' Nettie gasped. 'Your tablets. I almost forgot them. It must be all that sherry I had before lunch. It's turned my brain to dishwater.'

'Not to mention,' Erica said, 'the wine we drank *with* lunch.'

'And,' Joseph added softly, 'the brandy in the coffee.'

Erica groaned. 'Joseph, you are a traitor. Now I shall have my niece, my own personal nemesis, bearing down on me in horror. She is fearsome, especially when she hasn't had a drink herself.'

'It's all right for you,' Helena said. 'Some of us have to drive. Honestly, though, I hope you're not going to get any bad effects.' She looked at her aunt anxiously.

'If I do, it will have been worth it,' Erica said. 'We've had a good day, haven't we, my dears? I must say, I feel unusually benevolent. But I also feel very tired, and I'm beginning to ache in every conceivable joint. I'd like just to take my pills, have a bit of a wash, and stretch out in bed. Would you mind very much? I feel sure I'll sleep like a stone. Nettie can help me, if she will, but you two carry on playing if you want.'

'I'm pretty tired myself,' Nettie said, 'after that marathon of cooking! I'll get you ready, Mrs P, and then pop off home and put my feet up and listen to the radio.'

Joseph stood up. 'I should go home too, really. There are a few things I must do before I go to my sister's. I can't go till Thursday now, because there aren't going to be any trains on Boxing Day. But the house is a tip. I should do some cleaning.'

Helena looked disappointed, but she said nothing.

'Will you have to come back for Sunday, Joseph?' Nettie asked. 'It doesn't give you long at your sister's.'

'No,' Joseph said. 'It's the usual thing for the exhausted incumbent to have the Sunday after Christmas off. I'll be back in the New Year.'

Helena pulled back the curtains and looked out into the darkness. 'It's still raining.' She turned to Joseph. 'Would you like a lift home? I promise I haven't touched a drop all day.'

'Oh, thank you. It would be good not to get wet all over again.'

He bent over Erica's chair and took her hand. 'Thank you for inviting me. You've saved me from a lonely Christmas.'

'I'm glad you came, Joseph,' Erica said, then spoiled the gracious utterance with a salacious wink. Joseph bit his lip and pretended not to notice. He kissed Nettie's cheek. 'Thank you for a wonderful meal. You're a terrific cook, Nettie, among all your other talents.'

Nettie blushed. 'Very ordinary ones, I'm sure.' She turned to Helena. 'Lovely to see you again, dear. I'll be off home as soon as I've got Mrs P settled.'

'Should I come back after I've dropped Joseph off?' Helena said to her aunt. 'Or will you be asleep?'

'I hope I'll be out for the count,' Erica said. 'And dreaming. No, you go and do…well, whatever you have in mind.' Her eyes were hooded, and she gave a tiny smile full of mischief.

Helena slapped her lightly. 'For heaven's sake, behave.' She bent and kissed her. 'Goodnight, Erica. Sleep well. I'll see you soon.'

Helena drove Joseph the short distance across town. The Christmas lights were all blazing, the shopping streets and main square full of light, but the whole place was deserted, its wet pavements reflecting the festive shop-windows that displayed their wares to nobody. Joseph watched Helena covertly as she drove, seeing her long white hands on the wheel, noting her quiet competence. She turned into Church Street and pulled up outside the Vicarage. Here, away from the centre, the road was dark, lit only by chinks of light behind closed curtains and the rain-hazed streetlights.

Joseph turned to Helena and saw that she was looking at him, her face serious. He made a decision. 'Why don't you come in for a cup of coffee? It seems a shame that you've come down from London on Christmas Day to have the day end so early.'

'I'm surprised Erica lasted as long as she did,' Helena said. 'She is brave, but pain exhausts her. And I guess Nettie has been preparing for days, so no wonder if she is weary.' She tilted her head. 'I thought you were terribly busy getting ready to go to your sister's.'

'I've got all day tomorrow,' Joseph said. 'And the house isn't so very disgusting. But I thought I should make my exit, to give the ladies a chance to do whatever they had to do in peace. So I would welcome your company, if you haven't got some wild party to go to tonight.'

'Ha! Actually, as it happens, I have been invited to a party this evening, by my brothers. I am glad of an excuse not to go. I know some of their friends, but they include too many ogling men who fancy themselves.' She switched off the car engine and doused the lights. 'I'd like a cup of coffee, thank you. But will the car be OK here?'

Joseph laughed. 'Are you thinking of my reputation? How kind. We could put the car on the drive and cover it with tree branches to camouflage it if you like.'

Helena's fine blond eyebrows arched. 'Perhaps I was thinking of *my* reputation.'

'Touché.'

Helena shook her head and smiled. 'Just kidding. My reputation would probably benefit from some sensible company. Shall we go?'

Joseph led the way up the drive, opened the door with his key and stood aside to let Helena in.

'Mm, it's nice and warm in here,' she said. She kicked off her driving shoes.

'I left the heating on low,' Joseph said. 'It's not cold, but this constant rain makes it feel damp and miserable. Besides, I get my bills paid. Come into the kitchen. I'll get the coffee on.'

Helena looked around. 'It's a nice big kitchen. Good colours.'

Joseph followed her gaze. 'My late wife's choice.'

'Oh. I never met her. She had good taste.'

Joseph smiled wryly. 'Perhaps not as far as men were concerned.'

'What rubbish,' Helena said quietly, then her cheeks flamed. 'Sorry. I didn't know her, of course.'

Joseph set the coffee going and sat at the table opposite Helena. 'Before you arrived today, Erica was telling me the story of the accident that disabled her.'

Helena nodded. 'I remember it. It was awful. The atmosphere in our house was ten times as bad as usual.'

'Oh?'

'Do you really want to hear our family troubles? It's a very dreary subject.' She caught her lower lip between her teeth.

'Erica was telling me how much she feels she owes to your father. He seems quite a remarkable man.'

'Yes, he is. Something's bubbling, Joseph.'

'Right.' Joseph got up and poured two mugs of coffee. He found a plastic carton of milk, half full, in the fridge, and put it on the table. 'Best cut glass.'

'Family heirloom?'

'Yes, at least a hundred and fifty years old.'

Helena chuckled as she stirred. 'Mummy actually *has* stuff like that. Far too precious to waste on the likes of Daddy and me, though.'

Joseph looked critically at the milk carton. 'I think I prefer the more modern design.'

'Me too.' Helena took a sip. 'You were asking about my father. You haven't met him, have you?'

'No, I'm afraid not.'

'He likes to keep a low profile here in Compton – so that Erica can have peace and quiet. But you're right, he is a remarkable man. Even I know that, and he's just my dad that I see every day of my life.'

Joseph folded his arms and leaned back in his chair. 'What seems to me most remarkable is his relationship with Erica. She told me that when she was first injured he travelled to Italy every week for four months to see her.'

Helena nodded. 'He did. He was desperately worried about her. At first glance it looks one-sided, I suppose – kind brother looking after helpless sister, etc. But it wasn't always so, and he is adamant that *he* couldn't do without *her*. She's some kind of anchor for him, I think. It all goes back to their childhood, but I don't know the details, because they never tell me anything. It's quite irritating how they all treat me as if I was a child.'

'Even Erica?'

'No, she's the exception, but even she is secretive.' Helena fell silent for a moment, drinking her coffee, her eyes distant. She sighed and looked up at Joseph as if collecting herself. 'I remember one especially hideous day,' she said, 'when Daddy was packing a bag to go to Italy to see Erica in the hospital. He and Mummy had the most ferocious row. They didn't know I was in earshot. Normally they were careful not to quarrel in front of us, but of course we knew. That afternoon the boys were out, playing rugby or some such thing. I was in my room, doing my homework. I tried not to listen, but it was impossible. Until then I'd have said Mummy objected to Daddy spending so much time and money and effort on Erica – I might even have seen her point. But after that day I realised she actually hated her. It was quite chilling for me.'

'How old were you?' Joseph asked.

'Mm...twelve, I think.'

'It opened your eyes?'

Helena nodded. 'After that I saw more and more evidence of the total collapse of their marriage. They kept up some kind of pretence, and maybe outsiders believed it. But we all knew the score. I don't think the boys were that bothered, as long as services weren't disrupted, but I hated it. I tried to spend as much time as I could at my friends' houses. Nowadays my parents just lead separate lives. We all do, in a way, except that Daddy and I still have a real bond. It's sad.'

Joseph scratched his chin. 'Why do you think it went that way? I hope you don't think I'm being nosy. It's just that some of what you're saying resonates with my own experience.'

'It's hard to say. I wasn't there at the beginning, of course. I've gleaned a few hints from Erica, but she's pretty tight-lipped. My parents should probably never have married in the first place. But Alex was on the way, and things were different then.' She looked at Joseph. 'Don't tell me your parents were the same.'

Joseph shook his head. 'No. I was conceived squarely in wedlock, fifteen years down the line. My sister's eleven years older than me. No, it was my own marriage I was thinking of. There was no reason for haste, but hasty we were, and both of us regretted it. Perhaps I shouldn't be telling you this.'

'I don't see why not,' Helena said softly. 'I won't be selling your story to the papers.'

Joseph winced. 'I didn't mean that. So what, in your opinion, makes for a happy family life? Where have we all gone wrong?'

'Hey!' Helena protested. 'I haven't gone wrong, not yet. I don't know, but at least you have to be sensible in the first place and get married for the right reasons, and then you have to be forbearing for ever after.'

Joseph laughed, and his whole face, normally self-contained, lit up for a moment. 'A tall order, I'd say. What are the right reasons, according to you?'

Helena's face was serious, but her eyes sparkled with humour. 'Well, of course, you must be madly in love and equally madly in lust.'

'I know for certain that what you describe is a recipe for disaster,' Joseph said.

'Oh dear,' Helena said, suppressing an unsympathetic grin. 'Well, that's not really what I think, of course. I've been in that condition once or twice but I'm extremely thankful I didn't make it permanent. I don't know, Joseph. Mutual tolerance, I suppose. Deep knowledge. Kindness. Honesty. You tell me.'

'No, I'm hardly qualified,' Joseph said. 'Total failure as a husband.'

'Perhaps to *that* wife,' Helena murmured.

Joseph said nothing, merely raised one eyebrow.

Helena thought for a moment. 'Joseph, would you do something nice for me?'

'Gladly, if I knew what it was.'

'You sound so worried! I just wondered if you'd play something from your new music.'

'Really?' Joseph said dubiously. 'I'd be sight-reading, so it might be terrible. And you should know that I normally only play when I am sad.'

'You don't seem sad today,' Helena said, looking at him sideways. 'Or are you just good at hiding it?'

He shook his head and smiled. 'No, on the contrary. I'm not sad at all. It's Christmas Day, my Lord's birthday. And I'm in very pleasant company.'

Helena got to her feet. 'Then let's be revolutionary, and play when you are happy.' She stretched out her hand, and despite his habitual misgivings he took it. Her skin was cool. 'Take me to your piano, maestro.'

2008: Compton

Louise Gordon slid into the driver's side and buckled on her seat-belt. She rested her hands on the wheel for a moment and turned to Hazell, who was lying back in the passenger seat, his long legs stretched out. She couldn't see his eyes behind his dark glasses, and for a moment she thought he was asleep.

'You all right, sir?' She switched on the ignition.

Hazell sat up and loosened his tie. 'Hot, that's all,' he said. 'This weather's nice if you can spend it in a sun-lounger in your garden with a cool beer and the crossword. Having to drive from pillar to post through traffic, and wearing work clothes, gets a bit trying. We could do with a storm.'

Louise drove smoothly out of the car park and on to the road. 'You might get your wish before the day's out, if the weather forecast is right. It's sticky enough. So – up to London again? The Fraser place?'

'The office, on Marlborough Street. The forensic team might even have got there before us. Scouring every last inch of those cars, I hope. Especially the four-by-four we're most interested in.'

'Well, if there's anything to find, they'll find it.' She came to a T-junction and slowed, then eased the car out onto the main street. 'Traffic's quite heavy,' she commented. 'Might take us a bit longer than usual.'

'No, you'll be OK once you're on the road out to the motorway,' Hazell said. 'This bit's congested because it's been market day. There's the council van, doing its clear-up rounds.'

'Local knowledge, I see, sir.' Louise sounded amused.

'Something like that,' Hazell said. 'If you don't mind, Louise, I'm going to shut my eyes for a few miles. Got a bit of a headache. You all right with the route?'

'I think so, sir. There's a bottle of water in the glove compartment if you need a drink.'

'Right. Thanks.'

'Just one thing, though – you never told me about your meeting with the mysterious Dr Carver. Did he shed any light? What's his connection, anyway?'

Hazell grunted. 'He doesn't have one, not really. He's a friend of the vicar, Joseph Stiles, and he happened to be visiting. I don't suppose he comes within sight or sound of murder in his normal life, and now he's been close to two dead bodies. So he got intrigued and did a bit of research. But what he said was very interesting. It looks like Eddie Squire's body on the beach is the chap from Ewan Fraser's past, and now we know he'd got form we're going to have to put some more people on that side of things. I've organised some men from Stockley to go down to Bickham and liaise with Eddie and his team. They'll report to Tom Rivers, and Tom will collate any evidence on his computer. I'm still not a hundred per cent convinced he's our man, but we have to keep him as a possible suspect. He's a nasty little crook, he's done time, he's capable of violence, we think he tried to blackmail Ewan Fraser and he knew both Fraser and Erica Pole from years ago. There's history there. The photos you took of the key that was round his neck might spark a bit of a reaction from Mr Fraser. We shall see.'

The black BMWs were housed in an underground car park, reached via a gated ramp off the street. Louise pulled up at the gate. 'We're here, Fred.'

Hazell heaved himself up. Louise wound the window down and spoke into a small grille at the side. 'Detective Inspector Hazell, Stockley CID,' she said. 'We're expected.' A tinny voice answered her and the gate swung slowly inwards.

'Over there, I think.' Hazell pointed to a far corner.

Louise brought the car to a halt where the four Fraser cars were parked side by side. One of the four-by-fours was cordoned off. Its doors were open and two figures in white coveralls were crawling in and out of it.

'They look like worms devouring a rotten apple,' Louise murmured.

Hazell raised his eyebrows. 'I'm sure they'd be delighted to hear your description.'

Louise looked at him in horror. 'Don't tell them, please! Knowing those two, they'd be only too chuffed to get their revenge.'

Hazell got out of the car and straightened his tie. 'My lips are sealed.' He walked unhurriedly to the cars and stood outside the cordon. One of the men saw him and approached, stepped over the barrier and peeled off his gloves. 'Hello, sir. Afternoon, Sergeant Gordon.'

'Rowley, isn't it?' Hazell said. 'Found anything?'

'Not yet, sir. Just one thing's odd, though – there's no satnav, and it looks like it's actually been taken out. Maybe even not very carefully. But we haven't quite finished. Give us half an hour.'

'All right.' He looked around. 'Who's in charge of these vehicles?'

Rowley pointed to a small office set into the wall. 'Man's in there, sir. Name of Moulton.' He made a face. 'Best of luck, sir. Not the most cooperative of individuals.'

'Thanks. Right, I'll let you get back to work.' Hazell led Louise to the office and put his head round the open door. A small, grey-haired man sat at a desk, its surface empty except for a telephone, a hard-backed notebook and a pot of pens. On a large corkboard in front of him numerous printed dockets were tacked in symmetrical rows.

'Mr Moulton?' The grey-haired man looked round sharply, pushing his glasses further up the bridge of his nose. 'Inspector Hazell, CID. This is Sergeant Gordon.'

The man swivelled to face them in his chair, but did not get up. 'I'll need to see your ID,' he said.

Hazell nodded, and both he and Louise produced their warrant cards. Mouton took his time inspecting them. Finally he looked up. 'I was hoping your colleagues out there might have finished by now. They've been here for a considerable time. It's disrupting, to say the least.'

'They're thorough, Mr Moulton,' Hazell said patiently. 'I need to ask you a few questions about your work here and how the cars are used.'

'Fire away, Inspector. The sooner you all finish the sooner I can catch up on my backlog.'

Hazell looked at him thoughtfully for a moment, and Moulton shifted uncomfortably in his seat. 'I'm sure you'll agree, sir, that your backlog is a small enough matter when investigating a murder.'

'Murder? What murder? I don't know anything about any murder!'

'No one's accusing you, Mr Moulton. We just need some facts, and you can supply them.'

Moulton gaped. 'All right.'

'Who is entitled to use these cars?'

'Anyone who works for Fraser's and needs one for work,' Moulton said testily. 'But they need proper authorisation.'

'Is there any exception to that, sir?'

'Exception? What exception?' Moulton's face reddened.

'A member of the Fraser family, for example.'

'Oh, I see.' Moulton exhaled noisily and he looked at the ceiling. 'Miss Helena borrowed one the other day. But she went through the appropriate channels. Mr Fraser himself has been known to use one on occasion, but I can't remember the last time. The young gentlemen too. Again, not for a while now.'

'Theoretically, could a member of the family take a car without your knowledge?'

'Theoretically? What's that supposed to mean? Of course they could, if they had a mind. Mr Fraser has keys to everywhere. Why shouldn't he? It's his business. The cars belong to him. But without my knowledge? Not likely, is it? Even I can count to four.'

'When are you not here, Mr Moulton? In this office?'

Moulton scowled. 'At the weekends. When I go to the toilet. When I take my annual holiday.'

'Can you remember what time you left work last Friday, sir?'

'Normal time, five o'clock.'

'Perhaps you can tell me the last time that four-by-four was taken out.'

'What, the one your men are climbing all over? I'll look.' He opened the notebook and ran his finger down the page. 'Wednesday. Someone needed it for a site visit.'

'Nothing since then?'

Moulton looked up, his brows a black line. 'Not according to my book.'

'What about the missing satnav, Mr Moulton?'

Moulton's eyes widened. 'What? I don't know anything about that. Nobody told me.'

Hazell sighed. 'All right, Mr Moulton. Thank you. Oh, just one thing. How long have you worked for Frasers?'

'Twenty-nine years. Mr Fraser himself took me on.'

'I see,' Hazell said gravely. 'Good boss, is he?'

'The best,' Moulton said, scowling even more darkly. 'They don't make them like him any more. Not in this business.'

'Well, I won't take up any more of your time. But perhaps you can tell me where Mr Fraser's office is.'

Moulton turned his back and studied his corkboard. 'Fourth floor.'

Hazell looked at Louise and shrugged. 'Thank you, Mr Moulton. You've been most helpful.'

The two officers made themselves known at the reception desk and were shown to the lift. As they walked away Louise saw the receptionist pick up the phone and speak into it. 'Mr Fraser is being informed of our visit, I think, sir,' she murmured.

Hazell pressed the button for the lift. In a few moments it arrived and the doors slid open. They went in, and the doors closed. 'What did you make of our friend Mr Moulton?' Hazell asked as they glided upwards.

Louise smiled. 'I am getting a clear impression of loyal employees,' she said. 'You were very patient, I thought, in the circumstances.'

'Hm. It seemed to me that Mr Moulton was worried. He knows something he's not telling us.'

'Worried about what, do you suppose?'

'I don't know yet. Maybe that he'd get someone into trouble. Himself, even. But we need to get onto that missing satnav. Get someone to make enquiries – when was it last seen, when was the vehicle last cleaned, the serial number, and so on. We'll get that started on our way back to Compton.' The lift came to a smooth stop. 'Here we are, Sergeant. Lead the way.'

A moment later they rapped on a closed door, and after a brief pause Ewan Fraser opened it. He was in his shirtsleeves, his jacket hanging on the back of his chair. 'Good afternoon, Inspector, Sergeant. Please, come in. Have a seat.' He indicated two chairs by his desk.

'Thank you, Mr Fraser. I don't want to take up too much of your time.'

'Have your men finished with my cars yet?' Fraser asked. He stood behind his desk, his hands resting on its polished surface.

'Not quite, sir. I'm sure they'll let us know when they have. But there's something I would like to show you, if I may.' He turned to Louise. 'Can I have the photos, please, Sergeant?'

Louise handed him the sheaf of prints she had taken from her camera, and Hazell laid them on the desk in front of Fraser. 'Do you recognise this, sir?'

Fraser stared down at the photos. When he looked up, his face was a mask of control, but his voice was hoarse. 'What is this? Where did you get it?'

'Answer my question, please, Mr Fraser,' Hazell said calmly.

Fraser lowered himself slowly into his chair and cleared his throat. 'It looks very like the key to my late father's strongbox. Missing for many years. Stolen, I believe, along with the contents of the box.'

'Is there a chance it could be any other key, in your opinion?' Hazell said.

'I suppose it could,' Fraser said, his voice low. 'But it was a very old box, which as far as I know had been in the family for generations. So the key was equally unusual.'

'Would it surprise you to know, sir, that this key on its chain was found on the body of a man called Neil Gilmour?'

Gordon watched the blood drain from Fraser's face, so that his light freckles suddenly stood out. 'Not surprised, no,' he said. His voice was scarcely above a whisper. 'I knew Gilmour had stolen the money. But you say it was found on his body? Gilmour is dead?'

Hazell studied the face of the other man before he answered. 'A body was found early yesterday on the beach at Bickham,' he said, his voice neutral. 'Fingerprints determined the man was Neil Gilmour. His prints were on file because he'd been in prison. But not, I think, for the theft you accuse him of, sir.'

'No,' Fraser said. He gazed down at his own hands, resting on the desk in front of him. 'He vanished after that particular episode.'

'But you've seen him since then, I think, Mr Fraser.'

Fraser looked up, his lips compressed in a tight line. 'You obviously know,' he said finally, 'so I suppose there's little sense in pretending otherwise.' He heaved a deep sigh. 'It was a long time ago, I can't for the moment recall just how many years, over twenty certainly. He turned up at my house, not the one I live in now, and tried to blackmail me.'

'What did you say to him on that occasion, sir?'

'I sent him packing,' Fraser said, his voice suddenly firmer. 'I reminded him that he had nothing to back up his claims but his own evil suspicions. That I had been completely exonerated by the Inquiry, to which he had failed to turn up when called as a witness. That I was a respected law-abiding businessman, and he had served a jail term for embezzlement, theft and assault. Oh yes, I knew he'd been in jail. So who was likely to believe him over me? When he could prove nothing?' He looked at Hazell with challenge in his stare.

'What was he trying to blackmail you about, sir?' Hazell asked, his voice as calm as ever, as if he had all the time and all the patience in the world.

Fraser suddenly slumped. He sighed, resting his head in his hands. 'He said he had seen me take a gun from the gun cabinet prior to the fishing expedition during which my father fell into the river and drowned. From that he surmised I had threatened my father with it and caused him to fall. He said the gun was not in its place when he left the castle, but that it had reappeared by the time he returned.' Fraser looked up, and his eyes were hollow and bleak. 'But I can tell you, as I told the Inquiry, that Neil Gilmour saw nothing of what happened at the river. He was behind some rocks and trees, vomiting. When he returned to the castle, some hours after I did, he was soaking wet. Perhaps he went into the water to see if he could save my father, though I doubt it. What is certain is that he could only have come by that key by taking it from a drowned man's neck. He used it to open the strongbox and make off with the contents.'

Hazell frowned. 'I wonder why he kept that key,' he said, almost to himself. 'And what he did with it during his years in jail.'

Fraser shrugged. 'Perhaps he kept it to use against me at some future time, though I can't see how. When he went to prison he probably gave it to his – what? Wife? Accomplice? Who knows? To look after it for him. I really cannot say, Inspector.' Silence fell then, and rested on them all for several long moments. Then Fraser frowned. 'I'm at a loss to see why Neil Gilmour, alive or otherwise, is of interest to the police. What has he got to do with your investigation into my sister's murder, Inspector?'

'Possibly nothing at all, Mr Fraser,' Hazell said. 'But we are obliged to cover every angle. And in the last couple of weeks a man answering Neil Gilmour's current description was seen on more than one occasion in the vicinity of Plough Lane in Compton. A neighbour of your sister's saw this man hammering on Mrs Pole's door, shouting.'

Fraser's head jerked up, and his jaw dropped. 'What?' For a moment Hazell saw wild hope flare in Ewan Fraser's face before he reasserted control. 'I knew nothing of this, I assure you.'

'I believe you, sir,' Hazell said implacably. 'But the reappearance of Gilmour is something we are obliged to investigate.'

The phone rang on Fraser's desk, and he picked it up. His hand was shaking slightly. He listened for a moment, then handed the receiver to Hazell. 'It's for you.'

Hazell took it from him. 'Yes?' Both Fraser and Louise Gordon stared at him as he listened intently. 'All right, Rowley. Good work. You know what to do. As quickly as possible, please.' He handed the receiver back to Fraser, who replaced it. Once again there was a silence – a silence in which possibilities and unanswered questions crackled. Then Hazell said, 'We may wonder what Mr Gilmour was doing, hanging around Plough Lane in the weeks before your sister's murder, Mr Fraser. That's assuming that it was indeed him. It seems probable his presence there wasn't random, that he had found out where she lived, and perhaps he was again trying to get to you, through her. We don't know, nor do we know what he wanted. Of course if there is a connection we'll go on looking for it. But something more concrete seems to have come to light.' Fraser looked up at him, his face pale, his lips a thin line. 'I'll be honest with you, Mr Fraser,' Hazell said, his voice as matter-of-fact as ever. 'Our friends downstairs have found some forensic evidence which may put your company car in the vicinity of your sister's house at the time of her death.'

Fraser stared down at his desk. 'I see.'

Hazell was silent, looking at Fraser steadily. He sighed. 'Perhaps you do, Mr Fraser.' He glanced at Louise. 'We'll be going now, sir. If anything occurs to you that might help the investigation, you know where to find us.'

Fraser looked up, ill-concealed horror on his face. When he spoke, his voice was a strangled whisper. 'Yes, of course.'

Spring 2008: Compton

'Helena, my dear, you're wet!'

Helena laughed and shook out her hair. A rainbow of droplets flew across the room. 'There was a sudden shower just as I got out of the car. I thought I could run up the garden and stay almost dry. Seems I was wrong.' She bent and took off her wet shoes. 'How are you, Erica? Is your cold any better?' She came over to where Erica sat hunched in her wheelchair by the kitchen counter, bent down and kissed her cheek. She frowned and took her aunt's hand. 'You feel cold.'

'Fuss, fuss,' Erica muttered.

'I'll get your shawl,' Helena said, ignoring her complaint. She padded down the passage to Erica's bedroom and came back with a woollen shawl patterned in brown and orange. 'There – wrap yourself in that.' She arranged the shawl round Erica's shoulders.

'I hate being treated like an invalid,' Erica grumbled.

Helena chuckled. 'Not an invalid – a precious treasure.'

'Some treasure,' Erica said darkly.

Helena went to the window. 'Did you know you had daffodils out already? I wonder who planted them.'

'Some previous occupant of this place, I dare say,' Erica said. 'It certainly wasn't me. I can't do anything in the garden now, not with these hands.' She looked balefully down at her hands, resting twisted in her lap.

'I know, and it's a great shame. You used to enjoy being outside,' Helena said. 'Come out to the conservatory and look. Daffodils are enough to gladden even your gloomy heart.' Deaf to Erica's protests that she would much prefer a cup of tea, Helena stood by the door, arms folded, eyebrows raised in challenge, until Erica gave in with a small groan and guided the chair into the conservatory.

'It's freezing in here,' Erica complained.

'We'll only stay for a moment,' Helena said softly. 'Just look at those brave little flowers – like flakes of the sun, shining through the hail.' Outside, the sky had turned black, and hailstones began to rattle on the conservatory's glass walls.

'Very poetic,' Erica said, 'but please, let me go back inside before I turn to ice.'

'All right, I give in,' Helena said. 'Why don't you huddle by the radiator and toast yourself? I'll get the kettle on.' She followed Erica as she trundled slowly back into the lounge.

Erica twisted in her chair and watched her niece as the younger woman busied herself in the kitchen, humming quietly. She saw how her hair rippled down her back with every movement of her lithe body. She took in the tight jeans that moulded themselves to her rounded hips and long legs, and the oatmeal jumper with a shawl collar. She thought how little Helena resembled anyone in the family, except for her red hair from Ewan. But it was a different shade and texture, and Erica wondered, not for the first time, what her own mother had been like, the mother she could barely remember. Her aunt Joan had kept a few photos of herself and her younger sister, but there were none of Eleanor as an adult. She sighed and pushed her thoughts away. The past was not a place for dwelling.

Helena brought a mug of tea, half full, and put it next to Erica on a table the same height as her wheelchair, and easily reached. 'Do you want a biscuit? You could do with fattening up.'

'No, thanks,' Erica said. 'I'll wait for this tea to cool a bit, I think. Then if I spill any I'm less likely to scald myself.' She looked at Helena covertly as she settled herself in an armchair opposite. 'Helena.'

Helena tilted her head. 'Mm?'

'If one dare ask, how is your love life?'

'What love life is that?' Helena said, raising one eyebrow. 'Are you referring to Adam? James? Or perhaps Toby? You're terribly out of date, I'm afraid. They're all history.' She made a dismissive gesture.

'Don't be perverse,' Erica growled. 'You know perfectly well who I'm talking about. I don't have the time or energy to be oblique and diplomatic. As I've said before, I want to know you'll be OK when I'm gone.'

Helena put her cup down, her face serious. 'If you're referring to Joseph, I'm afraid your schemes have crashed, my dear old matchmaker. He doesn't like me. Well, perhaps he does, but not as you would wish.'

Erica scowled. 'But do you like him?'

Helena flinched. 'Even to you,' she said softly, 'I am loth to admit to having any feelings for a man who clearly doesn't return them.'

'I'd call that a nice clear answer,' Erica said with a crooked grin. 'So what's your evidence for believing he doesn't like you?'

Helena sighed. 'I can see that nothing but chapter and verse will get you off my back. All right, then. He seemed very friendly at first – you know, after Christmas and New Year. I really thought he was thawing. But now? I can't figure it out. He's gone very distant, weirdly polite and correct.' She shifted in her chair, and her voice changed, speeding up and rising in pitch. 'But I don't know why you're so keen, anyway. I realise Joseph is a friend of yours, but what's the big rush? I'm not exactly middle-aged yet. There'll be others, as my dear mama is fond of saying. Except that she, of course,' she muttered, almost to herself, 'has her own weird agenda as well.'

'Of course she does,' Erica said sharply. 'Anyone could tell you that. She'll have some brainless overbred overpaid lout lined up for you, I don't doubt. You and your brothers will be dynastic projects to her. But Helena, you deserve better. Better than all the Jameses and the Adams.' She sighed. 'All right, let me tell you a story. Not a nice one, but a true one. About a young woman who was ten times as foolish as you, with a self-destructive streak as wide as the M1. A young woman who married the wrong man, had a baby she dearly loved, but lost because of her stupidity, who drank herself into more idiocies than you can imagine. Who had affairs with men who didn't care for her at all. Who, at an age when she should have been earning a living and raising a family, had an abortion because the child's father had done a bunk and she herself felt utterly useless and incompetent. Incidentally, that's one of the few facts I kept from your father. He would have been horrified.'

'Oh, Erica.' Helena left her chair and came and squatted down beside her aunt. Tears were dribbling down Erica's face. Helena took her hand gently in her own. 'You lost two children, not one,' she whispered. 'How unbearable.'

Erica sniffed loudly, and Helena fumbled in her pocket, found a tissue and put it in her aunt's hand. Erica blew her nose awkwardly. 'Perhaps you can understand why I want you to be happy, but not just happy – happy in the right way, useful, fulfilled, and in the right company. I don't want you to fall prey to your dear mama's schemes – that would be a terrible waste.'

'I won't,' Helena said. 'Not a chance. Frankly, I'd rather go into a nunnery.'

Erica smiled. 'Much as I admire the cloistered calling, that would be a waste in your case too.'

Helena shook her head. 'I can't make Joseph love me, Erica. Not even to please you.'

'You don't need to, my dear. I'd lay bets he already does. Or is at least teetering on the brink. Why wouldn't he?'

'I'm afraid the evidence for that is very thin.'

Erica thought for a moment, shifting slightly in her seat to find a more comfortable position, wincing with each movement. She sighed. 'From what I know of Joseph, his past life, his life here in Compton, what I've seen of him, the things he's actually said in an unguarded moment, I'd say Joseph is afraid. Afraid of another failure, afraid of being some kind of curse to women. I'll bet you he blames himself for Caroline's death. In fact, I know he does. He's also learned from that very tragic experience. If he ever commits himself to anyone else, she is going to have to realise where his first loyalty lies. She needs to share it too, really.'

Helena frowned. 'Not sure I'm following you.'

'Joseph is no career clergyman, Helena. He's very able, but I doubt he'll ever rise from where he is now. He loves his Lord above all else, and his first thought is to be a shepherd to his sheep, as far as in him lies. That's his priority, and where all his stubbornness is. He's had to learn to persevere, even though he has been very discouraged at times. But the poor man is also human. He needs someone to work with him, help him sort his ideas out, set him straight when he goes astray, put up with his rants, make him laugh and warm his bed. Joseph is not cold, Helena. He is one of the most soft-hearted people I know. But life has dealt him some hard blows, and he's afraid. I don't know what exactly has passed between you, but I'd guess he's blowing hot and cold, and that's tough for a straightforward person like you. Perhaps you signify hope to Joseph, but he's scared to reach out and take it, in case it all goes wrong. Yes, Jesus is his first love. But you have to convince him that you are a gift to him from God, which I truly believe you are.'

'Golly,' Helena murmured. 'You really have thought this all out, haven't you?'

'I get to do a lot of watching, and a lot of thinking,' Erica said. She gave Helena one of her sly, knowing looks, then sighed mournfully. 'I shall go to my eternal rest content,' she said in sepulchral tones, 'knowing that between you something of the nasty, destructive past can be put right.'

Helena laughed. 'What? "Eternal rest?" For heaven's sake! You'll last for ever. So what would you have me do? Propose?'

'How you go about it is your affair, my dear girl,' Erica said. 'Just believe in your own very considerable qualities and irresistible charms. Cheat if necessary.'

'You're truly dreadful,' Helena said. 'I shall do nothing of the sort. And now I am going to change the subject.'

'Before you do,' Erica said, pushing her wheelchair awkwardly to where Helena sat and plucking at the younger woman's sleeve, 'just promise me you will do *something*. Don't let all that promise slip away because of some failure of nerve. Conviction, that's what you need. Even if it's the last thing you feel.'

'All right, all right,' Helena said, holding up both hands. 'Anything to keep you quiet. Now, tell me what's going on in this hive of scandal.'

'Compton? Nothing. The most thrilling things this week is that Nettie has decided to change her brand of dog food. Ben has been having trouble chewing, it seems. Or perhaps you'd like to know who's arranging the flowers in church, and what colours she favours? Because that's the most exciting thing happening here at the moment.'

'And *this* is the life you want me to have?' Helena exclaimed.

'Ha! I thought you were changing the subject,' Erica said.

An hour later Helena got up out of her chair and stretched. 'I'd better go. I'm supposed to be helping Mummy with this dinner party she's giving. Ugh.'

'Do you have to stay for it?'

'Fortunately, no. That's Daddy's penance, the price he pays for peace.' She paused and sighed. 'You know, I do take on board what you say about miserable marriages. You had one, sounds like Joseph's wasn't great, and I live in the middle of one. It's not something I'd ever want to risk. And yet, you know, oddly, I'm not afraid. For some reason I have confidence it'll be OK.'

'So do I. And I'm not confident of much, as you know.'

Helena paused with one shoe on and one off. She hesitated. 'I've been having that weird dream again,' she said. 'After such a long time, he's back.' Erica raised her eyebrows enquiringly. 'You remember,' Helena said. 'The man with the snake eyes. The one that's been hovering somewhere in my memory for years.'

'Ah. Him,' Erica said softly. 'I wonder who he is.'

Helena bit her lip. After a moment she said, 'I think I know. Or at least, something came to me when I woke up. I saw the man looking at me with those eyes. But this time it was as clear as if it was yesterday. He was sitting at the kitchen table with Mummy, and I was watching from the stairs. I had a green pencil in my hand. They were saying something to me, but I don't know what it was.'

'Perhaps you discovered your mother with her lover when you were a small child, and you've suppressed the memory,' Erica said acidly.

'Do be serious, Erica,' Helena said. 'I told you, Mummy doesn't believe in fun. Now I must go, or I'll get it in the neck.' She kissed Erica's cheek and for a moment hovered close, her hair falling in a cloud all round both their faces. 'See you soon, dear old reprobate.'

1985: London

'I told you I never wanted to see your face around here again!' Ewan Fraser put his briefcase down on the front path leading to his house, and stood with his hands on his hips.

The other man smirked, his dark eyes darting restlessly from right to left. 'Your good lady invited me in, Mr Fraser, *sir*,' he said. He spoke with a strong Scottish accent. 'Made me a nice cup of tea, too, which is more than you ever did, even for old times' sake.' He laughed quietly, an unpleasant sneering sound that raised the hair on Ewan's neck and made sweat bloom on his upper lip. 'But I wouldn't want such a nice lady getting into trouble on my account, so I'll be going now, if you'd be so kind as to get out of my way.' He spoke softly, with a slick veneer of gracious manners that stung Ewan's ears like grit under the skin.

Ewan clenched his fists, keeping his arms rigidly at his sides. 'Did she pay you?' he said, his voice low.

The other man took a small step backwards, nearer to the front door. 'She made a small donation for my trouble, for which I thank her,' he said. 'Seeing as I'm a bit short of funds right now. But I'm sure you can afford it, Mr Fraser. I hear you're doing well in your business.'

Ewan took a deep breath. 'Get out now, Gilmour,' he growled, 'before I overcome my revulsion and lay you flat on the pavement.'

'Still got a temper, then? Still ready for a bit of violence, just like you were as a lad?' Gilmour sidled past Ewan, who did not move.

'Out!' roared Ewan, so loudly that Gilmour scuttled to the gate, almost tripping. 'Show your face near my family again and I'll have the police on to you, you lying snake. Go on!'

Gilmour grinned, showing broken and missing teeth. 'I'm away now, Mr Fraser. So very nice to see you again after all these years.' He sketched a little bow and trotted off round the corner and out of sight. Ewan picked up his briefcase and stood for a moment, trembling slightly. He saw a curtain twitch across the road and muttered a curse under his breath.

He turned and strode up to his front door, put his key in the lock and pushed the door back against the wall with a crash. 'Fiona!' He threw the briefcase down so that it skittered across the tiled floor. 'Fiona!' He pounded into the kitchen, breathing heavily.

Fiona was sitting at the table, a cup of coffee in her hands. She looked up at Ewan calmly and said nothing.

Ewan's eyes narrowed. 'What the hell do you think you're doing, letting that creep Gilmour into the house? Have you gone completely mad?'

Fiona took a sip of her coffee and shrugged. 'I saw him hanging around at the street corner. Thought I'd see what he had to say. I didn't expect you home so early. It's a pity you even saw him.'

'How could you be so stupid? You knew what he came for last time. He's a blackmailer, you know that. He'd like to see us come to grief. At the very least he wants to screw money out of us. Is that what you want? What did you pay him for? I don't understand you.'

'Of course you don't,' Fiona said contemptuously. 'And I paid him for information, which you could have given me for nothing.'

'What information? What are you talking about?'

'Oh, just the truth about how your father drowned,' Fiona said almost casually.

Ewan frowned. 'I've told you what happened.'

Fiona gave a knowing little smile. 'Mr Gilmour tells a different version.'

Ewan smacked his fist into the palm of his other hand. 'What are you saying? Do *you* want to blackmail me now? What are you hoping to gain?'

'Just a little knowledge, that's all.'

Ewan shook his head. 'What have we come to, that there's so little trust between us?'

Fiona laughed, throwing her blonde head back, revealing perfect white teeth. 'Trust? Surely even you aren't that naïf.' She pushed her chair back and got up. 'Anyway, now you're here, I'm going out.'

'What?'

'You need to look after your daughter.'

Ewan's expression changed instantly, from bewildered frustration to black fury. 'You had that snake Gilmour here when Helena was in the house? Now I'm certain you've lost it! What sort of a parent are you anyway?'

Fiona picked up her handbag and slung it over her shoulder. 'Frankly, *darling*, a very bored one. You stay and defend your precious child. I'm going shopping. I'll pick the boys up from school on my way back.'

She strode briskly past him out into the hall and through the front door, leaving it swinging wide. Ewan stood still for a moment, taking deep breaths till his shuddering subsided.

'Daddy?'

Ewan turned abruptly and his face cleared. A small girl stood in the doorway, holding a sheet of paper in one hand and a clutch of pencils in the other. He smiled. 'Hello, sweetheart! Have you been drawing in your bedroom? Can I look?'

'I've been drawing on the stairs,' the child said. She looked around. 'Where's Mummy gone?'

'She's gone to collect the boys from school,' Ewan said. He crossed the room and scooped her up in his arms, holding her upside down so that her long red hair hung down, its wispy ends almost touching the floor. Her serious little face broke into giggles. He sat her down at the table. 'Shall we have a drink, my honey? What would you like? And don't say "gin and tonic" like you did last time your grandma was here!'

Helena chuckled. 'That's what Grandma likes, isn't it? I expect it tastes nasty. I'll just have some juice, please, Daddy.'

'OK, and I'll have a nice cup of tea, and you can show me your drawing.' He crossed to the kitchen counter, filled the kettle and plugged it in.

He had his head in the cupboard, searching for biscuits, when the innocent piping voice of his four-year-old stopped him dead, and a cold prickle ran down his arms.

'Daddy, who was that man with the snaky eyes?'

Summer 2008: Compton

Joseph heard the doorbell from the back garden as he emptied grass-cuttings into a compost bin. He frowned slightly. Thursday was his day off, and only in a desperate emergency would one of his flock come to the Vicarage on a Thursday. People still rang, of course – people wanting their baby baptised, or enquiring about a relative buried in the churchyard, even asking about the times of services, which they could as easily have found out from the notice-board outside the church. The answerphone dealt with all of these. 'It's my day off. If you have a problem that can't wait, please contact the churchwardens.' People ringing the doorbell were another matter, and he had never quite been able to harden his heart enough to ignore the summons. He sighed, wiped his grassy hands down the sides of his trousers, and padded round the side of the house.

'Oh! Hello, Helena. What a surprise.'

Helena turned and saw him, and he remembered how he must look, his hair stuck to his forehead and neck from mowing the long, coarse grass on a sweltering afternoon, his shirt with grass-stains on it, his old tennis-shoes without laces. Then he forgot all that, seeing her pinched, tense face. He frowned. 'Are you all right?'

Helena bit her lip. 'Joseph, I'm sorry, I forgot it's your day off. I'll go away again.'

'Of course you won't,' Joseph said. 'Come round to the back. You've rescued me from a tedious task. I'll get us something cool to drink.' He saw her hesitate, and smiled. 'Come on. It's all right. I was only mowing the so-called lawn.'

He saw her glance through the glass pane into the hallway and frown. 'Joseph, what are all those – what are they – boxes?

All that…stuff? You're not going somewhere, are you? Not leaving?' For a moment her eyes seemed wide and wild.

'No, no, it's just stuff people have left. For the church fete. I haven't got round to shifting it yet. That's why I was cutting the grass. The fete is always held in the Vicarage garden, because of its size.'

'Where do you want it put?' Helena asked. 'I can help you move it.'

'You don't have to do that.'

'No, please let me.' Her voice was low, carrying a note of desperation. 'I need to do something practical, to be useful. I need to get my feet on the ground. Anyway, it doesn't seem fair that you have to do all this by yourself.'

'Well, all right,' Joseph said. 'We'll put it in the garage. I've cleared a space. But don't lift anything too heavy.'

Helena took off her jacket. 'I'm strong,' she said. 'Don't you start treating me like something delicate. It's bad enough with Daddy and Erica.'

He bit back a comment. 'I'll come through from the back and open the door.'

Together they moved bulging cardboard boxes of random things, items for stalls, crockery, craft work. When they had finished the hallway looked dishevelled and dusty.

'Where's your vacuum cleaner?' Helena said. 'It needs a going-over in here.'

'No,' Joseph said firmly. 'I can do that myself. I'm sure you didn't come here today to do my housework. Come through to the back and sit in the shade.'

She followed him into the garden, where the ancient mower stood idle in the middle of the grass. He found a garden chair and dusted the seat off with his hands. 'Sit down if you dare,' he said. 'I won't be a moment.'

A few minutes later he came out from the kitchen with two glasses and a jug of squash on a tray. 'Sorry, I don't seem to be too well-supplied.' He poured a glassful and handed it to her.

'Thanks.' She was staring down the garden, her fine blond brows contracted. He said nothing, found another rickety chair and sat facing her.

She seemed to collect herself. 'Isn't this the weekend your friends are coming to visit?' she asked. 'Is that why you're mowing?'

'Patrick and Bert, yes,' Joseph said. 'They arrive tomorrow evening. But I'm cutting the grass because it's unmanageably long, and this is the first opportunity I've had. And because it needs to be half-decent for the fete.' He took a sip. 'Is there something on your mind? Can I help?'

Helena looked at him. 'Are you in pastoral mode, Joseph?' she asked quietly. 'Are you treating me like a parishioner in distress?'

'*Are* you in distress?'

Helena looked away. 'Kind of, I suppose. But I was hoping more for a friend than a priestly counsellor.'

Joseph kept silence for a moment, sensing that he was somehow being criticised. 'Why don't you say what's worrying you?' he said gently.

Helena swallowed. 'Joseph, something's going on and they're keeping things from me.'

Joseph cocked his head on one side. 'Who are?'

'Daddy and Erica. I came down to Compton on the off-chance to see Erica. She didn't know I was coming, but I don't always say, in case something happens and I can't make it. I had a bit of a lull with work, I'd come to the end of a particular project, and I left early. Erica was surprised to see me – she seemed pleased as always, but I felt she was on edge. There was something on her mind, and I felt, I don't know, as if I was intruding, or in the way. Then I found out why. I'd been there about half an hour, and she was distracted, kept looking at the clock and not always answering when I spoke to her, and then the back gate opened and Daddy came up the garden. He was surprised to see me too, almost perplexed, although he greeted me kindly as always. I felt awkward, something I've never felt before with either of them. Normally if we're all three together it's nice, we're all at ease, and it's one of the few times I see Daddy relaxed and laughing. Daddy and Erica are always teasing and fooling around when they are on their own.' She paused, and her voice was fretful. 'But today it was different –

they weren't laughing, they were, I don't know, *intense*. They didn't say Go away, or anything like that, but I felt, I felt...unnecessary. It was clear to me that this visit of Daddy's was prearranged, that they had something private to discuss, and I wasn't included.' She turned to Joseph, and he saw hurt and bafflement in her face. 'There are things in my family that no one seems to want to talk about. I just wish they weren't so secretive. Why don't they trust me? I'm not a child any more.' Joseph said nothing, and stared at the ground, holding his glass loosely in both hands between his knees. When he looked up she was staring at him and scowling.

'Erica talks to *you*, doesn't she,' Helena said, her voice harsh. 'She tells you things. Things she'd never say to me. Am I right?'

Joseph hesitated. 'Well, she has – '

'Why does everybody baby me?' Helena interrupted. 'How can it be right that you know things about my family that are kept secret from me? Who the hell else knows?' Her voice rose indignantly. 'My mother and brothers? Nettie? The postman?' She put her glass down on the ground and stood up abruptly.

Joseph stretched out his hand towards her, then helplessly let it fall. 'Helena, please. Yes, Erica has told me things, things she said weren't even strictly *her* business either. She asked me not to say anything. It's not for me to break that confidence. If I went around blabbing to all and sundry no one would trust me.'

'What are you saying, "all and sundry?" This is *my* aunt we're talking about! Don't I have any rights at all? Must I always be the precious cossetted baby?' Helena's eyes blazed, and she stood with her hands clenched tightly at her sides, as if she was afraid of losing control.

Joseph sighed. 'Look, I'm sorry. I didn't choose my words well. But what would you have me do? And what purpose would it serve? As far as I can see Erica is trying to protect you from unnecessary pain and worry, and it's done from love, that I do know.'

Helena crumpled into her chair and held her head in her hands. 'But I'm even more worried not knowing what's going on,' she said, her voice muffled. 'It feels like nothing is stable, and I don't know who to trust. I always thought I could trust Daddy and Erica, but I see now they're just a little exclusive society of two and nobody else is welcome. Not even me.' Her voice broke.

Joseph leaned forward and took her hand in his. 'I know for a fact that you are immensely important to both of them,' he said quietly. 'Maybe they do have something on their minds at the moment, and they'll let you know when they can.' He paused, and cleared his throat. 'I don't blame you for feeling I haven't been altogether straight with you. It's not the way I like to be, believe me. It makes me really uncomfortable. I just hope you can see my difficulty, because I would hate to think you didn't trust me.'

Helena drew her hand away from his and folded her arms. She looked at him, almost imperceptibly shaking her head, and blinked away the last of her tears. 'Of course I think you are an honourable man,' she said bitterly. 'But perhaps I felt my peace of mind might be at least as important as your sense of honour. I'd come to trust you, to feel you were different – oh, I don't know!' She turned away, and held up her hands in a gesture that spoke of impatience and embarrassment. 'That's why I came here when I felt so, I don't know, disoriented. Of course I believe you are trustworthy, in general. But perhaps I thought – ' A flush rose in her cheeks, and she pressed her lips together. Joseph waited. 'I don't know, perhaps I thought you cared more than you obviously do. Look, I'm sorry, I'm expressing myself badly, I'll just go.' She stood up again, slinging her bag over her shoulder.

Joseph stood also, facing her. 'I wish you wouldn't go, feeling like this,' he said, his voice low. 'Of course I care, and I feel bad that I can't help.'

Helena drew herself up. 'Don't worry about it,' she said proudly. 'I won't be the first person ever to feel isolated. You should understand that, if anyone does. That's what surprises me, I suppose. But of course, it's my aunt that's your concern, if anyone is. Why should you care about me, or my father, for that matter? I'll get back to London now. Thank you for the drink.'

Joseph stepped back. 'You make me feel very inadequate,' he muttered.

Helena shook her head. 'That wasn't at all what I had in mind,' she said softly. 'Goodbye, Joseph.'

Summer 2008: London

At the corner of Marlborough Street a small service cul-de-sac turned back from the road at right angles. On one side stood a huge hotel, many storeys high; on the other, at the far end, beyond the bare brick wall of a department store, was a chapel, used for occasional services but also for meetings and modest conferences, and maintaining a small library of inspirational books. Ewan Fraser often slipped into the chapel on his way home from work: it was a minor detour as he walked to the Tube, and he liked the way the never-ending roar and grind of the London traffic suddenly faded and dimmed as he approached its doors. At this time of the late afternoon, with offices beginning to empty and the streets to fill with hurrying commuters and shoppers, it was a particular haven, as well as being a space to take breath and put on a mantle of spiritual strength before the inevitable stresses of home. Although it was utterly different from the monastery where he had spent two years in his youth, something about its atmosphere sparked a fleeting image of his life there. Today, as he pushed open the door and looked around, the memory was strong, and a surge of nostalgia washed over him, as if his hands were somehow reaching out to that lost place of blessing. The monastery, he knew, still thrived; the lost place was in himself.

The chapel was open, but there seemed to be no one about, and the space reserved for worship was clean, fragrant and empty. Tall yellow lilies stood, stately in brass vases, on each side of the altar, and the summer sun shone through the nineteenth-century stained glass, colouring the blond wood of the floor with red and blue and green. Ewan slid into a seat at the back and put his briefcase by his feet. He leaned forward, resting his elbows on his knees, and closed his eyes. No prayer came to him, only a wordless cry of anguish and bafflement, like a black swirling in his brain and a deafening clangour in his ears, fogging rational thought and choking articulate speech. He gripped his hands together to stop them shaking. Unbidden and unwanted there rose before his mental vision an image of Erica, white and cold and still in a hospital mortuary, and he shuddered convulsively. The darkness seemed to deepen around him, the noise in his head rose to a screaming pitch, and with a gasp he forced his eyes open and raised his head.

'Oh, hello, Mr Fraser.' A young priest was standing beside him. His soft-soled shoes had made no sound on the wood floor. 'Sorry to disturb – ' The young man took a step back, frowning. 'Are you all right, sir?'

Ewan shook his head. 'Not really, no.' He forced a smile. 'It's nothing I can really discuss, I'm afraid. But I'd welcome your prayers, Mark.'

The young man squeezed Ewan's shoulder briefly. 'Of course. Look, I'll leave you to it. I'll be in the vestry if you need me.'

Ewan nodded his thanks, and Mark strode up the nave and disappeared through a small door to the right of the altar. For a moment Ewan sat, feeling the blood pulsing painfully through his head. The only words that came to him were *Lord, help me, Lord, stay with me*, repeated over and over.

At last he sighed deeply and got up, leaning for support on the back of the chair in front. Then he picked up his briefcase and walked out, heavily and unsteadily like a much older man, and closed the door quietly behind him.

Fiona Fraser picked up the jangling phone. 'Oh! Hello, Janice, dear. How are you?' She listened, her expression darkening with every moment. 'You're saying they're there now? With my husband? Two of them? Not in uniform? And – what are you saying? They've been with Moulton?' She fell silent, listening. '*Who* are looking at the cars? Oh, I see. Well, I think I do. Thank you, Janice. No, my dear, you did absolutely the right thing. Don't worry, I'm sure it's all quite routine. Yes, thank you, it has indeed been a bad business, most tragic. All right,

Janice. Thank you for calling. Bye.' She put the phone down and stood still for a few moments, staring sightlessly at the floor, gnawing her thumbnail.

'Alexander.'

'Mother.' Even though he could not see her face, Alex knew from her tone and from her use of his full name that he was in trouble. Now, however, it was no longer the 'oops, she's found me out' feeling of his boyhood or the truculent '*now* what have I done?' of his adolescence, but a deep sinking in the pit of his gut, a sweat breaking out on his face, a chill winding around his heart.

Fiona's voice was steely. 'I've had a call from my friend at Fraser's, Janice, the secretary who keeps me informed. Apparently the police have been searching one of the company cars. Did you know that?'

There was a small silence, then Alex groaned. 'Bloody hell. No.'

'It doesn't take much to put two and two together, Alexander.'

'What are they looking for?'

'Evidence, I imagine. Listen. Pick up your brother and come over here now. Whatever you're doing, whatever he's doing, this is more important. We have to talk before your father gets home.'

'Right.' Alex put the phone down and wiped his hands over his face and head, smoothing the hair back from his forehead. The feeling of dread was receding, replaced by a shaky sense of relief. He was thirty years old, he held down a job, he had his own flat and car, his own circle of friends and a steady stream of girlfriends; but the dark hole he was in seemed to him too deep to scale, and the pinprick of light at the top, broadening now, was the sharp intelligence and inflexible resolve of his mother.

Fiona Fraser contemplated her sons. Alex lounged back, his chair tilted on two legs, his arms folded across his chest. Rob sat hunched, his head in his hands, snuffling, swallowing paroxysms of sobbing. They were almost alike enough to be twins, except that Rob was an inch or two shorter, his body more heavily-muscled. She found herself remembering both their births, little more than a year between them, and her joy among all the agony that they were tough noisy little boys with a shock of dark hair, resembling Sandy Beaton, the great bear of a father she had always lived to please. She took a deep breath, banishing the memories, and fixed her sons with an unsmiling stare.

'For goodness' sake, Robert, stop your blubbing. It doesn't help. Anyone would think you were five years old, not a grown man of nearly thirty. Alexander, you'd better tell me what you've done.'

Alex let his chair crash down. He picked moodily at the tablecloth. 'You started it, actually,' he said. He looked up at his mother with a challenge in his eyes, but her expression made him flinch, and he looked away. 'You said you'd met Mr Hamilton at that cocktail party, and he'd mentioned Dad going to see him and you didn't know anything about it.'

'Yes. Well, your father told me later what he'd done, but he didn't say anything beforehand. I was chatting to Julia Hamilton and Bob came up and said, "Hello, Fiona, how are you, family all right? How's that godson of mine?" Meaning you, of course, Robert, not that he's had much to do with you growing up. And then he said, "Good to see Ewan the other day, but I must say he's looking tired, perhaps you need to tear him away from that office and take him on a cruise, ha, ha." As if I'm likely to want to go anywhere with your father, let alone be stuck with him on a boat for weeks. So I said, "Oh, where did you see Ewan?" just in idle conversation, and he looked puzzled and said, "He came to see me last week, wanted to consult me as his solicitor. Sorry, Fiona, have I put my foot in it? Did you not know?" And I pretended that of course I knew, I'd somehow forgotten, but the Hamiltons weren't fooled, and I was very embarrassed. As I said, your father did tell me eventually, but I was angry that he hadn't consulted me, and it caused even more bad feeling than usual, especially when he refused to tell me exactly *how* the will had been changed. All I knew was that he'd left a substantial sum to *her*. Then he just left me to stew, as usual. "You'll be well provided for, Fiona," he said. "There's no need for you to worry." So damned lordly, as ever. He has no idea how much the whole thing rankles.'

Alex looked at his mother, saw her flushed face, heard her noisy breathing, and waited for her to calm down. 'Right. That's why Rob and I had the idea of finding out exactly what was in it,' he said. 'The will, I mean. Give you ammunition, in case you needed it later.'

'*You* had the idea, more like,' Rob cut in, his voice thick from crying. 'Now it's all gone wrong, I can see I was just your performing monkey, *as usual.*'

Alexander turned to his brother and thumped the table with his fist. 'So why did it all go wrong?' he shouted. 'Because you can't get *anything* right, that's why! You cocked it up! If you'd stuck to the plan none of this would have happened. D'you realise the shit you're in?'

Rob's chest heaved and his eyes welled with tears. 'Of course I bloody realise,' he growled.

'Enough!' Fiona interrupted. 'Let's please not fight among ourselves. Robert, control yourself. Alexander, just tell me what *actually happened.*'

Alex shrugged. 'I remembered Helena telling us about that carer woman, what's her name? Betty? I don't know, anyway, she takes, took, Aunt Erica out every afternoon if the weather was fine, around three o'clock, regular as clockwork. We thought one of us could poke around her place while she was out, take a look at the will, without anybody knowing. We worked it all out. I lifted Dad's key to her front door – he just leaves it on the hook, so it was easy. Rob got it copied while he was out on site one day, and I put the original one back and Dad never twigged. We picked a day when we knew Dad had been down to see her the day before. If it hadn't all gone wrong –' he shot a venomous look at his brother – 'this bit of it was a bit of a laugh, working out how we could cover our tracks. Like when we were kids. We had the idea of not using our own cars because they're kind of noticeable, also we could leave them in the Golf Club car park to prove we were there. So, we decided to book a round of golf, borrow one of the four-by-fours, park it out of sight somewhere near the golf course fence, then turn up at the Golf Club and sign in. Made ourselves a nice alibi. The idea was that one of us would hop over the fence, leaving the other one to cover for him this end, take the BMW down to Compton, rifle through Aunt Erica's place, take a photo of the will, and come back with no one the wiser. Then we were going to finish the golf, sign out of the club, pick up the work car and take it back. We even bought gloves so we wouldn't leave any prints. Not that we expected anyone to find out what we'd done. The only thing to decide was who was going to do it. We just tossed a coin and Rob got it. I wish I'd done it myself. I should have known he couldn't think straight in a crisis.'

Fiona frowned. 'How did you get past Moulton? The man who looks after the cars?'

'It's easy,' Rob said huskily. 'We've done it before. If we ever needed a car, he'd cover for us, and we'd slip him a twenty.'

'So we add bribery and perjury to the list, then,' Fiona said grimly.

'To be fair to Moulton,' Alex said, 'he's a crabby old git, but he's very loyal, and he couldn't have known what we were planning. When we wanted it before it was to take our mates out somewhere.'

'If our cars were off the road,' Rob said. 'Once it was just because we couldn't afford any fuel. And another time Alex's car was being valeted because one of his mates was sick in it after a night out.'

'But Dad doesn't like us taking the work cars for what he calls stupid reasons,' Alex said. 'And we're only supposed to borrow them at the weekends, and we're supposed to book them out properly, like everyone else. But we can usually get round Moulton.'

'All right, all right,' Fiona said. 'Please don't turn this into some kind of boyish prank. You two could be looking at prison, remember that. Go on, Alex, tell me the rest.'

'It all went off OK,' Alex said. 'Rob climbed the fence, hopped into the BMW and drove away. I waited for him on the Golf Course. But when he got back he was in a hell of a state. I couldn't get any sense out of him. He was yelling and crying and saying we were going to get done and it was all my fault. I don't see how, but he always blames me.'

'Robert, tell me what happened,' Fiona said sternly.

Rob looked up at her with pleading in his eyes. 'Mum, I never meant to hurt her. I swear I didn't. I know we all can't stand her – at least not you and me and Alex, I know she's got Dad and Helena eating out of her hand – and you've always told us she's a sponging useless layabout, and I was kind of annoyed because maybe she was going to get our money as well – but I wasn't going to hurt her. I thought she was going to be out, didn't I? So when I let myself in I didn't even bother to be all that quiet. Obviously I put the gloves on, parked the BMW round the back, out of the way, and I was careful no one saw me going in. But that road's so quiet, I needn't have worried. All the neighbours are ancient. That time in the afternoon they're all asleep in their armchairs. So I let myself in, went into the lounge and started going through the drawers. And then I got the shock of my life. I swear I nearly passed out. Because she was there, in the conservatory. I hadn't seen her – she was behind the wall, in that high-backed electric wheelchair of hers, with her back to me. There I was, going through the drawers – and I found the brown folder with all her papers in it straight away – when suddenly she spoke up. 'What in hell do you think you're doing?' she said in that growly voice of hers. I nearly had a heart attack, I tell you. Then she turned the chair around and faced me. 'You! What are you doing in my house? Going through my things?' She wasn't scared, Mum, she was furious, and she wasn't talking quietly. I could see the conservatory door was ajar and all the windows were open, so I was terrified the neighbours would hear and come running. She could have shouted for help any minute!

'Mum, I tried to shut her up. I tried to threaten her, but she wasn't scared. She was getting louder and louder. And then I heard a door open, and voices really close, and I saw her next-door neighbour coming out into his garden. Mum, he was only a few yards away! I panicked.' He flinched away from his mother's implacable eyes and studied the tablecloth. For a moment he was silent, breathing deeply. 'I lost it. Any moment I knew he'd see me. I didn't stop to think. I grabbed the ends of her scarf and pulled them tight. All I wanted to do was shut her up. But then, when she went quiet, I opened my eyes.' He looked up, and his face was bewildered and bleak. 'I shut them when I was choking her. I couldn't stand to see her face. But I swear, Mum, I swear on a stack of Bibles, I didn't mean to hurt her.' He lowered his head onto his arms on the table top and sobbed.

'But that's not all he messed up,' Alex said contemptuously. 'Tell Mum what else you did, Rob.' Robert, his voice strangled with weeping, said nothing. 'Well, I'll tell you, then, Mum. He thought it would be a good idea to steal her phone. He thought it might keep the police off our backs for a while. He took the whole package of her papers too, and trashed the bungalow to make it look like a burglary. So he thought. But what he did led them more or less straight to us, the fool.'

'Well, it probably wouldn't have taken them long to come sniffing round us anyway,' Fiona said sombrely. 'Please tell me you've disposed of the stuff carefully, Robert.'

'It's all right, Mum,' Alex said. 'I burned the papers and chucked the phone in the river, down by -' he stopped abruptly, seeing his mother's tanned face suddenly drain of all colour. He swivelled in his chair, almost toppling over. Ewan was standing in the doorway, staring at his wife and sons, his face a stiff mask, his eyes glazed.

'Dear God in heaven,' Fiona muttered. 'How long have you been standing there?'

Ewan looked at her, his expression unreadable. 'Long enough.'

Rob looked up, saw his father, and uttered a strangled cry. 'Dad, you've got to believe me! I didn't mean to hurt her! Please, say you believe me!'

Ewan looked at his younger son, his face a blank. When he spoke, his voice sounded strange, as if it belonged to someone else. 'Oh yes, I believe you, Rob,' he said slowly. 'I believe you are a bungling fool. I believe you have been manipulated by your brother, and both of you have been corrupted by your mother.'

Fiona leapt to her feet, scraping the chair legs against the wood floor. 'You hypocrite!' she hissed. 'How dare you blame me!'

Ewan turned his dead stare on her and spoke calmly. 'I do blame you,' he said. 'You have systematically poisoned our sons' minds against my sister – a woman who has never done any harm either to them or to you, except in your own warped mind. Out of jealousy and spite you have encouraged hatred at the centre of this family.'

'No,' Fiona spat. 'I don't accept any of that. It's your responsibility from the beginning. You have always favoured Helena. No wonder I have been left with the raising of the boys. And you have the gall to criticise *me!*'

'What you say is not true,' Ewan said. 'You deal in lies, as always. Lies and half-truths. From their childhood onwards you have taught our sons to think of a disabled relative as a burden, someone to be ignored, and now someone to be discarded. What's all this about? My will? Don't you have enough? Must you scratch and claw every penny, whether you need it or not? Frankly, your attitude disgusts me.'

'What right do you have to be so bloody high and mighty?' Fiona screamed, her face red, her eyes bulging. 'You can deny favouring Helena over the boys if you like, but you can't deny favouring your precious sister over me. You even killed to defend her.'

'You're talking rubbish, insane rubbish,' Ewan said coldly.

'No, I'm not,' Fiona taunted. 'Tell your sons how you drove your own father to his death.'

Now it was Ewan's turn to blanch. 'You know nothing,' he said, but his voice faltered.

'I know plenty,' Fiona said savagely. 'Because I had a conversation, many years ago, with someone who was there.'

'Neil Gilmour?' Ewan said. 'He didn't see anything.'

'Oh, but he knew you'd taken the gun,' Fiona said. Now she felt that she was gaining the upper hand her angry voice dropped, replaced by a silky slyness. *That* didn't come out at the Inquiry, did it? Perhaps if it had they mightn't have been quite so ready to absolve you of all responsibility.'

Alex looked from one parent to the other, frowning. 'What the heck are you on about? And what does it have to do with Rob and me?'

Fiona turned back to them, her eyes narrow, a half-smile twitching the corners of her mouth. 'I'd say it has everything to do with what's just happened,' she said. 'I'd say that's where it all began, when Lachlan Fraser fell into a freezing river and drowned because his son was waving a gun at him. So you see, boys, your father's nothing like as saintly and perfect as his admirers would have you believe. He's a bloody hypocrite.' She turned to Ewan, her voice hardening and rising as she smelt victory. 'We all make mistakes. But yours are on a grander scale than most. This is your fault – your neglect – your selfishness – your arrogance. You have created your own disaster.'

For a moment there was silence. The two young men stared at their father with their mouths open, and Ewan stood frozen in the doorway, his briefcase still in his hand, his face chalk-white. Then they all heard a door slam, and the sound of running feet, and Helena appeared at Ewan's side, breathing hard. She took in the scene, her brothers sitting goggle-eyed at the table, her father motionless in the doorway, her mother standing, leaning forward, with her fists clenched.

'What's going on?' Helena cried wildly. 'What's happening? Why were the police at Daddy's office? And why are you all here like this?'

Ewan dropped his briefcase on the floor and put his arm round her shoulders, murmuring something inaudible.

Helena looked at him and frowned. 'Daddy, tell me! Don't cut me out!'

'I've just observed to your brothers,' Fiona said, her voice harsh and jeering, 'that this particular plaster saint, your father, has, after all, despite his reputation, feet of clay.'

'For heaven's sake!' Helena cried. '*What* are you talking about?'

Ewan seemed to gather himself together. He turned to Helena, hugging her to him. 'Please, sweetheart, don't worry. I'll explain everything, I promise. But right now I have something very urgent to do.'

'Wait, Ewan!' Fiona said. 'You can't just leave, not like this! We have our sons to think of, their future. We have to hire a barrister, the best we can find. Maybe we need to get Rob out of the way, even out of the country!'

Ewan waved his hand impatiently. 'No. No, that would be stupid. It's like shouting, "I'm guilty!" from the rooftops. Just leave it to me, please. It's my problem, and I will deal with it.' He looked directly at Fiona. 'In your warped way, you have told the truth,' he said bleakly. 'I *am* to blame. Please, do nothing for the moment. Say nothing to anyone. I'll contact you when I can.' He turned to Helena, murmuring into her cloud of hair. 'Trust me. Don't be afraid.' Then he picked up his briefcase and was gone.

Helena stood frozen for several long moments, shaking her head slowly. Then she cried out, 'Daddy!' She raced out of the kitchen and into the hallway. The front door was open, and she saw his car roar out of the drive and disappear down the road.

She ran back to the kitchen, her hair flying, her eyes wild.

'All right,' she said grimly, 'it's time to come clean. Time to stop keeping me in the dark. Did I guess right?' She fixed her brothers with her bright blue stare. 'Did you two, did you…' her voice shook, '…murder Erica?' They didn't answer, their heads bent, their shoulders hunched, and Helena, her face and voice stretched with anguish and horror, whispered, 'You did. Oh, God, you did, didn't you?' She turned to her mother. 'And did you plan it?' she cried. 'Did you hate her so much that you set your bulldogs to kill her?'

Fiona sank down onto the chair. 'No, of course not. Helena, I may be many things, but stupid isn't one of them, I hope.'

'Is that all you can say?' Helena demanded in amazement. 'Your sister-in-law is murdered by your sons, and you feel absolutely no remorse? You may not be stupid, but you are certainly without human feeling. And your sons are both stupid and callous. As you have raised them to be.'

Fiona lifted her chin, but the defiance had gone from her voice. 'If they are stupid, then at least they are loyal.'

'Ha!' Helena cried. 'What do any of you know about loyalty? Or kindness? Or truth?' She turned away from them and ran out of the room, slamming the door behind her. For a moment she hesitated in the hallway, tears running down her face, gasping for breath; then with an exclamation she hurtled through the front door, wrenched open the door of her car where it stood on the drive, and flung herself into the driver's seat. She reversed, and paused at the gate, looking to the left, as if trying to guess the direction her father had taken. There was no sign of him. For a moment she sat, breathing deeply as the engine idled. Then she wiped the tears from her face and shook her head. Slowly she eased the car out onto the road and accelerated away.

Summer 2008: Compton

The Desk Sergeant at Compton Police Station, a man called Fenner, approaching retirement, with many years of largely routine experience behind him, looked up when the door opened, and showed mild interest. He was a Compton man, and there was rarely any excitement or drama in Compton. Even now, with a murder on the doorstep, he wasn't at the sharp end. Len Fenner had no problem with this; he was looking forward to tending his garden, perhaps taking more adventurous holidays, and spending more time with his baby grandson. Fenner looked with polite curiosity at the man who had entered, and was now standing in front of the desk, staring around with the look of someone who has suddenly found himself on another planet. 'Can I help you, sir?' He noted the visitor's immaculate suit and silk tie, then his worn and worried face.

'My name is Fraser,' the man said, and Fenner registered his slight Scottish accent. 'I have come to confess to the murder of my sister, Erica Pole.'

Fenner dropped the pen he had been using, and bent to pick it up, emerging red-faced from under the desk. 'Right. Um, sit down, please, Mr Fraser. I'll get someone to attend to you.' He went to a door behind him, opened it, and put his head into an inner room. He spoke to someone there. A moment later Constable Walsh appeared, straightening his jacket.

'Stay with Mr Fraser, Walsh,' Fenner said. 'I just need to go upstairs.'

Fenner bounded up the stairs at twice his usual sedate pace, strode along the corridor and knocked on the Incident Room door.

'Come in.'

Hazell and Louise Gordon were sitting at the table, empty mugs and scattered papers on the table between them. Louise frowned. 'Everything all right, Len?'

Fenner closed the door behind him. 'Glad to see you're still here, sir,' he said to Hazell. He cleared his throat, turning to Louise. 'There's a Mr Fraser downstairs. Says he murdered his sister.'

Hazell uttered an inarticulate exclamation and got to his feet. 'Is someone with him?'

'Walsh, sir.'

'All right, Sergeant.' Hazell paused for a moment, his lips pursed, his dark brows frowning. 'Here's what we do. Sergeant Fenner, you start the custody process. Don't ask Mr Fraser any questions at the moment, except the routine things. Find out if he wants or needs a solicitor. You know the drill. And, Sergeant – don't hurry.'

'All right, sir, understood. Where shall I put him?'

Hazell turned to Louise. 'You've got a Detention Room here, haven't you?'

Louise nodded. 'It's small, but then, we don't need to use it very often. Len, er, Sergeant Fenner knows what to do. We can leave it to him. What do you want me to do, sir?'

'Nothing at the moment,' Hazell said firmly. 'Just be here to take any calls that might come in from the lab, and to back Fenner up if he needs it, seeing as you know the ins and outs of the case and he doesn't. In a way it's better that he doesn't. Just fill in the paperwork, Fenner, and if you finish before I get back to you just give Mr Fraser a cup of tea, put a constable outside the door and leave him to sweat for a while.'

'Right you are, sir.' Fenner backed out of the room and closed the door.

'What are you going to do, Fred?' Louise asked.

'I'm going to ring my governor at Stockley,' Hazell said. A small smile twitched beneath his moustache. 'He's not one to interfere unless it's necessary, but he needs to know this latest development. He might well have something to say.'

'About anything in particular?'

'About that rare phenomenon,' Hazell said. 'The false confession.' Now the smile broke out, lighting up his dark eyes.

Louise's eyes widened. 'What? Are you sure it's false?'

'No,' Hazell said, sobering. 'I'm not sure of anything, and I won't be till we know the results from the lab. Maybe not even then. But do *you* think Mr Fraser murdered his sister?'

Louise shrugged. 'It seems unlikely, yes. But strange things happen, and he did have access to the BMWs, and by his own admission he was out of sight in his office for several hours on the afternoon Mrs Pole died, with no one to vouch for him. I find it hard to believe, but he could have done it.'

Hazell nodded. 'Which is why we keep an open mind, and why we keep Mr Fraser right here under our roof.' He paused at the door. 'Seems our little chat this afternoon has borne fruit, doesn't it? Sometimes it works, sometimes it doesn't. Right, I must go and ring my boss.'

Fiona Fraser picked up the phone in the hall and dialled. 'Julia, hello! It's me, Fiona. Yes, thank you, fine. How are you? Good.' She paused, half-listening, nodding. 'Yes, don't things like that *always* happen at the weekend? Julia, dear, is Bob about? He's just got in, that's great. Already provided with his evening tipple, I hope. Yes, please, just a quick word.' She waited. 'Hello, Bob. Had a good day?' She listened for a few moments, drumming her finger-tips quietly on the telephone table. 'Mm, yes, I can imagine. No, I haven't rung up just for a chat, nice as it always is to chat to you. I need you to be rather discreet, Bob. As our solicitor, but as a friend too. We do indeed go back a long way, and that's why I'm counting on you. We might need you to find us a barrister, Bob. Or perhaps it's a criminal solicitor we need. I'm not sure, but you'll know. Someone you can recommend.' She paused and listened. 'Well, I don't want to go into too much detail just now. But yes, it might have something to do with that will you did for Ewan, not directly, you understand. I'm sorry to be cryptic – I'm hoping things will pan out so we don't need legal advice, but I feel it's sensible to hope for the best and prepare for the worst, don't you? Just hold yourself in readiness, if you would. Give it some thought.'

Helena pulled into a service station off the motorway, parked, and switched off the engine. For a moment she sat quite still, her hands in her lap, her eyes closed. Then she heaved a deep sigh, brushed away a tear that had leaked from her eye, and took her phone out of her handbag.

With some hesitation she keyed in a number and waited. After a few moments the answerphone cut in. 'Christchurch Vicarage, Joseph Stiles speaking. There's no one to take your call at the moment. Please leave your name and number and I'll get back to you.'

Helena snapped her phone shut with a small groan.

Now what? Joseph, where are you? What do I do now? Why am I calling you, anyway? What can you do? Do you even care, except in a general way as a kind-Christian-vicarish person? The thing is, pathetic though it seems, I don't have anyone to talk to. If I told my friends what had happened, they would be horrified. Erica is dead. Daddy is nowhere. I don't have anywhere else to go. A sob heaved up from her throat, and she swallowed hard. *Stop feeling sorry for yourself, Helena. What would Daddy have said when you were a child in a fix? Pray, of course. But I'm not sure I have the right. I've not really given God much room in my life the last few years. Will he mind? That's another thing I could ask Joseph, if only he was there.* She sighed. *I'll go down to Compton and wait, even if it does make me look like a stalker. Who else is there?*

Joseph cycled round the corner, saw the blue Golf and came to a jolting halt. He got off the bike and wheeled it cautiously along the pavement. Helena was sitting in the driver's seat with the window rolled down. She was leaning back against the seat, and her eyes were hidden behind dark glasses so that he couldn't see if they were open or closed.

He cleared his throat. 'Hello, Helena.'

She sat up with a little gasp, and pulled off the sunglasses. Her eyes were red and puffy, and he felt something contract inside his chest.

'Oh, Joseph! I must have nodded off.' She leaned down and fumbled for her handbag which had fallen into the passenger footwell.

'How long have you been waiting?' Joseph said. 'I'm sorry – I was visiting Mrs Sivyer. She's housebound. And then I bumped into the chairman of the Parish Council and he buttonholed me about the churchyard.'

'It's all right,' she said quietly. 'You have to work, I know that. I haven't been here long, but it's so hot I couldn't stay awake.' She looked at him anxiously. 'Are you terribly busy?'

'I'm not busy at all,' he said gently. 'And I'm very pleased to see you. Come inside. It'll be cooler indoors.'

Helena wound the window up, got out of the car and locked it. Joseph thought she looked different, somehow crumpled, her uprightness and confidence gone. He went ahead of her, pushing the bike, and opened the front door with his key. 'Go on in – I'll just take the bike round the back. The study's probably the coolest place at this time of day.' He watched her walk into the hall, and sensed from everything about her that something was very wrong.

A few moments later he found her in the kitchen.

'I've put the kettle on,' she said. 'I hope that's OK.' She was leaning on the worktop with both hands.

'Good idea.' He hesitated. 'Helena, what's happened? Something has, even I can see that.'

She looked up at him, and her expression was bleak and slightly wild. 'What, apart from my aunt being murdered, is that what you're saying? Isn't that enough?'

'Of course it is – I didn't mean – '

Suddenly she seemed to cave in on herself, and she half-fell into a chair. She gave a low sound like an animal howling, and burst into a torrent of weeping, her elbows resting on the table, her hands in her hair.

'Oh, Helena. Whatever is it?' He came and stood beside her, and awkwardly put his arms round her heaving shoulders.

'I'm sorry, I'm so sorry,' she gulped, her voice strangled with sobs. 'I shouldn't have come. It's not your problem.'

He drew up another chair, sat in it, and pulled her into his arms. Her head rested on his shoulder so that he had a faceful of flyaway hair. He felt the weight of her, slumped against his chest. 'You did absolutely the right thing,' he said firmly. 'And it's as much my problem as you want it to be, whatever it is.'

Her sobs abated and she took a deep breath. She drew away from him and looked up. Her face was flushed, her eyes and nose running. 'Do you have a handkerchief?'

He pulled a wad of tissues out of his pocket and handed them to her. In the midst of his concern he almost smiled, because she looked so young and dishevelled. He watched solemnly as she blew her nose and wiped her face. 'Joseph, I came because I didn't know where else to go. I realised I don't have anybody, not any more. Erica is dead, and it looks like one or both of my brothers did it.'

'*What?*' Joseph's eyes widened.

'I knew something was up at work,' she said, her voice low. 'Someone said there were policemen in the car bay, forensic people going over one of the four-by-fours. I realised they suspected someone, I don't know, someone who worked there, or, worse than that, one of my family. I went up to see my father, but they told me he'd left. Daddy *never* leaves work early, Joseph. So I drove home. And I found them all there, my mother, my father, both my brothers. Rob was hysterical. Daddy was standing in the doorway, looking at Mummy all shocked, and then he, he…just left. Said there was something he had to do, that he would sort it out. And I chased after him, but he'd gone. And then I had this terrible thought – it was like a cold black cloud descending on me – and I went back into the kitchen, and I said to them, "You did this, didn't you?" and nobody protested, except my mother, who denied putting them up to it. Even then, oh, Joseph, even then, knowing that one of her sons is a murderer, she was so cold and calculating.' She shook her head. 'I just don't understand. Why?'

Joseph sighed. Her hands were in her lap, clutching the sodden tissues, and he took them in both his own. 'I don't know, Helena,' he said. 'But you were right when you said they kept things from you. More than you realised, I guess.' He shifted uncomfortably in his seat. 'Look, maybe this isn't the time, but I want to apologise.'

'What for?' She looked up at him, frowning slightly.

'For being so useless. For being a coward, for thinking about myself instead of you, for being no kind of help.' She stared at him, and he stumbled on. 'When you came to see me last week – Thursday, wasn't it? Erica was still alive then – you were worried and hurt and basically I just, I just – pushed you away. Why did I do that? Can you tell me? Why am I such a blundering, cowardly idiot?'

She was silent for a moment, blinking away the last of her tears. 'I don't believe you are any of those things,' she said. 'I think Erica was right. She said you were afraid. And perhaps you have every reason to be.'

'Well. You are very forgiving. But here I am again, talking about myself when it is you who have come for help.'

Helena bit her lip. 'What did you mean –' She hesitated, and he tilted his head enquiringly. 'What did you mean, just then, when you – no, never mind. Joseph, where did my father go? What do I do now?'

'Let me make a cup of coffee,' Joseph said. 'We'll think straighter with some caffeine racing round our veins.' He got up, and took two mugs from the cupboard above the sink. 'I'll make instant – it's quicker.' A few minutes later he put a steaming mug in front of her and slid back into his chair. 'Have you eaten?'

Helena wrapped her hands round the mug. 'I had a sandwich at lunchtime. I couldn't eat anything now. The coffee's a good idea, though.'

Joseph took a sip and grimaced. 'Ugh, I must buy better coffee. This stuff's like dishwater. OK – think, Helena. What do you suppose your father meant when he said he had something he must do? Was he implying that he was going to try and sort something out? Would he be going to see someone?'

Helena nodded. 'Obviously I don't know what went on before I arrived, what was said, how long Daddy had been there, how much he knew. But Mummy wanted to hire a barrister to defend Rob. She even said we should get him away, out of the country. Daddy said no, that he would deal with it. And Joseph, this is the weird part, he looked at Mummy with such a strange face, and he said it was *his fault*. How can that be? *He* didn't kill Erica. He would have given his life for her, I'm sure of that.'

Joseph was silent for a long moment. He shook his head. 'You and your father need to have a long chat, it seems to me,' he said. 'He has to trust you. Maybe now he will, because you are all he's got left. Think hard, Helena. He has, for his own reasons, accepted the blame for Erica's death. Why?'

Helena stared at him, her eyes wide. 'To protect the boys,' she whispered. 'Oh, Joseph! He's here, isn't he!' She leapt to her feet, scraping the chair against the floor. She paused. 'Here, or at Stockley. Where would he have gone?'

'There's only one way to find out,' Joseph said. 'Wait a moment.' He got up and left the room. A moment later he came back, holding a slip of paper in his hand. 'Inspector Hazell left his card when he came to interview me. Ring him, Helena.'

She sat down again, unhooked her bag from the back of her chair, and fished out her phone. For a moment she hesitated, then she looked at the card on the table and keyed in the number. She put the phone to her ear and waited. Her face looked pinched and pale, and Joseph tried to smile encouragingly.

'Hello, is that Inspector Hazell?' Helena said after a few moments. 'This is Helena Fraser. Is my father with you?' She listened, chewing at her lip. 'Thank you. I'll be there in five minutes.' She closed the phone. 'That's where he is, Joseph. The Inspector wouldn't say anything, but I know my father.' Her eyes welled with fresh tears. 'He's gone to the police to say he murdered Erica. I hope to God they don't believe him.' She got up again and started towards the door. 'I have to go and find him. He's making a terrible mess of everything.' She looked back at Joseph. 'You will come with me, won't you?'

'If you want me to, of course. I said your problems are mine, if you want them to be. I meant that.'

She stared at him from the doorway, frowning. 'I'm not sure I understand what that means. But we can't talk about it now. We must go to my father. I have to make things right – as right as they can be, anyway. We'll take the car.'

The five-minute journey to the police station went by in silence. Helena was pale, her hands gripping the steering wheel tightly. Joseph, watching her under lowered lids, saw the effort she was making to be resolute, to stay calm and focused. At some point during that short drive he allowed into his conscious mind the implications of his admiration for Helena, her loyalty to her dysfunctional family, her crusading spirit even in a lost cause, her bravery in the face of disaster. He silently admitted all this to himself, and knew that he could quite easily have swept her into his arms and confessed the tenderness of his feelings. It took an equal resolution on his part to do no such thing. He could not see how it could possibly help, and he kept quiet.

Helena parked outside the police station and sat staring out of the window, her hands still on the steering wheel.

'We'd better go in,' Joseph said quietly.

'Yes, of course.' She got out of the car and locked it. Joseph followed her up the shallow steps and through the doors.

Len Fenner looked up from behind the desk. 'Can I help you?'

For a moment Helena looked as if she had forgotten where she was and why she was there. Then she collected herself with an effort. 'My name is Helena Fraser. I believe my father is here. I would like to speak to him, please.'

'Well, Miss Fraser, I doubt that will be possible,' Fenner said in his rather pompous manner. 'Mr Fraser is in custody. I'll have a word with the Inspector. Just a moment.'

He picked up a phone, dialled, and a few seconds later spoke quietly into it. He replaced the receiver. 'Inspector Hazell will be down to see you, Miss Fraser. Take a seat, please.'

Joseph and Helena had barely sat down when they saw Hazell coming down the stairs. He strode over to them, his face serious under his dark brows. He shook hands with both of them. 'Miss Fraser, Reverend Stiles. How can I help you?'

Helena's voice was barely above a whisper. 'I need to talk to my father. Please.'

Hazell shook his head. 'I'm sorry, but that can't be done. Mr Fraser has made his statement. He has confessed to a most serious crime. The only person he'll be allowed to see, for now at least, is a solicitor, if he decides he wants one.'

Helena reached her hands towards Hazell in a pleading gesture. 'But he didn't *do* anything! His confession is false, don't you see? He would never do anything to hurt his sister. Not in a million years! He's covering for my brothers.' Her voice cracked, and Joseph took her gently by the elbow.

Hazell studied her, unsmiling. 'Miss Fraser, I understand your desire to defend your father. But how much do you really know? Can you prove your father was not involved, or that your brothers were?'

Helena shook her head, gulping back tears. 'It's true I don't know much. But I can tell you what I heard them say.'

'Them?'

'Yes. My father, my mother and my brothers.'

'When?'

'This afternoon, just before my father came here to tell you this terrible lie.'

'All right. Come upstairs to my office and I'll take your statement. You too, Mr Stiles.'

They followed him up the stairs and a short way along a corridor. He opened the door to a tiny room. 'Please come in and sit down.' He indicated two hard chairs.

'Just tell me what you saw and heard, please, Miss Fraser. Later on you can make a signed statement to my Sergeant. From the beginning.'

Helena swallowed. 'I was at work. Someone told me that the police were searching the company cars. I was afraid. I thought they, you, must suspect someone at Fraser's. Then I had the awful thought that you suspected one of the family. I knew my father had been in his office during the day and I went up to talk to him, but his secretary said he'd gone home. He never left early, never. He was, I mean is, a workaholic. I felt very confused, frightened really. I didn't know what to think. So I got in my car and drove home.'

Hazell nodded. 'Describe the scene to me as you recall it, in as much detail as you can. Exact words if possible.'

Helena shook her head. 'I can't remember everything that was said, not verbatim. They were in the kitchen. My brothers were sitting at the table. Alex was just sitting there. He looked shocked. But Rob had been crying, I could see that. My father was in the doorway. He still had his jacket on, and he had his briefcase with him. My mother said to him that he must hire a barrister, that they should think of their sons' future. She said "their" future – she meant both of them. Then she said they should get Rob away, even out of the country. My father said no, that it would be an admission of guilt, he said it would be like shouting "I'm guilty!" from the rooftops. So of course at that point I thought that Rob had done it, that he'd killed Erica –' She took a deep sobbing breath. Hazell waited, and Joseph tightened his hold on her arm. 'And that my mother wanted him defended, of course. I didn't know what had been said before I arrived, and I couldn't understand *why* Rob would have killed her. It was beyond my comprehension. But then my father said a strange thing. He looked straight at my mother and said something like, "You're right, I *am* to blame. Don't do anything. I will sort it out.' And then he left. I ran after him, but I was too late.' She looked up at Hazell, frowning in perplexity. 'At first it seemed simple. Awful, but simple. Rob had done it, and my mother wanted to protect him. But then my father said he was to blame. I didn't understand. But I didn't then, and I don't now, believe my father was responsible. Not for a moment.'

'Just the facts, please, Miss Fraser,' Hazell said. 'What did you do after your father left?'

'I went back to the kitchen. I said to my brothers something like "You did it, didn't you?" But they didn't say anything. They seemed dazed. I said to my mother, "Did you put them up to it?" Because, you see, Inspector, she has always detested my aunt. I don't really know why. The reasons I can think of don't seem enough for hatred like that.'

'What did she say, Miss Fraser? Please try to remember as exactly as you can.' Hazell looked at her levelly, his pen poised above his notepad.

'She said, "No, of course not. I wouldn't be so stupid." Not "I would never do such a wicked thing." Nothing like that. I accused her of being utterly callous and bringing up her sons to be the same. And then I left.'

'You came straight to Compton? Why? Did you think your father was here?'

'No, not then. I came because, because I – because I wanted to see Joseph. I didn't know what to do. It was when I was talking to Joseph that I thought my father would be here. I understood what he was thinking, or I thought I did.'

'You had no firm, factual reason to assume that he would be here, did you?'

Helena looked at Hazell directly, her chin lifted. 'I assumed it because I know him, Inspector,' she said stiffly. 'You may think I am biased, and of course I am. But you *don't* know him.'

Hazell sighed. 'Look at it from my point of view, if you will. I have to deal in known facts that can be substantiated. No one wants to think that someone close to them could be capable of a terrible crime. What you heard your father say could be a simple statement of fact – that he was to blame. And I'm afraid that's what he's still saying. That he killed his sister. He's made a signed statement to that effect.'

Helena groaned and held her head in her hands. Joseph felt her tremble with the effort of self-control. She looked at Hazell, her eyes wide and wild. 'The problem is, Inspector, that it just isn't true. It may be convenient, but it isn't true. You say people don't want to think of someone they love being capable of a crime. But you must remember that if it wasn't my father, then it was my brother – one of them, or both of them together. If my aunt had to die, I would much rather it had been at the hand of someone not related to me.' She stood up. 'I'll wait downstairs, if you don't mind.'

Hazell also stood. 'I will do my utmost, Miss Fraser,' he said quietly, 'to find out the truth. Not just what is "convenient." But the fact remains: your father has confessed. Your brothers have not.'

Almost an hour and a half later, her statement read back to her, Helena left the police station. She sat in her car in the car park, shaking uncontrollably. 'I can't believe this is happening,' she whispered. Joseph said nothing. Seeing her agony, he could think of nothing to say that might have offered some light, some grain of consolation. She looked at him. 'It's like a nightmare, Joseph. It's bad enough that Erica is dead, murdered by her own family. But that my father should be suspected – when he has spent most of his life supporting her in one way or another. It's unthinkable.' She gripped his arm. '*You* don't think he did it, do you?'

'No, I don't,' Joseph said. 'But don't forget, I've never met him.'

Almost to herself, Helena said, 'What story could he have spun? To make them believe him? What motive could he have had? Or don't they care? Is that all that matters? That *someone* is convicted? Even if they aren't guilty?'

Joseph shook his head. 'Maybe that happens sometimes. I don't know. I hope it doesn't, but we have to face the fact that we live in a wicked world. I don't believe that is what is happening here, though. From what I've seen of Hazell, I'd say he's an honest man.'

'Joseph, we have to do something. I can't let this go on.' She managed a smile, but it was bleak. 'I suppose you'll say we have to pray.'

'I do say so, of course. But I have been praying, for all of you.'

'Does it work?'

'Yes, certainly. Just not in the same way as a magic trick.'

'I think maybe you'll have to explain that to me one day.'

He took her hand. 'I'd be very glad to have the opportunity.'

Helena pulled her hand away and clapped it to her forehead. 'Oh! What am I thinking? What did the Inspector say? We have to get Daddy a solicitor! I'll ring Bob Hamilton now.' She rummaged through her handbag and found her phone. 'I'm pretty sure I've got his number in here somewhere.'

A moment later she was speaking very fast. 'Bob? It's Helena Fraser. Yes, it's a bit of an emergency. It's my father. He's in police custody, Bob. I need you to –' She came to a sudden halt, and Joseph saw her brows contract. 'What? What did you say?' She listened, and suddenly exhaled. 'Yes, I see. Well, thank you. Yes, I understand your dilemma. Goodbye, Bob.' She closed her phone.

'What is it?' Joseph said. 'What's happened?'

Helena turned to him. 'I should have thought,' she said, her voice breaking. 'How stupid I am, Joseph.' Suddenly her control was in disarray, and her eyes welled with tears. 'Bob said – he said – he can't help Daddy. Because my mother has already been in touch with him. She's asked him to find a barrister for Rob and Alex. Basically he's acting for her. He was so embarrassed, Joseph – he didn't know about Daddy confessing. Of course he didn't.' She bent her head and sobbed, her whole body rocking. 'How are we going to help him now?'

Joseph slid across the passenger seat and wrapped his arms round her, soothing her as if she were a hurt child. 'Helena, we'll think of something. We will. *And* pray.'

Frederick Hazell watched them, unseen, from the window beside the door of the police station. He shook his head and sighed. In a few short hours the case seemed to have taken a course he could not have predicted. 'Something needs to happen here,' he muttered to himself. 'Someone needs to start telling the truth.'

'What's that, sir?' Len Fenner looked up from the desk.

'Nothing, Sergeant,' Hazell said. 'If anyone wants me, I'll be upstairs with Rivers.'

'Right you are, sir.'

Hazell started for the stairs. Then he paused as the phone rang on the desk. He saw Fenner pick it up and speak, and he waited, tension in every muscle.

'Sir? I think you need to take this one. It's Sergeant Gordon. She's got some news.'

Hazell bounded back down the stairs and grabbed the handset. 'Yes, Sergeant?' He listened, and a slow smile spread over his face. 'Excellent. It's what I was waiting for. Now maybe I can get the warrant for the Fraser premises. I'm particularly interested in taking a look at the brothers' flats. Good work, Sergeant. Yes, get back here as soon as you can. I'm going to need you.' He replaced the receiver.

'Good news, sir?' Fenner said.

'Very good indeed, Sergeant Fenner. The lads found a fuel receipt in one of the cars they were looking at. Tucked down beside the seat. Name of the garage was on it, and the date, *and* the time. And a lovely little thumbprint.'

'A matching thumbprint, sir?'

'It looks very possible. A greasy partial, with just enough points to identify our suspect. Obviously it'll take time for full confirmation. But I'm cautiously hopeful. Now I must go and talk to Rivers.'

He was at the top of the stairs when the phone rang again. 'Sir, it's for you,' Fenner said. 'Do you want to take it up there?'

Hazell paused. 'Who is it, Sergeant?' He sounded impatient.

'A Mr Ronald Moulton, sir. From Fraser's. Says he has important information. Must speak to you *immediately*. Sounds rather a cross gentleman, sir.'

To his surprise, Fenner thought he heard Hazell chuckle. 'You could say that. Yes, I'll be delighted to speak to Mr Moulton. Put him through.' He paused. 'Oh, and Sergeant? When Louise Gordon gets back, send her up to me straight away. No hanging around to make tea or pass the time of day. We need to move a bit sharpish.'

Driving back to the Vicarage, Helena said suddenly, 'There's just one more thing I can do, Joseph.' She glanced at him, and he raised his eyebrows enquiringly. 'I'm going to talk to Rob.'

Joseph pursed his lips. 'It's worth a try.'

She parked the car outside the house, turned to him and took off her sunglasses. Her eyes were weary. 'You don't think it's a good idea?'

'I don't know your brother, of course. Perhaps it's best not to be too hopeful.'

She smiled sadly. 'Sometimes I think that's almost your motto, Joseph. Never be too hopeful.'

Joseph shook his head. 'It can be a battle, keeping hope at bay,' he said wryly. 'But come in. We'll melt out here. You can sit in the garden and call your brother, and I'll make myself scarce.'

She got out of the car and locked the door. 'Are you sure I'm not keeping you away from something important?'

'There's nothing more important at this moment than...' Joseph hesitated. 'Well, trying to get something straightened out here.'

Helena trailed after him up the path. 'If only.'

He let her in to the darkened hallway, smiling slightly. 'Now who's throwing hope away?' He led her out into the garden and set a chair in the shade of a pear tree.

'There's no need to go anywhere,' she said. 'It's only Rob. Just my fool of a brother.'

'I'll go and make us something to drink.'

A few minutes later he came out again, a tall glass in each hand. Silently he handed one to her. She was sitting quite still, her hands in her lap, holding her phone.

'Well? Did you speak to him?' Joseph said.

Helena took a sip. She seemed to speak with difficulty. 'Yes, for a very brief moment. I rang him on his mobile, but he's obviously still at the house with my mother and Alex. I asked him what was going on, and I think he was going to tell me. He sounded confused and, I don't know, bewildered, as if he doesn't really understand what's happened. He started to cry and say things like, "I didn't mean it, Nel, I didn't ever mean to hurt her." And then I heard my mother in the background, not what she said exactly, but her tone, sharp and cutting, and he mumbled, "I can't talk to you any more, I've got to go." But before he went I yelled at him, "Rob, you have to tell the truth!" And there was a silence, and I thought he'd hung up, but then he said, "I don't think I know what that is any more. Truth." And then there was a sort of scuffle, and the phone went dead. When I tried to ring him back it went straight to voicemail. So I never got the chance to tell him what Daddy has done.' She took another gulp of her drink, not looking at Joseph. 'He's been got at, hasn't he? She's told him not to speak to me. I never knew till now just how divided my family is. This has made it horribly clear.' She looked up then, and Joseph winced to see the hopelessness in her face. 'We're split down the middle, against each other. Mummy and Alex and Rob, against Daddy and me and Erica. Why did I never see it before? Why did it have to be like this?' She shook her head. 'I feel as though I've lost them all, in one awful afternoon.' For a moment she fell silent. 'You know who Rob reminded me of, Joseph? Pontius Pilate. Didn't he say something similar? Didn't he say, "What is truth?" Please tell me I'm not going crazy. There is such a thing, isn't there? It's not all just how each one of us sees it, changing every day, every hour, depending on the circumstances?'

Joseph shook his head. 'Of course I believe in absolute truth. But I'm not sure that now's the time for theological discussion. Helena, what are you going to do?'

She finished her drink, and set the glass down. She stood up. 'I'm going back to London, Joseph. But I can't go home, not now. As things stand I don't really have a home.'

Joseph stood also, facing her, his expression sombre. 'I wish you wouldn't go.'

'Well, I can't stay here, can I? Your reputation would go up in a puff of smoke.'

'Where will you go?'

'I'll ring my friend Becca. She'll let me stay with her for a while. She's very kind, and probably the most discreet of my friends.' She saw his expression and laid her hand on his arm.

'Don't worry. I'm not going to throw myself in the Thames or anything like that.'

'Please. That's a most terrible thought.'

'My father needs me, I think. Even if he doesn't know it yet. I have to stay sane for his sake.' She started towards the side gate, and Joseph followed her round the house to the car. She opened the driver's door, and a gust of hot air billowed out. 'Joseph, thank you for being there for me today. I really appreciate your kindness.'

'How can I contact you?' Joseph said. 'Something might happen at this end. Or I might think of something.'

'I'll write down my phone number, and Becca's address.' She scrabbled in her bag, found a pen and a scrap of paper, and hastily scrawled. 'Here.' She handed it to him, and he stared down at it, not daring to look at her. She brushed his cheek with her lips, and for a moment he smelled her perfume. 'Goodbye, dear Joseph.'

Inspector Hazell looked round at his assembled team. It was a small group of people, but the room was small and the day was already uncomfortably hot.

'Right, everybody. Are we all absolutely clear as to what we're going to do?' There were one or two murmured replies and throat-clearings. 'I'll just recap briefly, in case anyone was asleep earlier. Sergeant Gordon will take Win Davies and Barry Simmons in one car. Des Walsh will come with me in the other. He'll drive because I have some phone calls to make on the way. I'm going to call some old colleagues of mine in the nicks closest to where each of the Fraser brothers lives, and they're going to lend me a couple of bodies. One stationed outside Alexander's flat, one outside Robert's. They don't live together, but they're not too far apart, as it happens. Then I'm going to ring each of those two gentlemen in turn and tell them we have a search warrant to go over their property, and they're most welcome to attend if they choose. Somehow I think they'll be there. Meanwhile Sergeant Rivers –' he nodded to the Stockley sergeant who was leaning up against the window, his arms folded – 'will escort Mr Ewan Fraser to Stockley nick. I want to hold on to Mr Fraser senior for a few days yet, while we get this business sorted out – if we do. I don't want him here at Compton, there just aren't the facilities, but I want him out of the way and sweating. He's muddied the waters for us with this confession of his and given us more work we didn't need. Once Rivers has handed him over to the kind people at Stockley –' he grinned briefly – 'he'll pick up a couple of extra officers and join whichever one of us needs him. With me so far?' There was a rumble of assent. 'Are you all absolutely clear what we're looking for?' He looked around at them all, his gaze keen.

There was a moment of silence, punctuated by shuffling feet. 'Something to link the brothers to the murder scene,' Constable Davies mumbled.

Hazell nodded. 'Specifically, as far as the search warrant is concerned, we're looking for Mrs Pole's phone. It'll be nothing like something the brothers might own. It's big, a brick, with big numbers. And also a brown or beige cardboard folder containing documents – things like title deeds and birth certificates.' He sighed. 'But Win is right – we're looking for *anything* that might be used as solid evidence. Something the Fraser brothers can't wriggle out of. I'm pretty sure one of them did this, but so far I can't actually prove it. Unfortunately we have to face the possibility that we won't find anything. Maybe they've destroyed the stuff we're looking for. Which is why I want them there while we're searching. Neither of them is a practised criminal. They'll be worried. So we'll also be listening to what they have to say and watching their every move. It's all we've got, and the best we can do, so I'm counting on every one of you to have your eyes open and your ears flapping. OK?' Nods and muttered agreements answered him. 'All right, let's go.'

The team edged out of the small room, straightening jackets, adjusting belts and ties. Hazell and Gordon followed them down the stairs.

'Sir.' Hazell turned to Gordon, his eyebrows raised, seeing her frown. 'What if,' she stumbled, 'what if, as you said, we don't find what we're looking for?'

Hazell watched the team leaving, getting into the waiting cars. 'Then, Sergeant,' he said softly, 'we start again.' He paused. 'Mrs Pole was a believer, wasn't she?'

'What?'

'A Christian, used to praying.'

'Well, yes, I guess so. She attended the church.' She looked at Hazell, puzzled.

'Perhaps she can have a word with the powers-that-be, wherever she is now,' Hazell said grimly. 'See that justice is done.'

Gordon shook her head, smiling faintly. 'I don't know much about these things, sir. But something tells me that isn't quite the way it works.'

Hazell sighed. 'No, I dare say not. No point speculating anyway. Let's get to London.' A thought struck him. 'Hold on a minute. I want to catch Rivers before he goes.' He bounded down the last few steps and out of the door. 'Tom.'

Rivers turned. 'Sir.'

'Good, you haven't gone to collect Mr Fraser yet.'

'Just going to get him.'

'Once you've handed him over at Stockley, I want you to follow me to Robert Fraser's address. Bring whoever's with you. Don't hang about at Stockley any longer than you have to – they'll know what to do with Mr Fraser.'

Rivers nodded. 'Right you are, sir.'

'Good. Then we're on our way.'

Summer 2008: London

When Walsh swung the car into the access road that served the block of flats where Robert Fraser lived, the first thing Hazell saw was the police car parked at the kerb. A constable sat behind the wheel. Hazell also noted the red Lexus parked a few bays away, but he ignored it. As soon as Walsh parked he got out and went to speak to the driver of the police car. 'Morning, Constable. I'm Inspector Hazell, Stockley CID. You on your own?'

'No, sir. Constable Fernandez is outside the door of Mr Fraser's flat.'

'Oh. He sounds Spanish.'

'She, sir. British as you and me, Brazilian great-grandfather I believe.'

Hazell jerked his head towards the Lexus. 'You got here before them?'

'Yes, sir. Told them we all had to wait for you.'

'Good man.' He took a deep breath and walked the few yards to the red Lexus. As he approached the window wound down. 'Good morning, Mr Fraser. And Mrs Fraser too. What a pleasant surprise.'

Fiona Fraser rapped her elegantly-manicured nails against the steering-wheel. 'I wouldn't call any of this *pleasant*, Inspector,' she said coldly.

'Then we should get it over with as quickly as possible,' Hazell said. He turned to Rob, who sat hunched in the passenger seat, gnawing his finger-nail. 'You didn't drive yourself, then, Mr Fraser. Not at work this morning?'

Rob opened his mouth to speak, but Fiona cut in. 'My son was with me,' she said. 'He could hardly be expected to do a day's work with all this going on.'

'Mr Fraser,' Hazell said, not looking at Fiona, 'my search warrant allows me to break into your property. I've informed you of our intentions so that you can let us in yourself and be present while we work. However, only you will be coming in with us. I'm afraid, madam,' turning to Fiona, 'I must ask you to remain in the car.'

Fiona drew herself up. 'I don't see why.'

Hazell inclined his head politely. 'You don't have to see why. You just have to do as you are asked. Please don't make this more difficult. Come with me, please, Mr Fraser.'

'Wait a moment, Inspector!' Fiona said imperiously, her eyes glinting with suppressed fury. 'We have the right to see that search warrant.'

'Certainly.' Hazell drew an envelope out of his pocket, removed its contents and handed them to Rob, who hesitated before passing them to his mother. Hazell nodded to Rob, who clambered out of the car and stood beside him, his hands in his pockets, his shoulders slouched, a picture of abject misery barely hidden beneath a veneer of defiance. Fiona scanned the paper, smiled slightly, nodded, and handed it back to Hazell. She lifted her chin. 'You'll find nothing,' she said.

As she was speaking a second police car slid into place beside the Lexus. Sergeant Rivers got out, followed by two uniformed constables. 'You didn't waste any time, Tom,' Hazell said approvingly. 'Good. Indoors, please, Mr Fraser. Lead the way.' He followed Rob along a short path that led to the block of flats. As they approached the door opened and a young woman emerged, pushing a pram, struggling with the closing door. One of the young constables held it open for her, and she went through, her mouth open and her eyes wide. Hazell glanced back at the Lexus. Fiona Fraser was gesticulating, her phone clamped to her ear. 'We've stirred up *that* little pond well and truly, Tom,' Hazell murmured.

Rob opened the door of his ground-floor flat with his key. The young constable guarding the door saw Hazell and murmured a greeting, standing aside to let him through. Hazell looked round the flat from the doorway. 'Looks like you've had a burglary, Mr Fraser.'

Rob shrugged. 'Haven't had time to tidy up,' he muttered. Hazell turned to the team assembled behind him. 'All right, everybody, gloves on, get to work. You know what to do. If you've got any questions, ask Sergeant Rivers.' He watched as they fanned out into the sitting-room, then spoke to Rob. 'Do you have access to a garden, Mr Fraser?'

'Through the back. I don't use it much, because it's shared.'

'Show me.'

He followed Rob through the sitting-room where the officers were already working, into a disordered and malodorous kitchen, where dirty dishes lay piled in perilous heaps on the draining-board and fast-food cartons dribbled uneaten food onto the cluttered table. Rob turned a key in the lock of a curtained door at the back and gestured to Hazell to go through. A dried-up strip of grass ran the breadth of the building, peppered with rotary washing-lines, barbecues and children's toys. 'Any of this yours?' Hazell asked. Rob shook his head. Hazell looked at him, seeing the bleary, shifting eyes and the stubbly chin, and Rob glanced away. 'Are you feeling all right, Mr Fraser?' Hazell said. 'You don't look well.' Rob mumbled something inaudible and shivered. Hazell looked around for a few more moments. 'Right, we'll go back in.' He strode back into the flat. 'Perhaps you'd like to sit down, sir,' Hazell said. Rob subsided onto a stained sofa, kicking aside several empty glass bottles. He looked at Hazell and shrugged. 'Had a few people round night before last,' he said. His voice was hoarse.

'Stay where you are, please,' Hazell said crisply. He walked through to the kitchen where Rivers was going through cupboards and drawers with meticulous precision. He glanced at Hazell and pulled a face, wrinkling his nose. Hazell smiled faintly. 'Anything?' he said, his voice low. Rivers shook his head.

'I'll go and see how they're getting on in the bedroom and bathroom,' Hazell said. He was on his way into the corridor when his phone rang, shrill and jangling. He took it out of his pocket and put it to his ear. 'Yes, Sergeant?' Rivers looked up and saw him standing very still, listening intently. He stopped what he was doing and waited. Rob, sitting on the sofa, also looked up, his mouth hanging slackly open. For a moment there was silence.

'All right, Sergeant,' Hazell said at last. 'Bag it like it's the Holy Grail. Get someone to take it to the lab straight away, and tell the lab people what we're looking for. But complete the search. And tell Simmons well done.' He flicked the phone off.

Nodding to Rivers he went back into the sitting-room and stood before Rob. 'Mr Fraser,' he said quietly, 'I think you haven't been quite honest with us.'

Rob licked his lips. 'What?'

'You told us you were on the golf course that afternoon when your aunt was murdered, with your brother.'

'I was,' Rob said, his voice low.

'But you weren't there *all* afternoon, were you?' Hazell pushed on. 'You took one of the firm's cars and went to Compton, to your aunt's house.'

Rob shook his head violently. 'No.'

'We know you did, because Mr Moulton, the man who has general responsibility for the company cars, told us so on the phone a short time ago. You paid him to lie for you, didn't you? You, and your brother, had done it in the past and you thought it'd work this time too. But obviously Mr Moulton thought it over. Especially when he found out someone had been murdered. Sensible man that he is, he told us that you and your brother took the BMW that afternoon.

He's a loyal employee, is Mr Moulton, but even he draws the line at murder.'

Rob shook his head again, gulped, but said nothing.

'And then there's the gravel stuck in the BMW's tyres,' Hazell went on relentlessly, his voice even and quiet but quite implacable. 'A good match for the gravel outside the garages at the back of your aunt's bungalow in Plough Lane. Where a neighbour saw a black BMW that afternoon. Gravel is common, of course. Could have been any gravel, you might say. But then there's the CCTV image of a dark-haired man buying fuel for a black BMW, that same afternoon, at a garage not far from Compton, a BMW whose partial plates matched the one you borrowed. Not to mention the receipt for that fuel, dated that day, found down beside the seat of that very vehicle, with a nice tidy thumbprint on it. I'm thinking that will turn out to be your thumbprint, Mr Fraser.'

Rob looked up at Hazell, shuddering, his arms clamped round himself, his eyes dark. 'So I lied,' he ground out. 'So I wasn't on the golf course all afternoon. So what? You can't prove I...' he swallowed. 'You can't prove I murdered my aunt. Not from that. Just that I'm a liar. There's no law against lying that I know of.'

'You're right,' Hazell said. 'We can't prove you're a murderer, not yet. Tell me, Mr Fraser, does your brother sometimes call you a fool? Does he look down on you a bit? Does he think he's the clever one?'

Rob scowled and said nothing.

'Because now,' Hazell continued, 'it might be you cursing *him* for a fool. Especially if that stupidity and carelessness of his lands you in jail. Perhaps your brother hasn't been quite so clever as he led you to believe.'

'What?' Rob gaped, all swagger drained away. 'Have you, have they, found something at Alex's?'

Hazell nodded. 'On its way to the lab as we speak, Mr Fraser. We'll carry on here till we've done as thorough a search as possible. Don't think of going too far, will you?'

Rob staggered to his feet. His eyes were glassy. 'Oh, my God.' He pushed past Hazell and made for the front door, stumbling as he ran.

Hazell called after him. 'Oh, one thing, Mr Fraser.' Rob stopped, not turning, his head hunched down between his shoulders. 'Perhaps you should be aware that we also have your father in custody.'

Rob's head whipped round, a frown of utter bewilderment creasing his brow. When he spoke his voice was slurred, as if he was drunk. 'My father? Whadda you saying?'

'Your father has confessed to his sister's murder,' Hazell said calmly. 'He didn't say why, and we didn't ask. Because he didn't do it, did he, Mr Fraser? You of all people know that very well.'

Rob's arms flailed helplessly, and he uttered a strangled inarticulate cry. He made as if to come back towards Hazell, but then he seemed to change his mind, turned and lurched out of the door, scuttling down the path back to his mother's car.

Rivers appeared at his elbow. 'Boss. Shouldn't you have cautioned him?'

'All in good time, Tom. He's not going anywhere. Let's have him sweat a bit longer.'

'Your call. Just don't fall off the tightrope, that's all.'

'I think we've got him, Tom.'

'I hope to God you're right.'

Summer 2008: Compton, Stockley, London

Joseph was staring at the blank screen of his computer when the phone on his desk rang shrilly. He grabbed at the handset and sent it clattering across the desk's surface and on to the floor. 'Idiot!' he muttered at himself as he bent to pick it up. 'Hello?' Even to his own ears his voice sounded hesitant, almost nervous.

But it was not Helena – it was Bert Greville, keeping in touch, as he had promised. Joseph felt a pang of disappointment, then guilt.

After a few pleasantries Joseph said, 'It's good of you to call, Bert. Have you heard from Patrick?'

'He bends my ear once in a while,' Bert said. 'He has an unhealthy interest in your murder case. I keep telling him it's absolutely none of his business, but you know Patrick.'

'Yes, indeed. A terrier with a bone.'

'Sorry, Joseph – better go. George is at my elbow – some crisis. Good to hear you're doing all right.'

'Thanks, Bert. Bye.'

Joseph replaced the receiver slowly. The blank screen seemed to stare at him accusingly; it was already Friday, and Sunday's sermon remained stubbornly unwritten. He could think of nothing he wanted to say to his congregation – nothing that had any meaning. *Forgive me, Lord. I'm no use to you right now. Not much use to anybody, not even myself.*

He stared at the phone, willing it to ring. He had picked it up a few times in the last couple of days, had even keyed in Helena's number, but had stopped the call even before it had begun to ring. What did he have to say to her? Nothing that could be of any help. He wondered what she was doing. Was she going to work? Was there talk in the office, did people stare, did they stop what they were saying when she walked in? Was anyone helping her, was anyone on her side? He found it impossible to contemplate, and yet, try as he might, inevitably his ungoverned thoughts circled obsessively back, and his mental vision was filled with her pinched face, her shadowed eyes, that cloud of bright hair. He groaned softly.

With the thought of finding some inspiration for his sermon, he opened his Bible. But before he could decide what to read, the phone rang again. He picked it up, carefully this time, feeling his heart banging painfully against his ribcage.

'Reverend Stiles? Frederick Hazell.'

'Oh, hello, Inspector.' Joseph frowned, puzzled. 'Has there been some development?'

'Yes, sir, I think you could say that. But that's not why I'm ringing you. I have had an unusual request from Mr Ewan Fraser.'

'Is Mr Fraser still in custody?' Joseph asked. 'Has his daughter been able to see him? I know she was most anxious about him.'

'Mr Fraser is in the Detention Suite at Stockley police station,' Hazell answered. 'And that's where he'll stay until things are a bit clearer. I'm not letting anybody see him, for reasons which should be obvious, but you can tell Miss Fraser, if you see her, that her father is well enough in the circumstances.' He paused and cleared his throat. 'Mr Fraser has asked me if he can talk to a priest, Mr Stiles, and I'm inclined to let him. He seems disturbed. You're the only one I can think of, and you have a connection to the family. Will you come and talk to him? I'd have to have a constable in the room, of course, but otherwise you'd be reasonably private.'

Joseph hesitated. 'Would what he says to me be confidential, Inspector?'

'It can't be, can it, sir? You must see that. I'm not primarily interested in his spiritual state, but I have to know anything that's germane to my investigation.'

'So,' Joseph said, bristling. 'Am I being used as some kind of spy?'

Frederick Hazell answered as equably as always. 'Not really, sir, no. Just tell Mr Fraser not to say anything about the case. Then there won't be any problem. Will you come?'

Joseph hesitated. He looked again at his computer's blank screen, his open Bible. Then he said, 'Yes, of course. I haven't met Mr Fraser. But if he needs counsel, I'll do my best.'

'Thank you, sir. Are you free this afternoon? At about two thirty?'

Joseph thought rapidly. Was there a bus to Stockley early on a Friday afternoon? Whether there was or not, he would find a way. 'Yes, I can do that.'

'Then we'll see you later. The police station at Stockley is in Barham Road, in case you didn't know.'

The bus dropped Joseph in the centre of Stockley, and he walked to Barham Road soon after two forty. He pushed through the swing doors of the police station, and was met with a cool stare from the female officer behind the desk. Like many a law-abiding citizen before him, he felt a shudder of apprehension.

'Joseph Stiles,' he introduced himself. 'Inspector Hazell is expecting me.'

'Take a seat, please, sir. I'll ring up.' She dialled and spoke briefly into the phone on the desk. Then she looked up at Joseph. 'Up the stairs and turn right, Mr Stiles,' she said. 'Inspector Hazell will be waiting for you.'

'Thank you.'

He climbed the stairs and looked up a long, blank corridor. A door opened and Hazell appeared. 'In here for a moment, if you will, sir.' He held the door open and ushered Joseph into a small office. 'Do sit.' Joseph sat on the edge of a hard chair in front of a tidy desk, and Hazell perched on the desk and folded his arms. He looked tired.

'Thank you for coming, Reverend Stiles,' he said. 'I'm sure Mr Fraser will appreciate it.'

'I'm afraid I'm a little late,' Joseph said. 'I haven't got round to replacing the car that was written off. I don't seem to need a car these days, anyway. So I have had to depend on public transport.'

'I can arrange for you to be taken back to Compton later if you like,' Hazell said.

'The bus is quite adequate, thank you,' Joseph said stiffly.

'All right. Let me fill you in about Mr Fraser, as far as I can. He's sticking to his original statement, even though he's fairly sure we don't believe him. I have no choice, of course, except to behave as if we do believe him. It's rather a foolish state of affairs, and I can't move on until I receive a certain piece of information. Mr Fraser has been kept in the dark, and I think it's driving him crazy. He's very worried about his daughter, his family, his business.'

'I can't help him much,' Joseph said. 'I know very little myself.'

Hazell nodded. 'Even so,' he said, 'I think it will help him to talk to someone other than a police officer. Someone with whom he doesn't feel quite such a need to keep up a façade.'

'Why would he trust me?' Joseph wondered. 'He doesn't know me.'

'Perhaps not. But he knows you were friendly with his sister.'

'I suppose so.'

'If you're ready, I'll take you to him,' Hazell said, sliding off the desk and flexing his shoulders.

Joseph got up. 'Please do.'

Hazell led Joseph further down the echoing corridor and through another set of doors. He put his head round another door and spoke to someone inside. A moment later a uniformed officer appeared. 'This is Constable Swinton,' Hazell said. 'He'll keep the door while you talk to Mr Fraser. He's very discreet – you can pretend he isn't there.'

Joseph nodded to the Constable and all three passed through another door into another long corridor. Through the occasional window Joseph saw a school playground, deserted now, and the back of a parade of shops. Hazell stopped in front of a door marked Detention Suite, and knocked softly. A voice answered from inside, and he stood by as the Constable unlocked the door with a key on a ring at his belt. 'Stay here for a moment, Swinton.'

Hazell went into the room, and Joseph followed. He saw a modest-sized room, sparsely furnished. There was a neutral-coloured carpet on the floor, a high window with vertical blinds, a low table and two utilitarian armchairs. On the table was a tray with a cup and plate on it. A man got to his feet from one of the chairs. He was of medium height, slim and wiry, with white hair brushed back. The sleeves of his crumpled white shirt were rolled up, revealing well-muscled, freckled arms. His face was pale, his eyes red-rimmed.

'Mr Fraser, Reverend Stiles,' Hazell said. 'I'll leave you gentlemen to talk. If you need anything, speak to Constable Swinton.' He left the room, and Swinton came in and stood by the door. Ewan and Joseph shook hands.

'Good of you to come,' Ewan said. His voice was rough. 'Please, do sit down. I suppose they might bring us some tea later.'

Joseph lowered himself into one of the armchairs. 'Are you being treated well, Mr Fraser?'

'Please, if you feel able, call me Ewan. I almost feel I know you already – my sister spoke of you often.'

'Let me say how dreadful we all feel at Christchurch,' Joseph said, his voice low. 'Erica was a valued friend. I will miss her very much.'

Ewan gripped his hands together tightly. 'Thank you.' For a moment it seemed that he didn't know what to say, but when he began to speak his words came out in a rush, almost incoherently. 'You must think it strange that I asked the Inspector to see if you would come. But the fact is I'm going out of my head with worry. I've been in here for days, and the police are telling me nothing. I don't know how anyone is or what is going on. They treat me well, as far as it goes – they are civil and bring me food and drink and so on, but it's like a kind of torture being so out of touch. Anything could be happening!'

Joseph took a deep breath. 'I don't know much,' he said. 'Obviously I'm not in the Inspector's confidence. I can tell you how Helena is, and that's about all.'

'Is she all right?' Ewan's voice was pleading, almost desperate.

'Apart from being extremely worried about you, she is coping,' Joseph said. 'She knows you are here – she guessed, after you left London, and phoned Compton police to confirm it. Other than that I'm afraid I can't be of much help. Are you worried about your business?'

Ewan shook his head. 'No, not so much, not yet. I'm sure rumour is rife, but there are good people in place who can carry on quite well on their own. I organised it to run without me if need be. I'm concerned for my wife and my sons, but I suppose you know as little as I do. But you *can* help, if you will.'

'Gladly,' Joseph murmured.

'I need to tell someone why all this has happened,' Ewan said, and to Joseph's dismay his bright blue eyes, so like Helena's, filled with tears. 'You're an intelligent man. I dare say you don't believe I murdered my sister. Be that as it may – I am still responsible for this mess.' He took a deep breath. 'How much do you know? I'm sure you know some of it. What did Erica tell you?'

Joseph frowned. 'She told me she was very concerned about you. You were worried about your health, and convinced that you had inherited an illness from your father which would render you incapable of taking care of her. Hence the changing of your will.'

'Yes,' Ewan whispered. 'That's what set off these terrible things. If Fiona hadn't got wind of it – or if I had been more open with her, as I should have been – none of this would have happened. Perhaps...perhaps my dear sister would still be alive.' His voice choked and died, and he pulled a grimy handkerchief from his pocket and wiped his face. He looked up, swallowing, and Joseph saw the immense effort he was making to master himself. 'You see,' he said quietly, 'over the last few years I've been thinking. And doing a bit of research. I've come to the conclusion that my father – my mad, terrifying father whom I hated so fiercely as a boy – was not so much bad as ill. I became convinced that he was suffering from an undiagnosed degenerative condition which led to dementia.

There are a few illnesses that will do that, but I won't bore you with the medical details. The worst of it was that at least two of these conditions could be inherited. Hence my concern for my own health. But it's not just that. It made me feel even more conscience-stricken at what I did, all those years ago. How I drove him to his death, drowning in an icy river. I loathed him for years. It's only recently that I've seen there could be another side to it all: that he was sick and needed help.'

'But what could you have done?' Joseph said quietly. 'You were just a boy, away at school most of the time. How were you to know? You acted out of ignorance, perhaps, but also out of protective love for Erica. I know how terrified she was, how isolated she felt.'

'Yes, she said the same thing, and I've tried to convince myself of it,' Ewan said. 'Just recently, with all that has happened, not very successfully.'

Joseph stirred in his chair, trying to find a more comfortable position. 'If I may ask,' he said, 'have you had any medical tests, any results, anything concrete?'

Ewan sighed. 'Yes, lots of tests, and plenty of results – all but one. Everything has come back negative. Perhaps Erica was right – perhaps I have been suffering from paranoid delusions, perhaps it's all stress and fatigue, perhaps none of this needed to have happened. That one last test is probably the most crucial, and maybe those results are already in, but how am I to find out, all the while I'm detained here?' His fingers drummed on the edge of the table. 'Whatever the results may be, whether I am well or ill, I should have told Fiona what was going on. Why didn't I? Because I was sure she would react badly. How far back do I have to go? Being instrumental in the death of my father? Marrying the wrong woman because I'd got her pregnant at a drunken party? Whichever way you look at it, it's all down to me. And now I'm responsible for the death of the person I loved more than anyone else. But perhaps I've been wrong there too.'

Joseph shook his head. 'Love is not wrong. We all make many mistakes, and not all of them are our fault. You acted as you thought best, and it has rebounded horribly. But there are many things you have also done well, and many people who have benefited. And there is still one thing you can put right.'

Ewan looked up, frowning. 'What?'

'You can trust the daughter who loves you. You can treat her like the adult she is.'

Ewan groaned. 'Yes. My poor Helena – I have tried to protect her too. I have not been wise, have I?' He rested his head in his hands.

Joseph was silent. He glanced up at Constable Swinton, who was making a studied effort to be invisible, standing by the door with his hands behind his back, staring up at the high window. He looked back at Ewan, hearing his ragged breathing.

After a moment Ewan leaned back in his chair, his eyes closed. 'Joseph,' he said, 'do you have a Bible with you?'

'Yes.' Joseph fumbled in his pocket and brought out a small edition.

'Turn to Lamentations, if you will,' Ewan said. 'Read me chapter one, verse fourteen. Please.'

Joseph turned the pages and looked up at Ewan. 'Here we are. "He took note of all my sins and tied them all together; he hung them round my neck, and I grew weak beneath the weight." Is that how you feel?'

Ewan nodded. 'And there's that other bit in Jeremiah, where he's having that contest with the other prophet, Hananiah, wasn't it? There's something about a wooden yoke being broken and being replaced with an iron yoke. That's exactly it: all that weight dragging me down, and the worst of it is I deserve it.'

'But if we're looking to the Bible for answers,' Joseph said, 'you've conveniently forgotten the one who has the last word.' He thumbed further forward through the pages, found what he wanted and looked up at Ewan. 'This is Jesus speaking: "Take my yoke, and put it on you, and learn from me, because I am gentle and humble in spirit; and you will find rest. For the yoke I will give you is easy, and the load I will put on you is light." All the wrong turnings, all the blind stumbling, all the legacy of the past – he can deal with it. But I'm not telling you anything you don't know already, am I?'

Ewan shook his head. 'Of course I know it. I have known it for years. But just now I seem to have forgotten it. Just as I have forgotten my daughter, her loyalty, her strength. You're right, Joseph – there are good things I can still do. And she must be my priority. But my wife is wrong in one thing: I have always loved my sons as well. It's just that somehow I felt we weren't quite on the same wavelength. With Helena it was always so much easier.'

Joseph hesitated for a moment. 'Ewan, would it help, do you think, if we were to pray together? Now?'

Ewan swallowed. 'All right. But I'm not sure if I can find any words.'

'I don't think God cares what you say. He knows your heart. And I'll continue to pray for you, of course, when I'm away from here.' Ewan nodded, biting his lip. 'OK, let's be quiet,' Joseph said. He breathed deeply for a few moments, letting the silence gather. He glanced up at Ewan, who was leaning back in his chair, his hands folded in his lap, his eyes closed. 'Lord our Father, look in mercy on your servants who are confused and hurting. Forgive us our folly and our failures, especially our failure to come to you. Please draw close to your servant Ewan in his time of trouble and sorrow, and let him know that you are alongside him and those he loves. Help him to turn from everything that keeps him far from you, and show him how he can set wrongs right, with your gracious help.'

He paused, and Ewan cleared his throat and spoke. 'Lord, I am a sinner and a fool, and I ask your forgiveness. Thank you for sending Joseph to me today. Bless my lovely Helena and my boys as well, and help me to be a better father than I have been in the past. Lord, I need your guidance. Don't abandon me.' His voice ground to a halt, and as he looked up Joseph saw tears running down his cheeks. 'Amen,' Joseph whispered. He stretched across the table, took Ewan's hand, and for a moment gripped it. Then he let go, patted his shoulder, and stood up, stretching.

The door opened a crack, and Constable Swinton turned. Joseph saw him slip outside, and heard muttered voices. Then the door opened wide, and Inspector Hazell walked in.

'Gentlemen, I'm sorry to disturb you, but I have news.' His face was sombre. Ewan and Joseph stared at him, saying nothing. He sighed, thrusting his hands into his pockets. 'I have, this afternoon, heard from the lab. It was the last piece of the puzzle.' He turned to Ewan, his eyes dark, his brows contracted. 'We searched your sons' premises,' he said. 'And we found the partially-burnt remains of a brown cardboard folder in Alexander's barbecue – the folder that contained your sister's papers, including her copy of your will. There wasn't much of it, but there was enough: fingerprints were found, belonging to both your sons, and to Mrs Pole herself.' He paused, looking at Ewan's stricken face. 'As a result, we have charged Robert with murder, and Alexander with conspiracy. They are in custody now.'

Ewan gave a strangled cry, and crumpled into the chair. Joseph laid a steadying hand on his shoulder, and felt the other man's convulsive shuddering. The Inspector looked at both of them, his face inscrutable, and continued to speak. 'I must spell out for you, Mr Fraser, the implications of these latest developments. I did not for a moment believe that you murdered Mrs Pole, but I had no choice but to behave as if I did. However, you have at the very least wasted police time with your false confession, and it may be that you are also looking at the more serious charge of attempting to pervert the course of justice. We will see. Whatever happens, you will continue to be detained for the time being.' He paused, and there was silence for a moment.

Then Ewan croaked, 'Please, Inspector, will you now let me see my daughter?'

Hazell sighed. 'Yes, I think I can permit that. And I'll make sure she knows to bring you some fresh clothes, and whatever else you need, within reason. Now I have a great deal to do, so if you gentlemen are done, Mr Stiles needs to leave.'

Ewan gripped Joseph's wrist. 'Joseph, thank you for coming. For everything. Please, be where I can't be. Be with Helena. You're a good man, my sister trusted you, I trust you. Erica had her plans, I know. I laughed at them at the time, her fantasies, her matchmaking. Perhaps she was wiser than I realised. But

I'm not asking anything of you except to be a friend to my daughter. She needs someone she can trust.'

'You need have no worries on that score,' Joseph said softly. 'I've already told Helena – her concerns are mine. If that's what she wants. That part of it I can't be sure of. Now I have to go. Try to be of good courage, and don't forget to keep praying. Even here, shut away and lonely, you have the best friend there is.'

Ewan nodded. 'I know. Thank you for reminding me. Goodbye, Joseph.'

Joseph watched as Constable Swinton locked the door of the Detention Suite. In silence both he and Hazell followed the uniformed officer back down the corridor, hearing from behind the locked door Ewan Fraser's muffled howl, a sound so desolate that Joseph winced and stumbled. 'Inspector – '

Hazell held up a hand to silence him. 'Come to my office for a moment.'

He spoke briefly to Swinton, who nodded to Joseph and disappeared through a door. Again Hazell led the way, back to the room in which he had spoken to Joseph when he first arrived. 'Sit down, Mr Stiles. Would you like a cup of tea?'

'No, thanks. I'll wait till I get home.' He turned to Hazell and spoke urgently. 'Please, Inspector, what can I say to Helena? Is everything public now? When can she come and visit her father? You've seen the state he's in – well, she is distraught too, and she's done nothing wrong. On the contrary. And when will Erica's – Mrs Pole's – body be released? Will her brother be allowed to attend her funeral?'

'One question at a time, please, sir,' Hazell said. 'As to Miss Fraser, you can tell her what you think fit. She can come and see her father when she likes. For the rest, it's not necessarily under my control, as I'm sure you realise. I may have some influence, but that's all.' He frowned. 'I understand your concern. Believe me, I do. I understand Mr Fraser's actions – I am also a father. That doesn't mean I condone them. He has mocked and flouted the law, and I am a policeman. If he is charged simply with wasting police time, he can be bailed, and he can go to his sister's funeral. Whenever that takes place. If the more serious charge is brought – well, that's another matter. But he has also flouted the laws by which you, and he, profess to live, hasn't he? At the very least, he has lied consistently. I realise that Mr Fraser is suffering, and that his actions – however reprehensible – have been those of a loving father and brother. But the law must be upheld, or we will all be in trouble.' His tone softened. 'I understand your concerns too, sir, and they do you credit. But you must trust me to do my job. You'll hear from me soon. Just ask Miss Fraser to phone me. Any time.'

Joseph stood outside the police station in the sunshine, feeling at a loss. He looked at his watch, and an idea began to form. It was still early – barely three-thirty. Stockley, unlike Compton, was on a railway line. He could take the train to London and meet Helena as she left work. He could tell her what had happened that afternoon, face to face. He grimaced a little, aware that while this made sense and was kinder, it was still quite transparently an excuse to see her.

He walked slowly through the busy streets of the town towards the station, thinking about Ewan Fraser's life and the events and decisions that had shaped it; and he thought of Erica, whose life was now beyond such influences – beyond corruption, but also, in an earthly sense, beyond hope of change. He thought of his own life, seemingly stalled in a comfortable rut, but somehow poised between past and future, and he realised that he had the opportunity, perhaps uniquely, to consider deeply how things might be changed for the better.

He arrived at the railway station and looked at the timetable on the wall. He had a twenty minute wait for the next London train. He crossed the line to the appropriate platform and sat on a bench. Then another idea came to him. *Twice in one afternoon – I'm excelling myself.* He took out a dog-eared notebook from his jacket pocket, and found a pen which he poised over a blank page. *Sunday's sermon – could I use Ewan's experience, my own,*

Erica's – not named, of course – to say something about the limitations of human wisdom, the vastness of divine mercy? Something about the folly of pride, God's ready forgiveness, the necessity of turning to God, of leaning on him, of claiming his promises? Perhaps. I probably should say something about Erica anyway: she was one of us, people knew her. He remembered a conversation with Erica, more than a year ago. *It was the day after Caroline was killed. We were talking about forgiveness, about forgiving oneself, and I said, if I recall correctly, that I should learn to practise what I preach. Yes, that was it. Have I? Probably not. I have that in common with Ewan Fraser, that sense of being a hypocrite. Telling other people the best way, but far from living it myself.*

He began to scribble notes on the page, and to refer to the small Bible he always carried with him, and he continued to think and write, sitting in the train as it thundered through the countryside and the suburbs till it came to a sighing halt in the London terminus.

As he alighted from the train he looked at his watch again. It was a quarter to five – when did Helena finish work? He strode across the thronged concourse to a map of the Underground and plotted his route. He would need to hurry; he was only a few stops away from the Haven offices, but it was a busy time of day with people leaving work early for the weekend. He ran briskly down the steps and fought his way onto the crowded Tube train just before the doors squealed shut.

A short while later he emerged into the sunlight again, screwing up his eyes against the brightness, and turned a few times to work out his direction. Just after ten past five he found himself in a large paved square, surrounded by tall glass-and-concrete office buildings, and encircled by roads noisy with traffic. In the centre of the pedestrianized area grew a clump of trees, and beneath them were wooden benches. He made his way towards them, then stopped. He turned back to the Haven building and pushed through the revolving doors into a large, high-ceilinged reception area. He walked up to a long, polished desk and spoke to a young woman behind it. 'Can you tell me if Helena Fraser is still in the building, please?'

The woman looked at her computer screen for a few moments. 'Apparently so, sir. She had a meeting scheduled at four, and she hasn't signed out. Would you like to wait?' She indicated an area where there were leather sofas and low tables with magazines.

'Thanks – I'll wait outside.'

He found a space on one of the benches facing the Haven offices door, and settled himself next to a woman in dark glasses speaking intensely into her phone, oblivious of the outside world. While he waited, his eyes never leaving the Haven entrance, he carried on his train of thought. *I must tell Helena what I have been thinking – somehow it seems important, relevant to both of us, and to her family. But do such things interest her? Will she understand? I have no idea. There are so many things I don't know about her.*

At five thirty people started coming out of the revolving doors in some numbers, but there was no sign of Helena. Joseph took out his phone, looked at it for a few hesitant moments, then keyed in her number. It rang a few times, then went to voicemail. He could happily have rung again, just to hear her say 'Please leave a message, and I'll get back to you,' but he told himself not to be a fool. 'Helena, it's Joseph. Look for me when you leave work – I'm sitting on a bench under the trees outside your office.'

Five minutes later he saw her emerge, and watched her scan the area till her eyes alighted on him. She was wearing a short, sleeveless dress with a floral design, and her hair was tied loosely back. She waved and walked towards him, her large canvas bag swinging from her hand, and he got up from the bench. As she drew closer he saw that she had caught the sun: her cheekbones were pink, scattered with tiny pale freckles. He wanted to untie her hair and see it fly free, and he fought an urge to gather her up in his arms and bury his face in its floating brightness. *Whatever's the matter with me? As if I don't know.*

'Joseph, what a surprise!' She was smiling, but then her expression darkened. 'Has something happened?'

'I've been with your father.'

'Oh!' She laid a hand on his arm, and looked at him, her eyes wide. 'Is he still in custody? How did he seem?'

'Is there somewhere we can go that's a bit quieter?' Joseph said. 'It's like trying to talk on a station platform here.'

'Everyone's going home,' Helena said. 'Looking forward to their weekend.' She sounded wistful, and Joseph wondered what her weekend held. 'There's a little park a few minutes' walk from here. That should be a bit more peaceful. But don't keep me in suspense – talk as we go.' She tucked her hand in the crook of his arm. 'How come you got to see him, anyway?'

Because she was tall, only an inch or so shorter than he was, Joseph found it easy to walk in step. 'I had a call from Inspector Hazell,' he said. 'Your father was asking for me. Or rather, for some spiritual counsel, and I was the only person in the vicinity he could think of, I suppose. Maybe Hazell didn't see me as any threat to his investigation, because I don't know anything. Anyway, all the time I was with your father there was a uniformed constable in the room, pretending not to listen, so there wasn't much chance of anything untoward.'

'That was kind of you, to drop everything.' A thought struck her. 'How did you get to Stockley?'

'On a slow country bus,' Joseph said. 'And I came here on a train. It's no matter. Your father was worried about you, and your mother and your brothers. I couldn't tell him much, except that I thought you were coping as well as you could. He's well enough, and they're looking after him. But he is isolated and frustrated and anxious, and he wanted to tell me – or someone – how he was feeling.'

'But when are they going to let him out?' Helena cried. 'And when are they going to let me see him? This is crazy!'

'I'm coming to that,' Joseph said. 'Is this the park?'

'Yes, across the road. Be careful – the traffic is insane on this corner.'

In the end they had to run the gauntlet of the thundering cars and lorries, Helena grabbing Joseph's hand and pulling him after her. They came to a breathless halt in a small dusty park, and as they walked further in the sounds of the city quietened.

'Away from the ball games and the frolicking dogs?' Joseph said, looking at Helena with a small smile. She nodded, and he found an unoccupied bench under a plane tree.

'Well?' she said anxiously. 'Tell me everything, please.'

'I prayed with your father,' Joseph said. 'I hope that helped a little. But then Hazell came in. I'm so sorry, Helena. They – the police – found conclusive evidence. Your brothers are both in custody.'

Helena gasped, swallowed, looked down at her hands. 'Well,' she said quietly, 'I knew it couldn't have been Daddy. And we expected this, didn't we?'

'It's still horrible for you.'

'Do we have any details about the charges?'

'Rob has been charged with murder, Alex with conspiracy. That's all I know.'

'And where does that leave my father?'

'He's still being detained. For now, anyway. He'll be done for wasting police time, or maybe, and this is worse, perverting the course of justice. Hazell didn't seem sure of the outcome. But he will let you see him, whenever you want to. All you have to do is ring Hazell and organise it. Your dad will need a change of clothes, perhaps books, his Bible…you'll know.'

To Joseph's dismay Helena began to cry, her head bent, her shoulders heaving. 'Poor Daddy! This is a nightmare for him.'

Joseph took her hands in his, feeling them tremble. 'And for you,' he said huskily. 'When will you go?'

Helena took a deep breath. 'I'm so sorry, Joseph. I always seem to be crying, don't I? I'll get myself together soon, I promise.' She tried to smile. 'I'll have to go to the house and get his things. Perhaps tomorrow would be best. But I'll ring the Inspector now, and maybe he can tell Daddy and he'll know I haven't forgotten him.'

'He knows that already,' Joseph said.

'I'll ring the station now, then,' Helena said, fishing her phone out of the depths of her bag. 'I wrote the Stockley number down somewhere. Ah, here it is.' She tapped it in. 'I hope I'm not wasting your time,' she said to Joseph. He shook his head. 'Not at all.' Then she was talking to Hazell, arranging a time, sending loving messages to her father. She ended the call, snapped the phone shut and sighed deeply, leaning back against the tree trunk, her eyes closed. 'Oh, Joseph, what a mess.'

'Before I got the call from the Inspector,' Joseph said hesitantly, 'I was sitting at my desk, trying to think of something meaningful to say on Sunday, and coming up with absolutely nothing. A blank. But then, after I'd been with your father, I remembered something, a talk I had with Erica, over a year ago. She told me about when they were children, and her worries about your dad, and I said something about whether he felt forgiven. That got me thinking about the whole big subject of God's mercy, and now I have some notes and scribbles and maybe on Sunday that's what I'll preach about: your aunt, and her wit and wisdom.'

Helena looked at him wonderingly. 'I'd like to hear that sermon.'

'You're always welcome at Christchurch. No guarantees of spiritual insight, though. I don't think I'm really functioning all that well at the moment.'

Helena's eyes were searching. 'You talked about whether Daddy felt forgiven,' she said. 'Not that I know exactly what he needs to be forgiven for. I'd say he does, theoretically, but then it all comes back and hits him. I hope he'll be more open with me now. I feel so much in the dark.'

'He certainly feels responsible,' Joseph said. 'For pretty much everything.'

'Like someone else I know,' Helena said.

'What?'

'Well? Do *you* feel forgiven?'

'For what?' Joseph said guardedly.

'What was it you said?' Helena reminded him. '"Pretty much everything", wasn't it? Shout me down if you like, but don't you feel responsible for the things that have gone wrong in your life? Even though, like Daddy, you couldn't possibly have helped most of it?'

Joseph shook his head. 'Where did that come from?'

'You're not the only one who's been doing some hard thinking,' she said. 'And I'm going to try to persuade my father to tell me about some of those grisly family secrets that everybody but me seems to know.'

'I think he will.'

Helena got to her feet. 'Look, Joseph, I'd better get over to the house now and pick up Daddy's things, then I can go to Stockley early tomorrow. I don't want him to feel abandoned any longer than is absolutely unavoidable. If I go now there's a good chance nobody will be in, and I can slip in and out and not have to speak to anybody. Anyway, you have that sermon to write – I mustn't hold you up.' She paused, her gaze momentarily far away, then she seemed to collect herself, back into the present. 'Thank you for coming specially today – you've been so kind. I really don't know what I would have done without you.'

'As to that,' Joseph said with a crooked smile, 'my motives are only partially disinterested. As I'm sure you know.'

Helena rested her hand on his shoulder for a moment and looked down at him as he sat on the bench, her face serious. 'I think...I think we have a lot to talk about,' she said. 'Not just all this trouble, and my dreadful family. But now's not the time, is it? I have to see my father is all right. You do see that, don't you?'

'Of course,' Joseph said quietly. 'And there is no hurry.' He stood up, looking down at her intently as if taking in every feature of her face. 'But I want to know what happens tomorrow. Will you come down to Compton after you've seen your father?'

'Yes, of course. I'll come in time for lunch, and you can make me a sandwich and we can sit in your immaculate garden.'

'Done. Except scotch the "immaculate" part.' He paused. 'Helena, will you be all right? Tonight, I mean? Is your friend, Becca isn't it, going to be in? I don't want you to be brooding on your own.'

'I'll be fine,' she said softly. 'Thank you for thinking of me, though.' She leaned forward and brushed his face with her fingers. 'See you tomorrow.'

Helena was closing the clasps on a small suitcase, filled with spare clothes for Ewan, when she heard the crunch of tyres on gravel. She flicked back the curtain and peered out, in time to see her mother locking her car. *Bother, bother. Well, I can't really avoid her, short of hiding in the wardrobe.*

She went to the top of the stairs as Fiona let herself in. 'Mummy, it's me. Not a burglar.'

Fiona looked up at her, and slowly took off her sunglasses. Her hair was as perfect as ever, and she was dressed immaculately in a blue sleeveless top and crisply-pressed white trousers, but her face made Helena flinch despite herself: Fiona looked at least ten years older, and her eyes were dull. 'Oh, Helena. It's you. I was wondering where you'd got to.' There was no animation in her voice, as if all but automatic action had deserted her.

'I've been at Becca's for a few days.' She hesitated. 'Mummy, are you all right? You don't look well.'

'A bit late for sympathy, isn't it?' Fiona said. 'Your brothers are in custody, your father's vanished off the face of the earth, and I can't find out what the hell's going on.'

'Daddy's in custody too. That's why I'm here – to get him some clothes and books and stuff.'

Fiona frowned. 'What are you talking about?'

Helena picked up the suitcase and walked down the stairs to where her mother still stood in the hall. 'He's at Stockley, in the police station. I tried to tell Rob on the phone, but we got cut off.'

'Well, for goodness' sake, aren't you going to tell me why?'

Helena bit her lip. 'He confessed to murdering Erica,' she said, her voice low.

Fiona's eyes widened. '*What?* He did what? Why?'

'To protect Rob, of course. Alex too.'

Fiona laughed harshly, slung her bag over her shoulder and stalked into the kitchen. 'Well, he wasted his time,' she sneered. 'And now he's banged up too, is he? There's poetic justice for you.'

'Oh, Mummy, please, why are you so bitter? Can't you see he was trying to help them?'

'That's right, stick up for him, don't bother to see it from my point of view. You never have, so why start now?' She rounded on Helena. 'You call me bitter! My husband and sons are in custody, my daughter's deserted me, my friends all look at me pityingly, basically my life's in tatters. What's not to be bitter about? How have I deserved this? Tell me that!'

Helena put the suitcase down. 'Shall I make some tea?'

Fiona folded her arms. 'Perhaps it's best if you just go,' she said. 'Aren't you going to see your father?'

Helena nodded. 'Tomorrow, early.'

'And I dare say you'll be living at your friend's, won't you?'

'Yes, for now.'

Fiona turned her back, and her voice was strangled. 'I may not be staying here much longer myself. The humiliation of all this is getting to me.'

Helena took a step forward. Was her mother crying? She had hardly ever seen her cry. 'Mummy –'

'Just go, will you, Helena. There's no more to say. You've chosen what side you're on.'

'There shouldn't *be* sides!' Helena cried, her voice cracking. 'I care what happens to you and the boys – of course I do!'

'Whatever.' Fiona wrapped her arms around herself, still facing away. 'Don't forget your father's post. It's on the hall table.'

Helena sighed. 'Please, Mummy. Just tell me you'll let me know where you are, if you go away. Do you have any messages for Daddy?'

Fiona spun round to face her daughter. She held her hands stiffly at her sides, and her fists were clenched. 'If your father gets any message from me it'll be through a solicitor,' she said harshly.

'What?'

'Please, Helena. Go away. Go to your father. Don't bother coming back here, because I'll be closing up the house. No surprise, but ever since all this mess has been on the news the press have started sniffing round, and of course I'm in the front line.' She laughed sourly. 'Your father and brothers can't be got at, no one knows where you are, and if they try at Fraser's they'll just get 'No comment.' But they know where we live, your father's a public figure, and now the story's out I dare say they'll be crowding round the front gate. A reporter tried to stop me yesterday, in the street!' She exhaled loudly. 'Yes, I'll let you know where I am, when I know myself. It's been all over the papers – haven't you seen?' Helena shook her head, and Fiona shrugged. 'I don't know how you can have missed it. But you can see I have to be away from here as soon as possible.'

'I so wish it didn't have to be like this,' Helena whispered. Fiona stood silent, her chin up, her eyes red. Helena picked up the suitcase and walked through into the hall, stopping only to collect the pile of letters addressed to Ewan. 'Goodbye, Mummy.' There was no answer.

Saturday

At nine o'clock in the morning Helena walked through the doors into the Stockley police station lobby. She stood at the desk, suitcase in hand, waiting for someone to take notice. After a few moments the receptionist looked up. 'Can I help you?'

'I have an appointment,' Helena said. 'I spoke to Inspector Hazell yesterday. I've come to see my father, Ewan Fraser.'

'Ah. Yes,' the woman said. 'I'll take you up to Inspector Hazell's office, and he can let you into the Detention Suite. This way, please.'

Helena followed her up the stairs and along the long, blank corridor, feeling as if reality had somehow shifted sideways into an alternative universe. *Is this really happening? I wish I could wake up.*

The woman rapped on a door and was answered. She pushed the door open and gestured Helena inside. Helena tried to smile. 'Thank you.'

Hazell was standing behind his desk, leaning on it with both hands. 'Good morning, Miss Fraser,' he said, his face serious. 'You are early.'

'You understand, Inspector – I am very anxious about my father.'

'Yes, of course. Well, we'll waste no more time. Mr Fraser has had his breakfast, I believe. Come with me, please.'

Helena followed Hazell along corridors and through doors, as Joseph had done before her. Then Hazell stopped and knocked lightly. Helena heard her father's voice, and Hazell unlocked the door. 'All yours, Miss Fraser. I will have to lock the door after you. There's a phone in the room you can call me on when you need to leave.' He smiled.

'Thank you, Inspector.' Helena slid around the door, and there was her father, standing by the low table. The door closed behind her, and she heard the key turn in the lock. 'Daddy.'

'My darling girl, there you are.' Ewan crossed the room and wrapped her in his arms. 'Are you all right?'

Helena stood back. 'More to the point, are *you* all right? You've had me out of my mind, do you know that? Oh, but Daddy, it's so good to see you!'

'Come and sit down. With any luck they'll bring us some coffee later.' They sat opposite one another, with the table between them. Ewan sighed. 'I'm so sorry to have worried you, sweetheart. How did you guess I was here?'

Helena shrugged. 'I suppose I just put myself in your shoes, asked myself what you would do. Seems I must know you pretty well, despite everything.'

Ewan frowned. 'Despite everything?'

'Despite you never telling me anything, keeping secrets, cutting me out.'

Ewan winced. 'I know, I know, and I was wrong. I'm sorry.'

'Well, you're stuck in here with nowhere to go, so maybe today's a good day to tell me everything I want to know.'

Ewan nodded. 'Yes, I will. But first I need to know some things. Have you seen your mother?'

Helena took a deep breath. 'When the police said, finally, that I could come and see you, I went to the house to get you some things – clean clothes, books and so on. I hoped not to see anyone, but Mummy came home while I was there.'

'Aren't you living at home?'

'No. I've moved in with my friend Becca for a while. You remember her.'

'I see.'

'Well, anyway, I saw Mummy.'

Ewan bit his lip. 'How is she?'

'Bitter and resentful. Told me not to bother coming back, because she plans to close up the house. She didn't say where she was going, but she did at least say she'd let me know where she was, eventually.' She hesitated. 'Daddy, I asked her if she had any messages for you, and she said if she did it would be through her solicitor. What did she mean?'

Ewan leaned back in his chair and folded his hands on his stomach. 'Ah. I wondered how long it would take her. She's not wasted any time, but then, why should she? I suppose it's better this way.'

'What are you saying?'

Ewan sighed deeply. 'Helena, my darling, you can't have failed to notice that your mother and I hardly speak any more. Can you?' Helena shook her head, and her eyes filled with tears. Ewan leaned forward and patted her knee. 'She's wanted a divorce for years, actually. But I wouldn't hear of it, and perhaps that was wrong of me. I just wanted to keep a semblance of a home for you and your brothers, but she's never really been happy. The fact is, as I'm sure you're quite aware, we've never shared the same values and aspirations, and maybe I should have let her go long since, so that she could carve out another life for herself, something that suits her better. Well,' he added reflectively, 'now she has her chance, and she's taking it. I've been expecting something like this.'

'What a time to run out on you!' Helena choked.

'Don't look at it like that,' Ewan said. 'Just let her go. Back up to Scotland, I imagine, to your uncle Stuart. Maybe now she can have what she's always wanted – some ruin to refurbish, and a few acres of moorland.' He smiled. 'You don't have to look so sad, Helena. I don't mind, and neither should you. It's time the fresh wind of truth breezed through our family. If we can't let that happen now, we never will.'

'But what about you, Daddy? When are they going to let you out?'

Ewan shrugged. 'No idea. And I may have to go to prison. But maybe not, and eventually I will be free again, so I'm not worried about that. When it happens I'll get things organised with the business, and then I think I'll go back to the monastery for a while. You know, the one I nearly went into when I was eighteen. It's a blessed place, and I need to think and have space to pray.' He paused, as if summoning up his reserves of will and courage, and when he looked at Helena his face was bleak. 'Oh, my dear. It's been a terrible time. To have lost my Marjie was bad enough. But to have her murdered by the children that I myself brought into the world and raised…' His voice trailed away, and he stared at the floor.

'Children that you tried to save,' Helena reminded him gently. 'Children you tried to take the blame for.'

He looked up, and sorrow was written in every line of his face. 'Well, there was no bringing her back, was there?' he whispered.

Helena leaned forward and took hold of his hands. 'Daddy, please will you tell me about you and Erica when you were young? About the castle you grew up in? And your parents? I need to know.'

'Of course you do.' He stood up suddenly, smoothed back his hair that had flopped over his forehead, and walked a little unsteadily to the window. 'I keep trying to look out of here, but it's too high,' he muttered. He turned to face her. 'I'm going to ring down and see if they'll bring us some coffee,' he said. 'My throat is very dry.' He picked up the handset and after a moment spoke into it. 'Thank you.'

Hands in pockets, he began to pace the room. 'Well, now, where to begin? I'll tell you about my mother, your grandmother, Eleanor. They're the memories of a little boy, of course, and quite clouded by the years. She was tall and slim, and had beautiful ripply red hair, which she used to wear up most of the time. You are very like her, my dearest girl.' He smiled. 'She was softly-spoken, and very kind. Clever, too. And I and your aunt were the apples of her eye, no doubt about that.'

'What about my grandfather?'

'Hm. Well, I've had a lot of time to think and try to remember, so perhaps my memories won't all be bad ones. I hope not. I was always rather in awe of my father. He was so big – tall and wide in body, but also massive in personality. He dominated every room, every gathering. But I think that for the first few years they were happy enough, he and my mother. It was she who had most to do with us, because he was always busy, looking after the estate. He was an outdoors man. My mother told us stories, and that's where the whole Marjorie and Quintin thing came in. But you knew that.'

'Were you and Erica always close?'

Ewan nodded. 'Yes. But more so after our mother died.'

'Why did she die, Daddy? So young?'

'Cancer, I guess. I was only seven, so I didn't really understand. I do remember doctors coming to Mickle, and we children were kept out of the way and only allowed to see our mother from time to time, which was hard. We missed her. Erica cried every night, and I had to try to comfort her. Poor lamb, she was only four years old.' He paused. 'Well, anyway. Mother died. My father, I realize now, was in pieces. I guess, in his way, he really did love her, and without her he became morose and ill-tempered. Perhaps he was even then beginning to be ill. Because, you see, Helena –' Ewan stopped suddenly and turned to face his daughter – 'I have come to the conclusion that my father wasn't mad or bad, but ill. Progressively so, with an illness that was never diagnosed, that had physical roots but also affected his behaviour.'

'How did you come to that conclusion?' Helena asked.

'By trying to remember and piece together everything I experienced with him, all his oddities, which got more and more pronounced as time went on,' Ewan said. 'And by a bit of, I hope judicious, research on the internet. Be that as it may. He got much, much worse. He also started drinking heavily, which inflamed his temper at first and then rendered him comatose. It was no situation for young children. It was a confused time, you understand. There's so much I didn't understand, because I was too young. And it's so long ago, so my memory may not be altogether reliable.' He stopped pacing and sat down, leaning towards Helena. 'Erica and I went to the village school. We were often, too often, not taken. Questions were asked, I dare say. How we weren't taken away into care I don't know. I'm sure that if it were today we would have been. Father employed people, couples normally, the husband to help on the estate, the wife to teach us children. Most of them didn't last long. Sometimes we went back to the school in the village. We were woefully behind all the other children. Meanwhile my father grew more and more wild. He drank like a demon. Sometimes he hugged us and wouldn't let us go, crying and sobbing. Sometimes he chased us and if he cornered us we'd get a hiding. I was first in line, because he expected more of me – the eldest, and a boy. Often, too often, I had to stand in front of Erica and shield her. She was always small, skinny – no match for our bear of a father in his drunken rages. We lived in fear – but we knew nothing different. Mickle was, is, quite remote, a mile and a half from a decent road, a track across a bog. I had a vague idea, from the few contacts we'd made at the village school, and from story books, that we didn't live as other children lived. But I didn't really know.

'Then, one day, out of the blue, he announced that I was to go away to school. I was twelve, almost thirteen, and I dared to protest. Not that I didn't relish the idea of getting away, but I was afraid for my sister. He wasn't drunk that day, I think. He explained that Erica too would go to boarding school when she was older. I would see her in the holidays. Meanwhile she would have a decent woman to teach her. I had to be content with that. I was uneasy, but what power did I have?

'When I came home for the holidays, sometimes there were new people employed. Often by the time the next holidays came round, there would be someone else. Either they'd got fed up and left, I suppose, or Father had dismissed them. One holiday I came home and he'd employed the Gilmours: Neil and Catriona. They claimed to be husband and wife, but I wondered, even then. They seemed such an unlikely couple. He was much younger than her, obviously. But I had to admit that at first Erica seemed better cared for. She was clean and fed, and getting some sort of education. I had no idea at all what qualifications the Gilmours had, if any. But although I never liked them, it seemed a bit more normal for Erica when I was at school, rather than rattling around that draughty old place with just her crazy father for company. And when I was at home she never said much. It was the holidays, no lessons for either of us, and we spent every day together, keeping out of the way of the adults. If I ever asked her how things were, she clammed up. Perhaps she was waiting for the day she too would go away to school. But of course that never happened, and who knows if it was ever really intended? Poor Marjie. Much later, I found out some of what that poor girl went through.' He fell silent, and Helena waited.

'Well. One day I had a telephone call at school. Such things were not encouraged, I can tell you. Old Crundall was quite put out. That was the Headmaster. It was my sister, and she was distraught. She'd barricaded herself in her room and stayed there for two days. Heaven knows how she managed. I suppose she'd taken some food from the larder and a bucket for a toilet. She was absolutely terrified, and there was something new in it, something I couldn't quite pin down. You must remember, we weren't quite so *au fait* in those days. Children weren't. Well, full of big-brother adolescent pride, I swore to her that I would do something as soon as I could, when I came back to Mickle for Easter.' He groaned, and rested his head in his hands. 'What should I have done? Of course, I know now. I should have spoken to an adult, even old Crundall. I should have voiced my concern. But that never for a moment occurred to me. Perhaps I assumed I would not be believed. All I knew was that my beloved Marjie was threatened. The Gilmours drank with my father, constantly. They encouraged him. Whatever else, they were no protection for your aunt.' He hesitated, seeing Helena's appalled expression. 'I never, ever found out the details of what was happening,' he said softly. 'I know he beat her, because I saw the bruises. But her fear was somehow…wilder, more confused than I remembered. I never found out if he abused her sexually as well as physically. She would never say, and perhaps she simply didn't have the vocabulary. Later, of course, as an adult, she would have, but by then she had gone completely silent on the subject, and just lately, when I was talking so much about our father and what I believed to have been his illness, she hated hearing about it. She'd put it out of her mind, and she didn't want it resurrected.'

'Poor, dear Erica. How utterly dreadful,' Helena whispered. 'How did she keep so sane? How did she hang on to her sense of humour?'

Ewan smiled faintly. 'Well, she had great reserves of character. And for the last fifteen years at least she has had divine help, I believe.'

Helena shook her head. 'So what did you do?'

Ewan closed his eyes. 'I got myself included on a fishing trip, early in the morning. I stole a valuable gun and hid it under my coat. My father had been drinking most of the night, and he drove our rattly old pickup like a very demon of hell. Gilmour couldn't take it, was off puking behind some bushes when we got to the river. I threatened my father with the gun, and he fell into the icy water and drowned.' He looked at Helena, who was staring at him, eyes wide. 'Yes, dearest girl. If I didn't actually murder him, I certainly drove him to his death.'

Helena gulped. 'Would you have shot him?'

Ewan smiled, a twisted parody of humour. 'The gun wasn't loaded. But my heart was full of hatred, and perhaps that was just as bad as a bullet in the brain.'

Helena shook her head. 'But you got away with it.'

'Oh yes. Gilmour hadn't seen anything, so it was just my word. He didn't turn up when he was called to the Inquiry as a witness – by then he and Catriona had decamped, taking the pickup, the guns, and the contents of Father's strongbox. A verdict of accidental death was recorded. Catriona was never heard of again. But he, slimy bastard, turned up years later. He'd done a stretch in prison, and he came to our doorstep and tried to blackmail me.'

'How? What did he know?'

'He claimed he'd seen me take the gun, but that by the time he got back to the castle it was back in the gun-cabinet. He probably did see me take it. But it was my conscience he was appealing to, I think. With some success, though I never paid him a penny.' He paused. 'Horrible though this is, I think you may have seen him, Helena. You were very young, not even at school. He came to the house – your mother let him in.'

'Oh!' Helena cried out. 'Yes, I do remember! I've had dreams about him, because of the way he looked. The man with the snake eyes, I called him. That was Gilmour?'

Ewan nodded. 'I was so angry with her that day, letting that creep into the house when you were there.'

'But why did she?'

'For information, she said. Something to use against me, I'm afraid. She never really believed my version of events, and she was right not to, wasn't she? Your mother may have many faults, but she is far from stupid.'

'Daddy, what a grim story.'

'I know. And perhaps you can see why I never wanted you to hear it. To find out what I had done. The boy that killed his father.'

Helena leaned forward and laid her hand on his arm. 'It was a terrible thing to happen, and you acted from good motives. From love. Daddy, I really think you should let your conscience rest. You didn't know then that perhaps your father was mentally ill. All you knew was that he was doing bad things to the sister you loved. Please, now you have to be kinder to yourself.'

'But don't you see, Helena? It's where all this disaster has sprung from. From my actions – yes, taken in ignorance, but in hatred too.'

'No,' Helena said firmly. 'That's only part of the story. You can't claim all of it. Circumstances are in there too. The Gilmours had their part to play. And later my mother was a contributor. Rob and Alex are adults, not puppets. They didn't have to act as they did. No, Daddy. It's not all down to you.'

There was a gentle tap on the door, and the key turned in the lock. A young constable came in with a tray. 'Here you are, Mr Fraser.' He set the tray down on the table.

'Thank you, Constable. This is Constable Swinton, Helena. He's been looking after me most kindly. My daughter, Helena.'

'Pleased to meet you, Miss,' Swinton said. 'I'm afraid I'll have to lock you in again, sir.'

'That's all right. I quite understand.'

When he had gone, Ewan was silent, busying himself with milk and spoons. Then he looked up, and Helena could see the torment in his face. 'What would you have thought,' he said at last, 'if you had found all this out? Perhaps from someone else?'

'If I had found it out from my mother,' Helena retorted, 'I would have come and asked you if it was true. And I have heard it now, and it makes no difference. I suppose I did kind of hero-worship you a bit when I was younger. But I am grown up now. And you are still my dad, and I still love you and think you are a very remarkable person. I think about what you have done with your life, all the people you have helped, and how you have done your best to be a good father.'

Ewan gripped her hand. 'Thank you, my dearest. I don't deserve you.'

'Of course you do, just as much as I deserve you. But it isn't a question of deserving, anyway, is it?'

Ewan sipped his coffee. 'Perhaps not.'

There was silence for a few moments, a silence replete with the knowledge that there was still much to say and much to hear.

Ewan put his cup down, half-empty. 'I've met Erica's vicar, your friend, Joseph.'

'I know,' Helena said, feeling heat rise in her face. 'After he'd been to see you yesterday he came up to London specially to tell me. He knew how anxious I've been. And he made me promise to tell him how I've got on today. He's been very kind.'

Ewan looked at her under his sandy brows. His expression was serious, but his eyes said something different. 'So, is he just being kind, do you suppose, or is there more to it?'

'Not you as well!' Helena exclaimed. 'Erica was bad enough with her ridiculous matchmaking. Yes, there is more to it. But that's all I shall say on the subject at this moment.'

'If it makes any difference,' Ewan said diffidently, 'I liked Joseph. He seemed a good man.'

'Of course it makes a difference. And yes, he is. But Daddy, thinking about Joseph and what might happen in the future makes me so sad. Erica had a lot of fun at our expense, making us both very embarrassed and awkward, and now she'll never know the outcome of all her plotting.' Helena rubbed at her face with both hands, and her voice choked. 'How are we going to go on without her? Especially you, Daddy. Especially you. It breaks my heart just to think about it. How can we just go on living when she isn't there?'

'I don't know, Helena,' Ewan said softly. His face was expressionless, and he seemed to find it difficult to get his words out. 'But we have no real choice. We have to go on, and we each have to find something that makes our life worthwhile. That's all we can do.'

Saturday morning seemed to stretch out like an interminable desert, featureless, mile upon mile of nothing. Joseph had stayed up late into the night, and his sermon was ready. It had taken a long time to compose, interrupted by straying thoughts that had nothing to do with its subject or anything remotely edifying: thoughts populated by self-questioning, doubt, and hope; images of Helena and also, unbidden, of Caroline. He thought long about his brief, doomed marriage, and how he had failed, and he mourned Caroline's truncated life as he had been unable to do in the early days after her death, when he had felt only a kind of guilty liberation. *How sad for her that she had to die to be free of me. Forgive me, Caroline, wherever you are now. Truly I am a selfish man.*

In the few hours that he managed to sleep, the night so brief and hot, dreams had plagued him and left him exhausted. In the morning he looked in the bathroom mirror and was not encouraged. *You look every inch your age and more*, he said to the face that looked back at him. *Whatever could someone so young and fresh and glorious as Helena Fraser ever see in such a battered, disillusioned old ragbag? Even supposing she sees anything. I am a pretty dismal prospect.*

In the end he gave himself a stern talking-to, showered, shaved and put on clean clothes. He was munching on a piece of toast when his doorbell rang. He looked at his watch and frowned: it was not quite eleven, too soon for Helena to appear. When he went to the front door it was one of his parishioners, in the process of emptying the back of his van of several cardboard boxes.

'Morning, Joseph,' the man said. 'More stuff for the garden fete. Where do you want them?'

Joseph suppressed an impulse to reply, 'At the bottom of the river,' and smiled. 'Right, thanks, Mike, here in the hallway for now. I'll shift them later. Is there much more, do you think?'

'No idea, I'm afraid. But I think that'll be it for today.'

'Ah. Well, that's good.'

Between them the two men manhandled the boxes into the hallway and piled them up so that there was a narrow aisle for access.

'Would you like some coffee?' Joseph said politely, hoping Mike would decline; but his offer was accepted, and for the next half hour Joseph endured the man's chatter, silently berating himself for his lack of charity and wishing his visitor would leave. Eventually the phone rang in Joseph's study and he excused himself.

'I'll be off now, then,' Mike said. *At last.*

Joseph said a hasty goodbye, went into his study and picked up the phone.

'Reverend Stiles? Frederick Hazell, again. Sorry to bother you at the weekend, sir.'

'It's no bother, Inspector.' *Oh, but it is.*

'Just to let you know that Miss Fraser has been in to see her father, and has just left,' Hazell said. 'Unfortunately she'd only been gone ten minutes when I had a phone call from the States.'

'Oh?'

'From someone called Stephen Pole. Ring any bells?'

'Erica's son! Good heavens.'

'If Miss Fraser had still been here I'd have passed him on direct to her, but as it is, perhaps I could give you his number. I've given him the bare facts, but he needs to speak to a family member, and no doubt you'll have Miss Fraser's contact details.'

'How did he get hold of you, Inspector? And what has he heard?'

'From the internet, sir, no surprise. Don't forget Mr Fraser is a public figure. His sister's murder is news, and not just here in the UK. Of course we would have contacted Mr Pole as soon as we were able, I had hoped before it was all over the papers, but it seems he got there first.'

'I see. Well, of course I'll let Miss Fraser know when I see her.'

'I'll give you his number, then. Do you have something to write with?'

Joseph took down the number dictated by Hazell, and after a few more banalities rang off, leaning on his desk in something of a daze. *Nothing stands still.*

Joseph busied himself in the kitchen, making sandwiches. He thought for a moment, then went to a cupboard in the dining room and fetched a bottle of white wine, and put it in the fridge. *Don't know if this is a good idea or not.*

He was washing his hands at the sink, staring down the garden, half-seeing the shadows of the trees shifting in the sunlight, when suddenly she appeared outside the open kitchen window, smiling, a pair of sunglasses perched on her head, holding her hair back. She was wearing a loose cotton top in primrose yellow and azure blue cut-offs. Joseph stared at her unashamedly. 'You look like a twenty-first century angel,' he said.

She shook her head. 'Have you been drinking, Joseph?'

'Not yet,' he said. 'But I have a bottle chilling. Shall we sit outside?'

He moved a folding table and two chairs to the shade under a bowering cherry tree. 'I'll get some glasses.'

A few minutes later he brought a tray with the bottle, two glasses and the plate of sandwiches. 'As you ordered,' he said with a courtly bow.

'Lovely,' Helena said. 'I couldn't be bothered with breakfast, so I'm starving.' She helped herself to several sandwiches and began munching.

'How was your father?' Joseph asked, uncorking the wine with something of a flourish.

Helena sighed and finished her mouthful. 'He was very glad to see me,' she said. 'In pieces about the boys, of course. As you would expect. Wanted to know what had been happening, so I filled him in as best I could, even though I know very little. But then I asked him to tell me all those things I've wondered about, and guessed at, especially just lately.'

'Did he?'

She nodded. 'He told me the whole story. And he said he'd been wrong to try to defend me. You know about how he and Erica grew up in that castle, don't you, Joseph? And how his father died?'

'Some of it,' Joseph said. 'Erica told me, because she was so worried about him – your father, I mean, not your grandfather. But she made me promise not to tell you. I didn't like it, but I couldn't go back on my word.'

Helena smoothed her hair back away from her face. 'I understand,' she said. 'Poor Daddy, poor Erica. What a grim childhood! Perhaps if they hadn't been so isolated, hidden away in that ruin, someone might have realised what was going on with my grandfather Lachlan and rescued the children – before disaster happened. To think my poor father has been carrying that guilt all these years.' She stared down at her plate, distractedly playing with the breadcrumbs. 'I wish I'd known.' She shook her head and looked up. 'Daddy said I look like his mother, Eleanor. Erica didn't really remember her, but Daddy does. He said she was clever, and kind. He told me about their favourite story that she used to tell them – the original Marjorie and Quintin. I began to have a little inkling of their bond, him and Erica. United in adversity, I suppose. And it drove him to violence, didn't it, to keep her safe. Daddy's been doing a lot of that, defending his family, I mean. "Ring-fencing," he calls it. Not always wisely.'

'I tried to convince him to trust you,' Joseph said. 'To treat you like a competent adult, not a delicate treasure.'

Helena chuckled. 'Delicate I'm not,' she said. Her face grew serious again. 'Well, perhaps he will now. Oh, and he also said, when all this is over, whatever happens, even if he has to go to prison, he's going to go back to the monastery for a while, the one he spent a couple of years in when he was young, to take time to think, and pray, and heal. He's been in touch with the head man – the Abbot, is it? – even before all this –' she waved a hand vaguely '– happened. Because he'd convinced himself he was dying.' She sat upright suddenly, and put her half-full glass on the table. 'Which reminds me! When I went to our house to get him some clothes and things, I picked up his post that was lying in the hall. One of the letters was from his consultant. That test he was dreading? It came back negative! Oh, Joseph! He isn't ill at all. Of course I'm glad he isn't, but isn't it terrible? Do you realise, none of this needed to happen?' She shook her head. 'I can't bear to think of it, that my poor Erica might still be alive. My stupid brother might not be a murderer. Sometimes I think I'm going to wake up. But I am awake, and it's all real.' She fell silent, staring at the ground. Then she sighed and looked at Joseph, smiling wearily. 'Well, it's no use chasing all the what-ifs. What we've got is what we've got. Before I forget, Daddy said he would like you to conduct Erica's funeral. You will, won't you?'

'It will be my privilege,' Joseph said quietly. 'She was a good friend to me. Any idea when it will be?'

Helena shook her head. 'No. I just hope they'll let Daddy attend, even if he has to come handcuffed to a policeman.'

Joseph picked up the bottle. 'Can I top you up?'

'No, thanks. I have to drive later. Joseph, it's going to be me who has to organise the funeral. It's not something I've ever done. Will you help me?'

'Of course.' Then he slapped his forehead, remembering what he had to tell her. 'Forgive me, my brain is like a sieve. I didn't sleep well last night, that'll have to be my excuse. Just before you came today Inspector Hazell rang. He would have spoken to you but you'd already left. He had a phone call from your long-lost cousin, Stephen Pole.'

Helena's eyes widened. 'Really? How extraordinary!'

Joseph nodded. 'I think Stephen had seen something on the internet and realised it was his mother that was involved.'

'The mother he hasn't seen since he was six years old. The mother he can't possibly remember, not in any detail anyway.'

'Well, I don't know. But the Inspector gave me Stephen's number to give to you.' He felt in his trouser pocket and handed her the slip of paper.

Helena looked at it, and then helplessly at Joseph. 'Whatever am I going to say to him? This is awful, Joseph.'

Joseph reached over the table and took her hand. 'You'd have had to speak to him some time, I guess. Just remember, none of it is your fault.'

'I know,' she whispered. 'But it feels as if it is. He'll never know his mother now, because of what my brothers have done. What does he know?'

'Inspector Hazell said he'd told him the bare facts. But I'm afraid it's down to you to fill in the background.'

Helena sighed. 'Well, I'll do it later, tonight, when I'm quiet on my own. It'll give me time to think what to say. I don't want to spoil this lovely afternoon with any more gloom.' She bit her lip. 'But actually, there was one other thing Daddy said, while I'm in gloomy mode.'

'What?'

'When he'd opened all his post, and he'd finished beating himself up about what might have been if … well, all those what-ifs – he said he was surprised there wasn't a letter from Bob Hamilton, our solicitor.'

'Saying what?' Joseph prompted.

'Telling him Mummy was planning to divorce him. He's expecting it, any moment, he said. I was aghast, Joseph – I mean, I know they haven't ever really got on, if I'm honest, but what sort of timing would that be? But he's quite sure that's what will happen. He says if he knows Mummy at all, she'll take the opportunity to make another life for herself, apart from him. He said he didn't blame her, that it should have happened years ago, but he wouldn't hear of it then. According to him they never really valued the same things, and Mummy has never been happy. If it does go as he thinks it will, he'll sell the house in London. I saw my mother, briefly, last night. She's going somewhere, I don't know where, Scotland probably. Said she'd be closing the house up. To get away from the media circus that's bound to come, as much as anything.'

'How do you feel about that?' Joseph said. He still had hold of her hand, and she didn't pull away.

She heaved a sigh. 'I've never really thought of it as home, oddly enough. Too big, too shiny, not like our other house we had when I was small. I won't miss it. But it does feel as if my life is falling apart a bit.' She swallowed. 'I'm sorry, I promised not to cry, didn't I? And I won't, especially as it's mostly self-pity.'

'If anyone has the right to feel sorry for herself at this moment, it's you,' Joseph said. 'And speaking completely selfishly, it would give me the perfect excuse to hold you close and murmur consoling words.'

Helena threw back her head and laughed aloud. 'Honestly, Joseph! The way you talk anyone would think you were a crusty old colonel, not a…well, whatever.' She shook her head. 'You are such an idiot,' she said. 'You can do all that any time you like, but I'd much rather it was because you wanted to, not because I was wailing and you felt you had to be kind and uncle-ish.'

'I promise you, I have never, *ever* thought of myself as your uncle.'

Helena wiped away tears of laughter with the back of her hands. 'Thank goodness for that.'

Silence fell – a silence charged with unspoken questions. Joseph filled his glass up to the brim and took several large gulps. The bottle was more than half empty, and Helena had hardly drunk any. She watched him with a quizzical smile, twirling her own empty glass between her fingers.

He swallowed. 'I wish –'

She raised her eyebrows.

'I wish we could just go on doing this. Sitting in a sunlit garden, drinking wine. Forgetting everything else.'

'Except we would be falling-down drunk and it would get dark.'

He laughed. 'You're right. Sorry, that did sound ridiculously sentimental.'

'There's no reason, though,' she said, her face suddenly serious, 'why we shouldn't sit right here as often as we please, drinking the odd glass, talking. That sounds good to me.'

He gazed at her intently. 'Yes, it does,' he said softly. 'Helena, I need to say something, but I don't quite know what, or how.'

'I kind of gathered that,' she said wryly. 'Let me help. Is it that you think I am a needy nuisance and you wish I would go away and leave you in peace?'

'No,' he growled. 'Now you are mocking me. It's the absolute reverse. I want you to be here always. Maybe it's the wine talking, making me more reckless, I don't know. But I find I don't care.'

Helena frowned. 'I'd never want you to be reckless. It's too important for that. But I would like you to be more optimistic, more trusting, more accepting. I understand you are scared and over-cautious. I understand why. But Joseph, plenty of people get it wrong the first time around. They don't all go to ground and say 'Never again.' Sometimes they take a deep breath and take a chance – and sometimes it works out beyond what they hoped.'

He looked at her, his eyes wide. 'You make it sound simple.'

'You think too much. If it were so very complicated, the human race would have died out long ago.'

Now it was Joseph's turn to laugh aloud. 'I suppose you know, don't you? Your dear aunt had a great deal of fun at our expense.'

'Matchmaking. Oh, yes, I knew. *So* embarrassing.'

'It was. I could hardly look you in the eye.'

'Well, you seem to be managing it now.'

'Looking at you is very easy. And if I am honest, I have to say she wasn't wrong. At least, not as far as I was concerned.'

'That's an extremely roundabout declaration.'

'Come indoors and I'll try harder.'

Helena looked around. 'Why indoors? Are the neighbours peeping through the hedge?'

'Since the neighbours on this side are the dead people in the graveyard, that seems unlikely.' He glanced at the sky. 'No, but while we have been sitting here a large black cloud has been sneaking up on us. It's going to rain at any minute.'

Helena followed his gaze. 'Oh. You're right, and it's suddenly got colder. OK, I'll take the tray.' She gathered up plates and glasses with expert speed and half-ran indoors. Joseph collapsed the table and chairs and stowed them in the garage as the first fat drops pattered down. As the rain came down in earnest he closed the garage door with a bang, dashed across the slippery lawn and slithered into the kitchen. Helena was standing at the window, looking out as the rain bounced hissing on the grass.

She turned to him. 'Where were we,' she murmured, 'before all those dead people started gawking?' She slid her arms around his waist.

'I'm wet,' he protested feebly.

She said nothing, just looked up at him with the glimmer of a smile. Hesitantly he put his arms round her and drew her close, feeling the warmth and softness of her body. 'Oh, Helena,' he said, his voice muffled by her hair. 'I'm afraid I'm not a very good bet.'

'Joseph, for goodness' sake. That's not for you to say. Now please, stop talking and making excuses.'

He tangled his fingers in her hair and kissed her eyes, her cheeks, her mouth. He felt the heat build up between them, and with an effort pulled away, gasping. 'Sweetheart –'

'It's OK, don't worry,' she sighed, disentangling herself. 'I'll behave – on this occasion. I won't take advantage of you when you're not entirely sober.'

He held on to her, stroking her face with his fingers. 'A very big part of me wants to be taken advantage of,' he said. 'But we should be sensible. I suppose.'

Helena shook her hair out of her eyes. 'Sensible, *for now*. Not for ever. Or even for much longer. And perhaps you should consider making an honest woman of me, since you seem to be getting a bit carried away.'

He smiled, and deep laughter lines appeared at the corners of his eyes. 'Apart from your aunt, you are probably the most honest person I've ever met.'

Helena smacked him lightly on the chest. 'You know what I mean.'

'Yes, I do.'

'And?'

'And,' he said softly, 'it feels…miraculous.'

'So?'

He pulled her closer. 'So, dearest one that I adore to distraction, one day we will make dangerous promises and then you can take advantage of me whenever you like.'

'I'll hold you to that.'

He brushed his lips against her smooth neck, breathing in her scent. 'Please do. Any time.'

'But now,' she said, 'before I melt totally, I'm going home. Or what passes for home at the moment.' She wriggled out of his arms. 'Walk me to the door.' She took his hand and he followed after her. She stopped in the hall and surveyed the piled-up boxes with a jaundiced eye. 'More garden fete garbage?'

'Don't call it that – people will be offended.'

'Do you want help shifting it?'

'No, I'll do it when it isn't raining.'

'When is the fete anyway?'

'Next Saturday.'

'Should I come, or will it cause a scandal?'

'Not if you behave discreetly.'

'I'll try. I guess I'll have to start practising some time. Discretion, that is. Tough though that might be.' She paused, and her grin faded. 'Joseph, once Erica's body is released I'll get on with the funeral arrangements. Better sooner than later, I guess. You can probably recommend a firm in Compton.'

'Yes. There are a couple to choose from, equally efficient.'

She heaved a deep sigh. 'I hate thinking about the funeral. It seems impossible to think that I'll never see my crazy aunt again.'

'I know. But just think how she'd be laughing now.'

Helena smiled sadly. 'Clapping her hands and crowing, *I told you so*.'

'Probably.'

'I'm going now.'

He leaned past her and opened the front door, taking the opportunity to kiss her lingeringly. 'Ring me soon.'

'I'll let you know how I get on with Stephen.'

'Yes, please do. Now go – before it chucks down again. Or I get carried away – which could happen at any minute, if you're not very careful.'

She hesitated in the doorway, her hand resting on his arm. 'Did I actually tell you how much I love you?'

'Not in so many words. But I think I got the message.'

'Well, it took you long enough.'

'Go,' he said sternly. 'Or you will regret it.'

She ran to her car through the drizzle, laughing. 'What rash promises you make!' Then she flung herself into the driver's seat, started the engine and roared away, waving through the open window.

Helena rang just before nine o'clock that evening, as Joseph was slowly washing dishes and looking down the darkening garden, thinking about the events of the day. His head was throbbing dully. *I really shouldn't drink so much. Did I make a fool of myself? Did all that happen?*

He dried his hands and went into his study, flicked on the desk lamp and picked up the phone. 'It's me, your rather tarnished angel.' The sound of her voice seemed to knock the breath out of his lungs. 'Joseph? Are you there?'

'Yes, I'm here. I'd forgotten for a moment the effect you have on me. It's very worrying.'

She laughed. 'No, it's not. It's very encouraging. Anyway, enough of that. I've just been talking to Stephen.'

'Oh, you got hold of him – how was it?'

He heard her sigh. 'It was such a sad conversation, Joseph. Not as hard as I thought it might be – Stephen seems a nice guy and he certainly doesn't blame *me* for what happened. Or Daddy, for that matter. Thank goodness. In fact he was quite confused, and I had to tell him a lot of things he didn't have any idea about. But he was so devastated. We were both crying at one point. The thing is, he knew next to nothing about Erica. He said his father died about a couple of months ago, very unexpectedly, a stroke, I think. Stephen's been helping his stepmother sort out all the paperwork, and he came across a letter addressed to himself, from Erica. Did you know anything about that?'

'Yes,' Joseph said. 'She told me, oh, ages ago, that she'd written him a letter for his father to give him when he turned eighteen. Obviously he never did.'

'Maybe he just forgot all about it.'

'Or perhaps, 'Joseph said thoughtfully, 'he felt it would be better for Stephen not to be upset. Certainly that's what Erica thought. She said she decided not to interfere, not to complicate things as he was growing up. His father had remarried, a younger brother arrived after a year or two, and Stephen had a whole new life.'

'Yes, he mentioned his brother. He's about twelve or thirteen, I think.'

'It was desperately hard for Erica, the hardest cut of all. But she said she couldn't have taken care of him anyway after she had her accident. Apparently your father offered to hire lawyers to see if she could get access to Stephen, but she refused – for Stephen's own sake.'

'Poor Erica. What a life. But you know, she didn't feel sorry for herself, Joseph. She told me she'd been an alcoholic, kept very bad company, even had an abortion – did you know that?'

'No, I didn't.'

'She took all the blame for what happened, just like Daddy does. But I guess Stephen was never far from her mind – that's why she wrote the letter. And the awful thing is, he never saw it, till now. He said he'd been saving to come to England anyway, to see some of his family on his father's side. After he read Erica's letter of course he wanted to see her too. It's a pity he never got round to writing to her. Because then he saw the news item on the internet, and started digging, and realised that it was all too late. I suppose the police would have told him eventually, anyway.'

'Well, I'm very glad you spoke to him. You are the best person to explain everything.'

'He still wants to come here, Joseph – in time for the funeral. I promised to let him know the date when it's decided. He's got a bit of money his dad left him and he's going to make the trip he planned originally. I must give him plenty of notice, though, if I can, because he will need to get time off work.'

'What does he do?'

'Oh, he works in the same bank his dad was a leading light in. Just like I work for my dad's business.'

There was a small silence, then Joseph said, 'Are you all right, my dearest girl?'

'Yes, kind of. A bit punch-drunk, I guess.'

'Are you coming down tomorrow? To hear that sermon?'

'No, Joseph, I don't think I can. My friend Becca, you know, the friend whose flat I'm camping in at the moment? She needs my room back. I knew this was going to happen, just not when. She'd promised the room to someone else, but it was free for a little while. Now that other person wants to move in.'

Joseph frowned. 'What will you do?'

'I'm not exactly homeless, but it feels a bit like that,' Helena said. 'I don't want to go back to our London house, not with Mummy there, and anyway, she may already be clearing it out and leaving herself. I'll have to go and get my things, but I won't stay. I just can't face her. Not at the moment, anyway.'

'Tell me why,' Joseph probed.

'Because...because of her attitude to Erica, even though she's dead and no threat. Because of her ruthlessness, especially now, championing her sons. Daddy said she'd be like that, absolutely fierce and single-minded. He said she'd fight for them like a tigress. With a good lawyer Alex may get off more lightly, seeing as he only plotted to do a bit of breaking and entering, not murder. Leaving Rob to take the rap – as he should, I suppose. There are things I never really saw about my mother till now – her greed, her hardness. And how quick she was, getting Bob Hamilton on her side! It's so obvious she couldn't care less what happens to Daddy. I don't think she really cares what happens to me either. That's how it seems, anyway. It's awful to have to say this, Joseph, but my mother is really not a nice woman at all. Of course she has good qualities too – even people you don't like aren't all bad. Daddy always made excuses for her, always took the blame for everything. I don't say he is blameless, of course, but...' her voice faded.

For a moment Joseph held his peace, then he said soberly, 'Desperate as the last few weeks have been, they've also been quite instrumental, I think...debris cleared away, truth liberated. Hard to swallow, though.'

'Maybe I needed to grow up too,' Helena said quietly.

'You are just fine as you are.'

'I'm glad you think so. But I'm sure I could improve. So,' she added slyly, 'no regrets about this afternoon? Or are you going to tell me you were undone by alcohol?'

'Well, I probably was. But at this moment I'm not feeling regretful at all.'

'Maybe we need to keep a good stock of alcohol. In case your inhibitions come back,' Helena said, and Joseph could hear the schoolgirl snigger in her voice.

'My inhibitions, as you call them, are in complete disarray,' Joseph said sternly. 'The question remains, though – what are you going to do?'

'I need to clear my stuff from Becca's as soon as possible – tomorrow, in fact. Then I'll drive over to our house and fill my car up with my things. What I can't fit in I shall have to do without. If Daddy does decide to put the house on the market Mummy can send my stuff to a charity shop. For the time being I'm going to move into Erica's bungalow – it was Daddy's suggestion. It'll be weird, and sad, but I'll be near to him, and to you. I can take the train to work.'

'You'll be just a bike ride away.'

'People can get used to seeing me around. I'll come to church and listen to every sermon. I'm sure it'll do me good.'

'You can help me write them.'

'Hm. Not sure I'd be up for that. But I can make you cups of tea while you cogitate.'

'You'd be an irresistible distraction. I'd never get any work done.'

She chuckled. 'You think that now, but I'm sure a few years down the line you'll be ignoring me.'

'Impossible. You're much too loud, for a start.'

'Hey, easy on the charm! Look, it's getting late, Joseph. I'll ring you tomorrow night. You can tell me how that sermon goes.'

'I miss you already.'

'Well, I'll be an ever-present nuisance soon enough.' She yawned. 'I'm going to have a nice long bath and spend the next hour in my PJs gossiping with Becca. I shall tell her more good things about you.'

'I'm afraid that'll be a very short conversation.'

'You're a fool,' Helena said affectionately.

'You found me out. Goodnight, dearest tarnished angel.'

Wednesday

Joseph returned from taking an assembly at the primary school to find a message on the phone that sat on his desk. He had left the curtains closed to keep the room cool, and the red flashing light of the answerphone had a challenging, insistent look which added to his sense of unease. If he didn't know why he felt unsettled it was because he was consciously refusing to look for reasons. When he picked up the phone and heard Helena's voice, he was jolted, even though he half expected it to be her, and a thin film of sweat broke out on his face, as something very like fear turned in his stomach. *Oh Lord, what is the matter with me? This cannot be happening.*

He gripped the handset and listened to her message. 'Hi, sorry I've been off the radar the last few days, it's been absolutely crazy at work with so many people away on holiday. Just wanted to tell you I've heard from the police, and we can organise the funeral. Can we make a time when you're free to see the funeral directors? I'm at Erica's of course – it looks like a campsite! Can you ring me on my mobile? I'm around this evening.'

Joseph replaced the phone and collapsed into the chair. He pushed his hair off his hot forehead and rested his head in his hands, his elbows on the desk. *Lord, help me here. I don't understand myself. Here I am, almost forty, a childless widower, and this wonderful woman wants, apparently, to claim me for the rest of my days. Why aren't I pirouetting round the garden in a whirl of euphoria? Why am I so ungrateful? Do I want to stay the way I am? No, of course I don't. But, Father, I am so afraid.* He pushed himself to his feet with a quiet groan and went into the kitchen, set the kettle to boil and made a cup of coffee. He stared unseeing down the garden, tidy now in preparation for the fete, the grass remown, the hedges clipped. *I keep thinking about Caroline. I haven't thought* about her for quite a while, except fleetingly, but now –. So many images...Caroline in that frothy dress the day we were married. A very sunny day, I seem to remember. Caroline reordering this place, playing house, spending far too much money despite my protests. Caroline sulky and cross, demanding my company, bored and querulous. Or sly and seductive, wielding her power over me. Or weeping for hours, so that I was too wretched to work, or speak, or even stay in the house. Poor Caroline. What a terrible disappointment I was. I just wish she'd carried out her plan, left Compton, left me, and got on with another life. I wish my last memory wasn't of her lying naked under a sheet, a sheet which concealed her injuries but didn't stop my imagination torturing me. I wish I couldn't still see her poor white face. Oh, Lord, such a cruel end to her life, just when she might have been free. I know it's pointless to dwell on what Helena calls 'what-ifs', but I can't seem to help myself. What if Caroline had never met me? She'd still be alive. Perhaps she'd be happy.

He finished his coffee and put the cup in the sink. Then, with an exclamation of impatience, he left the house, slamming the door vehemently behind him, turned along the street for a few yards, crossed the gravelled courtyard and unlocked the door of the church. It was cool inside, and there were flowers on every ledge and pedestal, laying their summer scents on the still air. He slid into a pew, leaned back, and closed his eyes. No words came to him, no thought of prayer. He let the images unravel at random before his itching eyelids: Ewan in the Detention Suite at Stockley; Erica clumsily holding a mug in her crooked hands, looking up from her wheelchair with a glint of fierce humour in her eyes; Caroline curled up in bed, sobbing, the quilt over her head; and Helena, laughing, her eyes bright and full of hope. *I can't do it. I can't bear it if she is miserable too, because of me. After everything that has happened. I don't know if I can be the man she thinks I am, or the one she wants me to be. I'm afraid she'll die too. Even if not physically. There are other ways to die. And she's already lost so much.*

With a sigh he pushed himself to his feet and left the church, locking the door as he went. As he came to the road he saw a familiar car parked outside the Vicarage: Nettie's sky-blue Beetle, with its matching dented wings. He smiled despite himself. He found Nettie herself bending over by his front door, depositing a large and unwieldy cardboard box on the ground. She straightened up and saw him, her hot red face breaking out into a smile.

'Oh, Joseph, there you are! I've brought the crockery round, ready for Saturday. All washed. Where do you want it?'

'Thank you, Nettie. Just leave it – I'll take it indoors. It looks heavy.'

'Heavy and awkward. A miracle I didn't drop the lot.' She peered up at him, squinting. 'Are you all right, Joseph? You don't look…I don't know, not quite the ticket.'

He smiled briefly. 'Hot. Stressed. Fete coming up. Will it rain, do you think?'

'It had better not!' said Nettie stoutly. 'Any news about –' her voice dropped to a whisper '– poor Mrs Pole? Poor Mr Fraser too. Oh, Joseph, what a terrible thing! I can't hardly believe it. Are they going to let the poor man out? When will the funeral be? And what about poor, dear Helena?'

'There should be news soon,' Joseph said. 'I'll let you know.'

'No wonder you're looking harassed,' Nettie said. 'I hope you're eating properly. And don't work too hard.'

'I'll try not to. Let's get Saturday over with, and then we can all relax a bit, perhaps. Are you all right, Nettie?'

'Mustn't grumble. And I'm very busy, as usual.'

'Baking?'

'Like it's going out of fashion!' Nettie giggled. 'But this year I shall have help on my stall. Helena has offered to keep me company. I get so flustered these days – must be my age. Having a quick young brain on board will be a huge help. She won't have time to do any baking, what with working every day. But it'll probably do her good to have something else to keep her mind occupied, don't you think? You knew she's living at Mrs Pole's now, didn't you?'

'Yes, I did know,' Joseph said.

'I must be off,' Nettie said. 'Lots more to do. I've written myself out a list so I don't forget anything – stuck it on the fridge door. See you soon, Joseph.' She patted his arm. 'Don't stay up half the night working, will you?'

He shook his head and smiled. 'See you, Nettie.'

Thursday

Nettie was beating the contents of a large old-fashioned mixing bowl with a vigorous rhythm, an expression of concentration on her face, when the doorbell rang. She frowned, put the bowl down, and wiped her hands on a towel. 'Now who could that be?' she murmured to the pair of sleepy dogs curled up together in a basket in the corner.

She thought about untying her apron, but then shrugged and kept it on. Perhaps whoever it was would see she was busy and not stop to chat. But when she opened the door and saw Helena on her front step she gave a little exclamation of surprise.

'My dear, how lovely! But why aren't you at work? Aren't you feeling well?'

'No, I'm OK, Nettie. I took the morning off to get the funeral organised, that's all. I'll have to catch the train soon – I've got a meeting this afternoon.'

'What am I thinking of, keeping you on the step?' Nettie said. 'Come in, dear.'

'I'm sorry, I know you're terribly busy,' Helena said as she followed Nettie down the hallway. 'Your freezer must be absolutely bulging with cakes.'

'It is rather,' Nettie said, beaming. Then she grew solemn. 'So when is the funeral to be?'

'We've pencilled in a week tomorrow: Friday, at eleven. They had a space. But I have to confirm it with my cousin Stephen. I told you about him, didn't I? He needs time to get things organised for his trip. Poor Stephen. This isn't at all what he thought he'd be doing when he first had the idea of visiting his English relatives.'

'Shall we have some tea, dear? I could do with a break from cooking.'

'You sit down, Nettie, and let me make it. You'll wear yourself out before Saturday.'

'Certainly not. You make yourself comfortable, and I'll be just a moment.' She peered up at Helena. 'You don't look your usual self, dear. It's been an awful business, you poor thing.'

Helena bit her lip. 'I think you must hate my family, Nettie.'

Nettie shook her head. 'Hate? Why should I? Oh, you mean what your brothers did. Yes, that was wicked, no two ways about it. It makes me angry to think about it, and dreadfully sad, of course. But I don't hate anyone, and I certainly don't blame you, or your dear father. What a disaster for him.'

'It is. And I am angry too, Nettie. But at the same time I feel pity for my poor idiot brother. Not Alex so much, but Rob. You know, Nettie, I believed him when he said he didn't mean to hurt her. I don't think he did. It was just a stupid, nasty plan that went terribly wrong. But whatever he meant, she is dead, and he's going to spend years in prison, and my father is broken-hearted.'

Nettie heaved a deep sigh. 'Let me get this kettle on. I won't be a minute.' She bustled about in the kitchen, and Helena stood by the window, looking out at the quiet street. A few minutes later Nettie reappeared, carrying a tray. 'Here we are, dear. Plus some biscuits I made yesterday. They came out a funny shape, so I can't sell them at the fete, but I think they're still edible.' She laid the tray down on a low table. 'Sit yourself down and relax for a moment.'

'I'm sorry, Nettie, I'm taking up your baking time,' Helena said. 'But I don't really have anyone to talk to, not now Erica's gone. I hope you don't mind.'

Nettie settled herself in an armchair opposite Helena. She leaned forward, took the lid off the teapot and gave its contents a vigorous stir. 'That needs to brew a bit longer,' she muttered. She looked up. 'Of course I don't mind. But I thought you'd found a listening ear in Joseph. He's nice to talk to, you know. Understanding.'

'That's just the trouble, Nettie,' Helena said, looking up. Her eyes were wide, her brow furrowed.

'What is?'

'Nettie, I don't know that I should even be talking to you about it, or to anyone – it seems almost disloyal. But I'm very confused. Something isn't right.'

Nettie frowned. 'Let me pour this tea. I think it's probably brown enough. You take milk, dear, don't you?' She splashed milk into the cups, poured the tea and handed a cup to Helena. Then she folded her arms and looked at her for several moments without speaking, her lips pursed. Helena sipped her tea, which was strong and scalding hot. She recognised in Nettie the signs of deep thinking, and held her peace.

Nettie sighed. 'Forgive me if I'm blunt, Helena,' she said. 'And I wouldn't want you to think I'm nosy. But I can't help you if I don't know what's going on.'

Helena put her cup down. 'Joseph came to the funeral directors with me this morning,' she said. 'At my request, because he knows about these things – obviously, it's part of his job – and I don't. But he is acting weirdly. It's happened before. Last Christmas, and into the New Year, you know, after he came to Erica's for Christmas Day, he was so friendly and warm and funny. Then he seemed to change and go all polite and distant. I wondered if it was something I'd said or done, and I mentioned it to Erica. But, Nettie, now it's different. Then we were just friends, you know? Now –' She came to a sudden stop and bit her lip.

'Ah.' Nettie nodded. 'I'm getting the picture, dear. Has something actually been said? I mean, something concrete?'

'Well, yes – I thought so.'

Nettie pondered, breathing deeply. Then she said, 'I've never wanted to pry. It's not my place. But you know, I'm not blind, and I'm very fond of Joseph. He's had a few knocks in life, and in some ways he's quite fragile. Not in others, of course. We all have our strengths and weaknesses, that's obvious. My guess is, if he's blowing hot and cold, it's all about Caroline.'

'That's what Erica said,' Helena muttered. 'More or less. But what do I do, Nettie?'

'Let me think.' Nettie picked up her cup, blew on it, and took a gulp of tea. 'Have a biscuit,' she urged.

Helena took one and nibbled it. 'It's very good, Nettie, never mind the shape.' She dusted the crumbs from her fingers, leaned back in the chair and closed her eyes. Nettie, watching her, saw the shadows there, the lines of loss, and she shook her head. 'Men are such fools,' she said.

Helena opened her eyes and laughed despite herself. 'I thought you said you were fond of this particular one.'

'I am, my dear, I am!' Nettie exclaimed. 'He's definitely one of the better ones. As good as gold, in my opinion. But still a fool. And it may be,' she said thoughtfully, 'that he's telling himself just the same. He's probably afraid of adding to your hurts and troubles. But of course, he hasn't really thought it through.'

'So what would you do, if you were me?'

'Sometimes, dear, we just have to fight back. Don't let him throw everything away because of some silly notion he's come up with. He doesn't believe in himself, does he? So you may have to supply all the faith and strength that's lacking. I'm sure you can – you just have to ask yourself if it's worth it. It could be an uphill struggle, you know.'

'I might need encouragement from time to time, Nettie,' Helena said with a small smile. 'When my courage fails. But as to whether it's worth it, whether he's worth it, yes, he is.'

Nettie leaned forward and patted Helena's hand. 'I'll back you up whenever you need it,' she said, beaming. 'You come along on Saturday to the fete, help me sell these cakes and make a lot of money for the church. You can get to know people in the parish, and be your usual lovely, charming, happy self – even if you don't feel it. Don't let on that things may not be quite as you'd like. Then we'll see.'

'Nettie, you are a treasure.'

'Nonsense,' Nettie said. 'But it's true I've been around this world for a few years and have seen some of the daft things that people do. It's funny,' she added after a moment, 'I thought Joseph wasn't quite himself when I saw him yesterday.'

'Really? When did you see him?' Helena asked.

'I was dropping off a box of crockery for Saturday,' Nettie said. 'And he appeared. On foot, from the direction of the church. I guess that figures. He does sometimes go into the church, I think – just for a bit of peace, I suppose, away from people and phones and suchlike. Let's hope he got what he was looking for.'

Saturday

At nine o'clock Helena looked out of the front window of what had been Erica's bungalow, onto a deserted Plough Lane. She was still in her pyjamas, sipping a cup of coffee, her tangled hair tied loosely back. The sky was uniformly overcast, the air warm and humid. Helena sighed. She had promised to be at Nettie's by ten to pack cakes into her car and take them to the Vicarage. 'Why so early, Nettie?' she had asked on the phone. 'Won't they all wilt and melt and generally fall apart? It might rain – then you'll have wet cakes.'

'No, no,' Nettie had said. 'It won't rain, even if it starts off a bit grey. I've been praying for sunshine – you'll see. And we must get set up in good time. Some people start arriving before twelve, you know. We have to be ready. Mr Beech will be coming round at eleven thirty with the floats, anyway.'

'The what?'

'You know, dear, money for change. He gives us each ten pounds' worth and we return it to him afterwards.'

'I see. And then what?'

'Well,' Nettie said doubtfully, 'I suppose he either puts all the money in the safe or…no, he must go home and count it straight away, because there's always an announcement in church on the Sunday to tell us how much we've raised.'

'He's a busy man.'

'He certainly is.'

'And you're sure it won't rain?'

'Have faith!'

'What should I wear, Nettie?'

Helena heard a sly chuckle. 'Something really pretty. Perhaps a little perfume as well, and have your lovely hair loose.'

'Nettie, I suspect I am hearing a plot here.'

'Well, dear,' Nettie said innocently, 'we can't go into battle without weapons.'

By eleven the Vicarage garden was a scene of purposeful chaos, and Nettie's faith in the power of prayer had been vindicated by the appearance of the sun. The damp grass was drying, and a light breeze freshened the heavy air. Nettie had set up her cake stall with Helena's help. 'Much easier this year, thank heaven,' Nettie murmured. 'Normally Cyril – he's one of the churchwardens – insists on helping me, and he's so doddery it takes for ever. He means well, but he's over eighty and not very steady on his legs.'

'I think we did a good job, Nettie,' Helena said, casting a critical eye over the table, spread with a white cloth and groaning with the results of Nettie's baking, and other people's too. 'I can't believe we will sell all this.'

'We certainly will,' Nettie said. 'Unless the citizens of Compton are all on sudden diets. If previous years are anything to go by, this lot will be gone by two o'clock.'

'Don't you feel tempted to keep anything for yourself, Nettie? You've worked so hard.'

'Don't you worry,' Nettie whispered. 'There are a few things hidden away in my freezer.'

Joseph was there, strolling from stall to stall, talking to people, encouraging their efforts, helping to put up gazebos or cart boxes. Just before twelve he came by Nettie's stall and surveyed her wares. 'You have been busy as usual, Nettie,' he said, smiling. 'It all looks wonderful.' He turned to Helena, and his smile was somehow painful. 'Hello, Helena. Good of you to help Nettie out.'

'It's no chore,' Helena said breezily. She smiled at Nettie. 'We've been having fun, haven't we, Nettie?' She turned back to Joseph. 'I've been in touch with Stephen again. He's approved the date and time of the funeral, so I'll ring the directors on Monday. Nettie suggested we should have a small reception at the Red Lion, so I've spoken to them and got them to cater. I don't suppose many people will come, will they? Stephen's left it up to me to organize the wreath from the family – himself, me and Daddy. He liked the idea of inviting contributions instead of flowers. He suggested a charity for spinal injuries, which I thought was a great idea.'

'Yes, that's very appropriate,' Joseph murmured. He cleared his throat. 'When is he arriving?'

'Wednesday, late afternoon. I've said I'll collect him from the airport. He can come and stay with me at Erica's for a couple of days. But after the funeral he's got plans to visit other people too, relatives of his dad's. Will you need to talk to him? He said he couldn't really add to what Daddy told you, for the eulogy – he never really knew his mother, did he?'

'If he needs to talk to me, ask him to ring me as soon as he can after he arrives. He might only get the answerphone on Thursday,' Joseph said. 'Now I must let you two get on.' And he was gone.

Helena stared at his back as he disappeared into the crowd. She turned to Nettie, frowning. 'Do you see what I mean? How strange he is being? Can you believe that only a week ago he was talking about, well, about forever?' She shook her head. 'What's happening, Nettie? He isn't the sort of person to say one thing and mean another. I don't understand. I know he'd drunk a few glasses of wine, but I thought it was just enough to throw out some of his inhibitions, not make him actually say stuff he didn't mean.' She looked at Nettie, her face bewildered and miserable.

Nettie shook her head slightly. 'Keep smiling, dear,' she muttered. 'Keep up the good work, never let the enemy see you defeated.'

'No, Nettie, don't be silly,' Helena said, managing a smile despite herself. 'Joseph isn't my enemy.'

'He is for now,' Nettie said stoutly. 'And *we* have to defeat *him*. I've been watching,' she added. 'Discreetly, of course. That dress was a good choice, you know. His eyes were all over you. And you should have seen him scowl when you mentioned your cousin Stephen!'

'You're imagining it, Nettie!' Helena protested. 'Next thing you'll be telling me he's jealous of someone he's never met!'

'Of course he is. If he thought about it for a moment, he'd know how stupid he's being. Maybe he does know, and that makes him feel worse. Poor Joseph.' She took a deep breath. 'But I'm not going to feel sorry for him. We have to have, what's it called? A strategy, that's it.'

'I don't know, Nettie,' Helena said. 'It's all beginning to look a bit hopeless.'

'Nonsense! You have to keep your courage up. Tell me, what did Mrs P say about it – God rest her soul?'

'Ha! She said I had to convince Joseph that I was a gift from God. I guess if he believed that then he couldn't send me packing without feeling ungrateful.'

Nettie nodded thoughtfully. 'Your aunt was a wise woman.'

Helena smiled. 'She was a conniving, unprincipled, shameless plotter. Oh, Nettie, we are going to miss her.'

'Yes, dear, we certainly are. But between us we will carry out that plot of hers, if it's the last thing we do.' She patted Helena's arm. 'Now I think we'd better shape up – our customers are arriving.'

Friday

At a quarter to eleven Joseph was in place in front of the church doors. It was a morning of bulbous grey clouds and moist gusts, and though he stood unnaturally still and stiff the breeze whipped at the hem of his surplice, making it billow, somehow adding to the already charged atmosphere. Apart from murmured greetings the small group of parishioners stood clumped together in an uneasy silence, awkward in collars and ties, polished shoes, black coats. Only Nettie stood close to Joseph in unspoken solidarity.

'It's a sad day, Joseph,' she whispered.

'Yes.'

'Worse than most, I'd say.'

'Indeed.'

'Is Helena all right? I've barely seen her since Saturday.'

'Nor have I. Her cousin is here now.'

His terse responses dissuaded even Nettie, and with a glance at his stern face she fell silent.

A car drew up at the kerb, and its doors swung open. A moment later Inspector Hazell got out, doing up the buttons of his suit jacket. He was followed by the driver, Louise Gordon, formal in black, wearing unnecessary sunglasses. From the back of the car Constable Swinton appeared, in uniform, and then Ewan, whose dark suit and white shirt were offset by a startlingly bright tartan tie. With Swinton close behind, Ewan walked up to Joseph and wordlessly shook hands. His face was raw with strain. Louise Gordon appeared at Joseph's side.

'Good morning, Reverend Stiles,' she said. 'OK to leave the car there?'

'Yes, as long as there's room for the hearse.'

Then a blue Golf slid into place behind the police car. Everyone's eyes swivelled towards its occupants as they emerged: Helena, in a dark blue dress, accentuating her tall, lithe figure, her hair tied loosely back, and round her neck the scarf that Joseph had given her for Christmas; and following her a dark-haired young man, of medium height and slender build, his face pale and set.

Joseph heard a strangled sound somewhere to his left, and turned his head to see Ewan lay a brief hand on Constable Swinton's jacket-sleeve, then surge forward, arms outstretched, his face a mask of anguish. 'Stephen!' He wrapped the young man in his arms, and when they parted both men were weeping. Ewan pulled a handkerchief from his pocket and offered it to Stephen, then turned to his daughter. 'Hello, my darling.' He hugged her close for a moment.

Helena looked to the road. 'Daddy, the hearse is here.' Joseph heard Ewan choke, and Helena murmur, 'Be brave.'

Everyone stood back from the church doors as the long black hearse rolled to a smooth halt in front of the police car. Joseph saw how Ewan and Helena had grouped themselves one on each side of Stephen, as if to protect him. Constable Swinton stood back with his colleagues, but his eyes were on Ewan.

The funeral director got out of the car, resplendent in his formal attire. He nodded a greeting to Helena, then spoke a few quiet words to Joseph. From inside the church came the sound of solemn music as the organist started to play. A few drops of rain whisked down in the wind, dampening hair and shoulders. A second car drew up discreetly, disgorging three black-coated pall-bearers. The funeral director went to the rear of the hearse and two more pall-bearers emerged and joined their colleagues. He opened the rear doors and slid the coffin out on its rollers, and in a moment of expert adjustment the five men, one at the front and two on each side, took it on their shoulders and stepped onto the church forecourt. Joseph nodded to them, turned and walked towards the doors, followed by the funeral director, then the coffin. Stumbling slightly, but instantly correcting himself, Ewan followed, his gait stiff and straight, then Stephen and Helena, hand in hand.

Joseph began to walk slowly up the nave of the church, holding his Bible in both hands. When he spoke, his voice seemed unusually loud and ringing, and Helena felt a frisson ripple over her skin. '"I am the resurrection and the life. Those who believe in me will live, even though they die; and all those who live and believe in me will never die."' Helena felt Stephen's hand tighten on her own. '"I am certain that nothing can separate us from his love: neither death nor life, neither angels nor other heavenly rulers or powers, neither the present nor the future, neither the world above nor the world below – there is nothing in all creation that will ever be able to separate us from the love of God which is ours through Christ Jesus our Lord."'

Joseph arrived at the altar step where a trestle waited, and stood aside in silence as the pall-bearers slid the coffin to rest. Then they, and their leader, bowed to Joseph, and to the coffin, and walked back down the nave, hands folded respectfully in front of them. The organist played a last soft chord, and the doors ground shut.

Joseph looked up at the small gathering scattered among the pews. His gaze slid over each one, and when his eyes rested on Helena his expression was unfathomable. She looked back at him with a fearlessness she did not feel.

'We have come here today,' Joseph said, his voice returning to its normal low timbre, 'to remember before God our dear sister Erica; to give thanks for her life; to commend her to God's mercy, and to commit her body for burial. We have also come to offer one another such comfort as we can, tempering our human grief with the hope that we have in the death and resurrection of Jesus Christ our redeemer. So let us pray. Please do sit down.'

There was a shuffling as people organised themselves, and Joseph waited. He looked down at the book in his hands, and after a quiet moment began to pray. He prayed for God's compassion on all who mourned, remembering how Jesus himself had wept at the grave of his friend Lazarus. He prayed for hope to lighten the darkness, and strengthened faith, and as the service wound its predestined stately way he prayed for forgiveness and mercy, and for the faith that claimed Christ's promise of eternal life. Helena sat in the pew, her head bowed, hearing beside her Stephen's muffled weeping; and the sound of Joseph's voice as he carried out his customary office with solemnity and practised confidence awakened in her feelings that were totally inappropriate. She suppressed a guilty smile. *Wouldn't Erica have found it hilarious if she knew – anyway, who's to say she doesn't? Perhaps even now she is grinning that wicked grin of hers – that here I am at her funeral, and she's dead before her time, murdered by her own nephew, which should make anyone feel appalled and horrified, and of course I am, but seeing Joseph in his own place, hearing him speak with such gravity, just makes me lust after him even more! What a sinner I am. What a good job no one can actually read my thoughts. Sorry, Erica. Sorry, God.* She looked up and saw her father on the other side of Stephen. Ewan's eyes were closed, and every line of his face spoke of unutterable loss. From her father her thoughts ranged inevitably to her mother and her brothers, and to the ruin of all their lives, and she was chastened.

She heaved a deep sigh and looked up. Joseph was opening his Bible. 'I am taking a reading from the Psalms,' he said. 'These words were favourites of Erica's, and I believe they speak to us all. Psalm 103, beginning at verse six. "The Lord judges in favour of the oppressed and gives them their rights. He revealed his plans to Moses and let the people of Israel see his mighty deeds. The Lord is merciful and loving, slow to become angry and full of constant love. He does not keep on rebuking; he is not angry for ever. He does not punish us as we deserve or repay us according to our sins and wrongs. As high as the sky is above the earth, so great is his love for those who honour him. As far as the east is from the west, so far does he remove our sins from us. He knows what we are made of; he remembers that we are dust."' He closed his Bible and looked up, again letting his gaze rest on each person there.

'Erica's family have asked me to speak about her on their behalf, which I gladly do, as well as for myself as her friend. But before I begin let me also invite you all, after the service here in church and the burial in the churchyard, to join the family for refreshments at the Red Lion. All of you know where that is, I think.' A few smiles greeted this small spark of humour. He paused, and a faint smile crossed his face, and was gone.

'All of us here knew Erica, but of course we knew her in different ways and in different degrees. It was my privilege to have her friendship, and I valued it greatly, even when she was deflating me in some way, or telling me off for some folly.' He looked rueful for a moment, then became serious again. 'But there are some here who knew her very well, who loved her, and for whom her death is an unmitigated catastrophe. I ask you all to remember her family in your prayers in the coming weeks: her devoted and beloved brother Ewan, Helena who was more of a very dear daughter than a niece, and her son Stephen, whose particular tragedy was never to have known his mother beyond the memories of early childhood. Most of us are aware of the circumstances of Erica's death, but it is not my intention to dwell upon them today. Rather, I would like to tell you a little about her life, and the lessons we can draw from the way she dealt with the difficulties and disappointments of that life.

'Erica was born in Scotland and spent her early years in a remote castle in Perthshire. The death of her mother when she was just four, and the increasingly difficult relationship with her father, made for an unusually strong bond between Erica and her brother Ewan, older by three years. That bond was never broken; it remained strong until the end of her life, and I know that the love and devotion of her brother was something for which she was always deeply thankful. It is an example, I believe, of how often from the sorry messes that we humans make, even then, something beautiful can arise and endure – the work of the Holy Spirit. Erica told me that she owed her Christian faith to her brother: arguably his best gift to her. She clung to that faith through thick and thin – and as we know, things were pretty thin for Erica for many years. The accident that robbed her of mobility and independence was another disaster that befell her, but although she suffered constant pain, and although she could often be sharp of tongue, she never felt sorry for herself. Her sense of humour rescued her time and again from self-pity. In her weakness she was strong. She was the first to confess that she had made many mistakes – but from those follies sprang wisdom and compassion for others. She wasn't perfect! As Nettie can attest, she could be crabby to the point of abusive. But she remained alive to other people, especially those closest to her.

'There is much more that I could say about Erica, many memories of my own among them, and you will each have your own particular thoughts. But what can we draw from this one woman's example? What can we take away from today's sadness, and ponder on in the days ahead? I believe that the answer lies in her reliance upon her Saviour and Lord, her friend and companion. When the nights were long and the pain sharp, when no one was there to help or comfort her, it was in communion with him that she found the strength to endure. She knew that we are dust, as the psalm says, but in the teeth of pain and distress she rejoiced that we are beloved dust in God's eyes.' He took breath, and his gaze came to rest briefly on Helena, so that for a fleeting moment she felt her heart beat against her ribs with alarming loudness. Then his voice lowered. 'None of us knows how long we have remaining to us on this earth. Our decisions here have eternal consequences, and the most important decision of all, one that Erica made and never relinquished, is to follow Christ.'

He closed his Bible and put it on a small table. 'Now let us pray. Let us give thanks for Erica's life, let us pray for those who mourn, and let us ask God to help us live our lives in the light of eternity.'

Through the prayers that followed Helena sat in a daze, hearing the words, registering their solemnity, but not really taking them in. *Another time. There is so much to deal with, and this is just the beginning. My father. My mother. My brothers. My cousin. And Joseph.*

Then there was a general scuffling, and people were standing up as the pall-bearers came back into the church and took the coffin up on their shoulders. Again Joseph led, and everyone followed. Now Ewan walked with his arm round Stephen's bowed back, and Helena walked alone until Nettie caught up with her, held her arm and looked up at her with anxious affection. The organist started to play again as they came to the church door and out into the hazy sunlight of an ordinary lunchtime in Compton. Whoever died, whoever saw their life broken in pieces, the planet orbited the sun and the heedless world went on.

Joseph led them round the side of the church to a plot at the back where a new grave had been dug and a mound of earth was covered with a green cloth. The tiny congregation gathered round, and Helena found herself next to her father, and wrapped her arms round him. They watched as the coffin was lowered, slowly and carefully, into the grave.

'We have entrusted our sister to God's merciful keeping,' Joseph said, a catch in his voice betraying his own heart. 'We now commit her body to the ground: earth to earth, ashes to ashes, dust to dust.'

Helena barely registered the rest of the brief ceremony. She was vaguely aware of symbolic actions: the rattling of dry soil on the coffin lid, white roses falling, hands of farewell, and all the while she held on to her father, giving him her strength. Finally it was over, and she came back to herself like someone waking from a puzzling dream, or coming up out of dark water into sunlight. She looked at Joseph and he nodded briefly, his face set, then walked away in the direction of the Vicarage.

Half an hour later, in the function room at the back of the Red Lion, down a carpeted corridor off the bar, people were beginning to feel easier: to undo buttons, loosen ties and talk more normally. Parishioners were eating and drinking and chatting in a cluster, shyly glancing towards Ewan and Stephen, sometimes offering a brief comment of condolence to Helena. Ewan and Stephen sat side by side on a lumpy sofa and talked as if they had known each other all their lives – *which, in a queer kind of way, they have,* Helena thought. *How like Erica Stephen is, how strange that must be for Daddy. He knew Erica as a child, as a young woman, before the accident robbed her of health and youth. He knew*

Stephen too, as a little boy. I only have the vaguest memories of him – we rarely saw him, and then he went to America. Out of all this awfulness, the two of them sitting talking gives me heart. She glanced round the room and frowned. *Where the heck is Joseph? He should be here.*

Nettie appeared at her elbow. 'Where did Joseph get to?' she asked quietly. 'I thought he would be here by now. He hasn't actually met your cousin, has he?'

'I think he went home to change,' Helena said. 'He would hardly want to come to a pub in cassock and surplice.'

Nettie shook her head. 'If I was you, dear, I'd go and find him. The way he's been, I wouldn't put it past him to have gone on a long bike ride.'

'You're right.' Helena hesitated. 'Shoot a prayer up for me, Nettie.'

With a last glance around the room, Helena slipped out of the door, down the corridor, through the bar and out into the street. It was no more than a five-minute walk to the Vicarage, but she was suddenly possessed by a sense of extreme urgency. *What if he really has gone out on his bike? Is that possible? Probable?* She found herself half-walking, half-running along the pavement, dodging startled shoppers, and came to a halt outside the church hot and out of breath. *For heaven's sake, Helena.*

She hesitated for a moment, then breathed deeply and walked up the Vicarage path with an air of resolution that was completely deceptive. She crossed in front of the window and through the side entrance to the back garden, and felt a wash of foolish relief to see Joseph's bike leaning up against the shed. Gingerly she approached the back door, which was open wide. Pausing in the doorway she had a moment of intense weakness, so that she had to lean on the door frame to steady herself. *Get a grip, idiot. What's the matter with you? It's just Joseph, not Godzilla.*

She crossed the threshold and was about to call out when she stopped mid-stride. From the other side of the house came the distinct sound of a piano. As she crept closer she heard the melody: something she vaguely recognised, stately and elegiac. She found her way to the room at the back of the house where Joseph had played for her at Christmas, and peered round the open door. The room was quite bare: there was a carpet on the floor, and curtains at the windows, but otherwise just the piano and its stool. Joseph was sitting there untidily, one leg wrapped round the chair leg, the other stretched out, and as he played, barely looking at the music on the stand, he bent over the keyboard, his hair flopping over his forehead. Helena felt a wave of tenderness so strong that she wanted to hurtle into the room and throw her arms around him. But there was a remoteness about him, an almost forbidding preoccupation, that made her hesitate.

He stopped playing, and sighed, and turned, half-rising from the stool. He saw her, and his eyebrows shot up. 'Hello. How long have you been standing there?' he said mildly.

'Only a minute. What were you playing? It was lovely. Sad, though.'

'Oh, that.' He waved a careless hand at his music. 'It's the Sarabande from Grieg's Holberg Suite. Some of the other movements are more cheerful.' He pulled himself upright, steadying himself on the lid of the piano.

Helena took a few wary steps in to the room. 'Joseph – is it significant, your playing? Does it mean you're sad? Aren't you coming to the pub? I hoped you might come and see Stephen. He's anxious to meet you.'

Joseph shook his head, and said nothing for a long moment. Then he spoke almost reluctantly. 'I don't know what I am, Helena. Sad? Not really, apart from having to bury a good friend, of course. Anxious and confused, more like. I hardly know which way is up.'

Helena held her arms tightly by her sides, her hands clenched, and fought down an impulse to weep. 'Why are you confused, Joseph? Is it about you and me? Or something else?'

Joseph groaned softly and looked away from her, out of the window. 'I'm just…trying to do the right thing. But I'm not sure what it is. I know I'm not happy with myself, how I've behaved.' He turned to her suddenly and spoke in a rush, as if he needed to blurt everything out before his courage failed. 'The bottom line is, by any reckoning, I'm just not good enough for you. I am too old, too poor, too battered, too prone to gloom.' His voice was low, and held a note of desperation. 'I never told you, did I? Hardly anyone here knows. I was actually hospitalised once, for depression.'

'How long ago was that?' Helena asked, trying to keep her voice neutral.

'Well…quite a long time. After I left university.'

'Fifteen years, then, at least? Not since?'

He shook his head.

'Oh, Joseph. Age is not important. Well, it would be if you were eighty, maybe. Twelve years is not a big deal. As to "too poor", ask anyone who knows me, I don't care about material things. Anyway, I can go to work. And as to "too battered," how's this?' Her voice rose. 'My father and both my brothers are in custody. One of my brothers murdered my aunt, who was also my friend, and is likely to spend many, *many* years in prison. My parents are probably getting a divorce, my family home, such as it is, is to be sold, my father plans to lock himself away in a monastery. Isn't that battered enough for you? You make me out to be some unchipped cotton-wool-wrapped little egg!'

Joseph stretched out his hand, then let it fall. 'No, no – of course you have suffered, I don't underestimate that for a moment. Especially just lately. But that's just it – I couldn't bear to be another burden, adding to your troubles.'

'Joseph, you've got it *all wrong!* Helena cried out. 'The idea is to be a help to each other! You're making yourself out to be some kind of leech, sucking out my carefree youth – that's absolute rubbish!'

He stared at her, but it was as if he hadn't heard. 'And then,' he said falteringly, 'then I saw you today, with Stephen. Someone your own age, someone you've been getting to know these past few days, someone already close by family ties, and I thought, what am I doing?'

'Joseph, for heaven's sake! You are such an idiot. Stephen is a *boy*. He's my cousin, but I barely know him. He has a long-term girlfriend. He lives in America, and he's going back there in a few weeks, to take up his life again – a life I know nothing about, a life in which I am not involved. I've tried to be kind to him, of course I have, because of what's happened, and because he's family. That's all. How can you be such a complete fool?'

Joseph allowed himself a small smile. 'And you want to saddle yourself with a fool?'

Helena shook her head. 'Well, of course I'd prefer you to be sensible. But I'd rather have you, even being a fool, than anyone else on this earth.'

'My darling, how can you possibly know?'

Helena folded her arms. It was a gesture of defiance that made her look suddenly much younger, and Joseph suppressed a smile. 'I know enough to be going on with. That's all any of us can hope for, surely? And it's not as if I haven't had...um, other men in my life. For comparison.'

Joseph raised his eyebrows. 'When were you going to tell me about *them*?'

'Maybe never. But shall I tell you what Erica said?'

Joseph leaned back against the piano. 'What about?'

'About you and me. She said I had to try to persuade you that I was a gift from God. I suppose she thought if you believed that you would have to take me seriously.'

'My goodness. That sounds exactly like her. Did you enter into this plot?'

'Of course not. And anyway, even if she was right, that's only half the story.'

'So what's the other half?' Joseph said. Seeing her serious expression, he forbore to grin.

'She didn't seem to consider that you might be God's gift to me. But I believe you are. I think God, in his wisdom and generosity, not to mention his sense of humour, has given us to each other. To hold each other up. Maybe we can be a force for good in this funny little place.'

'We might not always be here, you know,' Joseph murmured. 'You get moved around in this job.'

Helena shrugged. 'I don't have anywhere I'm attached to. I only came here to see Erica, and then you as well. I don't really have a home, so I guess it'll have to be wherever you are.' She paused. 'That's if you aren't determined to send me away out of some crazy notion of what's good for me. Patronising or what!'

Joseph said nothing for a moment, just looked at her with a half-smile on his face. 'And if I *were* determined?'

'To self-destruct? Well, Daddy would be disappointed. Nettie would be aghast. I would have a broken heart. You would be lonely for ever. Maybe even God would be cross with you because of your ingratitude. And Erica would be *furious.*'

Joseph looked at the floor. 'You know, I haven't done at all well in the marriage stakes,' he said quietly.

'It takes two. You can't shoulder all the blame. And you can't possibly be responsible for the accident. Of course it was horrendous, and very bad timing. But the poor thing could have been killed on her way to the shops.'

For a moment a laden silence reigned in the room. Then with a frown that was also, somehow, a smile, Joseph straightened up and stretched his hand out to Helena. She crossed the room in three swift strides, and he held her tightly. She rested her head on his shoulder, and a tear strayed down her face.

After a long moment he said, 'We do have to talk about Caroline, you know.'

Her voice was muffled, half-buried in his shirt. 'Of course we do. But not today.'

He looked at her and shook his head, smiling faintly. 'You are irresistible, but if I said I wasn't worried I'd be lying.'

'I understand. I wouldn't want you to lie. But it might be nice, even if it's just today, if you could cover up the worst of the truth.' She sounded sober, but her eyes were alight.

Joseph groaned. 'I'm sorry. You're right to call me a fool. Please, don't doubt for a moment how much I love you, how badly I want it to work. Just lately I've been thinking about Caroline a lot, and it's scared me.'

Helena pulled away a little and looked at him, her eyes wide and bright. 'But I'm not Caroline. And just maybe you aren't the same man that you were when you married her.'

Joseph nodded. 'Maybe, indeed. So, my dearest girl, what now?' His gaze was fixed on her face, and his smile was unfeigned. 'Do I ask your father for your hand?'

Helena grimaced. 'Certainly not. It would be inappropriate today. Besides which, my father doesn't own my hand. *I* do.'

'Then I must ask you for it.'

'You can have it. Plus the arm it's attached to, and all the rest. Top to bottom. Inside and out.'

'Stop. I'm getting dizzy.'

'Good.' She stretched up and kissed him briefly, soft and tantalising. 'Come on, then. Let's show your face in the Red Lion, and you can talk to Stephen for a while, and perhaps tell him some of your memories of Erica. He's got so few, and they're all second-hand.'

Half way to the Red Lion Joseph stopped mid-pavement. There were people about, and some of them had nodded or murmured a greeting.

Helena frowned. 'What?'

'Wait a moment.' He brushed her face with his fingers, and very deliberately bent and kissed her, pulling away only, and reluctantly, when someone wolf-whistled from across the road.

Helena gaped at him, her eyes wide. 'Joseph, whatever are you doing? You're wearing your dog-collar!'

'So I am. I just wanted you to know that I am not all negativity and feebleness. I promise not to do it again.' He tried to sound contrite, but ruined it by laughing.

She took his hand and pulled him along the pavement. 'Don't make promises I don't want you to keep,' she said sternly. 'Of course you will do it again. But please, not in the street.'

2011

Stockley railway station on a cold afternoon in late November: it's already dark, and a sly wind is whipping round the platform at ankle-level. There are few people waiting. Among them is a tall man in a dark coat. One of his hands rests on a baby's buggy laden with paraphernalia; the other holds a well-wrapped infant against his chest, and he rocks gently from one foot to the other, the instinctive motion of a parent encouraging a child to sleep. Anyone close enough might also have heard this father humming softly. Someone who knew might have recognised the strains of a popular modern hymn.

At last the London train rumbles into sight, a dark shape punctuated by lighted windows, and grinds to a shuddering halt. Dedicated shoppers and early-departing commuters straggle from the open doors, swarm across the platform and make for the exit. A tall, lithe woman emerges from the crowd, her bright hair escaping from under her black woollen hat.

'There you are,' murmurs Joseph, brushing her face with his lips. 'Long day?'

'Very,' Helena says, attempting a weary smile. She holds out her arms, and Joseph transfers their sleepy son to his mother with expert ease. The baby's little hands, encased in mittens, flex and clench. 'How's he been?'

'Fine,' Joseph says. 'Eats like a navvy, just occasionally looks anxious.'

They walk out of the station, Helena holding the child, Joseph pushing the buggy with one hand and resting the other on her shoulder.

'Who had him when you were at your meeting?'

'Nettie, of course. So he's been very well looked after.'

'Spoilt is the word for it.' Helena's smile fades. 'I worry about Nettie. Sometimes she looks, I don't know, haunted.'

They reach their parked car, and Joseph opens the boot, folds up the buggy and puts it inside, together with several bags. 'Sometimes that happens,' he says. 'Someone seems to be coping well at first, but as time goes on the shock deepens and then, little by little, starts to work its way out.' He opens the rear door and Helena lays her son in his car seat and clicks the straps into place. He whimpers for a moment then goes back to sleep.

'I think she has nightmares sometimes,' Helena says. She plants a kiss on her baby's soft cheek before getting into the front passenger seat. 'I guess for such a kind-hearted person as Nettie it must have been a horrific shock to have discovered Erica's body, especially in the circumstances.'

'Mm. Something like that never quite goes away,' Joseph says. 'The ripples keep on spreading. But people usually learn to deal with it in the end, just for the sake of survival.' He switches on the engine and the car growls into life. He looks closely at his wife. 'Are you all right? You look pale.' She has pulled off her hat, and he runs his free hand lightly over her hair.

She yawns. 'Tired is all. Let's get home. This boy of ours will need some supper and playtime.'

'There should be some good aromas in the kitchen when we get in,' Joseph says, reversing out of the car park and pulling onto the road.

'You're an angel,' Helena says. 'When did you have time to cook?'

'While eating lunch standing up, at the same time feeding Tim and doing a sort of hornpipe to entertain him. And you weren't calling me an angel yesterday, if I remember correctly.'

Helena laughs. 'No one's an angel *all* the time, not even you. I like the image of the hornpipe, though.'

'Tell me about today,' Joseph prompts as the car picks up speed. 'How was your father?'

Helena thinks for a moment, biting her lip. 'He's OK on the surface. I'm sure the monastery did him good, gave him something to hang on to, and I'm glad he goes back there from time to time. But Joseph, there's something missing. Part of Daddy just isn't there.'

Joseph frowns. 'The same as Nettie, in some ways.'

'But for him it's not just shock and horror – it's part of his life, part of what makes him the man he is, that's been taken away. He doesn't say much, but I'm sure he misses Erica more as the years pass. You know, sometimes I think there'll be no real rest for Daddy, not in this life.'

'Is he coping, though? With the business?'

'Oh yes, I think so. And he has very good staff, loyal supporters. But what really keeps him going is his mission to the boys. He's doing everything in his power to save them from the consequences of their actions. He can't actually free them from prison, but he's trying to ensure prison doesn't make worse men of them. That's how he puts it.'

'Is he succeeding, do you think?'

'With Rob, I think he has a chance. Rob is so contrite, so grateful that Daddy has forgiven him and keeps on supporting him, he'd do almost anything. He's still studying, you know – at this rate he'll have a degree before he's released, and he was always a lazy boy at school, couldn't wait to dash off a hasty piece of homework and get out on to the playing-field. He still works out, so he's keeping fit, but meanwhile he's got quite a library in his cell. Daddy takes him books regularly. Maybe it's that that's keeping him – Rob, I mean – from going crazy. Perhaps he just refuses to think about how long he's still got to go. Poor Rob – by the time they let him out he'll be almost fifty.'

'At least he'll have a job to go back to.'

'Yes, he's better off than most. Most lifers.'

They sink into silence for a few miles, until Joseph swings off the dual carriageway on to the Compton exit. He looks sideways at Helena. 'What about Alex?' he says quietly.

Helena heaves a sigh. 'Well, of course we didn't actually see Alex today. He's so far away – a hundred and twenty miles. I'll see Alex next time, maybe.' She pauses. 'Daddy says Alex is still very bitter. He's still appalled at the length of his sentence, still rants on about how he only intended a bit of breaking and entering, how they chose that day specifically because they thought Erica wouldn't be there, and how could that have been so glossed over at the trial – you know how he goes on. He blames Rob for the whole disaster, especially as it was covering up for Rob, lying to the police, destroying the evidence, that got Alex into the most trouble. Daddy has had his work cut out with Alex, but he's still so patient with him. And I know he prays for them all the time, especially for Alex at the moment. Daddy probably feels his time's running out.'

'When's Alex due for release exactly?'

'February, he says. Then it'll be a toss-up whether he stays in London and goes back to work for Fraser's, which is what Daddy wants, or whether he decides to decamp to Edinburgh and work for Uncle Stuart. Once he gets back into the Beaton orbit Daddy thinks he'll lose him for good.'

'Your father is a most remarkable man,' Joseph says thoughtfully. 'Once I might have been astonished at how he has worked for your brothers so tirelessly, considering how they robbed him of his beloved sister. How could he forgive them for that? Now maybe I understand a bit better. Now I have my own child. Even so...' He negotiates the last corner and turns into the Vicarage drive with a crunching of gravel. The baby yawns, wakes, begins to wail. 'You take Tim in, I'll bring all the gear.'

Helena climbs out of the car, unstraps her son and pulls him out into her arms, rocking him. 'I haven't got a key.'

Joseph empties the boot and closes it with a thud. 'I'll open up.' He leaves the buggy and comes to stand beside her in the porch. He puts his key into the lock, pushes the door wide and snaps on the hall light.

'Sweetheart, you look exhausted,' he says.

'I feel it. Even though I haven't really done much, except sit in the car while Daddy drove, and listen to him talk, and contribute the odd comment.'

'Hospital visiting is draining enough. Prison visiting must be worse.'

'I don't think it's just that.' They walk through to the kitchen, where it is warm and redolent with cooking smells.

Helena takes off Timothy's padded suit, gloves and hat and hugs and tickles him till he gives up wailing and gurgles.

'I'll warm him some milk, keep him going till supper's ready,' Joseph says. He pauses and frowns. 'What do you mean – you're not ill, are you?'

Helena laughs, her eyes crinkling. 'I'm hardly ever ill, you know that. No, this feels distinctly hormonal. It's a very good job you're having such a ball being a father, because I suspect I might be cooking Tim's little sibling.'

Joseph's eyebrows shoot up. 'Really?' He closes the fridge door with the baby's bottle in his hand. He puts the bottle in the microwave, comes round the table and takes his wife and child in his arms. 'That's wonderful news, but we really must work out what's causing it. Before we wind up with the tribes of Israel.'

'Funny man. I'll do a test next week and make sure.'

Still hugging them, Joseph sighs. 'Is Ewan lonely, do you think?'

'Let me put this boy in his high chair.' Helena disengages herself. 'He probably is, though he'd never admit it. He has an air of calm which doesn't seem quite natural. Have you seen it? Anyway, at least I persuaded him to come to us for Christmas. Perhaps we can warm him up, in those places where he feels cold and alone.'

'He's always at ease with you.'

Helena straps the baby into his high chair. 'He loves to talk to you too, and Tim always cheers him up. Yes, all right, hungry monster, it's coming.'

She takes the baby's bottle from the microwave, shakes it, tests its heat, and puts it into his outstretched hands. As he sucks she turns back into Joseph's willing arms. 'It's a bit torturing,' she says, leaning her forehead on his shoulder, 'seeing Rob in prison, dreading what might happen to Alex, seeing my father so...stretched and taut, somehow. It's as if he's afraid to let anything out in case he might howl and scream and throw things.' She looks up at Joseph and heaves a sigh. 'I thank God I can come home to my warm kitchen, and listen to my baby glugging milk, and hang out with my mad husband.' A smile twitches her lips. 'Who, apparently, doesn't know where babies come from.'

'From the place of all blessings,' Joseph says, lightly stroking her cheek. 'God's hands.'

'Do you see now?' Helena says softly. 'It was right, wasn't it, Erica's agenda?'

Joseph shakes his head. 'She can't have known she was going to die, my darling, and in that horrible fashion.'

'No, but she knew very well the fault-lines in our family. In her own way she was doing just the same as Daddy: preparing for the future. Which is why I couldn't let you get away, those times when you were getting cold feet. We have to keep a little place of warmth and light. It's not just for us and our children, but for others – Daddy, Rob, Alex, Nettie, maybe people we don't even know yet.'

Joseph kisses her with infinite tenderness. 'I'm thankful you didn't let me get away. And you're right: a place of prayer as well.'

A loud banging comes from behind them, and a yell. Helena pulls away reluctantly and turns to see her son's empty bottle crash to the floor. She grins. 'Supper-time, I think.'